What Next...

A River Road Series

M. J. Hughes

Also by M. J. Hughes

Trigger Warnings

This book contains mature themes and language that may not be suitable for all readers. It includes explicit sexual content and strong language. Talk of depression and substance abuse are included in this book. Reader discretion is advised.

Prologue

Paul

Bubbly, kind, innocent, and a friend; that's how I see her. *For the most part.*

Yes, she's breathtakingly gorgeous; yes, I'm mostly excited for tonight because I get to see her, and yes…it's possible I've imagined how many ways I'd like to show her exactly how *experienced* I am, but as I once told Jake, she isn't for me and I sure as shit ain't for her.

When he asked why, I told him I don't want to sleep with her. It's as far from the truth as something could be, but *she* deserves so much more than *me*. And again, she is my friend, hell, probably best friend.

I don't do relationships, ever. The guys can attest to me being a fuckboy and I own that with pride; I love making women feel good – it gives me pleasure. The reasoning behind my *I won't settle down* rule? Something I don't discuss.

"Are you ready, dickhead?" Jake asks from my left, his arm wrapped tightly around his girlfriend, Leah.

"Been waiting for your sorry ass," I chirp back.

"That…may have been my fault. We uh–uh got carried away, sort of?" Leah begins to blush, looking at Jake.

"No, no. No sex talk under this roof," Clay adds, joining us.

"Lighten up, dude. Maybe if you got laid, you'd relax a little," Liam says as he grabs Clay by the shoulders. "Trust me, it helps."

I roll my eyes as Clara makes her way to my left, linking her petite arm through mine. With her and Leah basically living here, we've become…close. Our shared secret of our guilty pleasure, *Jersey Shore*, solidified our friendship.

"I think they both need girlfriends," she winks at me, "but we'll unpack that another day because the other three are here and ready to go!"

We all file out of our River Road house, talking about the night ahead of us, when I'm stopped dead in my tracks by the beautiful girl in front of me. Her short, jet-black hair and piercing green eyes wandering around our group then falling on me. I can't help the smile that spreads across my face as she makes her way over to us.

"You look ready to party," Susie nudges me with her shoulder as she stands close to me.

"You look ready to nurse a drunken Lucy," I gently nudge her back, knowing my height and weight could send her flying.

"Anything to keep her relaxed around Clay," she lets out a low sigh, "but I am excited to party with you, Pauline," she winks.

"Back at you, Susie Q," I say as I gently pull her hair.

It's nice this…friendship we've formed. And no matter what strange, foreign feelings may creep in every once in a while, that's all this will remain.

A friendship.

Three Months Earlier

Chapter 1

Susie

"You guys, this is ridiculous," I say as I sit on the mat, looking around at all the other girls. The word I should use is ludicrous, this is freaking ludicrous.

Clara leans over, gently hitting me in the shoulder. "Suse, respectfully, shut up. This is the exact talk we said not to do today."

Suse, a nickname the girls gave me, making sure to let the guys know to correctly pronounce it "Sues" not "Sus" to which all of them have but Paul. He has his own little nickname for me. I'm not naive to how it makes me feel…but it's Paul. He has a nickname for every girl, that's how he is–

"Did we lose you?" Leah asks as she holds her hand out, a smile spreads across her face.

I take it as I stand, fixing the cheeky spandex shorts I have on, continuously tugging down my sports bra to make sure there's no underboob.

"Nope, I'm here, petrified and sort of ready for tomorrow."

The big day. Tryouts.

How I let these four talk me into trying out for cheer is

absolutely beyond me. Never have I ever cheered a day in my life. Art has always been my thing. Painting, drawing, sketching, you name it. I didn't care for sports in high school and I don't particularly now, but I must admit, watching my four best friends compete in Daytona last year did look somewhat fun.

Imagine my surprise when they all bombarded me about their grand scheme a few weeks after we returned – a few weeks post-aftermath of Jake and Leah – which thankfully got worked out and the two are happier than ever.

At first, I didn't think they were serious. Me trying out for Barker's cheer team? The team that just became NCA National Champions? Hah, yeah right. Except they were. Clara, Sara, Lucy and Leah with their bright eyes wanted me to join the team and share their experiences. It only took them two weeks to convince me, and even now I haven't fully convinced myself. Still, their confidence has never wavered in me.

I wish I could say the same. Confidence isn't in my vocabulary. That's not to say I'm some gal who's down on herself *all* the time...I just struggle in certain aspects. Believing in myself? Hit and miss. Trying new things? I hesitate at the thought. Relationships? Even worse. I'm hoping that by putting myself in this situation, I'll grow in all three.

I'm trying out as a backspot, it was the one position they felt I'd be strong in. I'm too tall to be a flyer but not strong enough to be a base; we tried giving it a shot over the summer, it ended with a black eye from Clara falling on me – a fault of my own. However, when I stepped in as a backspot, it came natural. My tallness helps reach higher on the girl's leg, not to mention over my dead body will I let a girl hit the floor.

The girls recruited several stunt groups to practice with us over the summer before tryout camp – helping teach me the basics with various girls and groups; all were surprised at how well and quickly I learned the position. Including me.

Then came the matter of tumbling…the bane to my existence. I despise everything about it. In no life should it be possible to flip through the air without touching the ground, yet my best friends make it seem so simple. We spent many, many days and hours working me up to a simple standing back handspring and running back handspring, both still appear to resemble that of a slow-paced turtle mixed with a newborn foal trying to walk. Still, I have the skill and it's the minimum requirement for the team. The girls keep reassuring me that tumbling is continuously worked on throughout the season and will not be a make or break situation, but I'm not so sure Coach will see it that way tomorrow.

Still, no matter what, I'm proud of trying. With my lack of self-confidence, it took a lot for me to do this for myself.

"You'll do great, Suse," Lucy adds as she wraps her arm around my shoulder. "Now, can we please go eat? I'm starving."

As we make our way outside, we spot Liam's jeep in the parking lot in what has become our normal end to a practice. A little evening tradition that consists of IHOP and decompressing from our very stressful evening.

Immediately, all four of the boys hop out as we make our way to the car. To no surprise, Liam instantly embraces Clara in a very, very long kiss while Jake has engulfed Leah in an incredibly tight hug. I love seeing my friends happy – Clara and Leah are so incredibly loved by their men, and truly, it brings my heart joy. I just also wish I had that–

"And how was today, Susie Q?"

Susie Q. Only one person calls me that. I turn to my left to see those honey-filled eyes smiling down on me.

"Well, Pauline. It could've gone a lot worse. How was your practice?" Paul scrunches his nose at his nickname. His dark brown hair perfectly pushed back on top of his head. How does it always look like this man just came from the perfect windstorm?

Ever since Clara and Liam started dating last year, our friend group has become intertwined and I've come to know and like all of Liam's friends: Jake, Paul and Clay. However, Paul has become one I'm more comfortable with. I'm not sure why, I'm just relaxed around him and most importantly…I can be myself. Don't get me wrong, my gals make me feel the same way, but when the ghost of your high school self weighs heavy on your mind, all thanks to a boy, it's hard.

But not with Paul.

"Pauline the Saltine. It fits so perfectly," I tease, "I like it."

He gently taps my nose as he says, "Whatever you say, Susie Q."

"Mhm," we hear Lucy cough beside us, standing there with her arms crossed. Beside her, about two arm lengths away, as that's about as close as he can get without getting his head ripped off, stands Clay.

"Can we go eat now please? And once again–"

I cut her off, knowing exactly what she's about to say, "You aren't riding with Clay," I look at her and roll my eyes, "we know, Lu."

Clay doesn't bother looking her way, instead he scoffs and motions towards Paul.

"I'll take Paul and Susie."

Paul gives me a sideways grin as he holds his hand out in front of him like a proper gentleman.

"After you."

* * *

"That's bullshit," Liam laughs as he leans back, stretching an arm behind Clara. "You really think Rogers would suck Coach Watt's dick if it means he could be captain instead of ol' Clay over here?"

Next to me, Paul shrugs his shoulders. "I'm just saying what I heard, dude. Although I wouldn't put it past him. The dude's a complete–"

"Kiss ass," Sara adds as she rolls her eyes, wrapping her arm between mine. "We've heard."

Her subtle outburst causes us all to laugh. It's not often Sara speaks up in the group. In fact, she's been so busy lately she hasn't been around much outside of cheer practice and occasionally joins us for girls night. I can't blame her; she's a senior balancing an internship for her interior design program, work, and cheer. She joins when she can, but it's rare.

"Just so there's no question about it," Jake adds while looking at no one but Leah. The man is so smitten with our girl and I'm here for it. "The dude is a complete kiss ass."

Paul flips him the finger while directing his attention to Clara. "Enough about us and hockey. Tomorrow's the big day, how do you all feel?" He nudges me with his shoulder. "Will Susie Q be a Beavers cheerleader soon?"

I shake my head, not because I'm saying no, but because I'm trying to shake off all this stress and freaking anxiety. I want so badly to make the team, not necessarily because I care so much about being a cheerleader, but because I care to prove to myself that I can.

"I think Suse has a really great chance!" Clara winks at me from across the table. "Not to mention she looked smokin' hot in the uniform when we had fittings the other day."

If there's one thing about my girls, it's that they'll forever believe in me even when I don't.

"Like there was ever any doubt," Paul throws out there without looking up from his food. Earlier on in our friendship I would've assumed his flirty attitude meant something, but I've come to know that's just Paul. A sweet-talker hockey player who's only care is what puck bunny he'll be with that evening. That's who he is and there's nothing wrong with that – to each their own.

"I don't know," I say while pouring syrup on my waffle. "I'm not the best by any means but I'm going to go out there tomorrow and give it my all!" I've heard the same spill from my mom twenty times since I told her about me trying out.

"Hell yeah Suse!" Jake says with a smile. "No matter what happens, we're all proud of you."

Then the whole table erupts with excitement which includes a lot of "fuck yeahs", "you got this", and my personal favorite, "fuck em' up, Q."

* * *

It's nights like tonight I'm semi-thankful to have the dorm room by myself. Clara basically all but lives with Liam at his River Road house, but she does make an effort to still come and check on me every other day. But tonight, I'm happy to be alone.

Tonight I am focusing on tomorrow. I've practiced the cheers at least twelve times, not to mention the silly facial expressions I've been making in the mirror for the last ten minutes. I'm glad no one is here to see how badly I want this; that would make tomorrow's rejection that much more painful.

I'm getting ready to hop in the shower when I hear my phone chime.

PAULINE

How are you really feeling?

A sweet question, but discussing my nerves is the last thing I want to do right now.

Seriously, I'm fine. Nervous, of course. But I'm ready and excited!

PAULINE

If you say so. You'll do great tomorrow. Can't wait to see this uniform the girls were talking about. G'night Q.

I swear the only thing this man knows is flirting.

Thank you, Pauline. Goodnight.

Chapter 2

Paul

W hen I found out Susie was planning to try out for the cheer team, it made me nervous for her. I don't know why I care so much? I mean sure, Susie and I have gotten close over the last few months and yeah I consider her one of my good friends, but why I care so much about her making the damn cheer team is beyond me. I can only assume it's due to me knowing how it'll go for her once she does.

Susie Cobble is sweet and kind. A junior with me, Liam and Clara, and from what I can tell, she's incredibly naive. I'm not saying that to be rude, I'm saying that because just last week at the restaurant the girl was oblivious to the waiter flirting with her. Hell, I could practically see the fucking hard-on he had, yet she didn't bat an eye. One could guess maybe she wasn't interested, but considering she was staring at him like she was also into him, I'm going to say she had no idea about his subtle hints of flirting.

Becoming a cheerleader at Barker University will basically be similar to throwing her into shark infested waters, and I'm not sure she knows how to swim. Again, it isn't my business and I sure as hell ain't going to voice my concern but should a motherfucker mess around and hurt her, it won't just be the girls on his back.

But hey, that's what friends are for.

"Has Clara texted you?" I ask Liam who's currently sporting a stupid-ass grin. The girls are currently in there awaiting the tryout results and we're all anxious to see how it went.

"Dude, she sent me the cutest dog for adoption, look."

"Are we still on the subject of a dog?" Jake asks, peeking over the driver's seat to see the photo.

I swear they've turned into women since getting girlfriends. Their dicks? Gone.

"I was talking about tryouts–"

"Holy fucking shit balls! Paul, Clay. Guys, look at this dog," Jake yells while grinning from ear to ear. It is inevitable that soon our house will be getting a dog. I'm not entirely against it, but I haven't told them that yet. I love making Clara sweat that it may not happen if not everyone's on board. As for Clay, I don't know how he feels.

I roll my eyes as I lean over, preparing myself to not react too excitedly to where Liam will tell Clara. He tells her everything…

"Holy shit that's the cutest dog I've ever seen." Well, there went my plan. But seriously, the statement stands. "Clay, dude. You have to see this dog."

"Really, Paul. You too?" He asks as he reluctantly leans forward. "It's a–"

And then he goes quiet because even cold, heartless Clay can't resist those cute eyes. It's a little black and brown dachshund with the word "Chiweenie" underneath it. I don't know what the hell a Chiweenie is, but I want this dog.

"It's not the ugliest thing in the world," Clay adds as he

shrugs his shoulders. He tries to turn away, but not before I catch the smallest smirk on his face.

"I wouldn't be completely opposed if this little guy came to live with us," I say as I go back to checking my phone, waiting to see if a text from Susie appears.

I remember when she first started coming around with Clara. I may have openly flirted with the girl and I still do, but as my reputation precedes me, that's not out of the ordinary. I flirt with everyone. And although it is just harmless flirting, I can't deny the fact that I enjoy being around her. But that's as far as it goes.

"Then it's settled," Liam says. "I'll let her–oh shit…she's calling."

He quickly hushes us as he answers the phone. It's a very quick call, one which gives no answers about how tryouts went.

"What she'd say?" Jake asks. "Did they all make it?"

He points towards the door of the athletic center as he says, "Ask them yourself."

We all immediately rush out of the vehicle and begin heading towards them. None of us were worried about Clara, Sara, Lucy or Leah – I'm pretty sure being part of the winning NCA Championship team helps prove your abilities – it's Susie we're all anxious to hear about.

As we approach the girls, their faces aren't showing much. There's no tears, but also, no smiles.

Fuck.

"Ladies," Liam says as he immediately pulls Clara into a kiss. "How did it go?"

Susie looks around at her friends, none of them saying a word.

"Well, it could've gone better," she admits while looking at me.

"That statement stands for all of us," Lucy adds as she intertwines her arm with Susie's, "but you did great Suse!"

I give her a wink because as Lucy said, I know she did great.

"Even I shit a brick," Clara says as she wraps her petite arm around Liam. "I don't think there was a single cheerleader in there that didn't mess up."

"Okay, okay," I quickly add, "people fuck up and everyone can do better, but did you make the team?" The anticipation is killing me.

"Oh, we don't know," Sara chimes in. "They won't send out information until this evening. I thought we told you guys that?"

Are you shitting me? I look over towards the other three who are as confused as I am.

"Uh, I don't–"

"I dare you to finish that sentence, Wiley," Leah says as she gently cups his chin, "I told you last night, remember?"

Judging by the look on his face, he most definitely does not.

"Of course, of course, darlin'. How could I forget anything you tell me?"

She, along with the rest of us, roll our eyes as Susie moves next to me while the others begin to talk.

"It was pretty nerve wracking," she admits as she leans closer. My six-foot-one figure towers over her five-foot-oneish build which gives my nose perfect access to all things sweet and Susie. She smells like berries mixed with flowers and vanilla – just as sweet as she is.

"All tryouts are, Susie Q. I bet you did great," I gently nudge her shoulder. "Freshman year of high school, I was convinced I wouldn't make the hockey team because of an error I had on a drill I've been doing since seven. Yet here I am years later, the best goalie BU has had," I wink.

"Oh, Pauline," she places her hand on my shoulder. "I admire your humble attitude but–"

"Are we ready?" Clara joins our conversation. "Our tradition of IHOP continues on. Plus, at least if things go to shit with tryouts we can eat our emotions with pancakes and syrup!"

I wrap my arm around Clara's shoulder as we both keep looking at Susie who is now sporting a small smile.

"First," I say, pinching Clara's cheek with my other hand, "it won't go to shit. Second, pancakes sound good. Whatcha think, Q?"

Her smile grows bigger as her little dimples begin to show. One of the prettiest smiles I've ever seen.

"Like I have a choice," she says as she walks past us. My head automatically turns to follow her.

"Paul," Clara's voice brings my focus back to her.

"Yes, Sandra D?" referencing a costume she once wore over before her and Liam were a thing, and I, loving to piss Liam off, jokingly flirted with her about it.

She hesitates for a moment before her lip slightly tugs upward. "Never mind, I'm hungry. Let's go."

* * *

Just like every night before, our group has found its way to the same corner table in the same seating arrangements. When we first came here after the girls first practice, it was like playing musical fucking chairs to keep everyone happy. The girls wanted to be close enough to one another to talk but also sit with their boyfriends. Then we had to make sure Lucy was far enough away from Clay so she wouldn't stab him with a knife which landed me next to Susie with Clay on my left.

"Dude," Clay nudges my shoulder. "The waitress hasn't stopped staring at you. It's ridiculous and sad watching her drool over you. Can you please–"

I look over, not realizing I haven't been focusing on anyone or anything other than the girl next to me, and see a taller, sunshine-blinding blonde eye-fucking me; something I'm used to and happily welcome. But being around Susie… and the girls…I don't necessarily find myself wanting to bring her home.

"She's cute," is all I say as I direct my attention to the menu.

"Who's cute?" Susie leans forward looking at Clay and I. Her eyes wander around the restaurant until she settles on the same blonde who is still looking in my direction. "Ah, she is cute! And," she pats my knee, "I think she's staring at you, Paul."

"Honey, all the girls stare at me. Don't you know who I am?" I return the favor by patting her knee, offering my most charming smile.

"Good lord," she shakes her head as she waves the waitress over.

"What are you doing?" I ask her, eyebrows pressed together.

"Helping a friend out. Not that you need help, I mean you are Paul Simmons. But the poor girl was looking pretty desperate and that's just sad," she winks as the waitress approaches.

"Hi, I'm Lindsay. Did you need something?" she asks, still looking directly at me. She's even more gorgeous up close, but still…I'm not entirely interested right now.

"Just another Dr. Pepper. Please, Lind–"

"My friend here is being shy. He thinks you're quite cute, he said so himself," Susie adds.

I quickly twist my neck towards her, as do all of our friends who are now very aware of what's going on. I think the girl's cute, yes. But I don't really give a shit. Strange, I know.

"I–uh–" what the hell do I say? "I do think you're cute," I finally manage to get out there, "but–"

"Everyone shut the fuck up the results are in," Lucy practically screams for the entire restaurant to hear, which is perfect timing for this disaster with Sidney, Lindy – I don't remember. Susie immediately grabs my hand, squeezing it tightly. It instantly draws my attention from the waitress to her. Her gorgeous, concerned eyes widely staring at me.

"Sorry Lindy, we're good. Thank you."

And with that, she walks off. Judging by the look on her face, I don't think her name was Lindy.

"You just scared off your puck bunny for the evening," Susie says, still holding onto my hand.

I gently squeeze it back as I add, "She doesn't matter right now, you do." I motion towards Lucy with my head. "What's the results say, Lucy?"

Jake has his arm wrapped around Leah's shoulders while Clara is clinging to Liam's arm like a sloth to a tree. Sara is on the other side of Susie holding her arm with Lucy directly in front of them biting her nails. Everyone is eager and nervous to know if Susie will be joining them on the sideline next school year and potentially in Daytona... including me.

"Well," she says as she looks around at everyone. "I'm sorry to say you boys will have to get to games early from now on because you no longer have someone to save you seats. She'll be too busy cheering on the sidelines," she finishes with the biggest smile I've seen Lucy wear since winning the competition a few months ago.

The entire table erupts with cheers as the girls begin clapping and quite literally jumping up and down in the booth. Even Liam, Jake and Clay are smiling. Me? I'm carefully watching for Susie's reaction. I know how much she wanted this and I'd imagine she'd be screaming from joy right now, but she isn't.

"Did you–" I begin to say but am quickly cut off.

"I'm a freaking Beaver cheerleader, Pauline."

I realize she never let go of my hand, she's only squeezing it tighter. I smile as I nudge her with my shoulder, her eyes bright.

"Yes you are, Q."

Present

Chapter 3

Paul

What a wedding. In all honesty, I never thought we'd be here; Liam Russell and Clara Lowe *finally* tying the knot. It's fucking ridiculous it took Liam as long as it did to get his shit together and tell Clara how he feels, but that's Liam. Shit at communicating, but a damn good friend.

Am I still pissed at him for not being his best man? Hell yeah I am. But…I understand. If it were up to me, it would've been strip clubs and Vegas for the bachelor party, not some country cabin filled with fishing and corn hole, which is exactly why he chose Jake. Ever since Leah, the man's become calm and tame. No more parties, no more puck bunnies. As much as I hate losing a fellow friend to tag along and play wingman, I am happy for both of my best buds. Clara and Leah are exactly what the two needed in their lives, and seeing them so in love is equally disgusting and somewhat cute.

Which leaves Clay and I.

He's now taken on the role of being my wingman and vice versa. Although it's really only him being my wingman as he is on a strict *"no relationship"* rule due to hockey. He just got named captain of the team which has turned that rule into more of a goddamn commandment for himself.

Me? I'm content with puck bunnies and the one-night stands. Fuck around, never tied down – that's what I've lived by. But tonight, there's only one girl that keeps catching my eye. The gorgeous Susie Cobble.

She's a walking picture of sunshine and happiness wrapped in absolute beauty.

"Paul Simmons doesn't always wear sweatpants?" Clara's slurring voice interrupts my thoughts as she links her arm through mine.

"A rare occurrence for a special day," I unlink her arm and wrap mine around her shoulders, pulling her into my armpit. "And no, you can't fuck with me about it or everyone will find out about your dirty *Jersey Shore* secret, bestie."

"That's *our* secret. You'd go down too, Paulie."

Paulie. A stupid nickname the boys gave me last year that Leah and Clara now use as well.

"My word against yours," I tease.

"Touché."

We stand there for a moment, watching our friends on the dance floor. Our very shit-faced friends.

"Clara Russell has a nice ring to it," I say, turning towards her with a smile. "I'm happy for you tw–"

"Do not make me cry right now," she interrupts before I can finish my sentence. "But you are right." She pushes me away with her elbow just as a slow-paced song comes on.

"Excuse me, but can I grab my wife now?" Liam appears out of nowhere, grabbing Clara's hand.

"By all means, buddy."

I step aside as I watch the two take the dance floor, followed by Jake and Leah. I immediately turn around heading towards Clay who is at a table by himself with a deathly glare looking past me. I turn to follow his eyes and see Jake with his hand very dangerously close to Leah's ass with Lucy and a random man next to them. I'm unsure why he'd be glaring, the two do much worse in front of us.

"Harp, dude. Your eyes could burn a hole through the wall," I say as I sit next to him. Still, his gaze is locked.

He cuts his eyes my way, most likely annoyed by the nickname, but he doesn't mention it.

"Do we know him?" he asks. I now realize it isn't Jake and Leah he's glaring at.

"Uh I–"

"Doesn't matter." And with that, he's gone.

I sit here, basking in just how amazing their wedding turned out to be – especially for it being planned in four months. Truthfully, the two could've gotten married in a barn in the middle of butt-fuck nowhere and it would've been a great time.

"No puck bunny to dance with?" Her soft voice catches me off guard as I turn to see Susie taking the empty seat beside mine.

Holy hell she's gorgeous.

She has a long, red dress with a very low-cut neckline and two very thin straps holding it on her shoulders.

"Not tonight, Q. Tonight I'm admiring other things," I drag my eyes up and down her body, licking my lips.

She fidgets in her seat, laughing as she slightly turns away. "You're such a tease."

"Clearly I'm talking about the decorations," shaking my head back and forth, I stand and hold out my hand. "Dance with me?"

I shouldn't. Being this close to Susie with how she looks makes my mind not think clearly, but again…I like being near her.

"You–you want to dance?"

"Only with you, Susie Q."

She stares at my hand for a moment before carefully taking it. Immediately, I begin walking to the floor, trailing her behind me as we make our way close to the rest of our friends. When we find an empty spot, I spin around and pull her close to me, gently placing my hand on the small of her back. She's being very cautious in leaving a space between us, causing me to let out a small chuckle.

"And why are you laughing?" she asks with an attitude. A *cute* attitude.

"Because you're staying away from me like I'm the plague," I pull her tight against me. "There."

"I–I didn't want people to think–"

"That we're a thing? It's a simple dance with one of my best friends, that's all Q. Fuck what everyone else thinks."

I finally feel her relax and lean her cheek against my chest as we continue to sway to Chris Stapleton's "Tennessee Whiskey." It reminds me of all those months ago when she fell asleep on my shoulder on our way home from Daytona. I didn't have the heart to tell her I was uncomfortable, and truthfully, I liked the feeling of having her there.

"I'm nervous, Paul," she says, interrupting me from the memory.

"About?" I pull back, looking into her gorgeous green eyes.

"Being a cheerleader. I–I didn't really think I'd make it and now that I have I'm worried I won't be good..."

I begin shaking my head. "None of that shit. You made the team for a reason," I hook my finger under her chin. "You're going to do great."

A faint smile comes across her face along with a light shade of red on her cheeks. "Much easier said than done. But thank you," she says leaning in, wrapping her petite arms around my waist. "I'm glad to have a friend like you, Paul."

I lean down, placing my cheek against the top of her head. "Yeah, you are pretty lucky."

Her chest begins shaking up and down with laughter as the song comes to an end and she pulls away. Smiling Susie is a lot better than doubts herself Susie, and I'm not sure if it's the alcohol or the fact that she was just so close to me, but I grab her hand before she turns to walk away.

"You're beautiful, Susie. Inside and out, and that, along with your hard work, is why you're going to be a great cheerleader."

She goes to open her mouth but something behind me catches her eye.

"There's a girl behind you undressing you with her eyes. You better go before she thinks you're taken," she squeezes my hand before pulling away. "Thank you for the dance, Paul."

I watch her walk away, taking a moment to admire her very perfect ass before I finally peel my gaze to find who she was talking about. Immediately, I'm met with a dark brown stare belonging to a girl with big tits and a sinister smile. She's sexy and might as well be wearing a neon sign that says *"come fuck me."* I take one look back at Susie who is now surrounded by the girls before making my way over to the mystery lady. My game has been off lately, but I have no idea why.

So, I'm on a mission, for myself, to prove I still got it.

Chapter 4

Susie

I thought Paul was kidding when he asked me to dance, but as I'm making my way back to my friends, I was clearly mistaken. And it's taking a very strong voice in my head to convince me *not* to turn around to see him most likely already cuddled up beside the girl with the *take me home* expression written all over her face.

Any girl with eyes and common sense can look at Paul and see how handsomely attractive he is. His chocolate hair is always perfectly messy and even a freaking bear could fall for his honey eyes, which make him *appear* all innocent-like, yet I know that's entirely the opposite of who Paul Simmons is.

Clearly, he's good with the ladies. From Clara's stories, which she learned by being around them since freshman year, he's all down for puck bunnies, one-night stands, and meaningless sex. She's never seen him with the same girl more than once and he usually doesn't care to know their names. *"Fuck around, never tied down"* is the saying I heard Jake use once to describe Paul when we were all out at a bar a few months ago. He claimed Paul wasn't *"being himself"* and had to remind him of who he truly is. It, along with the stories I've heard, is the reason I and most likely every female within Evanston, *probably the surrounding areas*, would categorize Paul Simmons as a *fuckboy.*

Still, he is my friend. And no, I am not slut-shaming him, he can do what he wants, I've just never been able to be like him. Flirtatious and carefree. And I know that's a result of what happened in high school.

I wasn't popular, didn't care to be, and it wasn't until the summer going into senior year that I experienced what one would call a *"glow-up."* And one night shattered any ounce of confidence I had in me. Flirting with boys wasn't on my radar, and honestly, it's safe to say that all these years later I wouldn't know what to do if the opportunity presented itself.

"Cough cough," Sara says. "Are you with us, Suse?"

I realize that at some point I did turn around, and my eyes have been glued to the dance floor where Paul and fuck me girl are dancing. And it isn't a slow dance. It's an ass grind, hands trailing, definitely not suited for young eyes type of dance.

Thank god for Liam and Clara making this an eighteen and older wedding.

"I'm here. I was lost in my own world," I say while looking at Leah who's sharing the same mischievous look as the other three.

"What?"

"We see who you're staring at, Suuuuuuse," Clara draws out very dramatically.

I roll my eyes as I lean over, grabbing Leah's arm.

"An unintentional stare," I quickly add.

"Still a stare," Lucy chuckles as she looks over at the two still grinding on the dance floor.

"He asked you to dance not even five minutes ago and now he's letting another girl grind on him?"

I laugh, grabbing my fork and *finally* diving into the cake everyone claims is so delicious. I'm embarrassed to admit that with the first bite I take, a moan escapes my mouth because yes…it *is* that delicious.

"We're friends, Lucy. He can grind and dance with whomever he wants." The words come out jumbled as I continue to shove my face full of this freaking cake.

She goes to open her mouth but Clara cuts her off.

"What do you guys think of the wedding?" Her voice is laced with worry and concern. For what? I have no idea. It's absolutely stunning.

They settled for a very elegant, classy, inside venue to fit their gigantic number of attendees. The floorplan is very open, leaving enough room for dancing, *apparently club style*, with three very tall, very breathtakingly gorgeous arched windows and a godly-extravagant chandelier. Still, Clara deserves the wedding of her dreams and I'm so incredibly happy for the Russell's.

"Clare bear," I say sincerely as I reach over and grab her hand, ignoring her eye roll towards the nickname she loathes. "Your wedding is absolutely stunning and putting this together in a span of four months is freaking bananas." *I couldn't even imagine.*

"She's right, Clara," Leah adds. "I only hope my wedding is as beautiful as yours and Liam's."

"Your wedding?" Lucy asks with a slight quirk of her brow. "Anything to share with the table, Leah…darlin'."

I chuckle; Leah despises when Lucy pokes fun at Jake for his "*darlin'*" nickname. Me? I think it's absolutely adorable.

"I know that Lucy…I just mean in gen–"

"She's pressing your buttons," Sara adds. "Like she always loves to do."

"Sara," Lucy quickly says, "you're gone ninety-nine percent of the time. How would–"

"My internship is kicking my ass," she flips Lucy off, "but I have missed you guys."

As the conversation continues, I again find my eyes drifting to the dance floor where I no longer see Paul and *bunny. Short for puck bunny that is.* I find the floor now empty, and before I can even begin to look around, I feel a hot breath spread over my neck from above me.

"Do you need a ride, Susie Q?"

Looking behind me, I see Paul standing there with bunny's hand interlaced between his.

"Uh…"

"Have you been drinking?" His voice serious and… concerned?

"Well I…uh–uh yes but–"

"Come on," he drops the girl's hand and stretches it out for me. "I'll give you a ride home."

"Paul," the girl whines. "Aren't we heading back to your place?"

"Not if–"

"Actually," I quickly interject, "I can't leave yet. Bridesmaids are responsible for helping clean up afterwards. And typically," I give him a pointed look, "so are the groomsmen."

His bottom lip slightly pulls into a smirk.

"Then a ride after?"

I look around at the girls who, of course, have disappeared.

"Paul, really. I'm just teasing you. I'll catch a ride with Lu–"

"Lucy is as shit-faced as you. And Leah is coming back to the house. Which leaves Sara who is always MIA," he shrugs his shoulders. "Looks like I'm your only hope, Q."

"Are we not–" the poor girl can't even get her sentence out before Paul cuts her off.

"Sorry, Jessica–"

"It's Jenny."

"My friend here needs a ride. Maybe another time." He doesn't bother looking at her while he talks.

She looks at me, then back at Paul, staring at him a moment before finally walking away with a not-so-happy attitude. When she's gone, I look to Paul with my brows pinched together.

"You didn't have to do that. I could've found a ride, Paul. Go get bunny back for your fun night of talking and movie-watching," I laugh saying it out loud because we both know that's not what they were going to do.

He holds his hand out for the third time tonight and just like before, I hesitate for just a moment before grabbing it.

"Bunny, huh?"

"Puck bunny. Bunny for short," I stop, tugging on his hand. "Really, Paul. I can get a ride home."

"I don't want her," he says abruptly as we begin making our way over to the rest of the group.

"That is not how it looked out on the dance floor, bud," I say as I pat him on the shoulder, walking past him.

"She–she was just–"

I toss a look over my shoulder, nudging my head for him to join me and our friends.

"Pauline, I'm just teasing you. Come on, let's finish out the night with drinks and–"

I am cut off by the very familiar sound of Chappell

Roan's "Hot to Go" accompanied with the high pitch shrilling of my gals in front of me.

I immediately reach back, grabbing Paul's hand as I tug him to the group, letting go as I join Leah, Clara, Sara and Lucy as we begin jumping up and down. At first, the boys share a look of confusion until Jake shrugs his shoulders, joining in the dance with his girlfriend, sending a ripple effect of Liam, Paul and even Clay singing and dancing.

All four of my best friends have a gigantic smile plastered to their face as they scream their hearts out – looking so flaw-less and carefree. And it's at this moment I'm reminded by how incredibly lucky I am to have a friendship like theirs.

Then I turn to my left. The boys have their arms wrapped around each other's shoulders looking at one another trying to keep on beat, laughing more than they are singing when my eyes connect with Paul's. A smile as wide as mine on his face.

And it's at this moment I'm reminded that not only do I have the best four girlfriends a girl could ask for. I also have Paul. And he's a good friend, too.

Chapter 5

Susie

One Week Later

It's just a mixer. That's all it is. With every single football player on Barker University's team. Am I nervous? No. *Yes*.

I only just made the team a month or so ago, still not entirely sure how, but this is my first outing in my cheer uniform with the whole team and all the players; I'm not just nervous, I'm absolutely terrified. Fears are on overdrive.

What if I don't look good in the uniform? I'm not as skinny as my friends. My left boob is bigger than my right and my thighs are on the larger side – muscle is what Clara calls it – still, there's things about my body that I love and things that still live in my mind from *that night*. But like my mom tells me, I am beautiful inside and out, and beauty does not a body make.

So, here I am getting ready with my girls, trying to ease my nerves while convincing myself it'll be a good time.

"Did you hear me, Suse?" Leah asks from in front of me where Sara's doing her hair.

"Oh–I…no. I'm sorry. I was–"

"Overthinking?" Lucy asks, leaning as close as one can to the mirror without touching it.

"I–I–I'm just nervous." *And yes, overthinking.*

I *never* spend this much time doing my hair or makeup. The short cut is simple enough to just wake up, add a few products and call it good. I do very minimal to my face and am out the door in a total of fifteen minutes. I don't even know where to begin right now.

"Can a bow even fit in my hair with how short it is?" I yell, accidentally. "I can't do half-up half-down like Leah because mine isn't long enough. I can't pull all my hair up either. And what if it won't stay in and I can't wear a bow at all? Do you think Coach will be mad?" I take a deep breath and continue to word vomit.

"And my makeup? I've never, ever done as much as y'all are doing and I don't necessarily want to but will if you guys think I should. And what should I expect tonight because it's only been a few months and I haven't mastered all the cheers and if we're stunting what if my hands are too sweaty and–"

"Honey, take a breath," Clara comes around to my front, grabbing my shoulders.

"You do as much and as little as you want to do with your makeup, you are radiant as is. As for your hair, no stress! The girls and I researched many different ways to get it to stay – that sucker won't be going anywhere," she winks as she lets go of my shoulders, moving to sit behind me. "Now, do you want to straighten or curl it?"

I can feel my eyes begin to burn, refusing to allow a tear to escape…but I truly have the most thoughtful friends.

"Curl, please, Clare Bear."

She gets to work on my hair as Lucy finds her way in front of me to do my makeup.

"What did you decide? Natural looking?" she asks while rubbing her lipstick together.

"I want to look like myself with a hint of sexy," I wink. And like a proud mother, she clasps her hands together and says three words, "Let's get started."

I sit here, following every instruction she gives me while Clara continues to add little curls in my hair. My fear? I'll resemble Shirley Temple, but I am trusting the process.

It's only been a week since Clara Lowe became Clara Russell and we're still living on the high of her wedding.

"So, Lucy," Sara says with a smirk on her face. "Did you end up going home with Mr. not-so-subtle last Saturday night?"

Judging by the eye-roll, I'm going to guess no.

"Please," she says, "I just wanted–Suse, keep your eyebrow still–I just wanted to dance and he was there."

"Oh, we know," Clara adds. "We had the privilege of hearing him describe just how well he'd take care of you if you would have let him take you home. He wasn't bad look-ing, but he was my cousin's date and she was definitely not happy," she giggles.

"You know who else wasn't too happy?" I ask, making sure to be as still as possible. Before giving them a chance to answer or to hear Lucy snap at me to be still, I add, "Your brother, Leah."

Her neck snaps to mine.

"Why? Because Jake's hand was on my ass? That's bull-shit. We've done way worse around him."

"I overheard him asking Paul about the guy Lucy was dancing with," I open one eye to gauge her reaction.

"Why the hell would he care who I was dancing with?"

"He was curious who he was, I guess?"

"What's it to him? He's an arrogant asshole – sorry Leah

– who thinks he can do anything, say anything, and get anyone he wants. He probably wanted to warn the poor bastard away from me. Ugh, he's such a dick."

I look around at the girls and mouth *"sorry"* as she continues her rampage. I don't know why or when, but early on in our group friendship, those two decided to hate each other, and it hasn't faded since.

"Okay, okay," Sara cuts her off, "you hate Clay, he hates you. Trust us, we get it," she cocks a brow over Leah's head. "I'm more interested to hear about you and Paul's ride home, Suse."

Well, I saw this coming.

"It was just a ride. A ride from a friend who wanted to make sure I got home safe."

Still, it was a very enjoyable ride home.

* * *

"Here," Paul says from beside me. "It's chilly outside, take my jacket."

Without waiting for my reply, he drapes it over my shoulders. It's fifty-five degrees out here, not the coldest, but I still find myself wrapping it around me as we make our way to his truck.

What a wedding. And now, I'm exhausted.

The two love birds left about an hour ago and we spent the remaining hour cleaning up. Now, everybody has gone their separate ways. I made a beeline for Sara after cleanup was done, but Paul kept insisting on driving me back to the dorm, which is how we got here. Him helping me into his tall-ass truck.

He gets into the driver's seat, immediately turning on the radio as he angles towards me with a smile on his face.

"You hungry?"

"Well, I mean...kind of? But it's midnight and–"

"McDonald's or something else?" He raises his eyebrow, insinuating he once again will not be taking no for an answer.

"I could eat a whole twenty-piece right now," I chuckle. "I'd love McDonald's."

"I could tear up some McDonald's, too," he winks as he pulls out of the parking lot. "I know it's supposedly fake-ass chicken, but it's my favorite fast food restaurant and I am not ashamed to admit it, Q."

With that, we let the silence wash over us with only the soft hum of music filling the truck, but I don't mind. Tonight was exceptionally loud and...a lot, a little breather is nice. Paul must feel the same; he hasn't said a thing.

As the song ends and we're pulling into McDonald's drive through, he turns the radio off.

"You want the meal or just the nuggets?"

"Paul," I say, getting him to look at me. "If you think I'm going to pass up McDonald's french fries, you're insane."

He swipes his tongue over his bottom lip while shaking his head up and down and says, "Noted."

After getting our food, and him yet again not taking no for an answer when it came to paying, we're now sitting in the parking lot stuffing our faces.

I watch as this man devours twenty nuggets, two mcdoubles, and a spicy mcchicken while I'm still on nugget number ten. I'm fairly certain my mouth is hanging open as I watch him pull out his two large fries next.

"Q," he says without turning towards me. "Is there something I can help you with?"

"I–I just...where–where does it go? Seriously, Paul.

You're all muscle and a solid stomach. If I just ate like you did I'd be bloated and at least gain four pounds."

Now he faces me.

"You think I'm all muscle?" He pats his stomach. "Aw Susie Q, you're feeding my ego. Be careful or I'll think you're flirting with me."

I feel my cheeks instantly turn red. I know Paul flirts with me, but that's Paul. Me? I'm not a flirt and if he thinks I'm flirting he's going to think I want something and if he thinks I want something he won't want to be my friend and I–

"I'm kidding. Tell your wheels in there," he reaches over tapping my forehead, "to slow down."

I let out a huff of air without even knowing I was holding my breath to begin with.

"Good, good. I–I didn't want you to think I wanted more or anything. You know, didn't want to lose you as a friend and I am definitely not a flirt. Wouldn't even know how," I throw my hands up in innocence, wishing I could shut up. "Haven't flirted with anyone in ages, literally I'm like a grandma."

A grandma? What the hell am I saying?

He chuckles as he reaches over and grabs my hand.

"Susie, you're spiraling," he gently squeezes. "Not a flirt and not flirting with me, got it."

Something foreign paints his face, a look that I can't explain but it's gone before I can dwell on it and his usual smug smile is back. He lets go of my hand, turning back to the steering wheel.

"I should let you know that all my flirting is completely innocent. You too are my good friend and if it ever makes you uncomfort–"

"It's who you are, Pauline. You couldn't stop if you wanted to," I tease.

He shrugs his shoulders in agreement as he continues

scarfing down french fries. Just as I think the conversation is over, he clears his throat.

"Hey grandma," he says in a hushed voice. "If you ever need practice, I'd willingly be your guinea pig."

I roll my eyes, looking over at his shit-eating grin.

"As if," I say.

* * *

"If it was just a ride, why are you grinning from ear to ear?" Leah sticks her finger out, wiggling it like a little school girl.

Damnit, I am smiling.

"I promise that Paul and I are just friends," I shake my head laughing. "He's a good friend and makes me laugh, that's all."

And he just so happens to be extremely handsome and caring…

"And when did you and Paul become such good friends?" Lucy raises an eyebrow.

Honestly, I'm not sure how to answer that. When did we become such good friends?

"Well, I considered us friends before Daytona, but I think the trip was when our friendship really grew."

Lucy nods, motioning for me to continue.

"I was stuck in a car with him for seventeen hours one-way, sitting right next to the dude." I think back to our game of twenty questions on our way home to Evanston. It was so quiet in that car thanks to the events that occurred between Jake and Clay, you could've heard a pin drop, so we texted back and forth sharing embarrassing confessions and talking about our favorite foods.

"And then when we got back it just…continued. I think he's become one of my best friends," I chuckle.

The girls don't say anything, but I see the looks they're sharing with one another.

I twist my head to Clara. "I swear it's not a big dea–"

"Okay, okay," she says as she turns my head back. "They're just giving you a hard time. Turn around, I'm almost done," she rests her head on my shoulder. "And then we can head to the mixer and all the boys will be dying for a chance to talk to Susie Cobble."

Probably not true, but the thought alone terrifies me.

Chapter 6

Susie

"I –I think I left something in the car," I turn around to hustle back, hoping to lock myself inside away from the field we're about to walk onto.

"Oh no you don't," Sara grabs my arm. "You are a cheerleader now, Susie. Own this shit. Plus, you look super hot."

I scratch my head as I reluctantly let her drag me along. When I originally asked the girls for the reason behind the mixer, they said it's been a tradition for forty-five football seasons, one the coaches take very seriously. Apparently it's a way for the players and cheerleaders to meet, mingle, and get excited for the season because in the words of Coach Bates, the football coach, "What is football without cheerleaders?"

The mixer is strictly for staff, coaches, football players and cheerleaders – no outsiders – which did not settle well with the boys. In fact, we're still getting messages in our *"Dudes & Dudettes"* chat; super original, I know.

JAKE WILEY

Fucking ridiculous, just saying.

LIAM RUSSELL

I mean I do agree. C, babe. Are you sure
you can't sneak us in? Pleaaaseeee.

"Clara, can you convince your man that it is not happening?" Lucy asks while she mutes the chat. As you can guess, she and Clay don't participate much in the conversations.

"The man doesn't hear anything other than when I tell him I love him and that I can't wait to suck his di–"

"No," Sara slaps her hand over Clara's mouth. "Don't finish the sentence, just text back."

CLARE BEAR

Leon, my love. You guys really need to get
over it. We'll see you all at the bar
afterwards.

She has a point guys. It's a FOOTBALL
mixer - see you boys later!

PAULINE

I agree. Bullshit. Plus, hockey players are so
much better. Hotter, tougher, sexier,
stronger, bigger dicks. You get the point.

SARA

We don't care about your dick size, Paul.

LEAH

Well, I do care about one person's dick in
this group chat

Clay Harper has left the group chat.
Pauline has added Clay Harper to the group chat.

CLAY HARPER

No talking about dicks in this chat.

LU

I never thought I'd say this, but for once, I agree with Clay.

CLAY HARPER

Hey sweetheart, you're learning.

Lu has left the group chat.
Susie has added Lu to the group chat.

"You know he just likes fucking with you," Clara says as we're making our way into the gates, nudging Lucy on her shoulder.

"I don't give a shit. He's annoying, basically a Neanderthal, and overly–"

"Not that I disagree," Leah says next to me, looking towards Lucy, "but can we stop talking about my brother and enjoy our first mixer together?"

We finally step into the bleachers, overlooking the field, and it's even more insane than I could imagine. The football team consists of about one hundred players; not all see an ounce of time on the field, but of course all were required to be here tonight. It's a bit intimidating, looking down at the sea of people, but I feel a bit of relief knowing I'm not alone.

* * *

It's been thirty minutes. Thirty minutes of me giving the same speech to every new person I meet. Thirty minutes of me wishing I could go back to only hanging out with the girls. And thirty minutes of me constantly pulling at my damn skirt.

When someone came over the speaker stating that "speed friending" was about to begin, I can only imagine how wide my eyes were. See, the girls didn't tell me that the mixer came with organized activities, such as spending an entire hour of "speed friending" to get to know the entire football team…

Us cheerleaders were instructed to find a seat as the players switched to a new person every five minutes. Considering there are significantly more players than cheerleaders, when they made their rounds and claimed they were finished, they had to turn in their signed card before being released from their "duty."

Thankfully, the girls and I are sitting semi-close to each other, so even through this awful hour, we're still able to somewhat go through it together.

"How was the last guy?" I yell to Clara who's the furthest away with Lucy next to her, followed by Sara, me and then Leah.

"Well," she rolls her eyes, "he at least didn't smell like an onion." She shrugs her shoulders as the next few players begin making their way to us. There's no mistaking when it's time to switch when someone, I'm assuming Coach Bates, blows an air horn into the overhead speaker.

I watch as Lucy leans over to Clara, chuckling about the boys who are now approaching them as I turn my gaze to Sara who is staring straight ahead with a smile on her face. I follow her eyes to the very familiar footballer approaching her table, one of Barker's most handsome players, Chase Ryker. The same Chase Ryker that dated Clara, took the break up like a champ, and still wished her well. All in all, he seems like a decent guy. Just as quickly as he approaches, I watch the twinkle in Sara's eye disappear as she gently shakes her head.

I open my mouth to ask if she's okay when the sound of someone clearing their throat in front of me captures my attention. I snap my head towards the noise and am met by gorgeous blue eyes, broad shoulders, and a very muscular body with a messy head of blonde hair.

He's absolutely gorgeous.

"I'm sorry," I say as I nervously run my hand over the top of my hair, "I didn't see you there."

He giggles, a very adorable sound, as he pulls out the chair in front of me. In true speed dating fashion, the coaches set up a table and chairs to make us more comfortable…

Except nothing about this is comfortable.

"No worries, sweetheart. You notice me now, that's all that matters," he winks.

"A smooth talker I see." Grabbing my chair, I sit down. Suddenly becoming very aware of how sweaty my palms are. He's extremely cute, and it's not that I'm not around cute boys – I mean Paul, arguably one of my best friends, is as cute as they come – but still…I wasn't prepared for *this* guy.

He leans back in his chair, stretching his arms up and above his head, revealing what I already knew. Chiseled, muscular, very detailed abs.

"So, tell me about yourself, Mr…" I pause, hoping he'll fill in his name for me.

He laughs as he shoots forward, sticking his arm out.

"Where the hell are my manners? I'm Jamee, spelled with two e's because mom wanted to be different, Locke. And what's your name, sweetheart?"

I reach out, grabbing his hand as he shakes it up and down twice before slowly letting go. "I'm Susie. Susie Cobble, but my friends call me Suse."

"Well, Suse. I hope it's okay I call you that as I do already consider us friends," he flashes me a smile that definitely makes panties drop, "tell me about yourself."

I start the normal speech: I'm twenty-one, have two

younger brothers, both idiots, it's my first year as a cheer-leader, I'm majoring in psychology, love art and hate peas.

When I finish my short but just long enough autobiography, I'm expecting him to start telling me about himself. Instead, I find his eyebrows raised with an unsure look.

"Yeah, yeah. All that is awesome and I love CrimeJunkie so psychology is definitely cool, but what about the real Susie Cobble? The one who doesn't give this animated answer? Who is she?"

I swear I feel my cheeks heat.

"What–what do you mean? That's who I am," I say nervously, fidgeting with the bracelet on my wrist. The same bracelet I've had since graduating senior year: a simple chain with a thin engraving of *"love yourself."* A graduation gift from mom and dad, words they hoped I'd live by.

For the most part, I do.

He leans forward, his blonde hair falling just perfectly in front of his eyes. "Tell me something you hate, Susie Cobble. Something that isn't part of your speed-friending answer. Something real," he reaches up and boops me on the nose, "about you."

Well, this isn't how these conversations usually go. All rounds up to now have been five minutes of me listening to the footballer tell me all about his high school experience, his NFL dreams, with the occasional flirting. Not once since this whole thing has started has someone actually seemed... interested?

"I hate assholes," I say quickly and honestly, which earns me a giggle from Jamee.

"Do you think I'm an asshole?" His tone sincere.

"Truthfully," I shrug my shoulders, "I don't know but–"

The sound of the air horn over the speaker announcing the

next switch interrupts my sentence. Still, we don't break eye contact and Jamee doesn't hurry to get up.

"But I hope you aren't," I say while sticking my arm back out, just like he did at the beginning of the round.

He looks down, a smile plastering his face as he grasps my hand. And after a moment of us standing there, he finally pulls away, walking off, not saying another word.

Jamee Locke. Cute, kind, mysterious. And if I wasn't so horrendous at the whole flirting thing, maybe I would've attempted to keep the conversation going...but it's me we're talking about.

Susie Cobble. Shy, lacking in confidence, and shit at flirting.

Chapter 7

Paul

"What do you mean you don't know what you want to do after graduation?" I poke Liam in the chest. "Even I know what I want to do after graduating."

That earns a look from all three of my buddies. I know, I know. How surprising that the playboy, the one who never talks about academics or plans, knows what he wants to do. But Meme made sure I always thought about the future, and for that, I'm thankful.

"And what's that?" Jake narrows his eyes as he yells from beside Clay.

It's pretty fucking loud in this bar, so yelling is a must.

"Play for the Razers, obviously," I hold out my shirt, motioning to the logo center of my chest. The Illinois Razers are a top team in NHL – part of the Western Conference, Central Division – a hard division to be part of. They've been mine and Meme's favorite team since I can remember and playing for them isn't only for me, but for her as well.

Clay wraps his arm around my shoulder, "We're already there, bud."

Harp has been open about his plans post-graduation; all

the man does is eat, sleep and breathe hockey, it was no shock he was given the captain role with Jake right by his side.

He was drafted by the Razers right out of high school, the asshole was impressive enough he had the opportunity to head straight to the NHL, but being the overachiever he is, he decided to develop more throughout college and earn his degree.

Me? I had to work my ass off as goalie, attend several showcases and exhibition games, ask a favor from Coach to specifically request a Razer's scout to be there, and finally received the news that I have a spot waiting for me on my favorite fucking team.

My dreams are so close, I can hardly wait, and as excited as I am to be there with Harp, there's nothing I want more than for our whole gang to be together. Again.

"Well," Jake says as he runs his hands through his hair, "I–I mean you all know I have a few teams that are interested, but I…I haven't made up my mind."

Jake Wiley has only ever been sure of one thing and that is his love for Leah Harper. Still, I'm surprised he isn't more excited about his many opportunities.

"Dude," I say as I run my hands over my face. "You have the Razers, Wisconsin Vipers, and the Michigan Miners offering you a spot on their roster. Your pick of the fucking litter."

I turn my attention to Liam.

"And what about you?"

Contrary to popular belief, although we all breathe hockey, the guys and I don't talk much about post-grad plans. I think we're too busy living in the now, and to be honest, it's terrifying thinking of a life after this with my friends. Including the girls.

"I'm not as popular as Jake, that's for sure," he slaps

Wiley on the back. "But the Razers and the Miners have shown some interest," he shrugs his shoulders, "I–I don't know either."

I know both Liam and Jake love hockey as much as Clay and I do, but I also know they have other reasons for not being so sure about their plans. Reasons that are walking through the front door of the bar right now.

I nudge him with my shoulder, pointing towards the door. "I think I know why that is." I watch my love-struck friend's eyes literally light up as Clara walks towards us.

As for me? I'm too busy smiling at the gal walking next her. Judging by their outfits, they most definitely stopped and changed because Susie is now wearing skin-tight jeans paired with a tight red crop.

Pure sunshine wrapped in beauty.

Within a moment, the girls are surrounding us: Leah, Clara, Susie, Lucy, and even Sara.

The entire gang together – a rare occurrence with Sara's new internship – but one I'm happy for.

"So," I inch closer to Susie, "how was it?"

She gently wraps her arm around mine, something she does quite often.

"I'm freaking exhausted," she looks at Clara, "and these assholes didn't tell me we'd be doing a speed dating event."

I quickly turn towards Clara who's looking around at the other girls.

"Oh come on Suse. It wasn't *that* bad," she winks. "Plus, I heard you and Jamee Locke got along real well."

And something in me doesn't quite like how she wiggled her eyebrows as she said that. Why? Because I've heard stories about Jamee. Stories from fellow football players about how the only thing he's faster at than running a route is going through women.

I look down at her, her arm still snaked through mine with her other hand on my bicep.

"Jamee Locke, huh?"

She rolls her eyes as she takes a step away.

"It was literally nothing. Can we get a drink now?"

"Hell yes," Lucy says, grabbing her arm and pulling her towards the bar.

Out of our entire friend group, the only poor soul not twenty-one is Leah. Although this bar has never seemed to care about age – we've been coming here since freshman year. As long as you keep it civil, they don't question IDs. Shitty? Probably. But what college kid is going to question them if it means getting to drink?

As the two disappear in the sea of people, the rest of us make our way to the usual spot in our favorite bar, *The Jungle Book.*

Tonight's packed with all kinds of Barker students, but when the front door opens and in walks Chase Ryker with Jamee Locke beside him, my mood immediately sours. Especially when I see Locke spot Susie and make a bee-line.

Not that it should matter, but it does.

* * *

"Did you hear me?" Clay asks as he leans towards me from the table.

"It's pretty hard not to when you're yelling in my ear," I joke.

Clay, Sara, Lucy and I are currently sitting at the table while the rest of the group are out there dancing. I think it more closely resembles dry-humping on the dance floor, but who am I to judge? I scan the bar looking for my bob-headed best friend when her pitch black hair catches my attention, her face lit up in one of her signature smiles, but not towards me.

No, no. She's smiling because of Jamee. I know I shouldn't be pissed about it. She's happy right now, and as her friend, I'm happy to see her happy. But the thought of it being Locke that's causing her to beam? Um, no. I don't find that appealing.

But, it's Susie's choice...and unless it's apparent the asshole is hurting her, making her uncomfortable or she gives me *the look* – the one that says help me – I'll keep my distance. For now, at least.

"Sara," I hear Lucy say, snapping my attention back to the table. "Aren't you going to go talk to a certain you-know-who?"

Clay and I share a look of uncertainty, not sure who the girls are discussing, and although it isn't my business, they're my friends as well and I'm a nosy son-of-a-bitch.

"Who's the you-know-who, Sara?" I tease, knowing she's already fed up with the conversation.

"No one," she says quickly, giving Lucy a warning look.

"It's definitely not no one," Lucy leans a bit closer to Clay and I. Unfortunately for Lucy, Clay is the closest. I watch as she exaggerates leaning as far away from him as possible as she tries to whisper to us. "It's Chase Ryker."

I swear to god I almost spit my drink out.

"As in Clara's ex Chase Ryker?"

Sara reaches across the table, slapping my hand which causes Lucy and Clay to laugh.

"Can you not?"

I pull my hand away, not acknowledging the sting that this petite cheerleader caused.

"Are you two," Clay cuts in, "like...a thing?"

"Harp, dude. A bit personal, yeah?" I roll my eyes, immediately adding, "But are you?"

This time, Sara drags her hands over her face as she mumbles. "We're in the same class, that's all."

I look towards Chase who is already looking this way. "The dude is an interior design major?" Not that anything is wrong with that, I just didn't expect it.

She chuckles, "No, no. I had to take a stupid elective to fulfill a requirement and we just so happened to take the same one."

Lucy opens her mouth to say something but their eyes land on the seat next to me, almost immediately as I feel it dip and a body brush against mine.

I turn my head to see Susie, who is trying her hardest right now to appear happy.

"So," Sara says, "how did it go with Jamee?"

Why do these girls care so much about Susie and Jamee?

"It was…good," she answers with a tight-lipped grin. Not to mention she completely hesitated to answer which tells me one thing: it was not good.

"Care to elaborate?" Sara winks.

"Uh…"

"I think Clara is waving at you guys," I quickly point behind them to Clara, who is most definitely not waving, but I can tell something's up with Susie and it's not something she wants to go into detail about with the whole group around.

"I don't see her waving?" Lucy adds as she stares in Clara's direction.

"She was." *Definitely wasn't.*

"Well," Sara adds, looking at Lucy and Susie. "Maybe we should go check on her?"

The two are already getting up to head that way while Susie stays plastered to her seat.

"Are you coming, Suse?" Lucy asks, holding out her hand.

She looks towards me and then around the bar before answering, "I'm going to sit for a bit."

The girls wander off towards Clara while Clay stays seated. I gently nudge his foot with mine to get his attention, motioning my eyes towards Susie, hoping he'll get the hint so I can find out what's going on. *If that motherfucker upset her.*

I watch as the realization finally washes over his face. "Well, I need to go take a leak. Be back in a bit," and just like that, he's gone.

Not a second passes before Susie looks at me with her eyes narrowed.

"Clara wasn't waving at them and Clay didn't need to go to the bathroom, huh?"

I shrug my shoulders in response. "I don't know what you're talking about, Q."

She places both hands on top of the table as she begins picking at her fingernails. She may not be saying anything, but I can all but hear the wheels in her head turning.

"Now that everyone's gone, do you want to tell me what happened?"

She looks up quickly, a shocked look on her face.

"I–I didn't say anything happened?"

"You don't have to say it. You're one of my best friends, I can just tell."

She rolls her eyes, but not before her dimples make an appearance.

"I don't know what you're talking about, Pauline."

I reach out, grabbing her hand. "I think you do."

"I–" she starts to say, but pauses to take a deep breath. "I fucked it up."

I can't help the small laugh escape me at her bluntness as I'm slightly taken aback. It's the first time I've heard Susie say the word "fuck"...*and I find it oddly attractive.*

"You're laughing?"

"I don't think I've ever heard you say fuck before," I nudge her with my shoulder, "it was cute," which earns me another eye roll. "What could you have possibly fucked up, Susie?"

"I told you it's been ages since I've tried flirting with anyone. I–I had no idea what to say, how to act, how to be sexy? Talking at the field was easy, we traded questions back and forth. But here? I don't know how to read signs so when he'd step closer, I'd inch away because I thought the man was just trying to get comfortable and I didn't want to be in his space," she lets out a deep breath as she continues.

"He'd throw out a flirty comment and I wouldn't know how to respond. Like he told me I looked beautiful and I literally didn't say anything. I completely changed the subject. I barely said any words to him because I had no idea what to say. He did all the talking and the man probably thinks I don't even like him because of how uninterested I seemed. I started off okay and then got into my head and it just kept going downhill from there."

"Then," she inhales, huffing as she exhales, "he told me he had to leave for the night, code for *get me the hell out of here.* I mean, he did give me his number but what am I supposed to do? Text him and apologize for being so damn awkward tonight? He probably just did that to be kind and–"

"Susie," I interrupt because she is quite literally spiraling right now. "I'm sure it didn't go as bad as you think," I say, trying to get her to slow down.

"It *was* that bad, Paul."

Whether or not Susie was bad at flirting shouldn't mean jack shit to Jamee Locke. She's absolutely gorgeous and funny and the kindest person I know. And considering he gave her his number, there's two possible motivators behind it: one, he sees what I see or two, he's looking for a hookup. If his motivation is anything other than wanting to get to know the amazing Susie Cobble, I'll make sure he won't have any working arms to catch a damn ball.

She's back to fidgeting with her fingers, watching her friends on the dance floor. Gone is the usual happy Susie, in her place is a Susie I never want to get used to seeing.

"Hey," I say as I gently squeeze the hand still wrapped in mine. "You're the greatest catch, Q. And judging by how he gave you his number, he thinks the same."

I don't want the asshole to be with her, but it's the truth, and Susie doesn't need to be down on herself just because she thinks she bit the bullet tonight.

Her face lights up with my words. "You don't think I completely blew it?"

"Fuck no. I guarantee you if you texted him right now he'd immediately reply." *But I hope you don't.*

She softly bobs her head while she chews on her bottom lip.

"I–I still need to work on my flirting skills," she softly chuckles.

I see the group walking back towards us, the signal that it's time to leave. So, I quickly lean over and whisper, "Like I said, I'd gladly be your guinea pig," knowing damn well I mean it.

She doesn't say anything, just shakes her head as she shoves me away. Her smile is wider and brighter; the only way I ever want her to be.

Chapter 8

Susie

As I'm lying in bed, replaying the embarrassment from the bar in my head, I can't help but think back to the dipshit, prick, goddamn freaking asshole who caused the downfall of my confidence...Lane Ross. The one who decided one night he wanted to break me in every way.

And I let him. Almost four years later and I'm still partially broken.

I remember it like it was yesterday. The party at Tracie Summers' house. Me in a pink tie-dye bikini, sipping on a Coca Cola, sitting next to my high school best friend, Maya, with not a care in the world going into senior year.

I remember Lane taking a seat next to me. The confusion Maya and I shared because Lane Ross never slummed it with the non-popular kids, which was most definitely us. So, when he sat down and draped his muscular hand over my thigh, we weren't exactly sure how to react. I vividly remember forgetting how to breathe for a moment.

Lane Ross was one of the most popular boys in high school with a face that every girl loved to look at. Muscular, sexy, confident, and he knew it. Of course I was one of the girls that had a stupid crush on him…who wouldn't?

I remember him asking if I wanted to take a swim. Maya's face was full of excitement when he grabbed my hand, trailing me behind him. Like I mentioned, I wasn't the version of pretty everyone had in mind throughout school, but that summer? I felt like I was. I wore just enough make-up that made me feel good, my hair was longer, and I felt gorgeous in my body.

I remember us wading into the water, him never letting go of my hand. How my heart started racing when he reached around, cupping my ass as he pulled me close to him. The feel of his sculpted hips as I wrapped my legs around his body. His laugh as we joked and talked, Maya's wide eyes as she watched us, me beaming with happiness…thinking that after three years, he finally noticed me.

Sure, I had boyfriends here and there, I was always as awkward as ever and they never truly amounted to anything, but Lane Ross? Just the idea he was giving me the time of day was mind blowing. Flirting with me? Holy shit.

And then, when he asked me if I wanted to go somewhere private, for once in my life, I let go of the fear. I–I still don't know why I said yes. That wasn't who I was, who I am now. But I was going into my senior year and I was tired of being so…scared? Shy? I decided to just live in the moment, and the moment royally fucked me.

I remember the heat that trailed where his hand skimmed up my back and neck, a moment I thought was meant to be sweet and affectionate. I remember the look on everyone's faces, the noises of their hysterical laughing, their fingers pointing at me when my top fell down.

Immediately, I covered myself with my arms, turning towards Lane to shield myself, frantically looking around the ground for my top. I didn't know what had happened, but was sure it was some mishap, an accident. It had to have been.

I remember the tears that began streaming down my face when I saw my top in his hands, his eyes looking at my boobs. Him pointing and laughing right along with everyone else. As if that wasn't enough, I still, to this day, remember the words he directed towards me but said out loud to everyone.

"Holy shit y'all, it's worse than we thought. Ugly and no boobs!"

The fear that I felt that day has forever been unmatched. I turned to run to Maya, but he gripped my arms, holding them down to my side, my body on display for everyone to see. I still think of his hot breath in my ear as he leaned in and whispered.

"I can't believe you actually thought someone like me would be into someone like you. No one will ever be into you, Susie Cobble. You may think you look different this year, but you're still the same ugly girl. And who'd want to date an ugly girl with an ugly body?"

And that's when Maya appeared with a towel, shoved him away, and we took off.

Yes, of course I told my parents, who in turn told the police and school. But Lane Ross wasn't held accountable in any legal sense, unfortunately there wasn't much that could be done for bullying, but the school expelled him, making it to where he couldn't return senior year.

So, my summer was spent leaning heavily towards depression. As one could imagine, being humiliated in front of everyone while practically naked takes a toll on your mental health. My self-thoughts became almost completely negative. I wore baggy clothes, I stopped taking care of myself and worst of all? I believed Lane.

Thankfully, I have parents who talked with me every day about my self-worth and advocated for therapy. I was hesitant at first; I wasn't suicidal and I wasn't quite sure how it would help me. But, I figured it couldn't hurt or make things worse. So, I began seeing Mrs. Baker once a week. We discussed the *event* – that's what we began to refer to it as – and how it affected my opinion of myself. We discussed how to build that opinion of myself back up and how to handle going back to school, facing the aftermath.

It wasn't easy, we did a lot of practice regarding positive self-talk, and going back senior year sure as hell wasn't fun, but I made it. Maya and I remained close friends up until we departed for college, and we still talk every once in a while, but we aren't as close as we once were and that's okay.

Mrs. Baker and I continued our sessions all throughout senior year and I still remember the one valuable lesson she taught me: what happened had changed me – it broke a lot of confidence inside me – but I don't have to let that change control me. I try not to. I try to remember that I will find someone one day who thinks the world of me and that inch by inch, my confidence will come back.

So far, it's still mostly broken. And tonight? Tonight I question if Lane's words are true. How can anyone be into me if I can't freaking flirt or show I'm interested. But, then there's Paul's words that shine bright in the dark: *"you're the greatest catch, Q."*

No one knows what happened in high school. Since I *try* not to let it define me, I don't open up about it a lot. Still, it's as though Paul can read my inner thoughts and calm the storm that no one but me can see.

That's how it's been since meeting him. Him in my corner, cheering me on; he's a really good friend and one I'm thankful for.

As soon as I finish the thought, my phone vibrates, as if his ears were burning.

PAULINE

I hope you aren't letting tonight get to your head, Q. Need some pointers? You know who to ask

I smirk as I type out a response.

You think Clay would mind me reaching out for help?

PAULINE

Sweet dreams, Q.

Chapter 9

Susie

I don't think I can breathe.

Today's practice was more brutal than it's ever been and I think that's highly due to the fact that tomorrow, like… one sleep away, is our first home game; my first game as a college cheerleader, ever. We've had plenty of practice and I've had plenty of time to come to the realization, but with the day quickly approaching, it's becoming more and more real.

But I think I can do this.

The exact words I've heard from the girls, and Paul, is that, *"Coach wouldn't have put you on the team if she didn't think so. So stop overthinking it. You're great,"* yada, yada. It's nice to hear, but believing it is entirely different.

However, I've worked my ass off in practices and I truly feel like I've grown in my position as a backspot. My stunt group has seen my improvement as well and we've truly started to mesh together. Still, nothing beats the nerves of this Friday being my debut game.

I didn't truly feel like much had changed since tryouts – I'm still the same Susie Cobble. However, when I sported my first BU cheer attire, a cute black cropped sweatshirt, to class on Monday, it really put my new status into perspective.

* * *

I'm ten minutes ahead of schedule, enough time to stop at the campus Starbucks to get my normal – White Iced Mocha with two extra pumps of white chocolate. I'm not one of those who must have coffee to function, but Monday mornings calls for some extra help.

Apparently everyone else thinks so as well because the line is ridiculous.

As I'm standing here waiting, I notice a guy – a fairly attractive guy – about two people in front of me, looking my way. Not a quick, glancing look, but a deep stare. I can feel his eyes roaming my body as I try to act like I'm looking at the sign slightly to the left of him. But he's not looking away...

Finally, and very reluctantly, I look directly into his bright blue gaze. His hair is a dirty blonde color with his black t-shirt stretched across his broad chest while his lips are curved upward.

I flash him my dimples in return before looking to my right, as if I'm scanning the shop for a seat. I see the people in front of me shift a bit, bringing my attention back towards the mystery guy who is no longer two people ahead of me, but standing right in front of me.

"Uh..." is all I can manage to say as I gawk at him. He's tall, not necessarily the tall I'm used to with all the hockey boys in our group, but tall nonetheless.

"Hi there," he says in a deep, raspy voice. The type of voice that screams he's in the same boat as me with needing the extra energy.

"Um, hi?" The word comes out more as a question than statement.

"I saw you and couldn't help but to introduce myself," he holds out his hand, "I'm Jay."

I cautiously reach my hand out. "I'm Susie."

His smirk is wider now. "Well, Susie. May I?" He motions to the register as we step forward.

"May you cut in front of me?" I ask with my brows pinched together. "You were already ahead of me in line?"

Maybe he needs the energy because he drank himself silly last night and is still slightly drunk?

He chuckles, but the confusion on his face mimics mine.

"May I buy your coffee, Susie?"

Oh. OH. I–I wasn't expecting that.

"Oh I–I guess so?"

Could I sound less interested? Jesus Christ.

After I give my order to the barista and Jay so kindly pays for our drinks. We take a seat as we wait for our names to be called. And as always, I'm pretty dang awkward.

"So, Susie," he breaks the silence, "you're a cheerleader?" His tongue swipes across his bottom lip in what I think is an attempt to be...sexy?

"How did you–"

"Know?" He finishes the sentence for me while motioning to my shirt. I quickly look down, remembering the cropped sweater I threw on this morning as I was rushing around.

I let out a nervous giggle. "Duh," I say while shaking my head. "Yeah, it's my first year on the squad."

His eyes rake over my body, again, before he answers, "Well, I'm sure you're as gorgeous in your uniform as you are right now," he winks.

My cheeks immediately heat. "Oh well, thank you, Jay."

Our names are called, and as I start to stand, he places his hand over mine and says, "Can I get your number, Susie?"

Well, this is…unexpected.

"Oh, uh–sure."

He hands me his phone and I put in my number under "Susie Cobble – Coffee Girl" just in case he forgets who I am. Something tells me this man most definitely does this a lot.

When he takes a look at my contact, his eyes meet mine again with a heated gaze.

"You think I'd forget where I met a girl as gorgeous as you?" He bends down, whispering in my ear, "I could never."

✳ ✳ ✳

I'm gathering my things as I physically shake at the cringey memory from only two days ago. At first, I didn't necessarily think of the situation specifically being related to me being a cheerleader until twenty minutes after that while in class, *the same class I've been in for about three weeks,* a classmate of mine, who usually sits in the back, decided to sit next to me.

The classmate being one of the hottest guys in our class, who I know for a fact, thanks to the two girls sitting behind me, has already hooked up with three girls in our classroom and is an athlete on our men's competitive swimming team. When he plopped down next to me and the first words out of his mouth were, *"I didn't know you were a cheerleader, Susan,"* I didn't think twice before grabbing my things and moving to the next row.

I suppose people look at you different when you're part of an NCA National Championship tea–

"Suse," Clara's voice startles me out of my thoughts. "Are you coming?"

"Cominggggg?" I ask because if the girls have been talking, I most definitely have not been listening.

"To eat, you goof," she teases as she grabs my bag, slinging it over her arm. "Us athletes have to fuel our bodies to keep growing strong," she says in quotation marks with a sarcastic tone.

I laugh as I sit down to tie my shoes. "And whose wise words are we living by?"

"My husband's," she laughs. "Ever since he and the boys came to Daytona in April, all I've heard is how strong we are and how I need to continue fueling my body to grow my muscles and do more flippy things," she laughs. "His exact words."

I don't think I've heard Clara use Liam's name since their wedding, unless he needs a reminder he's on thin ice, then the name comes out. Usually, it's husband, and I think it's adorable.

"Oh, I could definitely go for some food!"

Not five minutes later, all of us are walking hand-in-hand into Evan's Diner.

* * *

"Guys," Leah says as she shoves a fry in her mouth. "Can you believe that tomorrow is our first game? Isn't it insane!" She beams as she wipes ketchup off the corner of her mouth. Insane is one of the best ways to describe tomorrow.

"I don't know which is more insane," Sara says. "The fact

that tomorrow is the first game or the fact that tomorrow is Lucy and I's last first game..." she trails off.

I love our friend group more than anything, but I hate knowing we all graduate at different times. Sara and Lucy will be graduating this school year, Clara is a junior like me, and poor Leah is a baby sophomore. It's a scary thought to process – that after this year two of my best friends won't be here with us – but I know it's not the end of our friendship, just the end of this chapter here at Barker.

"Don't remind me," Lucy rolls her eyes. "I–I know I'm what one would call–"

"Emotionless?" Clara cuts her off with a wink.

"Not good at sharing feelings," she cuts a look to Clara, "but you girls are my absolute best friends and–and my college experience would've been shit without you four."

I look around at the girls surrounding me, knowing I feel the same.

"Aw," I gently pinch Lucy's cheeks, "that was the sweetest thing you've said to us." She swats my hand away, narrowing her eyes at me.

"And until graduation, it'll be the last."

"Okay, okay," Sara chimes in. "Enough about this sad shit of us leaving. Susie, how are you feeling about tomorrow?"

Like I'm going to throw up all this food throughout the entire day.

"Honestly," I take a deep breath, "I feel like I'm going to shit my pants," I chuckle. "But I'm also excited to be cheering with my best friends."

The entire table erupts with laughter and of course, it's Clara who speaks up first.

"We all," she looks around at the girls, "are so proud of you for trying out with us, Suse. Granted," she softly laughs, "we didn't give you much of a choice, but Coach Hawkins saw something in you. You made the team for a reason, remember that, babe."

And as I'm lying in bed, mentally preparing for tomorrow's festivities and the big game, I'm starting to gradually allow myself to believe her words.

Chapter 10

Susie

"Did I blink?" I ask the girls as we're standing on the sidelines, waving at the boys in the stands.

The last three hours were a blur. I think I cheered? There's the possibility I was flailing my hands and arms around in the air but I think Coach would have pulled me off the sideline if that was the case.

Right?!

Stunting, from what I remember, went great! My group hit everything we put in the air, but most importantly? I had a freaking blast. During halftime, Liam came down to the gate and took our group photo, the girls and I wrapped tightly around one another, which I can only imagine includes me being wide-eyed with an enormous grin from ear-to-ear, but that's exactly how I felt today.

Happy.

All the worrying, the stress, the nerves…I enjoyed cheering for our football team, but more than that, I enjoyed doing it with my best friends.

"Suse," Leah shakes my shoulders as we're making our

way to the locker room, "you killed it!" She pecks a kiss to my cheek.

Lucy, who's directly behind me, hugs my waist. "And you looked hot as fuck while doing it," she tickles my side.

I slap her hands away, a blush creeping up my neck from the compliment. "I wouldn't say I looked–"

"Finish that sentence," Clara says, "I dare you."

We're heading to the locker room when a hand gently pulls me to the side. "I thought that was you, Suse."

I look to my left and see a sweaty, football player. I don't recognize him at first, but when he takes off his helmet letting his blonde hair fall down, I immediately know. Jamee Locke.

"Did you see my catch?" He asks, still holding my arm with a cocky smirk on his insanely attractive face.

"Umm…" I reach up, running my fingers through my hair, "I–I was a bit too busy making sure I didn't mess up the cheers," I admit. "But I heard the crowd chanting your name when you did, if that makes a difference?"

He tilts his head to the side, finally letting go of my arm.

"Did you participate in the chanting?"

Shrugging, I say, "I may have jumped up and down, cheering with a *go Jamee* thrown in there." I swear my face is on fire.

"My own personal cheerleader," he winks.

Okay…is this flirting? I–I think it is but what do I say to that? And…why would he keep trying after how horribly I messed things up at the bar? My mind goes blank, my mouth is dry, and I'm frozen in place as this incredibly handsome man continues to smile at me, waiting for me to say something.

After a moment, his smirk falls and I'm sure he's about to walk away. Hell, I'm about to run, but then he takes a deep breath and closes his eyes.

"Okay. Maybe you aren't into me, maybe by you not texting me after the bar that was your cue for me to take the hint, but I'm going to shoot my shot here and ask if you'd like to go grab dinner with me after the next home game in two weeks?" He opens his eyes and I imagine my face shows just how I feel: shocked.

"I think you're gorgeous and would like to get to know you more," he shrugs his shoulders. "What do you say, Suse?"

I'm fairly certain my mouth is hanging open and entirely convinced I misheard him.

"You want to go on a date? With...me?" *Could I sound any more surprised?*

"Absolutely," he answers without a second thought.

Well, this isn't how I figured my first ever game day would end, and as much as I want to say yes, I'm freaking terrified. I don't know what to do or say now, how the hell would I know how to handle our date?

"Locke," someone yells his name near their locker room, "get the hell over here before you're benched for the next game."

I go to open my mouth, but he quickly cuts me off.

"Don't break my heart out here in the open, Suse. Text me later." He begins heading towards their locker room but quickly turns around and yells, "Think about it!"

And as he disappears through the door, I'm met with whistling not too far from me. I turn to see the girls standing by our own door with wide grins on their faces as I begin making my way towards them, knowing I'm about to be met with twenty questions I don't know how to answer. Because I still don't know what the hell just happened.

"Susie," Lucy calls out as she walks through the door next

to me. "Care to explain what the fuck just happened back there?"

I don't answer, and instead, shrug my shoulders, sitting to gather my things. Tonight we continue our game night routine of Buffalo Wild Wings or IHOP, depending on what everyone's feeling. And I don't want to dive into the possibility of going on a date with Jamee Locke right now…I just want to eat followed by wallowing in my bed with my self-doubts, convincing myself why I definitely *should not* go out with Jamee.

As I continue packing my bag, swapping my skirt out with our cheer sweats, I continue to remain silent. That is until Clara bends down, shoving her head in front of my face.

"Suse. We can't just let that go," she moves my bag away from my hands. "Jamee Locke, the same guy who came to the bar, found and talked only to you the whole night, just sought you out again at the game. He definitely has a crush on you!"

I drop my shoulders with a sigh, rolling my neck as I continue gathering my things.

"Look," Leah says as she sits next to me, "we want to know because we love you, Suse. And–and we haven't seen you really around any guys other than our group and it could be nice for you to…get out…with someone other than us?" She gently squeezes my hand.

"If that's something you want to do," Sara interjects. "We don't care either way, but we want to support you and encourage you if you do."

I look around at my girls, knowing that without a doubt if they knew what I went through in high school they'd help me with how I'm feeling. They're the best friends I could ever ask for, but…I don't want to burden them with this. All of them are busy with their own lives, the last thing they need to do is take on the topic of my relationship skills. My past is my past and although it still affects me, it isn't how I want people to know me. So, I can share just enough to get them off my back without needing to tell them the underlying factors.

"He–he asked me out after the home football game in a few weeks." I don't dare look up to gauge their reactions, but the squeal that comes out of Leah is enough to tell me what they would look like.

"Oh my god, oh my god, oh my god!" She keeps repeating. "How? And what–what did you say?"

"Do we know much about Jamee?" Lucy directs the question to the girls. "I know he hangs out with Chase and he's a good guy," she looks at Sara. "Right, Sara?"

Sara's eyes go wide as we all turn towards her, and her face? Fifty shades of red.

"I–I wouldn't know," she looks at Clara. "I swear, Clara. We aren't – that's not a thing. Me and him. I would nev–"

"Sara," Clara laughs. "Chase is a great guy and should that ever be something you want to explore, you don't need my permission babe," she winks.

"Well, I–I'm not looking for a boyfriend right now," she looks around at us while waving her arms through the air. "Anyway, this isn't about me. This is about you, Susie Cobble, and this date in a few weeks."

"I don't know if there will be a date," I say as I grab my bag, hoping to escape this conversation.

"Did he upset you, Suse?" Clara whispers from beside me.

I scrunch my nose as I shake my head. "No, absolutely not," I quickly say. "I–I just don't know is all."

The girls share a look around the room at each other; a look that is their way of calling bullshit without outright saying it, which I appreciate. After a moment, Lucy breaks the silence.

"Well," she says while putting her backpack on, "the boys are waiting for us outside. I'll sacrifice myself to go let them know you all will be out soon."

As we all begin grabbing the last of our things, I feel a gentle hand land on my shoulder. Turning to my right, I see Clara smiling at me.

"I'm not going to give you a speech," I narrow my eyes as she leans in to hug me. "But I want to remind you how beautiful, smart, and kind you are, Suse. Jamee Locke would be lucky to have a date with you and if you like him, I think you should go for it."

"And if you don't like him," she adds, "then don't." She steps away, grabbing her own bag. "We'll support you either way, but it could be good for you to get out with someone other than us and the obnoxious boys."

"The obnoxious boys include your husband, you know," I tease as we walk outside. A few feet away from us is our group. The girls are talking with Jake while Liam has Paul in a headlock with Clay trying to break them up.

"Trust me," she grabs my hand. "I know."

Chapter 11

Paul

Buffalo Wild Wings is what the group decided tonight, and now we're packed in our vehicles like usual as we head to the restaurant. Liam drove which means it's Susie, Lucy and I in the backseat. I'm not as tall as Jake or Clay. Liam and I both are about six-foot-one, but if there's anything being a goalie has given me, it's thick fucking thighs and broad shoulders. Both of which are currently pressing against Susie all because of Lucy's huge-ass bag. Am I complaining? Hell no.

"Since last year, I've officially attended more football games than I ever planned to attend in my life," I say. "I still stand strong to my statement of how they'd get their shit rocked in a fight with us."

"I'd stand strong with that statement if the now quarterback didn't knock me on my ass last year," Liam says with a chuckle as he grabs Clara's hand. "With every right to do so, but he did pack a hell of a punch."

"Were you prepared to be punched in the face?" Lucy asks.

"Uh, no. I didn't expect Chase Ryker to emerge from the shadows like fucking Batman and sock me in the face."

"He did knock you on your ass," Clara adds while laughing.

I watch as Liam brings her knuckles to his mouth, kissing each one and then saying, "I deserved it."

Ew, gross. Love.

I open my mouth to ask Susie how her first game went when my phone begins ringing. I can't help but grin when I see Meme's contact, answering the call and putting her on speakerphone.

"Meme? Isn't it past your bedtime?" I tease, knowing how irritated she gets when I acknowledge her being on the older side. My meme, who's given name is Charlotte Simmons, sits at the young age of sixty-seven, and is the woman who raised me and loved me as her own, given her own daughter wouldn't…

"Is that Meme Charlotte? Tell her, her favorite says hello!" Liam yells while looking at me in the rearview mirror.

"That doesn't sound like Jake?" I hear her snicker through the phone. *"Hello, Liam. Taking good care of my boy?"*

His smile is wide as he answers, "Always, Char."

I roll my eyes as I turn towards Susie, shrugging my shoulders and shaking my head.

"Did you call to talk to me or flirt with my best friend, who by the way, is married now, Meme." Clara giggles from the front seat, knowing exactly how Charlotte is.

"Paul Henry Simmons!" She yells through the phone. *"I would never–"*

"Yeah, yeah. What's up, Meme? Did you need something? Is everything okay?"

"Yes, Henry," another snicker, *"everything is fine and*

dandy. Can't a grandma just miss her grandson and want to call to shoot the shit?"

I'm hesitant to look up at my friends around me, knowing damn well how they tease me every time she uses my middle name.

"Must you use my middle name?"

"Yes."

"And what shit did you need to shoot?"

I notice Susie smiling next to me. Apart from the guys, no one knows about my upbringing with Meme, more specifically...the reason why. I don't care if people know, I just don't openly talk about it. I feel like by doing so, I'm giving *her*, my egg donor, more attention than she deserves.

"That fucking neighbor, Billy Randall, let his dog shit in my yard. I know it was his dog because the shit was the size of a goddamn dinosaur, same as that gigantic pain in my ass german shepherd. You know—"

"The one who eats your tulips every year," I finish for her.

I turn to see the girls' eyes wide as they listen to Meme continue her rant. I mute the call, knowing she'll continue on even if I don't say a word.

"What?"

The girls look at each other, some unspoken looks that seem to end in nominating Clara as the spokeswoman of the group.

"Your grandma...she–I–see where you get your language skills," she chuckles.

It's true. Ol' Charlotte Simmons has always had a sailor mouth and Clara is most definitely right – it's one trait of hers that I most definitely have.

We're pulling up to B-Dubs and she's *still* going on about Billy Randall's asshole dog.

"Hey Memes," her casual nickname, *"I hate to cut you off, but I am out at dinner with friends. Can I call you tomorrow?"*

"Oh, yes, yes. Of course. I love you, boogie."

Boogie. The nickname she gave me since I've been in diapers because apparently I had a real problem staying out of my nose when I was younger.

"I love you. And don't do anything to wind up in trouble, Memes."

"No promises."

And with that, she hangs up.

As we file out of Liam's jeep, Susie latches onto my arm, like always, as we walk inside.

"Your Meme seems adorable," her eyes are crinkled from how wide she's smiling. My favorite sight.

"Adorable, sassy, sarcastic, you name it," I wink.

She goes quiet, focusing on the ground as she chews on her bottom lip. I know she wants to ask so I choose to spare her. She doesn't need to know all the particulars, but a brief explanation wouldn't hurt.

"Charlotte, my Meme, raised me."

She nods in understanding as I hold the door open for her.

"And, if you don't mind me asking, what about your mom?" It's a question I haven't had to answer since I told the boys about my past. But, going into detail about how Lisa Simmons is a woman who continuously chose drugs over her own son isn't something I want to dive into during dinner.

I offer a small shrug as I motion for Susie to climb into the gigantic booth along with our other friends.

"Charlotte is the only mother figure I've ever known and needed."

* * *

We've finally stuffed our faces full of wings and french fries, sitting here now discussing the events of the game.

"Okay," Lucy says while leaning over, wrapping her arms around Susie's shoulders. "Can we all just acknowledge how fucking amazing our girl was tonight for her debut game as a cheerleader?"

All I can think about is fucking sleeping – I'm exhausted and tired of football. However, I do want to hear about Susie's first game day, so for her, I'll suffer through.

And it's true. She was phenomenal. I don't know anything about cheerleading, but I know Susie looked damn good on the sideline tonight and really fucking happy.

"I think you looked great, Suse," Liam says while holding out his fist – their signature handshake.

"I have to be honest," Jake chuckles as a smile stretches across his face. "I didn't watch anyone but my girl, so I truly don't know," he pulls Leah's knuckles to his mouth, "but I have no doubt you killed it, Susie!"

"And what did you think, Clay?" Lucy asks. I know she enjoys pissing him off and I for one, enjoy watching it happen.

"I think you did great, Susie," he pauses and looks Lucy up and down. "However, I saw you fuck up at least once, Lu."

She exaggerates an eye roll, bringing her middle finger up to her lips as if she's applying lipstick.

"How original," Clay smirks. "Don't worry, you'll do better next time."

She returns that same smirk and adds, "All I gathered from this conversation is that you were watching me cheer."

I watch as his jaw tightens, like he wants to say something, but is cut off by Susie as she turns towards me.

"What about you?"

I look over at her, finding it adorable how she's interested in what I think. I can't exactly tell her my true thoughts – of how she looked incredibly sexy in her uniform, or how more often than not I found myself staring at her – that doesn't seem like the *friendly* thing to say.

"I think you looked amazing and did fucking phenomenal, Q," I smirk as I gently ruffle her hair.

"You aren't the only one who thought she looked amazing," Lucy wiggles her eyebrows at Susie.

"LUCY!" Susie all but yells while her face turns red.

Lucy ignores her, shrugging her off, turning towards the rest of the group. "Susie here got asked out on a date," she tickles Susie's side as she finishes her sentence.

"A date?" Liam asks as he rests his head on his hands. "Do tell."

While everyone seems interested and excited for her, I can't help but feel slightly…annoyed? Happy but…um… what's the word? Jealous? Why the hell would I be jealous if Susie is going on a date? I don't know how the fuck I feel, but I know I'm not exactly excited.

"There's nothing to tell," she glares at Lucy, "Jamee asked me to go out after the next home game, and I didn't answer. That's all."

"You didn't give him an answer?" The question is out of my mouth before I have a chance to think about it.

"I stood there like a deer in headlights," redness starts creeping up her neck and to her cheeks.

"And what did you decide?" Jake asks.

Susie looks around the group, her eyes landing on me with a sigh. "I'm not sure yet?"

The group starts conversing with Susie, offering their input of how supportive they are for her and this *potential* date. Don't get me wrong, as Susie's friend, I am also supportive. As a guy, I find Susie attractive, sweet, and the fucking sunshine to a cloudy day, so I'm hesitant to *want* her to go on this date.

At the end of the day, me being her friend outweighs me just being a guy. And judging how our conversation went at the bar, I have a feeling that worry is what's preventing her from saying yes. So, I find myself saying something I don't necessarily want to, but need to.

"Jamee Locke would be lucky to go on a date with you Q. And I think it could be a good thing for you."

"You sound like the four of them," she motions to the girls with her head, taking a moment before answering, "I'll think about it."

And although I hate hearing it, Meme taught me the best thing to do for a woman is to support her, and that's exactly what I'm doing for my best friend.

Chapter 12

Susie

J ust text him, Susie. It's just one date.

All the encouragement from my friends at tonight's dinner is fresh in my mind and that's the only reason I'm considering saying yes to Jamee.

One date can't hurt, right? Scare the shit out of me? Yes. Make me anxious enough to vomit and skyrocket my nerves? Sure.

But the girls, and I hate to admit it, even the guys, are right. It would be good for me to get out with people other than my group. And when I crash and burn with my dating-slash-flirting skills, I can fail knowing at least I tried.

As I'm getting ready to send Jamee a *"Hey it's me, hope you haven't forgotten what you offered"* text, my phone vibrates with a message.

PAULINE

Just wanted to check in with how you're feeling, Q.

Abboutttt?

Not a minute passes before he answers.

PAULINE

The idea of a date with Locke? Do you want
to talk about it?

Talk about it? No. But, maybe taking him up on his initial offer of being my guinea pig wouldn't be so bad. I chuckle to myself thinking back on the conversation. Paul, one of my best friends and Barker University's most well-known fuckboy, wants to be my guinea pig and I–

Wait a minute.

What if that's exactly what I need? A, dare I say, dating coach? Paul doesn't even date so I'm not sure if it's fair to call it that, but I suppose he could be like…my teacher?

I'm struggling with flirting, ultimately my self-confidence, two areas in which Paul knows extremely well. I'm convinced English is his second language and his native language is smooth talking. I have no idea what this would look like, but I know I could trust him to be sincere in teaching me and keeping it between us two. And before I give myself time to change my mind or think about how incredibly embarrassing this will be, I quickly answer.

Think you could meet me Wednesday at the
coffee shop in town? 3:00?

Two seconds later a response comes through.

PAULINE

I'll be there.

Chapter 13

Paul

"**D**ude," Jake plops his ass next to me and begins stretching. "What are you doing?"

I look up to him, my weight on my elbows with my hands above me, knees spread to where it practically looks like I'm about to start fucking the floor, but its technical term is the frog stretch.

"I'm stretching my hips and groin, Wiley. A stretch I do literally every fucking time before we begin practice."

"I've never seen it before," he winces in pain the further down I push my hips.

"It's Laurie's favorite," I wink. Laurie is his mom, and for a lady her age, she's not bad looking, but I'm most definitely not interested. What I am interested in is pissing Jake off for the fun of it.

"You fucking–" he's cut off by Liam and Clay stopping in front of us.

"Are you two ready to skate or do you need some more time to suck each other's cocks?" Clay snaps.

It's cute how seriously our newly appointed captain is taking his role.

Liam holds his hand down to me. "Come on. Coach is doing that thing where his vein is popping out of his neck like he's about to yell."

I grab his hand, all of us turning to face Coach who sure enough, is probably a millisecond away from yelling at us to get our asses in gear. I skate over to my home on the ice, the familiar peace taking over.

I wasn't always a goalie, but out of every position on the ice, it's what I became best at.

It started when Meme all but forced me to the local arena one Saturday morning. She was tired of me running around the house, driving her up the wall with my energetic attitude. I still remember the conversation she had with Coach Herbert; she was worried that the situation with my mom would lead me down a path of anger and hate with nowhere to funnel my feelings because I sure as hell didn't talk to her about it. She wanted me to have a sport to lean on, something other than her that encouraged me to be good, *better*, than the path that was made for me.

The feeling of stepping onto the rink that first time lives in my head; it's the same feeling I get when my blade hits the ice for game days. Excitement and a sense of belonging. Coach Herbert coached my club league until I started playing in high school, and if it weren't for him and Meme bringing hockey into my life, I'm not sure where I'd be.

I move to the left and right side of the net, back and forth as I continue to think back on *those* days.

Those days refer to the days of my mother. She was a younger mom when she had me, mixed up with the wrong crowd. My father? Fuck if I know. Meme's always been adamant that Lisa, the egg donor, never knew. And although I don't remember every detail about my younger childhood days, I do remember Meme being the best damn mother figure I could've had. Not to mention the memories of continuous disappointment brought by Lisa and her many broken promises throughout my elementary and middle school days.

I'm not ashamed to say that it probably fucked me up more than I realize, but I'm thankful for Meme taking me out of Lisa's care when I was only a baby – there's no telling the shit I would've gone through. Still, it's not my favorite topic to discuss…and if I'm being honest, Lisa is the reason for the whole *'never tied down–'*

"Simmons!" Coach yells at me from the sideline, dragging me out of my thoughts. "If it's okay with you and your damn daydreams, I'd like to begin practice now."

Daydreams? Anything related to Lisa Simmons is more like a fucking nightmare.

"Sorry, Coach. I'm ready."

And as practice begins with a game-like drill, I'm back to reality. I don't usually let my mind wander too far back to how it was when I was younger, but when I do, it can be overwhelming. But here, right now? Watching Jake slam Liam against the boards, knocking him back down when he goes to get up while Clay skates past both of them with the puck heading straight towards my goal, I remember that no matter the shit I went through, I'm right where I'm supposed to be.

* * *

"Yo, Paul," Clay's sitting next to me, taking off his skates. "Are you coming with us to grab some food?"

I'm standing at my locker with a towel wrapped around my waist, my hair still drenched from my shower. "Nah, I'm meeting Susie for coffee," I drop the towel to put on my boxers, just as all three of my friends turn towards me, staring with questionable expressions.

"Are you just realizing my dick's the biggest out of every-one's?" I ask as I pull on a pair of grey sweats, slipping my black shirt over my head. "Don't worry boys, I'm sure the ladies think yours is *just right*," I wink.

Liam shakes his head, mumbling something under his breath which sounds a lot like how Clara thinks his dick is so much better than *just right* before finally speaking loud enough for us all to hear.

"More like confused because I swear you just said you're going to have coffee with Susie? As in Susie Cobble, Clara's best friend?" He narrows his eyes as I roll mine.

"Yes, dad. I'm going to have coffee with Susie as in C's best friend Susie," I grab my backpack from my locker and look at the other two who are still staring. "Do you numbnuts have something to add?"

"Like–uh…" Jake opens his mouth, closes it, and opens again. "Like a date?"

I angle my chin to my chest, knowing where they're going with this.

"Is this a *let's all date one of Clara's friends' cult* that I wasn't aware of? Because I didn't sign up for that shit," Clay says as he stands. "And no offense to Sara, but she isn't my type."

I turn towards him, raising one eyebrow as I say, "But Lucy is?"

He scoffs. "Over my dead fucking body would she ever be my type," he says while chuckling. "I can't–"

"Stand her," I finish his sentence, "so you've said." I pick up my gear bag, feeling the sudden need to clarify this coffee thing between Susie and I. "It's not a date. Not that it should matter to any of you shits if it were, but she just asked me to meet for a coffee. We're just friends."

"I just…" Liam trails off. "I just wouldn't want you to hurt her is all."

For fuck's sake. He may not have explicitly stated it, but I know the underlying meaning of the comment. He knows all I do is fuck around; I don't date, never have, and he doesn't want that to hurt Susie. Although I don't care to hear Liam's concern, it is valid. I never see the same girl twice and have never once cared for something more than a hookup. But also, his concern is not needed considering that Susie would never think of me like that.

"That's not what this is," I walk over, placing my hand on his shoulder. I think after the big shit-show with Jake and Clay due to Jake dating Clay's younger sister, Leah, who also happened to be one of Clara's best friends…Liam's been on edge with needing to feel like he's protecting not just Clara, but everyone. Especially because the whole thing almost blew up our friend group.

He nods his head up and down and I can tell it's because he's contemplating how to say whatever it is that's on his mind.

"I don't think any less of you because of your lifestyle with women, Simmons." I always know when Liam's being sincere because it never fails he uses my last name. "But Susie doesn't seem like the type to be down for a casual hookup and I can tell her friendship means a lot to you so–"

"Liam, I get it," I cut him off. "It's just coffee with a friend…"

"Hm," Jake finally speaks up, "that sounds a lot like what Liam said when he tried convincing us he and Clara were only sharing a class and working together as partners."

I give him a pointed look because this is nothing like Liam and Clara's situation, not even in the slightest.

"Susie hasn't kissed me," I say as I wave. I'm not sure who says it, or if I even heard correctly, but it sounded like a *not yet* comment came from somewhere behind me.

But they're out of their minds because there is absolutely no way in hell Susie Cobble would ever be interested in me, let alone want to kiss me. I've already acknowledged I flirt with the girl, I flirt with everyone. Yeah, she's a fucking knockout, but I'm most definitely not *her* type.

That's not to say that if the opportunity arose, I wouldn't take it. What idiot wouldn't?

But it won't, so there's nothing to worry about.

Chapter 14

Susie

I think I've picked up my coffee and sat it down a total of fifty times since the moment Paul sat in front of me. I've been anxious for this all week; so anxious that even the girls picked up that I was on edge. Did I tell them what for? Hell no. I will not be telling *anyone* about this little arrangement that Paul could or could not accept.

And truthfully, I don't know which he would choose. He technically offered, but I doubt he thought I'd actually take him up on it.

We started with small talk – him asking about cheer, me asking about hockey – as if he knew I needed to ease into the reason I asked him here today. Now, our muffins are gone and my coffee is almost empty, so I better get to the point…

"Thanks for meeting me here today, Paulie," I giggle as I use the nickname he pretends to hate but deep down I think he secretly loves.

My suspicion is confirmed when his bottom lip barely twitches upward before being replaced with a dramatic eye roll.

"I'd rather you call me Pauline."

My nose wrinkles at the unfortunate nickname I gave him.

"Pauline is much worse than Paulie."

His full lips pull into a wide smile, and as always, it's one that is entirely too attractive for his own good. "Not when it's the nickname given by you."

Now it's my turn for the eye roll.

"Alright, Q-T," he says. "Tell me what's going on."

Hm. That's new.

"Q-T?" I ask with my eyebrows drawn together. "What's with the new nickname?"

He shrugs. "Just trying a new one out. Don't like it?"

"I don't know what it means," I admit.

"Well," he takes a deep breath in, "Q for the traditional Susie Q and T for terrific," he says matter of factly.

Well, when he puts it that way, of course I love it.

"I like all the nicknames you give me," I confess. "Although you may distance yourself after the idea I'm about to throw your way…"

His face twists in confusion. "Why would I ever distance myself from you, Q?" The way he's genuinely taken aback like that would ever be a thought in his mind is…cute.

I look around, making sure no one we know is nearby, and lean in motioning for him to do the same. His six-foot body is stretched outward, giving his knees space so he doesn't hit the table, which is pointless because as he quickly leans closer, he whacks the table and almost sends my coffee to the floor.

"What's wrong, Susie?"

"Nothing's wrong, Paul. I just…umm…I was wonderingifyou'dbemydatingcoach?" I ask very quickly and in a very hushed breath.

The look on his face tells me he has absolutely no idea

what I said. I run my hands over my face before repeating myself.

"I was wondering, and saying no is totally okay and completely understandable, but would you like…I was thinking…would you maybe be my dating coach?" I mouth the last two words, not wanting to embarrass myself completely, yet.

"Be your hating coach? Q, what does that mean? Is there someone you hate and you need help telling them off? Who is it and what the fuck did they do–"

"My dating coach, Paul. Would you be my dating coach and help me with my self-confidence and flirting skills?"

His eyes go wide as he sits still not saying a word. Meanwhile, I'm nervously running my fingers through my hair. We stay frozen for what feels like five minutes – I'm not sure if I broke him or what – but the man is not budging.

This was a huge mistake. What was I thinking?

I shake my head as I say, "You know what, I'm sorry Paul. Forget what I just said, I don't know what I was thinking." I scoot back so fast I knock my purse down, everything spilling out of it. I don't bother looking up as I move with lightning speed to gather everything.

"I'll see you later, Pauline!" I'm trying to act as normal as possible after just asking my guy best friend if he'd be my dating coach. "Next group hang out, yeah?"

I salute, because how else could I embarrass myself more, and hastily take off out the door. As soon as I step into fresh air, I take a moment to breathe and truly reflect on the major issue I could've just caused. Paul didn't say a word, but what if I just ruined our friendship? What if he's awkward around me now, or worse…what if he doesn't want to be around me at all?

Shit. Could this affect our group? Would he tell–

"Susie!"

I turn around as I see Paul bust through the door frantically looking around. When he spots me, he lets out a puff of air and reaches me in one step.

"You took off without letting me say anything."

"Paul, you don't have to say anything. Your face said it all," I motion where we were just sitting. "Your silence was enough and really, it's okay. I just don't want my stupid question to mess with our–"

"You're misunderstanding my surprise for an answer, Q."

Now, it's my turn for confusion. "Your answer isn't no?"

He looks around, probably for the same reason I did just minutes ago, and then begins running his hand through his loose waves.

"Can we go talk in my truck?"

I don't say anything, and instead, bob my head up and down. He grabs my hand, leading me the short walk to his truck and only lets go when he's opening the door for me. I'm still not entirely sure how this conversation is going to go, but I feel better that we're at least going to talk about it.

I meant it when I said I'd understand if he says no – the last thing I want is to lose him as a friend.

As he gets in the driver's seat, I don't say a word. Truthfully, I've already said too much and I'm waiting to see where he goes with the conversation. For what feels like several minutes, I stare into my lap feeling my heartbeat through my ears.

"Susie," his gravelly voice cuts through the silence. "Tell me exactly what it is you're asking me, please.

Chapter 15

Paul

I had to have misheard her, or at least that's what I thought when I stared in silence. *Would you maybe be my dating coach?* I thought surely that couldn't have been what she said.

But when she all but sprinted outside, I knew I heard right and I knew I had to make things clear. Over my dead fucking body would I have her thinking she embarrassed herself or that I wouldn't be willing to help her. And now we're here, sitting in my truck as she works up the courage to tell me the specifics of what she's asking.

"I need help with my self-confidence…I think it's why I struggle with flirting," she admits without looking at me. "I panicked when Jamee asked me on a date because I don't feel confident enough to go."

Hearing her admission sends what feels like a knife through my heart. How could a girl so amazing, so beautiful, struggle so horribly she felt like she needed me to help her?

"You need my help with your…confidence?" I repeat, making sure I'm understanding correctly. She still hasn't made eye-contact with me, but her head gently nods up and down.

"Who broke this self-confidence of yours, Q?" I ask with a bite in my tone. Not towards her, but towards the asshole that caused this for her.

My sunshine girl has clouds of her own and that I can't settle for.

"It doesn't matter who," *fucking knew it,* "all that matters is that it did. As much therapy as I've done for what happened, as many times as I tell myself it doesn't control my life, there are parts that it does and I'm tired of that."

Therapy? She may not be ready to tell me the story, and that's okay, but whenever I find out who caused this pain of hers, I will not rest until they hurt worse.

"I'm going to go out on a limb and assume the push for this is wanting to prepare for your date with Locke?" I ask, knowing damn straight that's a contributing factor, and not necessarily thrilled to know I'd be helping her with her date.

But I would be helping her and that in itself is enough to put my ping of – not jealousy, but not happiness – aside.

"I want to go on a date without being anxious or nervous or full of self-doubt," she turns her body towards me, finally connecting with my eyes for the first time since we started this conversation. "I want to feel sexy and powerful and confident."

I nod, understanding what she wants and needs, but oblivious to where I come in.

"I already think you're all of those things," I wink, hoping to make her smile. I'm awarded with a faint and quick tug of her lips. "But I have to ask Q-T," short for cutie but she doesn't know that, "where do I come in?"

I offered a few weeks ago to be her guinea pig if she

needed to brush up with her flirting skills and I'd still be more than happy to be that, but this seems much deeper.

"You're the epitome of self-confidence wrapped in human form, Paul," she silently laughs, "I couldn't think of anyone better to teach me how to be confident in myself than the hockey team's no-strings-attached heartthrob."

I suppose she isn't wrong. Getting a girl to come home with me has never been an issue – I've always been sure of myself and not to sound like a complete prick, but my hockey-toned body and good looks just adds to this confidence of mine.

Not to mention I know what women like in and out of the bedroom.

"Fair point," I finally say, realizing I've been quiet this entire time. "You think I'm the hockey team's heartthrob?" I tease with a smug grin.

"I think that I could learn a thing or two from the man who never has a problem being so full of himself," she winks.

Not that I need convincing to spend any extra time with Susie, I'm definitely a willing participant. Spending time with my best friend whom I find to be extremely fucking attractive and want to be around anyways? Um, yes. For my own selfish reasons? Abso-fucking-lutely.

Still, I want to be a good *"dating coach"*, so I need to know exactly what she's wanting from this. Self-confidence? Yes – I got that. But what is she expecting? How do I live up to what she's needing from me?

Which has my mind circling back to the *"dating coach"* term. I don't like it. One, I don't want to think of Susie on a date with another guy and two, I've never dated anyone myself and definitely am not equipped in that realm.

"So," I clear my throat, "you want my help in teaching

you how to be confident in yourself so that you feel ready to go on a date?"

She takes a big breath as her head moves up and down.

"And what do you want that to look like, Q?"

Her brows scrunch together as she begins chewing on her bottom lip. "Whatever my dating coach thinks it should look like? Whatever you think I need to learn to be sure of myself. If you were to agree."

"I don't want to be your dating coach," I say too quickly, realizing once the words have left my mouth how fucking shitty it sounded. I watch as her mouth slightly opens and sadness spreads across her face.

"No! Fuck. Shit," I reach across the dash and quickly grab her hand. "I want to do this, Susie. I want to help you, I just don't think a dating coach is the right term."

"You're–you're going to help me?"

For my own reasons. "You're one of my best friends, Q. Anything you need, I'm here."

She squeezes my hand as she lets out a relaxed breath.

"Why not call you my dating coach?"

"I'm not necessarily helping you with dating, Q-T. I'm just helping *you.* We could call me Mr. Flirtatious, Professor Charming–"

"How about just…my teacher?" She laughs. "My own personal teacher."

I'll take anything as long as it doesn't involve preparing her for dating someone.

"Works for me, Q."

She glances down at her phone, her eyes turning wide.

"Shit. I have to hurry to practice! It's about a ten minute walk and I can't be late. Can we talk sometime soon about… our little…yanno?" She motions between the two of us as she goes to hop out of the truck.

I gently grab her forearm before she gets completely out of the door. "I'll take you to practice and we can discuss this," I motion between us just like she did seconds ago, "on the way there."

"I can't ask–"

I turn my head towards her with my eyes slanted. "Ask me to take you to practice after you just asked me to be your teacher? Come on Q," I tease.

Her face immediately reddens followed by a chuckle. "I suppose you're right there, Pauline."

Chapter 16

Susie

Would I have ever imagined I'd be sitting in Paul Simmons' truck discussing the details of our little… arrangement? I mean, I suppose part of me knew it was a real possibility, but I still find it humorous this is legitimately happening.

Me, Susie Cobble, with my own personal teacher to help me win back my self-confidence, which I'm hoping will help with my other skills, a.k.a. flirting with the male species.

I half expected him to laugh in my face, but when he asked me who caused me to be so broken with my own confidence, it caught me off guard. No one has ever asked *who*, it's always *what. What happened? What did I do?*

He's the first person who immediately assumed someone else broke me. He's the first person, outside of my parents, to immediately become protective of me.

And did my heart flutter for a moment? Yes, yes it did. A completely normal reaction for anyone when a guy comes to their defense, especially someone with the face and body like Paul.

I hate that I accidentally spilled the beans about therapy…

but I'm so glad he didn't push the subject. I know there will come a time I'll have to share more of my story, but today is most definitely not it.

"Did you hear me, Q?"

Paul's rich voice fills the truck, snapping me out of my thoughts.

"No, I'm sorry. I was caught up in my head. What did you say?"

He clears his throat as he repeats himself. "Your date is in two weeks? How often are you wanting to meet to go over these…um..le–lessons?" He takes one hand off the wheel and runs it across his cheek. He may not outright say it, he may be trying not to show it, but Paul Simmons is nervous.

And I think it's absolutely adorable.

"Um," I say as I wipe my hands up and down my thighs, "I–I'm not sure? I don't want to take away from hockey or overwhelm you on top of practices and school. Three days, three lessons? Wow, saying it out loud seems like a lot… maybe we should–"

I stop mid-sentence when I feel his hand cover mine on my leg. And I can't quite ignore the small, very tiny ounce of electricity that prickles my skin from his touch.

"Q-T," he chuckles, "you're spiraling. No need to spiral," he pats my hand before pulling away. "I can do this Friday, and next Monday and Thursday after practice ends. I can come over to your dorm, since Clara all but lives with Liam now, and go over everything there?"

I can't help the small smile that breaks free. He seems so…invested in this.

"That's a lot of time during the week, Paul. Are you sure?"

He winks as he says, "I'm always sure of myself, Q."

"That sounds perfect," I say as I nod, trying to laugh away

the nerves that are settling in at how concrete this plan is becoming. "What will our…um…lessons look like?"

He chews on his bottom lip for a moment, thinking hard. I can see it in the way he's squinting his eyes as if he's talking to himself and weighing the options. I sit patiently as we get closer and closer to the gym and finally, as he pulls his truck into a parking space, he lets out a deep breath and answers.

"If you're wanting to build your confidence, I say we focus on three important aspects, or at least they're important aspects to me," he holds up his pointer finger as he continues.

"One. Attitude," he shrugs as if that's a no brainer.

"Two. Yourself – we'll flush out those details later. And last but not least…how to be sexy. Everyone knows you won't be confident in yourself if you don't believe you're sexy."

I mean…I suppose that makes sense?

"Ass," he beams.

"One of our lessons is about…my ass?" I wasn't going to question his methods, but that can't be right…

His eyebrows pinch together as he quickly shakes his head. "No, no. Our lessons are called A.S.S. Attitude, self, sexy. Simple enough," he smirks.

"What will that look like?"

"You'll see when we get there," he points to the gym. "Better get going before you're late, Q."

I look towards the gym, the realization of what's happening hits me at full speed. Almost as if I'm a turtle trying to cross the street just to see a gigantic ass semi-truck barreling towards me. I want to cross, but it's scary. And I expected a car or two…but a semi-truck?

It's Paul. Paul and his incredible confidence is the semi-truck…

Does that make sense? Am I spiraling in my own head right now?

"You're really willing to help me with this? I–I can't promise to be an easy student. Self-confidence is something I've struggled pretty hard with after…" I trail off, not wanting to finish the sentence.

I watch as Paul's jaw tightens, his hand closing and opening where it lays on the center console.

"I love hanging out with you, Q. And the fact you asked me to help, knowing that it means so much to you, means a lot to me. So, yeah. I'm not just willing, I'm thankful you chose me."

He sticks his hand out to me, holding it open. "And I promise I'll do everything I can to help, Q-T. You're safe with me."

I fit my hand in his, not needing to think before saying, "I know."

"It's a deal. I'll see you Monday, Teach," I wink as I hop out of his truck.

I'm quickly making my way inside when I hear him yell, "Get ready to talk about your ass, Q!"

* * *

"Is it like this?" I repeat the motions to Clara, making sure I'm doing it correctly.

It's been two hours of us learning competition material for Daytona and my mind is absolutely fried. I'm exhausted, my muscles are aching, and all I want to do is soak in a bubble bath and sleep for forty-eight hours. Thankfully, practice has officially ended and we're gathering our things.

"Fucking perfect, Suse!" Her lips pull tight as she wipes the sweat from her brow.

I know what you might be thinking. Why the hell is a cheerleader sweating during practice?

I'm half convinced that people assume we sit around talking about hair and bows all the time. I don't think people quite understand the exhausting work that goes into cheerleading. Especially for NCA champions with a title to defend...

"Coach has really high expectations for us," Leah says from beside me as she twirls a strand of hair around her finger. The worry in her voice is strong, laced with anxiety. "Do you think I'll–"

"Bitch," Lucy interrupts, "if you're about to ask if we think you'll make the competition team, I'll punch you in the tits myself."

That causes Leah to relax, a laugh erupting from her chest.

"I ask Jake all the time if he thinks I'll do as good as I did last year," her cheeks turn slightly red. "He also threatens me for doubting myself, but his threat includes tying my hands to the bed and–"

"No, no," Sara says as she violently shakes her head. "I do not need to know the sexual secrets of the youngest baby in the group."

Leah rolls her eyes as we all head outside to our separate vehicles.

Paul wasn't wrong earlier, with Liam and Clara married, she all but lives at the River Road house now with him and the boys, while Leah stays over all the time as well.

Sara and Lucy share a house off-campus, which leaves me all by my lonesome in the dorm. Not that I'm entirely complaining; not having a roommate means being able to do whatever I want around the dorm and not having to cover my ears with a pillow at night...

"You guys want to come over to the boys' for dinner?" Clara asks as she throws her bag in the back of Leah's car. She considered finally biting the bullet and getting one herself, but Liam said it would be pointless when he would still drive her everywhere she needs to go.

The boy is smitten for my best friend, and I love it.

"And spend additional time with Clay when it's not needed?" Lucy's quick to respond. "No thank you."

Sara cuts her a look as she answers, "Nothing against the boys for me, I just need to get some homework done."

Her and Lucy take turns going around, saying their goodbyes before getting in Lucy's car and driving off.

"And you, Suse?" Leah asks.

And see Paul so soon before I've had the chance to truly think about what the hell I asked him to do? Nope.

"I'm pretty exhausted. Rain check?"

"I'm holding you to it!" Clara says as she pinches my cheek. "Go soak in your bath you old lady," she winks. "We'll see you tomorrow?"

I wave her off as I walk towards the dorms yelling, "Love you guys!"

I have one full day to prepare for our first lesson and although I'm extremely nervous for what it'll look like, I truly feel at ease knowing that it's one of my best friends helping me through it.

Chapter 17

Paul

I've had time to prepare for what I'm about to start with Susie and I'm still fucking nervous.

I–I want this to be perfect for her. I want my best friend, *my girl*, to feel good – sexy – to understand what I see in her and feel that in herself. Maybe that's why I've spent the last two days being more thorough and organized than I have ever been in my entire life. I came home Wednesday with a new purpose, and helping Susie isn't something I'm taking lightly.

Meme would most definitely be proud right now.

Just not about me lying to myself and my best friend about the weird underlying feelings I have. I don't know what the feelings mean, I just can't shake the constant desire to talk to her, to see her, to catch a glimpse of her entirely too cute dimples.

So, yeah, I quickly agreed in hopes that being around her will help me get my head straight while also benefitting her.

And although I've been friends with Susie for about a year now, I don't know much about her personally, which is a must for our lessons.

Or at least that's what I told myself yesterday morning when I called her on my way to a workout.

"*Hello?*"

The sound of her sweet but raspy voice fills my speaker.

"*Well, good morning Q. How's it going?*"

"*Are you okay?*"

Her immediate concern confuses me. I've called Susie before to shoot the shit, I'm not sure why she'd immediately think something's wrong?

"*I appreciate the worry but why wouldn't I be okay?*"

"*Because it's 4:30 in the morning and no one in their right mind just calls someone this early if they aren't okay?*"

Fuck.

I tend to forget not every athlete has to get up at the ass crack of fucking dawn for their workouts.

"*Shit, I'm sorry Q. I didn't even consider how fucking early it is. Everything's fine, I just had some questions for you that I was needing you to answer for tomorrow's first lesson. Can I text them to you?*"

"*Well, my heart is already racing so I'm not sure going back to bed is an option,*" *I hear her yawn.* "*What kind of questions?*"

I feel my lips pull into a small grin. I wish I could say I feel bad for waking her up, but not when it means I get to talk to her.

And that is how I learned all things related to Susie Cobble.

Favorite food? Chicken, but specifically chicken tenders.

Her favorite color is blue, but only a pastel blue, and she's a sucker for Disney movies.

She has two younger brothers – Will and Landon – both currently in high school and both playing hockey. She was born and raised in a town here in Illinois called Quincy where she grew up learning to value family above everything.

Now, an enormous part of me really wanted to pry into what had happened that forced her into therapy, but I refrained. Instead, I focused my questions on her – what she likes, hates, anything she wanted to share with me.

Turns out Susie Cobble has a love for art. She mentioned how when everything happened with the *event*, that's what she kept referring to it as, art helped her express herself in ways words couldn't. It helped take her mind off the shit that occurred and focus on something she enjoyed.

She opened up about cheerleading and how tryouts were one of the most nerve-racking days of her life but how she's grateful the girls pushed her outside of her comfort zone.

She talked about her parents, Daryl and Tricia, and how she's always been close to them. Daryl, her dad, works as a realtor for Quincy and the surrounding areas while her mom manages a boutique right outside of their town. She again briefly mentioned her past with no specific details but how her parents advocated for her, fought for her, and got her the help she needed for what she went through. I feel like I'm going out of my damn mind not knowing the specifics but I also know it isn't my place to ask. So, when I finally got out of my head about whatever this asshole did and focused on all the stories she told of her and her family, I found myself wishing I had stories like hers to share.

That I could explain what my mom does for a living without having to use the fucking words "drug" paired with "addiction." Hell, it'd be nice just to know my sperm donor's name. And when I hear about parents like Susie Cobble's who sound like they'd burn the world down for her, it reminds me how shitty mine truly are.

But then I remember my Meme and how she is the one person who will love me unconditionally and that's enough for me.

When I asked her what she thinks her strengths are, it was no surprise she couldn't find any. Seeing your own strengths is hard enough without some asshole tearing you down. As an outsider, it's easy to see Susie's. I'm not sure what it's called – I don't think there's one word to describe it – but she has this calming sense about her that makes people feel welcomed, like they could sit and talk with her about anything and everything without feeling judged or ashamed.

I know it's a strength of hers because several times I've found myself almost opening up about my past, about me.

Anywho, back to the task at hand. I finally, *after a shit-load of crumpled up paper,* constructed our three-part plan to help my best friend. Are there lesson plans? Hell yes. Why? Because I'm taking this fucking seriously.

So, here I am. Standing outside Susie's dorm, notebook in hand with two things on my mind. One, helping out Q. Two, being alone with her.

Chapter 18

Susie

"Coming!" I yell as I stumble towards the door, knowing who it is on the other side.

Friday came much quicker than I wanted it to. Not because I wasn't looking forward to hanging out with Paul – the man always makes me laugh and smile – but because I'm not quite ready to completely embarrass myself in front of him.

Attitude is the first lesson. I tried the last two days to get him to spill what exactly tonight would look like, but the man wouldn't budge…

All he would tell me is that our lessons will probably be an hour or two long and food is required. He's coming from practice, so I took the liberty of already having dinner waiting for him – food I know he *loves*.

I hover my hand over the doorknob, taking one final deep breath before slowly pulling it open, immediately taken aback by the man standing in front of me. I was expecting to see a post-practice Paul – the Paul I've seen many, many times since becoming friends last year – but this Paul? Holy hades.

He is the walking model for a girl's ideal man. Grey

sweatpants that tightly hug his thighs. A shirt that stretches across his broad muscles outlining the entirety of his abs, which is at least an eight-pack, with his damp hair that exaggerates his slight curls. And you guessed it...a goddamn backwards hat.

You know in those romance novels when they say a man in a backwards hat does things to them? I was never able to truly picture or understand just exactly what they meant. I understand now. And apparently I'm just gawking because a cocky grin begins to spread across Paul's face.

"Are you going to let me come in, Q, or just gawk at me like eye-candy all evening? Don't get me wrong, I'm flattered, but it's not very professional considering I'm your teacher," he winks.

I immediately snap out of it.

"Oh! I wasn't–I didn't mean to–"

"Q," he steps past me in the doorway, "I'm fucking with you. You know I love making women drool over me."

"I am not drooling over you," I protest as I shut the door, leading him towards the kitchen.

"A guy could hope." He plops down at the kitchen island, reaching for the McDonald's bag. "Did you go and grab my favorite fake food?" His tongue dashes out of his mouth, licking his top lip like he's been a starved man for days.

And damn the backwards hat curse for making every move hot.

"Well, I figured it was the least I could do for you helping me out."

He pokes his head in the sack, sprawling all the food out on the counter as he shakes his head.

"You're my friend, Susie. I don't need payment with food or anything else," he looks at me, taking off his hat and smoothing out his hair. "I just want to help you. Whatever happened back in high school clearly fucked with your head," he reaches up, patting the top of my hair. "A head that is too gorgeous and smart to feel that way and if I, your best friend, can help you gain your confidence back, I'd feel on top of the world knowing I had any part in that."

Well, damn. I didn't expect such a sentimental statement to come from Paul. Don't get me wrong, he's as nice as they come, but I've never heard him care for something so much outside of hockey. If the man ever decides to settle down, I have a feeling he'd be quite whipped for his girl.

I should say something, thank him for caring so much about helping me, maybe explain what happened that got me here, but as quick as the moment came, it's gone. Because he's now shoving a handful of fries in his mouth going off about tonight's practice.

"Our first game is next month and shit-for-brains Brandon can't get it together. He's the left-winger, replacing Liam when we switch lines, and he's missing the drop pass every... fucking...time," he exaggerates. "Clay even turns around to check and make sure he's there, gets his ass chewed every time by Coach, and the dude skates right past the puck. How in the hell is he on a college scholarship, let alone for Barker? I mean–"

"Paul?" I quickly cut in as I'm staring at him. "I have no idea what you're saying?"

He chuckles as he dumps his fries on the counter.

"I forget people don't sleep, eat and breathe hockey like I have for all my life," he begins breaking apart his fries and elaborately laying them across the table. "Let me show you what I mean."

Thirty minutes later, Paul has now explained, in detail, every position in hockey along with how line changes work and what a drop pass is, which is exactly as simple as it sounds. And as he gets up to throw his trash away, I know the moment I've been anticipating is finally here…

"Alright, Q. Where would you be most comfortable to get crack-a-lackin' on this lesson of ours?" He stands, holding his hand out for me. I grab it and hop off the barstool, wrapping my arm around his bicep as I do so often, and lead him to the sofa.

We take a seat next to each other and I watch as he pulls out a notebook, flipping it to a page with *A LOT* of words. Again, my heart is full seeing how much he cares about this.

"Okay," he takes a deep breath in and blows it out, "a few things before we get started, Q." He turns towards me as he brings his leg up on the sofa where it's now resting against my thigh.

"I will do my best to help you but you have to know this isn't a one and done type thing, Q-T. We can't just practice these things here with me and assume they're fixed. You have to put what we go over into practice anywhere and every-where you go."

He places his hand over his heart. "I know I make confi-dence look simple and easy." I roll my eyes at his humble-ness. "But everyone's confidence falters at times, and even I have to take time to focus on these things every once in a while."

I grin at Paul, knowing that in his own way, that was him trying to ease my nerves.

He lowers his eyes, raising his eyebrows as if I'm supposed to answer what he had just said, not knowing there was a question in there…

"Oh ummm. Am I supposed to insert a speech here too?" I tease as I shove him with my elbow. "I'm kidding. I under-stand, Pauline. Practice makes perfect. I am a college athlete you know? Hockey players aren't the only athletes that practice often."

"Hey," he places a hand on my thigh, "after watching the girls compete at Daytona last year, I'm fairly positive you guys probably practice more than us."

"I just hope I'm enough to make the competitive team too–"

"And we have arrived at our lesson," Paul interjects. "This is a good place to start. Attitude, Q. Attitude."

"Okay but all I was saying–"

"You were saying you *hope*," he emphasizes the word, "that you're good enough. Confidence is based on attitude and attitude is based on many things, but we're focusing on two key factors," he points to the notebook as he says, "self-talk and assertiveness."

I scrunch my nose at the words. Assertiveness? Who is she?

"You can't build your confidence if you're constantly tearing yourself down and not being clear with your communication. You said it yourself after talking with Jamee at the bar the other night, you had no idea if he was flirting or what to say. This is to help with that."

My lips begin to curve upward while he goes into detail of what tonight entails, his fingers skimming over the notes he has written down.

Paul Simmons may be a flirt, but he's the most genuine friend.

Chapter 19

Paul

"I wrote some questions down and I want you to answer with the first thing that comes to mind."

Susie nods her head in agreement as I begin reading off the list. Mostly simple questions, but it's meant to demonstrate how easy it is to allow negative self-talk to override the good. A concept I grew up with.

Lisa left because I asked too many questions. Lisa doesn't come around because I annoy her. Lisa didn't come over today because I'm too loud.

Meme quickly nipped that in the ass and helped rebuild my thought process, it sure as shit wasn't an overnight job, but we got there.

Lisa left because she isn't well. Lisa doesn't want to be around because of her own choices. Lisa didn't come over today because she chose not to.

And as I go down the list of questions, I see in Susie what I had in myself – doubt.

The questions aren't too deep, just enough to get a feel of her default response.

"Coach Hawkins pulls you aside after practice and says your group did well today. What's your immediate response?"

"Um…" she begins to think.

"No thinking. Quick answer, Q-T."

She rolls her eyes as she says, "I'm just the backspot. It's Kristy, the flyer, who made us look good."

"Last question," I sit the notebook down, looking directly at her. "Leah comes up to you tomorrow saying you look gorgeous, what's your immediate response?"

"I have amazing friends so this is something they say often," she blushes, "but I always respond with doubt? Like, asking them if they're sure it fits right? Is it too much? Usually questioning their judgement," she hangs her head. "I see where you're going with this, Pauline."

"Then by all means, explain away."

She turns completely towards me, pulling her legs into her chest. Her oversized sweatshirt bunched up on her thighs with her fuzzy cat socks pulled over her black leggings. I know I should be focusing, but for just a moment, I let my eyes roam over her body. Her hair is pulled up with a claw thing, no makeup, completely relaxed…absolutely stunning.

"I didn't answer a single thing with any type of positive comment. Even if I didn't outright say something bad about myself, I didn't imply anything good either. It's just…it's my automatic response, you know?"

Strange, because my automatic response to Susie is the complete opposite. Perfect in every way. Beautiful every day. And she has no idea.

"I think it's everyone's automatic response and we have to rewire our brain to think differently. So, now we're going to go through your answers and reword them in a way that does think positively about yourself."

And we do. We spend the next fifteen to twenty minutes discussing the questions and how she can take the time to acknowledge that in everything I asked, there is something positive.

"I suppose for Coach Hawkins' comment it isn't just Kristy that makes it look easy. As a stunt group we work together to ensure the stunt stays in the air. If it begins to fall, we all fight for it. The group did well which means yes, I also did well."

I wipe an imaginary tear from my eye as she finishes her sentence, being rewarded with one of those adorable laughs.

"Shut up," she says. "You know it'll take time for me to consistently think like this, but it's nice to see I can."

"It isn't just seeing the positives in what people say to you, Q. It's looking in the mirror and being able to say the positives to yourself. It's having a rough day and being able to say it's okay, tomorrow will be better. It's having a rough practice and being able to tell yourself it was a bad day, not that you're a bad athlete."

Where in the fuck is this shit coming from? Have I turned...emotional?

She smirks as she asks, "Does Paul Simmons stand in front of the mirror, admiring his eight-pack and tell himself he's the greatest goalie Barker University hockey has ever had?"

I laugh as I lean forward, lowering my voice. "Honey bun," *why did I just say that,* "Paul Simmons doesn't have just an eight-pack," I tease. "Now, how are you feeling about moving on to the second part of our lesson?"

She scrunches her nose, and I can only imagine it's towards my horrendous excuse of a nickname I just gave her, but I don't feel like making an ass of myself by asking, so I choose to move on.

"Alright," I slap my thighs, standing from the sofa and holding out my hand, "we're going to stand for this next lesson." Why? Not sure...but it sure as hell *isn't* an excuse to grab Susie's hand again.

Without thinking, she takes it, springing to her feet, and some odd part of me loves knowing she trusts me so easily.

"How does one teach someone to be...assertive?"

"Great question, Q," I tap her nose. "By role-playing, duh."

She opens her mouth to talk but I don't let her get a word out before I launch into phase one, part two.

"Hey baby," I reach up, cupping her chin. "You come here often?"

As I say it, I realize how fucking cringey it sounds and how unfortunate it is that I've used this line much too often.

Not recently though...

Her eyes move to my hand that's still holding onto her chin while her eyebrows are pinched together with a faint splash of red crawling up her neck.

"Uhhh. What's happening Paul?"

"Role playing, Q-T. You can't learn to be assertive if you don't practice when you need to be." I take a step closer, almost chest to chest, and holy shit balls her eyes are so fucking mesmerizing and sure, I could easily kiss her right now–

No, no, no. That is not what I'm here for.

"Do you trust me, Susie?"

She's staring into my eyes as she answers, "Yes."

And I think I had a very minor heart palpitation for a moment. Is it because of how vulnerable she looks or how there was no hesitation to answer? I don't know, but we're going to ignore it and move on.

"Well, then role play with me...baby," I wink.

She laughs, shrugging her shoulders for me to continue on.

"I want you to become comfortable with situations in which you should be assertive, cue man in the bar hitting on you not knowing how to take a hint."

I take my hat off, running my fingers through my hair as I push it back. "Hey baby, you come here often?"

"Uh, no?"

"I figured. I would've remembered a sexy girl like you," I begin walking her backwards until her back hits the wall, placing my hand above her head.

It's just a scenario. NOT REAL.

"Like what you see?" I motion up and down my body, my cocky fuckboy attitude shining bright.

"Yes," she answers quickly. So quickly that I immediately snap my eyes to hers as I see them widen in realization. "Should I say yes or no for the lesson?"

"Well, as much as I love hearing yes," *from her especially,* "let's go with no for this lesson, Q."

"You're…okay," she immediately jumps back into the situation, "but I really have to get back to my friends."

"I can walk you back to them," I lean close to her ear, "and then afterwards I can walk you back to my place."

She sidesteps away from me with a lopsided smile. "No, that's okay. I can manage." She tries to step past me, but I reach out and grab her wrist. Suddenly, I'm pissed off just thinking about the possibility of someone acting like this to her.

"I insist, sweetie," I drape my arm around her shoulders, walking her towards the kitchen without an ounce of pushback from my sunshine girl.

"Uhh–uh okay."

I drop my arm, stopping in my tracks turning Susie to face me.

"No, no, Q," I shake my head. "Assertiveness is not agreeing to something after you've already said no. Assertiveness is holding your ground, telling the dickhead to fuck off because you aren't interested. Holding your own and becoming confident in saying how you feel."

"Okay, okay…I know I'm a little go with the flow of things and I should speak up more," she begins chewing on the inside of her cheek.

"Give me an example."

She squints her eyes as she begins to bite her top lip. I can tell she's thinking hard and it's truly adorable.

"I love my girls to death, but sometimes when we all go out they insist on what I wear and–and I typically hate their outfits," she breaks out in a hysterical laugh and I can't help but join in on the infectious sound.

I think back to the most recent bar trips. Sure, Susie Cobble looked as breathtaking as ever, but the more I think about it, the more I remember how uncomfortable she looked. Constantly pulling down her skirt, always fixing her top. Gorgeous, but she didn't seem like Susie.

"Why not say something, Q?"

She shrugs her shoulders as she says, "They're always so excited to help me dress up and I love making my friends happy."

And that right there is why Susie Cobble is my sunshine girl. I know beyond a fucking shadow of a doubt that she would sacrifice her own happiness for those around her, but with me – with our group – there would never be a reason she'd have to do that.

"Susie," I cup her chin again, "I can guarantee you that

Clara and them could give two shits about picking your outfit. They're happy because they think you're happy with what they choose." She looks up at me with her green eyes shining bright. "Plus," I drop my hand and head back towards the sofa, "you're gorgeous no matter what outfit you're in, Q. Now, come on and let's practice some more assertiveness."

Chapter 20

Susie

"That fucking door is definitely big enough for both of them," Paul says as he shoves more popcorn in his mouth, his eyes glued to the TV.

We finished our lesson three hours ago, it's 11:30 p.m., and we're almost finished with *Titanic.*

I'm genuinely impressed with how serious Paul is taking this whole teacher role, and not only that, but tonight was super beneficial.

I know I have a tendency to immediately think negatively, my brain has been wired that way ever since the *event.* Mrs. Baker and I worked on it quite extensively when I first began therapy, but I suppose since moving to college I've lost my techniques. It was a nice reminder from Paul that I am in control of how I view life.

As far as being assertive…I've always struggled with that. My personality has always been heavy with the *whatever you want* attitude or the *sounds good to me* gal. It's not that I think my friends wouldn't care what I have to say, it's just that it's much easier to go with the flow than against it.

I'm sitting on the sofa with my legs curled underneath me

while Paul is leaned back, legs stretched out with his hands behind his head. And I guarantee you that if I were to google *"attractive man on sofa"* this is the image I'd get because *GOOD GOD* does he look good.

But I'm also going to blame that on the lesson earlier. His fake flirting, calling me baby, the chin grab…

It's all fake, it's all fake, it's all fake.

He is one of my best friends and it's of course normal to feel attracted to a man as good looking as Paul but it's a harmless attraction.

"What do you think, Q?"

Shit, did I say something out loud?

"Abouutt?"

"Was the door big enough?"

I stretch out my legs, my feet pressing against his thigh. I know I should move them, but not being scrunched up feels too good.

"I think Rose could've tried a bit harder for sure," I yawn as I finish the sentence. "But can I be honest with you?"

He angles towards me with a smirk on his face. "Is this you being assertive in your opinion, Q?"

I chuckle as I sit up, pulling my knees to my chest. "I don't like the movie at all." I hide my face in my arms, afraid to look at his expression because we literally just talked about me speaking up and here I am, watching a movie I don't like…

After a moment of silence, I slightly lift my eyes to meet him, caught off guard by his extremely white teeth shining bright at me.

"I–uh–I thought you would be upset that I didn't tell you before we watched it?"

He shakes his head as his lips tug higher, gently brushing a loose strand of hair out of my face and softly placing it behind my ear. I choose to ignore the jolt of electricity that shoots up my spine because it's simply insane it's even there.

"You may not have told me before I chose the movie, but you told me, and that my Q-T, is a big step. And I'm proud of you," he says as sincerely as possible with a twinkle in his eyes.

"You're…proud of me?"

He pats my knee as he stands, "Always, Q. Now, I guess I better get out of here since it's," he pulls out his phone, "11:50 and I have seventeen missed texts and five missed calls from the guys. Hell, they've probably called the police by now," he chuckles as he begins grabbing his things.

"How–how did you feel about tonight's lesson?" He asks without looking at me.

I walk over to him, grabbing his arm so he'll meet my gaze. His eyes go to my arm first and then trail up to my face where he stands straight up, his muscular body towering over me.

Without saying anything, I wrap my arms around his waist, hugging him tight, my emotions almost breaking free.

"I can't explain how much this means to me, Paul. Tonight was great. It reminded me of what Mrs. Baker and I used to discuss and…I–I really needed that reminder. As for assertiveness, it gives me something new to work on," I take a deep breath as I prepare to share just a small piece of me, now aware that his arms are wrapped around me as well.

"Mrs. Baker was my therapist after what happened and she quickly realized there was nothing but negativity in my mind," I squeeze his body tight as I think back to the broken girl I was. "We worked really hard to get to where I am today but I think since stepping away from her sessions, I lost my techniques and let some of what I learned slip away. Tonight reminded me of those things all thanks to you,

Pauline," I lift my head but continue to keep my arms wrapped around him.

His honey-filled eyes are beaming down at me, but it's not a smile he's wearing now. It's…concern? Anger, maybe?

"Paul, are you–"

"I struggled when I was younger with being positive to the point where I thought everything that happened was my fault. My Meme wouldn't settle for that and she taught me everything I know about changing my outlook on things, understanding where to see the good," he closes his eyes like he's trying to hide from me.

"I didn't know any better, you know? That's how Lisa was. It wasn't necessarily because of me but because she chose who she wanted to be." He finally opens his eyes, his gaze locked on mine. "Anyways…I–I had a good time tonight, Q. And I'm glad the lesson was helpful," he pauses as he releases me, reaching down to grab his backpack. "Helping my best friend is all I care about. Well, that and hockey," he shoots me his signature wink.

I follow behind him to the door and it's taking all of my inner strength to not ask about his mother–Lisa. A woman who seems very, very shitty. I open my mouth to thank him yet again for tonight but he beats me to it.

"Thank you for sharing with me, Q. I–I can tell whatever happened really fucked with you and, for that, I'm sorry. And although I hate that you need this type of help, I am glad I'm the one helping you. I'll see you again on Monday for the next lesson of Paul's three steps to sexy confidence," he teases.

I know it's his way of taking away the seriousness of the last few minutes, but I also need him to know how thankful I am.

"Paul," I say as he grabs the doorknob. He turns around,

his usual well-groomed hair a bit messy from him running his hands through it during the movie. "I'm glad you're helping me, too. I wouldn't want it to be anyone else."

He smiles, a genuine smile, as he turns back around and heads out the door and there's one thing I know for certain after tonight's lesson.

There's a lot more to Paul Simmons than what meets the eye.

Chapter 21

Susie

"**A**re you sure that's what your boss said?"

I'm sitting on the floor of Clara and Liam's room with all the girls for *pajamas and drama*. Every Sunday evening we come over, kick Liam out of his room, and have a girls night which typically consists of talking about the week's events.

Truthfully, it's my favorite night of the week…usually. This past Friday with Paul definitely takes the cake. And still, the girls have no idea about our little…arrangement. For now, it's going to stay that way. Not because I'm ashamed of Paul helping me, more so because I'm ashamed I even had to ask.

The other part of that being that for some reason I can't quite get Friday evening out of my mind…

The fake flirting, I get. It was part of the lesson. Him asking if I wanted to watch a movie after? Normal. He's one of my best friends. The movie-move of brushing the hair behind my ear? The comforting me and sharing with me?

My poor, poor mind is having a hard time coming to terms that it meant nothing more, and besides, I wouldn't *want* it to mean anything more.

Right?

Paul is a great friend but…I'm not his type. Can't be.

"I'm pretty fucking positive," Lucy says deadpan. "I guess it's some new requirement for a core class that they need to put in some volunteer hours and the shelter offered to be a partnering business…and each of us practicing vet techs have to be a mentor."

"A mentor?" Sara asks. "Like you're overseeing the volunteers?"

Lucy huffs, shrugging as she says, "I suppose, I don't know. They're still ironing out details and said it'll start next semester. Who the fuck knows…"

"You know," Leah shakes her finger back and forth, "Clay mentioned something about his class having some type of internship thing where he has to put in so many hours or whatever. I wonder if this is similar?"

Lucy scoffs, "I pray to God it isn't, I'd feel pretty bad for whatever soul gets stuck with him."

I'm not sure when, and I'm not exactly sure how, but Clay Harper and Lucy Hayes are sworn enemies. I *thought* that as time went by maybe whatever hatred they had for one another would disappear, but unfortunately, it's only grown stronger.

She shakes her head back and forth. "I can't–"

"STAND HIM," Clara cuts her off. "We know Lu, you say it all the time, but have you ever really told us why?"

We all scoot closer as she huffs out a breath.

Lucy Hayes is the picture-perfect example of a beautiful, confident, hard-headed but lovable gal. Her rich chocolate hair and brown eyes with peppered freckles is the icing on top of a tall, striking figure. She's majoring as a veterinarian technician, currently working at Evanston's local animal shelter. She may not have the patience for certain individuals, but she has the biggest heart for animals.

"Because he's…infuriating. He thinks he's a hot shot that can get whatever and whoever he wants. He's arrogant, he was an asshole to Leah when all that shit went down, and he just fucking annoys me," she finishes waving her hands around in the air, clasping them in her lap with a relaxed breath. "And that's that."

"You know," Leah says while rummaging through the snacks laid out in front of us, "he doesn't actually get whoever he wants because he doesn't sleep around."

"I'm sorry," Sara coughs as she tries to swallow her drink. "You're telling me the captain of the hockey team doesn't fuck around with the puck bunnies that follow the boys around like their Gods?"

Honestly, I'm just as surprised as anyone. But come to think of it, I don't think I've ever actually seen Clay take a girl home?

"Why not?" Clara asks. "Isn't that part of the perks of being captain?"

Leah shrugs her shoulders as she answers, "He's always been that way. Sports first, love never," she laughs. "Honestly, we're convinced he'll never have a girlfriend."

"Whatever. He's still an arrogant asshole and I'd rather shove my face in a cage full of angry kittens than spend a fucking second longer than I have to with him."

"Okay, okay," Sara interjects. "Let's talk about something more happy like…" she trails off as she turns to Clara, "when we're going to have a baby Russell running around?"

The sudden change of topic causes Clara to almost choke on her food while we all erupt in laughter around her.

"We've been married for like a month, Sara! We aren't– we aren't even ready for a baby!"

"Someone's a little defensive…do you have something to tell us Clara?" Lucy teases.

"Trust me. If I was pregnant I wouldn't be able to keep it from you bitches. You'd be the first to know. Of course Liam and I have talked about it. A little boy or girl with his curly hair running around? Thinking about it hurts my fucking ovaries but no, we aren't trying and don't have plans to try anytime soon, ladies."

"But how's it been?" I quickly ask. "The married life with your former crush turned enemy turned epic lover?" I nudge her with my elbow. "Is it everything you thought?"

The glow on her face says it all.

"It's more. It's waking up to my best friend knowing I get to spend the rest of my life with him. It's feeling safe and confident and loved even on my bad days. It took us a while to get here but the journey was worth it to have a love like ours," she looks towards Leah. "How about you two lovebirds?"

Oh, Leah. Our baby sophomore. The one who fell for her brother's best friend and fell hard. In hindsight, the two did a great job at keeping it a secret. No one had any idea until the Daytona trip and everything blew up after an accidental post she made with his tattooed arm in the picture. Safe to say the fallout was ugly, but it got better.

And it's safe to say that Jake Wiley has it bad for our girl. The man is a human golden retriever. Leah walks into a room? His eyes are shining bright. Leah needs to go to the restroom? He's standing outside the door.

I could sit here and listen to my best friends talk about their happiness all day. I love to see them happy. I love knowing that they found the one for them. What I don't love is feeling like I'm about to pee myself.

"Guys, I hate to interrupt but I seriously have to go pee before it's all over you and Liam's room. I'll be right back!"

I quickly stand, brushing the popcorn crumbs off of my

black satin night set, and begin heading to the restroom down the hall. Usually my pajamas consist of plaid bottoms and an oversized sweatshirt, which I of course wore as a layer on the way here, but I got this as a gift from Sara last Christmas. I'd never worn it and figured it was time. I even did the whole positive self-talk into the mirror thing before heading here today.

And I feel it. I'm not sure if it's the color, the way it fits, but I feel good. That feeling may differ if I were around anyone but the girls tonight, the shorts are just a tad bit cheeky, but that's not something I need to worry about because the boys are out.

So, you can imagine my surprise when one minute I'm running down the hall and the next I'm lying on top of a bare chest, a chest rumbling with laughter.

"AAAAHHHHHH," I yell as I slap my hands over my eyes. "ARE YOU NAKED?!"

I feel long fingers grab my wrist when an all too familiar voice underneath me says, "I'm not naked, Q."

I reluctantly peel my hands away, already fully aware who's underneath me, as I lay pressed against his very muscular chest. "What–what are you doing here?"

Paul's gorgeous brown eyes are looking up at me with a crooked grin on his face. *Have his eyes always had specks of gold in them?*

"I wasn't feeling the best so I came home early. Shit. It's pajama night isn't it?" He looks over my shoulder. "Where is everyone?"

I realize I haven't moved an inch but am becoming very aware of every outline of his body. A body that feels very, *very* nice…

Okay, time to get up.

I begin pushing myself off of Paul, standing and

smoothing my pajamas and hair. "They're in the room, I just had to–

"Holy shit," he cuts me off.

"What? Is–is there something in my hair?" I begin brushing through with my fingers.

"No, no. Umm…you just look…your pajamas. Black. Good," he throws his thumb up with a lopsided grin as he mumbles something under his breath, something that sounded a lot like *fuck*. "You look good in your pajamas, Q."

I can't help the heat that spreads across my face, and I may be crazy, but his face looks a shade of red as well. It must be hot in here?

"I hyped myself up in the mirror," I lean in close, "something my teacher taught me."

God he smells good.

He pulls his face slightly to the right with his eyes beaming down at me and I know I shouldn't, because it's pretty damn obvious what I'm doing, but I let my eyes wander. His face, his hair, and like a woman with no control…they make their way down his body. And holy shit how can a man be built like this?

Chiseled. Outlined to every fine detail. There's a small scar above his left hip, which I imagine came from skating, and he was right about the eight-pack…definitely more–

"Q?"

My eyes immediately snap back to his, knowing damn well I've been caught.

"Ye-yeah, Pauline?"

He leans even closer, so close that his cheek is basically pressed against mine.

"I don't mind you looking, I was looking too."

He pulls away, no trace of a joke to be found, and begins to walk to his room. Me? I'm frozen solid because there's no way Paul just admitted to checking me out too. Sure, he's flirted with me before. I always felt he did it without even thinking.

But that seemed…intentional?

"Oh and Q-T. I'll see you tomorrow."

Then he's gone and I'm left wondering what the hell just happened and how in the hell do I calm the butterflies fluttering around in my stomach?

Chapter 22

Paul

After last night's fiasco, I – Paul Henry Simmons – am…nervous…to be around a girl.

This is Susie we're talking about…one of my best friends.

But last night? Seeing her in those little pajama shorts and her satin tank top showcasing a sliver of her silky skin? Uh, yeah. My attraction to her fucking skyrocketed. Every attraction I've ever felt, if I can even call it that, has been purely physical. Nice ass, big boobs, fuckable.

This is different. She's a goddamn knockout, sure. But she's also caring and kind and trusting, and it only fuels whatever strange, foreign feelings I have. Feelings that have me daydreaming about her like a fucking psycho.

Let me preface this by saying I am *trying* to keep this one hundred percent professional.

The other night when things got personal and I found my eyes bouncing between hers and her mouth? I looked away. Last night when she was on top of me? I was good. I didn't let my hands wander, hell, I didn't even take my eyes off hers until she stood up and I allowed myself a split second to admire her outfit. Just enough to compliment her and then I'd be on my best behavior.

And then she checked me out…

So, naturally I did the same.

And fuck did I like what I saw.

I probably shouldn't have said what I said, it's the thought that's been in my head since the words left my mouth. What if I made her uncomfortable? Did I cross a boundary? Fuck, I'm not used to this. I don't even know what *this* is.

Typically I'm all for crossing boundaries. But this isn't typical. I care about Q.

So, I suppose it's time to stop standing outside her door and grow a pair. I'll know in the next five minutes just how badly I fucked up last night.

After six knocks I'm convinced she's regretting her whole decision of trusting me. I'm just about to pull out my phone and call her, ready to apologize profusely, when the door swings open and Susie stumbles out.

"I'm sorry, I'm sorry," she says as she wipes her hair out of her face. Her wet, damp hair. "I didn't hear over the shower. I thought I had time but clearly I didn't," she grabs my hand, pulling me inside.

"There's food on the counter, I have to finish getting dressed."

And that's when I notice that Susie Cobble only has a fucking towel wrapped around her. My eyes immediately shoot to the ceiling. One, so I don't ogle her and two, to ask god why he must torture me.

"You answered the door in only your towel, Q?"

"Well, yeah. I knew it was you."

Duh. And why would she be concerned about her friend who's here to help her looking at her any differently?

I hear her feet patter down the hall as I turn to head to the barstool.

Don't do it, don't do it, don't do it.

But I do. I turn around, taking in the view as her hips sway side to side. She may not be confident in herself, but Susie Cobble is a fucking goddess and I won't rest until she knows that.

Also, I think I'm royally fucked because I know damn well I shouldn't be thinking the way I am right now about what's underneath that towel.

* * *

Dinner was delicious. She opted for Panda Express tonight, and I'm fairly certain I scarfed mine down within five minutes then ended up eating what she had left. We've spent the last ten minutes talking about how cheer's going and how they've been gearing up for their big competition announcement this Friday, which always aligns with the announcement of our starting line. It also aligns with Susie's first date with Jamee, but that's not important.

And just like last year, it'll be a huge celebration, which typically takes place at our favorite bar, *The Jungle Book.* Except this year there should be no strange shit going on.

Liam and Clara are together so there should be no weird unspoken sexual tension like there was last time.

Jake and Leah are publicly together so he won't be moping around.

I know all the girls will make the team and I'm fairly confident in us guys being together on the first line again.

I love hockey, but I love hockey even more knowing I get to do it alongside my best friends.

And just as I'm about to get into today's lesson, my phone

rings. I plan to ignore whichever asshole is calling to ask if I'll pick up food on the way home, but it's not them. It's a FaceTime from Meme and I'll never not take a call from her.

"Q-T, I have to take this. It's Meme," I stand to walk outside her dorm but she gently places a hand on mine.

"You can take your call here, Paul. You don't have to leave."

I raise my eyebrows as I say, "If I let it slip that I'm here with a girl, even just a friend, Memes will want to talk to you."

"If you let it slip and she insists, I will happily oblige," she flashes her signature smile.

I shake my head as I answer the call, my grandma's face lighting up the screen.

"*Memes, what's up?*" I try to get only my face on the screen, hoping she doesn't notice I'm somewhere different.

"*Henry,*" she coos, "*why can I see up your nose?*"

I see Susie muffle her laugh out of the corner of my eye.

"*Because I'm just–just getting ready for bed.*"

She lets out a sigh, one laced with disappointment. "*It's 9:30 p.m. Henry. I know sure as shit you ain't going to bed right now.*"

"*I'm naked gram. I don't–*"

"*You're over at a girl's aren't you?*"

"*No Memes. I told you, I'm not seeing anyone.*"

"*Bullshit,*" she scoffs. "*I'm not an idiot Paul Henry. Is she there? Can she hear me? Let me see her.*"

All my life she's always been able to call me on my bullshit. I suppose she got an itch for it when her daughter started to lie and sneak around…

I turn my head to the right where I'm met with Susie's beauty as she mouths the words *"hand me the phone."* I shake my head no, which does no good, because before I know it, she's ripped the phone out of my hand and is now on FaceTime with my grandma.

"Hi, I'm Susie Cobble and I've heard so much about you," she says with her faint dimples showing. *So fucking adorable.*

"Well my god you're a pretty thing. No wonder why Paul chose to finally settle down."

And there it is.

Susie's cheeks turn visibly red as she tries to find the right words.

"Oh, no–no ma'am. We're–we're just friends. He's helping me with a...project!" Susie all but shouts.

Meanwhile, I can't help but to laugh. I did try warning her, now she's on her own to fend off the grandma who's always wanted a nice girl for her grandson to bring home.

"HENRY!" A loud shriek comes through the phone. I don't answer and instead, walk behind Susie, wrapping my arms around her shoulders in a hug. Something I often do.

"Please don't start. She's my friend, one of my best friend's," I ruffle Susie's hair, *"and we are in fact working on our project so we really have to run but this has been fun."*

"That's how they all start, you know–"

I don't give her time to finish whatever bullshit she's about to spew.

"I love you Memes. Talk to you tomorrow," and then I hang up.

As I lay the phone face down, because there's no telling what she'll text me now, I realize I still have one arm wrapped around Susie. And I don't quite want to let go...

But it's pretty fucking weird of me to stay here like this, so I softly lower my arm, taking a step back.

"Well, sorry about that," I laugh as I walk to the sofa. "Meme can be...a lot sometimes."

"I like her," she says as she walks towards me. "She seems funny, cool and kind. Just like her grandson," she pats my knee as she sits next to me. "And I can definitely see the resemblance. It's in the nose," she scrunches hers, "and it's adorable."

You're adorable.

Oh, fuck me.

"She used to always tell me I looked just like my birth mother and then I think she realized how much it pissed me off to know I resembled her," I confess. Why? I'm not sure, I've never told anyone that before.

"I don't want to pry, but do you mind telling me a bit of what–what happened?" Q asks, sincerely and wholeheartedly.

"A truth for a truth?" I stick out my hand. I want, *need*, to know more about what it was in her past that left her so fragile and broken.

She doesn't say anything as she fits her hand into mine. And for the first time since telling the guys, I'm about to share a piece of me no one else has known.

"My birth mother was, I suppose still is, a drug addict," I say, never taking my eyes off hers. "And I never refer to her as my mother because there was never an ounce of time she spent being one."

Susie's face isn't quite what I expected. I would've guessed sad? Disturbed? But she looks…angry.

"Sus–"

"I know it may not be my place to say this but–but I don't like her. How could she do that to her son? How could she do that to you, Paul? What kind of–"

I place my hand on her knee, which is still shaking up and down. Trying to ignore the swell in my chest of how much she cares.

"It's a question I spent too much of my life wondering, Q.

And I–I'm fine, you know? I have one hell of a grandma, great friends," I nudge her with my elbow, "so fuck her, honestly. She's the one missing out on my life."

Did her constant absence and consistent flaky attitude probably affect my choice of having anything meaningful with a woman? A therapist would say yes.

Don't get me wrong, I adore all the ladies in our group. Hell, I would do anything for them, especially Susie. But having a girlfriend is entirely different than having a girl as a friend.

Having a girlfriend means *this*. Opening up to her about my past. Sharing my dreams. And for what? For her to leave like Lisa? Fuck no. I'll take no-strings-attached, please.

Susie doesn't say anything; it's as if we're sharing the same wavelength and she understands there's much more to the situation than I'm letting on. Instead, she takes a deep breath with a long exhale and begins talking.

"I don't think I'm ready to share all of what happened," she looks down as she picks at her fingernails. "Not because I don't trust you but because it's–it's embarrassing and I promise I will. One day I will share the whole story but for now," she stops, crossing her arms over her chest, "just know that what happened to me was a very public thing and really freaking humiliating." Her voice becomes softer as she adds, "And it included me being displayed for all to see."

I can feel my jaw clenching in anger. Pure fucking rage as I soak in the details of what she just told me. A million things race through my mind. Where was she? Who saw? Did–did anything happen to her? But the top of that list is who's the asshole that's going to get murdered?

But she respected my truth, I need to respect hers and trust that she'll share with me when she's ready. Hell, maybe

I'll even share more…it felt nice talking about it; something I never thought I'd say.

There is one thing I must know for the sake of our lessons.

"Q," I say softly. "You don't have to tell me anymore than you already have but I do need to know one thing. Last lesson I grabbed your chin without even thinking or asking. Fuck Susie, there's no telling how often I grab your hand or touch your cheek. I–I don't know what happened but if me touching you in any way offended you or–"

Her head immediately snaps up. "Oh no, no! It wasn't… like that…and you touching me definitely did not upset or bother me, Paul. But–but thank you for checking. That means a lot."

That's a fucking relief.

"I just had to make sure. And for the record, should I ever find out who this fucking asshole is, you might as well have my bail ready."

There it is. Her contagious laugh.

"Now, how about enough truth for the night and we focus on tonight's lesson? Which honestly, this whole sharing of our life thing is a great segue for tonight because tonight, my Q-T, is all about you."

Chapter 23

Susie

"What the fuck!" Paul screams at the TV. "You're telling me he spent all this time trying to get her to remember just for him to crawl in her bed and die with her?!"

Sweet, sweet Paul. I've experienced the same emotions…

"It's true love. He didn't want to live without her. Her time was also his time–"

"Fucking Noah and Allie. I loved and hated it," he pouts.

Once again, we finished tonight's lesson two hours ago, but Paul insisted on watching yet another movie. This time I chose and you bet your ass I put him through the emotional turmoil of *The Notebook.*

I don't know if it's because I got the nerves from our first lesson out of the way or because I just love being around Paul, but tonight was…great.

It was all about me, and at first I didn't quite know what he meant, but when he started grilling me with this or that questions, I caught on pretty quickly.

* * *

"If you want to be confident in yourself, Q. You have to know what you like and dislike. You have to know those two things to be able to stand up for yourself."

"Are we talking about like...flirting or..." I leave the question open-ended because I don't quite know what he's asking. If he's talking about what I like and dislike sexually... I too would love to know. But I wouldn't have any idea.

No, I'm not a virgin. Yes, I've had sex since the event. It's just been a while...

And if I'm being honest, I don't fully believe any of the ones I've been with before knew what they were doing because satisfaction was definitely one-sided...

"I'm not asking about your sexual likes and dislikes, Q," he leans in, lowering his voice, "unless you want to tell me about them."

I know he's kidding. I know Paul is just being Paul...but dammit. Why are there goosebumps all over my body and why do my cheeks feel warm?

"Likes and dislikes in general. Understood," I clear my throat. "But what does that look like?"

He's still leaning in close to me when he says, "Easy. I like when girls blush," he pokes my cheek, "I dislike when girls try to act like someone they're not."

Well, now my cheeks are extremely red.

"I'm assuming as the puck bunny magnet, you've had your fair share of those types of girls, huh?"

"One time I had a girl tell me she grew up playing hockey at her local YMCA, whatever it was she called it, and when she got back to my room, she saw one of my game winning pucks and asked if it was a miniature fris-bee," he shakes his head back and forth. "A fucking frisbee, Q."

I close my mouth tightly to keep from laughing but it's no use. I lose it, hunching over as I gasp for air. When I finally get it together, I turn to Paul as I wipe the tear from my eye.

"Tell me you kicked her out?"

He closes his eyes, scrunching his nose as he shrugs his shoulders. "I had needs, Q-T."

"No, Paul. You didn't," I tease.

"Enough of me," he says stretching back, his shirt revealing a sliver of his toned stomach. A stomach I know feels rock solid. "I'm going to throw some rapid fire questions at you and I want you to answer honestly and quickly, just like last time. Then, we're going to practice some scenarios," he stands, reaching out his hand. "Ready?"

Like always, I instinctively fit my hand in his as I stand, "Hit me, Pauline."

"A guy approaches you in the bar and immediately hits on you before introducing himself. Yay or nay?"

"Ummm..."

"No, no. Answer quickly, Q."

"Nay," I blurt. If you don't care to ask my name first, you're probably after one thing.

"A guy compliments your personality before your appearance?"

"Yay." I love a man whose main focus isn't physical beauty.

"You're on a date, a date that went really well, and when it's time to leave he goes in for a kiss?"

"I'd kiss him back."

"He's big on public display of affection?"

"Yay." Show me off, baby.

The questions go on and on, but honestly, they're super helpful. Mainly because I've never thought of them before and wouldn't know where I stood on some of these things if it weren't for Paul asking me.

Then they end and in come the scenarios. After Sunday evening...I'm on edge. Why? Maybe it's because when I look at him, I see his muscular chest, feel the grasp of his hand on my arm, the heat from his smooth skin beneath me.

It's just an attraction – that's all it is. He's an extremely attractive man, someone I've been around quite often lately, and he's sweet. I'm attracted to him, doesn't mean I have to be interested in him.

"I'm going to get flirty, Q. The whole point of this process is to help you become more outspoken about what you like and dislike."

I nod. "You're always flirty, Paul. Nothing new there."

It starts simple. The role? I'm at a bar and he's trying to get me to come home with him. We do the same situation multiple times with variations of him approaching me, talking to me, and leaving the conversation.

"What are you doing here alone, Sarah?"

I chuckle, caught off guard by his slip up, knowing it's for a reason based on the eyebrow raise he gives me.

"It's Susie."

"Sarah, Susie," he shrugs his shoulders, leaning forward to whisper in my ear, "it's all the same when you're screaming my name."

I peer up at him from the corner of my eye. "I doubt that and if you'll excuse me, I need to get back to my friends."

He smirks as he pulls away. "Did I detect some sass, Q?"

"A man forgets my name and tells me it's all the same? Yes, you definitely detected some sass."

I'm finishing the last word of my sentence as Paul cuts in and says, "You deserve much more than an asshole at the bar calling you the wrong name, Susie."

"Anyways," he continues, "tell me a few things you've found out about yourself tonight."

"I care more that a guy gets to know me as opposed to flooding me with compliments. I like affection," I take a quick breath and continue. "I don't care to be impressed. Oh, and I like when the guy takes charge but also enjoy knowing that I have a say."

I wrap Paul in a quick hug. "Wow, you're a great teacher, Pauline."

He wraps his arms around me tightly, but only for a moment before he pulls away and places his hands on my shoulders. "I appreciate that, Q. More than you know."

* * *

I see how it all comes together now. And I'm not saying my confidence is just magically fixed, it takes time and practice. But it's been two lessons and I already feel better about it – about everything related to my date this Friday with Jamee. And that's all thanks to Paul.

Paul who is *still* going on and on about *The Notebook.*

"Do you think I'm ready for my date with Jamee?" I blurt out, needing to know how he feels about it.

He's a little taken aback and I can tell he's frantically searching for the right words which immediately sends me spiraling.

"What? What is it? You don't think I'm ready? Do you think I'll make a fool of myself? You don't think I've made progress–"

"Q," he interrupts, grabbing my hand. "I know you're ready for your date. But it doesn't matter what I think, it only matters how you feel."

I know there's a soft side to this man, apart from his fuckboy facade, and I adore it.

"I feel like I understand what I need to do to feel confident in myself, and during our lessons I'm able to put it into practice, but what if I shit the bed when it comes to the date and I lose all sense of what I've gradually been gaining?"

I realize he's still holding my hand when he gives it an extra squeeze. "I'm not teaching you *your* confidence, Q. I'm teaching you tools to use for you to become more confident. How to look for the positive versus the negative, when to consider being assertive in what you want, learning to express your likes and dislikes. Never once have I been the one to give you the answers, Q-T. You've come up with those on your own."

Paul may have only come into my life a year ago, but from the moment he hopped out of his truck and all but told me I'd be sitting in the front with him, I knew he'd be a friend of mine. I don't necessarily think I knew he'd become one of my best friends, or that I'd feel this stupid fluttering in my chest at his words.

But here we are.

"If you need a career after becoming a professional goalie, you may have one as a life coach waiting for you out there," I lazily take my hand out of his, patting his knee as I stand and walk to the kitchen.

"Please," he makes his way to the barstool, "hockey's been my life since I was old enough in Meme's eyes to safely skate. I'm pretty sure it'll be my life until I'm too old for it."

I think it's endearing how a sport can mean so much to someone. How they can continuously work hard towards what they love. I suppose that's art for me. Not that I plan to make a living out of it, and it's not something I necessarily work hard towards, but it's what I love doing. I love cheerleading with my best friends, that's something for us. But art? That's entirely for me.

"You want to see something?" The girls have seen my

paintings before, they say it's something I should sell on the side, but I'm perfectly content with plastering them around my room and making them for friends or family as gifts. That's what brings me happiness.

"Q, I'm a nosy motherfucker. Of course I want to."

I grab his hand and take off towards my bedroom, realizing this is the first time I'm going to have a guy in my room since god knows when but feeling at ease it's Paul.

I throw the door open and walk Paul inside with a sense of pride, spinning around in a circle taking in the paintings plastered on my wall. I remember the feelings I felt when I constructed every single one of them. Some happy, some sad, but all me.

I hesitantly turn towards Paul, anxious to see his reaction. Some are completely abstract with no rhyme or reason to the naked eye. Some are of the girls and I, others just vary from things I love or have seen throughout my time at Barker.

His expression is hard to read as he drops my hand and walks around the room looking at my art – some paintings, some drawings. I'd say there's about ten hung around the room with a stack in the corner of pieces lined behind another. When he's done glimpsing through them, he turns to look at me.

"You did all these?"

Confidence, Susie. Confidence.

"Every single one of them and–and I love them."

He points to one above my headboard, a painting I know all too well and asks, "What's the story behind this one?"

The first painting after what Lane Ross did to me at the party; when I finally began seeing Mrs. Baker and she found out about my love for art, encouraging me to channel what I was feeling into something I enjoyed doing. At the time, I didn't quite know what I was painting, but when I stepped back it was clear as day. I painted me, in all black, with the brightest and most lovely background.

It was exactly how I felt at the moment. Empty. My happiness, carefree attitude ripped from me in an instant.

I don't entirely feel that way anymore, and I know some people may not understand why I have a reminder of the shit I went through hanging above my bed, but to me, it's a symbol of how I didn't let the darkness suffocate me.

"That was the first painting after what happened," I confess. "It reminds me of what I overcame."

"I think it's beautiful," he says, catching me off guard. I've heard remarks from my family about the painting, mostly about how they hate I ever felt that way, but never beautiful.

"Re—really?" I ask.

His slight curls sit perfectly on his forehead as his head bobs up and down. "All pieces of you are beautiful, Q. That," he points his head towards the artwork, "may hold horrible memories for you but for me? I see a girl who went through a dark hell and came out as a bright light."

"That's the realest thing I've ever heard about that painting," I confess, trying to ignore my heart beating faster. "Thank you, Paul. That–that means a lot to me."

He reaches up, brushing his knuckles down my cheek, his eyes never leaving mine. I watch as his Adam's apple bobs up and down, his eyes moving between mine and my…mouth?

And for a moment, I feel like Paul might kiss me. And I think I want him to?

No. NO. This is Paul, the man who's helping me prepare for a date this Friday.

I quickly step back and away from his touch, clearing my throat. Trying to act like my heart isn't racing, like I'm not thinking about kissing him right now because that's a disaster waiting to happen.

He chuckles as he puts one hand in his pocket and the other pointing towards the door. "I should probably get going. The boys turn into concerned girlfriends after 11:00."

"Yeah, yeah. Totally," I squeak. "And I'll see you Thursday?"

His lips pull tight as he says, "See you then, Q."

And as I watch him walk out the door I realize one thing: I'm not ready for these lessons to end because I don't want these moments to end.

Chapter 24

Paul

*W**hat the fuck was I about to do back there?*

Kiss Sussie Cobble is what I was about to do and I know damn well I would have if she wouldn't have stepped away.

I need to get my shit together. I can't be having those feelings for her, not when I'm helping her with something so personal and meaningful. There's one lesson left and then we're back to being around each other with the group, the normal friend things and I can go back to my harmless flirting.

Except this is this most intimate lesson of all and I'm supposed to stay level-headed during it?

Fuck me.

I'm pulling into the parking lot of our River Road house ready to face the wrath of the guys. They've been giving me shit recently for being off my game, and even more so when I came home early from the bar last night.

I told them I didn't feel well, but truthfully, I just couldn't look at a girl without thinking of Susie. She's been consuming my mind to the point that it's absolutely fucking pathetic. So, I came home hoping to talk some sense into myself and of course, there she was in her damn pajama outfit, and well, we know the rest...

But tonight? Her sharing such an intimate part of herself with her paintings? I–I got lost in the captivating, strong woman in front of me.

Whatever these weird ass feelings are, they're confusing the shit out of me. I just need to get them off my mind and what better way to do that than get drunk with my friends?

"Daddy's home!" I say as I fling open the front door. I don't make it ten steps before I feel something pulling on my pant leg and when I turn around, I see the cutest fucking thing.

"Holy shit!" I scream as I bend down, picking up the little fur ball. "Guys, there's a fucking dog here, is it ours? Please, please say it's ours."

It's fucking adorable. A long black body with a black and tan face, floppy ears, and little legs. "Actually, I don't care if it wasn't ours, it is now." As if the dog agrees, it begins barking.

"There you are!" Clara comes scurrying around the corner holding out her hands. "Dante, I was looking for you!"

I quickly yank the dog closer to my chest. "I just got it," I pout as I walk towards the living room, seeing all the guys sitting around playing FIFA. "Guys, there's a pwecious wittle puppy and Clara's trying to take it from me!"

"That's because it's Clara's puppy, Paul," Liam chuckles as he continues watching Jake destroy Clay.

"Ah," I say as I sit down next to Jake, sitting the pup on my lap. "You must be the Chiweenie. I'm Paul, your new best friend, and you are the cutest wittle puppy there is. Yes you are! Who's a good boy? You are. You are da goodest wittle boy aren't you–"

"Dude. If I knew getting a dog was going to make you talk more, I would've told C no."

"Ah, so Liam's a smart-ass now, huh?" I say to Jake.

"He's always been a smart-ass," Clay chimes in, "he's only recently become a funny smart-ass."

"Good one, Clay," Jake laughs while throwing up an air high-five. A true middle school expression.

"Jake," I say, still holding the dog. "You're already dating his sister, no need to kiss his ass more."

He laughs and then proceeds to punch me in the shoulder.

"JAKE! I am holding precious cargo. Be careful!"

He quickly puts his controller down, reaching for Dante. "I want to hold him now."

"Fuck you, I'm holding him."

"You've had him since you got home, give him to me or I'm telling Clara."

"I just got home dipshit!"

"Clarraaaaa!" Jake yells.

"Jesus fucking Christ," Liam gets up, walking over to me with his hands out. "Give me my dog and his name is not fucking Dante."

Reluctantly, I hand the fur ball over. "Clara called him Dante when I walked in."

"Well, she's–"

"She's what, babe?" Clara comes up beside Liam with her hands on her hip.

And that's when I see it. My friend's balls shrivel up right in front of me.

"My wife is absolutely fucking stunning and I love her and our pup very much," Liam bends down, planting a kiss on Clara's cheek. "But can we please not call him Dante? I'd much rather call him Rocky."

Now it's Clara's turn to hold out her hands, not requesting

but demanding the dog. "We can call him Rocky if you agree to take him out at night whenever he needs to go," she smirks.

Smart, smart girl.

I give her a thumbs up while Liam is clearly contemplating his options.

"House meeting," he says.

Clay looks around, draping his arm around his sister's shoulder. "Dude, we're literally all already here."

"I know I briefly talked to y'all about getting this dog a few months back," he pats Dante, Rocky, *I don't fucking know*, on his head. "And I know it's no easy task having a puppy running around but I want y'all to know Clara and I won't ever leave him unattended, we'll clean up any messes he makes and pay for anything he may ruin by chewing because the little asshole has teeth like a fucking shark."

"And thank you," Clara adds. "I've been begging Liam to adopt a puppy for some time now and I'm thankful you guys agreed to let us get one."

"Hold up," I interrupt. "But like…what if I want to hang out with the little guy while y'all aren't home? Dante–"

"Rocky," Liam quickly adds.

"Doesn't deserve to be kept in your room or kennel all day. If I'm home, I'd be happy to help!"

"Wait a minute, wait a minute," Clay interjects. "What–what if I want to keep him in my room while y'all are gone?"

"Fuck all of you. I was the best man, I'm definitely the Godfather which means I get to keep him while they're gone," Jake says while Leah gives him a disapproving look. "And of course my gorgeous girlfriend," he wraps her in a hug.

Meanwhile, Liam and Clara haven't said a word. They're

too busy wide-eyed looking at each other, probably wondering what shit show they just created.

* * *

Thirty minutes later and we have a schedule created that everyone's happy with.

My days with Rocky, *yes they settled on Rocky*, begin next week since they're Thursdays and I have my lesson with Susie, which was probably the best news for Jake since he gets to take over.

Jake and Leah get Mondays and Clay gets to take Sundays while the two lovebirds work.

We made it very clear to Liam and Clara that we're all here to pitch in whenever. I know they *think* this is only their dog, but this is a house dog whether they want it to be or not.

"Alright boys," Clara and Leah say. "We're heading upstairs, y'all have a good night."

"Leave Ro–"

"I'm taking the dog with me, Paul."

Dammit.

"Night C, night Leah!" I yell, ready to talk hockey with the boys. I don't give anyone a chance to say anything else before I cut to the chase. "Harp, what are you thinking strategy wise for our first game against Carnelly in a few weeks?"

We're fairly sure we know the starting line, but there's never a way to know what Coach is truly thinking. Friday's announcement couldn't come fast enough.

"Skate hard, pass good, make your fucking shots," Clay answers as if it's that simple.

"Is that the shitty pep talk you're going to give the whole team?" Jake asks. "If so, I'd recommend you come up with something else or Coach might beat you with your own hockey stick right then and there."

"And this is your first hype speech of the season, Clay boy. You don't want to let the team down, do you?" Liam teases.

"Fuck you," he spits back. "And for fuck's sake, can we stick with my name and stop with the Harp and Clay boy shit? I blame you for that, Paul."

Ah, yes. The nickname I gave him while we were out at the bar one evening. I was trying to teach him how to be a playboy – the man hasn't been with a woman since we've met him – but he says nothing is more important than hockey and nothing will take his focus off winning the Frozen Four his senior year.

But what he doesn't know is I remember him at the wedding staring daggers at Lucy when she was dancing with another man, but I'll keep that to myself.

So, instead of a playboy, he's Clay boy, or Harp, depending on the way I feel. Safe to say, he doesn't care for nicknames.

"Have you two numbnuts made a decision yet about the NHL teams literally fucking begging for you?" I ask, changing the subject.

"Yeah actually, I–I have," Liam clears his throat. "I thought it'd be fun to keep playing with you boys but then I figured beating your asses would be even better." *Typical Liam.* "So, I talked with Coach last Friday and signed with the Michigan Miners," he says as it's the most normal thing in the world to be drafted to a NHL team as great as them.

We all erupt in cheers as we celebrate, taking turns congratulating our best friend.

"Dude," I say as I hug his neck, "you're a seven hour drive from Clay and I, even closer when you're rich enough to own a jet. You bet your ass we're taking turns for monthly dinners, especially with that little pup you just got. We can't have him missing his uncles."

"Yeah, yeah," he waves me off. "What about you Jake? Have you made a decision yet?"

"I still have some things in the works that I'm waiting to hear back on but I think I'll have a decision before the end of the month."

"Look at us," I pretend to wipe a tear from my eye, "we're growing up fellas. What–what are we going to do when we aren't in the same house anymore?"

"FaceTime," Clay quickly answers, causing our heads to snap in his direction. "I mean…I'm just saying it's an option should someone–"

"Holy shit! You're going to miss us," Liam says.

"I'm not saying I need to–"

"No, you literally just said that," Jake interjects. "I'm man enough to admit I'll miss the shit out of you guys and am very happy to do weekly, hell even nightly, FaceTime calls," he shrugs.

"For fuck's sake," Clay runs his hands over his face. "I'm going to miss you assholes and yes," he lowers his head, "IwouldliketodonightlyFaceTimecalls."

We look at each other knowing damn well we're poking a bear but ready to deal with the consequences.

"What was that?" I ask.

He lets out a deep sigh, mumbling *assholes* under his breath before he repeats, "I said I would like to do nightly FaceTime calls. There, happy?"

Sitting here with my friends, with a specific girl on my mind? Yeah, I'm happy.

Chapter 25

Susie

"Okay, but pictures don't do you justice," I say as I snuggle Rocky into my chest. "No they don't, not for this itty bitty weenie body, huh buddy?"

Clara and I are out for a post-practice walk while the other gals are away studying. The walk quickly turned into us taking turns carrying Rocky due to his little legs not being able to keep up, but I don't mind, he's too adorable for his own good.

"God, please no more baby talk," Clara laughs. "I hear enough of that shit at home with all of the big, rugged hockey players."

I chuckle, imagining their household and all the boys taking turns talking to the little guy, probably spoiling him more than Liam and Clara. But my mind wanders to one rugged hockey player in-particular…the same one who I haven't stopped thinking about.

It's so bad of me, especially considering I've spent the week catching up with Jamee. School on top of practices has been the death of me, for him as well. But we've found time this week to text with the occasional phone call but this morning was something I wasn't exactly prepared for.

** * **

"A Grande Iced White Mocha with a double pump of white chocolate," the barista yells.

I make my way over to the counter, grabbing my drink as I hear, "I thought that was you." Lo-and-behold, I turn to see Jamee Locke and all his handsome glory standing next to me with a smirk.

"Hey Jamee," I manage to squeak out. "What are you doing here?"

He chuckles as he looks around. "Well, I was here to get a coffee but talking with a cute girl is much better than that. When's class?"

"Thirty minutes. How about you?"

"In about fifteen but I–"

"Do you want to maybe...grab a table with me until you have to leave?"

Holy shit. I just asked him to hang out. I, Susie Cobble, somewhat confidently just asked this man to sit with me. Attitude and assertiveness – shout out to my teacher Paul Simmons.

"Yeah, I'd like that."

** * **

And it went great. For once, I felt comfortable and although it may have been small, it felt empowering to see some confidence shine through.

Still, no matter how great it was. No matter how he made

me laugh or asked all the right questions in that short fifteen minutes…it was Paul I thought about.

It was Paul I kept comparing him to.

It was Paul I wanted to be flirting with me.

"Clare bear. Can I ask you a question?"

"I'm not pregnant Suse, I promise I will tell you guys first."

"I know, I know. I–I need help with a boy…" *Keep it ambiguous, Susie.*

"Oh, shit," she says, grabbing Rocky from me. "Susie Q needs help with Barker's own football star, huh?"

Something like that. "How do I know if he likes me?" *How do I know if Paul's just being Paul,* is what I really need to know, but this will do.

"I'm so glad you're asking me this of all people, Suse!" She squeals, scaring Rocky. "Let me teach you from my mistakes."

Her mistakes being that she was completely oblivious to Liam's feelings and I suppose her own? There was once a time Clara and Liam weren't even friends, thanks to him being an idiot on top of a shit communicator. But, here they are. It just took them longer than needed to get here.

"I'll take any help I can get…"

I mean honestly, do I even know my own feelings about him? He's sexy as hell. He's opened up to me about parts of his past, which I find to be more attractive than his looks, and let's not leave out that after I departed from our little run in on Sunday, my damn panties were soaked.

FROM FALLING ON HIM.

I either have feelings for my best friend-slash-teacher or I've confused myself due to us spending some one-on-one time together. And I'm going to go with the latter.

But having an idea of if this is Paul simply being Paul or

if he also may have feelings will help me sort my shit out. I think.

"Does he share the surface level shit or deeper shit?"

"Uh, well I suppose deeper shit?"

She nods as we head inside the dorm. "Give me some examples of how you think he's flirting."

I take a seat on the couch, the same couch that just a few days ago was the location of what I *think* was an intimate moment between Paul and I.

"Well, I think he's kind of a flirt to begin with?"

"Come onnnn," she says as she picks Rocky up, placing him on the blanket between us. "Give me something to go off of."

"Okay well…" I trail off as I think. Paul's always been a flirt but something's changed lately that's made me believe this is different. So, what is it?

"Let's say he grabbed my chin and told me I'm beautiful, shared a bit of past trauma, told me he was checking me out and then rubbed his knuckles down my cheek in a very intimate way that insinuated he wanted to kiss me?" I say in one speedy breath.

Her eyes narrow as she asks, "And what makes you think he's a flirt to begin with? And when the fuck did you and Jamee spend any time together for all this shit to go down? Your date is Friday!"

"Firstly, we saw each other in the coffee shop this morning and had some time to hang out before class," *not a lie.* "And when we first met he gave an '*I flirt around*' vibe? So how do I tell if it's just him being the person he is or if he's genuinely flirting with me?"

Without hesitation she says, "Oh, Suse. The boy is definitely genuinely flirting. That's the peak level of 'I'm into you.' You know how many times Liam pulled that shit after we became friends again? Don't be me and ignore the signs!"

I feel my heart race at the possibility that Paul may actually be flirting with me. Because if he is…what does that mean? Does he like me?

Does it matter?

No, of course not. I'm going on a date with Jamee, and once I do, I'll be over these weird feelings towards Paul and everything will go back to normal.

"It's not a bad thing Susie Q," she says as she stands, tucking Rocky into his little purse carrier. Yes, the dog has a purse carrier…she swears it's only while he's this small.

"And maybe this Friday we'll not only be celebrating us girls making the Daytona team or the boys and their starting line," she squeezes my cheek, "we'll be celebrating our little Suse having a great fucking date and hyping her up for the second one."

I swat her hand away as I walk her to the door, "We'll see Clare Bear. Tell the boys I say hi, get home safe, and for the love of god don't become the dog mom that walks around with a purse dog," I tease.

She holds up her purse with little Rocky still sleeping peacefully, "Too late!"

Chapter 26

Paul

Thirteen years ago

"Meme, Meme, Meme!"

It's here. Today's the day mom swore she'd be coming to see me. She even pinky-promised it, and according to Meme, breaking pinky-promises is like lying.

Meme is like my mom but not. She's my mom's mom and I've lived with her since before I can remember due to mom's sickness. I don't know what, Meme won't really tell me other than whatever it is, it makes her not think straight.

Meme also says that's why she's gone a lot and forgets to come over when she says she will...but not today. Today she'll be here because today we're celebrating my birthday!

"Yes, Henry?"

"Memeee," I hate when she uses my middle name.

"I know, I know. I'm sorry. What is it bud?"

"What time is it? Is she almost here?"

I watch her check her phone again, except this time she doesn't have a smile on her face.

"What's wrong Meme?"

"Dammit," she says, tucking her phone away. She walks over to where I'm standing, kneeling down as she puts her

hand on my shoulder. "Bud, I'm sorry but it looks like your mom won't be making it today after all. She–she got sick today."

"But–but she pinky promised she'd be here. Maybe she'll feel better later and we can go to dinner instead?"

I wish I could say this was the first time this has happened but it's not. Just last week mom didn't show up because she was sick.

"I don't think so bud. But you and I–"

"Why does mom not want to be around me? I freaking hate her."

"Paul Henry," she says gently, grabbing my chin. "Your mom not being around has absolutely nothing to do with you. She–she's sick buddy. A type of sickness that can't always be helped," Meme sniffles. "And I'm sorry she isn't showing today, Paul. I know–"

"I'm tired of her being sick! Why can't she just get better? It's stupid!"

I don't even remember the last time I saw mom.

"I know bud. It is stupid and it's not fair to you," she smooths down my curls. "But you and I can still go to Chuck-E-Cheese? I can beat you at basketball and do all the fun–"

"I'm over it Meme," I stomp past her and to my bedroom.

"Hey," she calls from behind me. One thing I've learned is to never ignore Memes so I turn around, arms crossed against my chest.

"Yes ma'am?"

"I love you Paul. Always," she blows a kiss.

I roll my eyes but say, "I love you too."

And when I get to my room, I shut the door, lying on my bed staring at the ceiling as a stupid freaking tear slides down my face.

Meme's been the only one to stay. What if no one else ever does?

Chapter 27

Paul

"Give me the dog," Jake pouts with his arms held out. "It's my night."

Since I'm unavailable tonight, Jake gets to take over Rocky duty and he's being a real bitch about it right now.

"I'm just saying bye to the wittle guy. A wittle guy who doesn't need to see his fwiend get beat up by his bestest fwiend."

"You think you could beat me up?"

I snuggle the dog to my cheek, turning us to face Jake. "Say yes I do. I do know I could beat you up," I answer in my normal dog talking voice which to Clara equals baby talk.

"You're out of your fucking mind if you think–"

"Clay beat you up, Jake. I most definitely can."

"I'd take Jake on this one," Clay pipes up as he walks by. "Sorry, Paul."

Rolling my eyes, I direct my attention to Jake and Leah. "What are you two doing tonight?"

"We're taking Rocky upstairs to watch Jake's movie pick," Leah grins as she walks over to me. "My turn, Paulie."

"Well, considering I like you better than Jake." I give

Rocky a kiss on the head, handing him over. "Take care of the good boy."

"Duh. He has his own bed and toys that Jake went and bought so he'll be nice and comfy all night," she says as Rocky bites down on a strand of her hair.

Leah may be Clay's sister, but the only similarity the two share is their somewhat same shade of blonde hair. No wonder why Jake never put two and two together.

"Alright, well that's my cue to head out," I say as I grab my keys. Tonight's the last lesson and I've come to realize that I don't want my evenings with Q to end.

I've also come to realize I think I'm into the girl.

Not just attracted to her, not some feelings I have of just wanting to fuck her.

I'm genuinely into her. Something I told myself I didn't ever need thanks to Lisa. But, here I am.

I've always kept girls at an arms-length. One night, one fuck, that was all. A girl can't find a reason to leave you if you don't give her the chance to stay.

But Susie? I don't want to keep her at an arms-length. Not that it matters…

I don't think I can do jackshit about it. This whole arrangement was created to help her with a stupid fucking date, and I just happened to be a casualty of catching feelings for my best friend. Telling her now would create issues. It would make things fucking messy and I don't want that for her. She hasn't let on that she's ever been into me, why would she be now?

She's not. So I won't subject her to the awkward shit. I'll help her tonight and we'll go back to our normal friendship.

* * *

"You're early!" Susie says, flustered as she flings open the door. "Dinner isn't ready yet!"

I sniff the air as I walk in; a strong, delicious smell filling her dorm, immediately causing my stomach to rumble. The last two lessons she's ordered in, but she insisted on making dinner as a thank you.

I told her there was no need for all that but she wouldn't take no for an answer.

"It smells delicious in here Susie Q. What's for dinner?"

She runs over to the stove and begins moving around frantically. "It's chicken alfredo but–but I'm starting to worry it's going to taste like crap."

I walk around the center island directly behind her. I know I shouldn't. In fact, I should distance myself from her tonight, especially considering this evening's lesson, but something possesses me and I don't necessarily want to stop myself.

Bending down, I reach around her, grabbing her hand as I lean in close and ask, "How about I help?"

It may be wishful thinking, but I swear she freezes. I swear her breath hitches and that she leans into me.

"Yeah," she clears her throat, "that would be nice. Do you want to uh–uh stir the noodles while I finish the chicken?" She turns around to face me, her body so close I can feel the rise and fall of her chest and fuck do I want to know what she looks like standing here in an oversized shirt of mine with nothing underneath...

"I can do that," I step aside, getting to work on my task.

We fall into a rhythm, a comfortable silence, and I think maybe this is what a relationship could feel like. Hell if I know, I've never experienced it before. A girl comes over, we fuck, I tell her I'm not looking for anything and she leaves. End of story.

When the fuck did this become different?

"So, Q. Big day tomorrow. Daytona announcement and your date. How are you feeling?" Not that I particularly want to talk about her date, I just want to talk to *her*.

"I–I think I'm ready? I mean, these lessons have definitely helped, and I actually had a mini-date with him yesterday morning which helped ease my nerves."

That catches my attention. I probably gave myself whiplash from how fast I turned my damn head.

"A mini-date?"

"Yeah, we ended up in the same coffee shop and had some time to hang out before class. I–I think it went well. In fact, I asked him if he wanted to join me!" She says proudly. As she should be, considering I know it took a lot for her to do so, but I have a strange feeling running through me right now. Something I don't know how to name.

I want to ask questions. I want to know everything – what he said to her, does she think he's funny, did they fucking kiss?

WHAT. THE. FUCK. IS. HAPPENING.

"And how did it go?" *Smooth, Paul. Real smooth.*

"Good, I think? We talked about classes, practices and the plans for tomorrow night," her dimples begin to show as she goes on about their conversation.

I fucking hate that he's the reason for her smile and not me.

Once she finishes talking about her date, we go back to silence as we wrap up dinner. And then we sit in silence as we eat. Not because I'm angry, but because I'm miserable.

I'm miserable knowing that tomorrow night she's going out with Jamee fucking Locke. Especially because I know I have to let it happen.

"Dinner was delicious, Q," I stand, walking to the sink to

rinse my bowl out. "You didn't have to cook, but I sure am glad you did because that right there was the best fucking pasta I've ever had."

She begins laughing as she walks towards me, brushing against my arm as she puts her bowl in the sink. "It was pretty good, huh?"

I hear what she says but my brain is too focused on her touch.

My eyes are too focused on her lips.

"Paul?"

"Are you ready to start tonight's lesson?"

Her brows crease together but are quickly replaced with a grin. "Ready as I'll ever be I suppose."

I nod as I turn, walking to what has become my spot on her sofa.

"Our last lesson," Q says as she curls up next to me. "I–I can't tell you how much I've enjoyed this Paul. Hanging out with you, having you help me. This has meant so much to me but I…I've also had fun spending time with you."

"Susie Q," I lean back, running my hands through my hair, "I have had the best time with you. You've been the best student," I tease, tapping her on her nose. "Now, let's wrap up these lessons and get you ready for tomorrow."

I stand like usual, holding out my hand as her grin turns into a slight frown. "What if–what if I don't want us to stop hanging out like this?"

My heart just malfunctioned because skipping a beat isn't fucking normal.

"You won't be able to get rid of me that easy, Q. Now, tell me what you know about being sexy."

She tucks a piece of hair behind her ear as she quietly answers, "I guess that appearance is a huge part?"

"It isn't just appearance, Q-T. Confidence is sexy. Taking

charge is sexy. Flirting is sexy. What do you find sexy about a guy?"

Her eyes trail me up and down, slowly, *I'd be lying if I said I didn't puff out my chest a bit*, as she says, "I think it's sexy when guys have genuine conversations. I think tight fitting shirts are sexy. I think it's sexy when a guy isn't afraid to tell you how he feels..." she trails off, her big green eyes peering up at me.

"What do you think is sexy about a girl?" she asks.

You.

I step towards her, watching as she takes a small step backwards.

"I think it's sexy when a girl is all about physical touch," I take another step, met by another step backwards. "I think it's sexy when girls blush."

One more step and this time, she ends with her back against the wall. "And I think it's real fucking sexy when a girl's nervous."

"But this isn't about me, Q." I put my hands against the wall just above her head. "This is about you and what helps you feel sexy. So tell me, if Jamee Locke is this close to you during your date tomorrow," I reach down to grab her chin, forcing her eyes on me, "what would make you feel sexy?"

I'm playing with fire, fitting for someone going to hell. Why? Because this isn't just about being her teacher anymore...

Without missing a beat she stands on her tiptoes, leaning close to my ear as she says in a playful voice, "I would say something about how I had a great time in my best sexy voice." Lowering to her feet, she slips her hand in mind, "And then I'd grab his hand so he knows I like physical touch."

I swallow, trying to keep my head straight.

Susie Cobble doesn't know it, but to me, she's always been sexy.

"How do you feel at this moment?"

Her eyes go big, and for a second, she's speechless. I'm not quite sure why? Maybe she didn't hear me correctly?

"Do you feel sexy right now, Q?"

She lets out a loud breath as she looks at our connected hands, raking her eyes up and down my body once more and then finally returning to my gaze.

"I–I think I'd feel sexier if I pulled you closer? If–if that's okay…I don't want to cross a line of the student-teacher relationship," she winks.

Cross all the fucking lines, baby.

"Anything you need or want to do, I'm yours to do it with, Q." *The whole truth.*

"Do I need to tell you what I'm going to do before I do it or just play it out organically?"

I smirk at her question, finding her worry adorable.

"Play it out organically, Q-T. Catch me off guard."

She won't hear any complaints from me. And I know it's shitty, but it's our last lesson. This is the last time I'll be close enough to Susie Cobble for her to have this effect on me. Sure, I'll always find her incredibly attractive and use my usual fuckboy charm on her, but I won't be around her enough to question what it means.

She brushes her hand up my arm, twisting the front of my shirt as she pulls me flush against her. I can feel her breathing – fast and nervous – and goddammit if it doesn't send blood rushing straight to my dick.

Now is not the time for you to make an appearance, I keep repeating to myself. This isn't about me, it's about Susie.

With me being this close, I find my brain short circuiting for a moment.

"I had a really good time tonight," she says as she reaches through my arm, rubbing her hand up and down my back. "I'd love to do it again?"

Fuck yes for my girl speaking her mind.

"Q? Do you want me to react how Jamee would in this situation? Because I have to tell you, it would involve me touching you more intimately than we have and–and I want you to be comfortable with that."

Her tongue darts out of her mouth, licking her bottom lip and I'm lucky my dick doesn't spring out of my fucking sweats because the sight alone is enough to send me over the edge. Without a word, she quickly bobs her head up and down.

I have to play this carefully. I can't come across as me being Paul but more so how any guy would react with an irresistible, sexy girl in front of them. *Easy enough.*

I gently drop her hand, resting my forearm above her head.

"I couldn't imagine tonight with anyone else, Susie Cobble," I move my hand under her chin again, forcing her to hold my stare. "I think you're fucking gorgeous, down to earth, and the kindest girl I've ever met. I'd be out of my fucking mind if I didn't ask you out again."

I lean in so close that if we so much as move an inch our lips would be on one another.

"I'd also be pretty fucking crazy if I didn't kiss you right now," and I should be playing the part, but I'm not. I want to kiss this girl so bad I'd be willing to drop to my knees and beg.

And I know I'm not imagining how she slightly parts her lips.

"I–I think I would like that."

I don't move. I'm too nervous to ruin this moment. All I am picturing is how her lips would feel pressed against mine. How I'd fist my hand into her hair savoring her taste. How easy it would be to pick her up and carry her to the sofa.

"Paul? Are–are we going to–"

"Do you think it would help you if we do, Q? I don't want–"

I truly believe the world stops fucking turning for a moment because Susie Cobble's lips are on mine. It's quick, short – *too short* – and she immediately pulls away bringing her hand up to her mouth, her eyebrows almost touching the top of her hairline.

"Oh shit! I'm so so sorry, Paul! I–I didn't let you finish that sentence. You could've been saying you didn't want to and I just kissed you. My best friend. I–I'm–"

"Q-T?" I cut her off. "Do you want me to kiss you back like Jamee Locke would?"

Fuck playing with fire. I'm burnt to a crisp.

"I want to practice feeling sexy and–and I think practicing a legitimate kiss with someone and how to move my body or what to do with my hands will help with that."

I reach up, brushing a piece of hair behind her ear. "Look at someone speaking their mind," I lean back so she can see my whole face. "If this gets uncomfortable for you or if it becomes too much, tap my left shoulder twice Q. I'll stop immediately."

Her brows crease in confusion as she goes to step towards me. I gently put my hand on her shoulder, "I need you to acknowledge that, Q."

"I will tap your left shoulder twice if I become uncomfortable."

There's no going back from this, and I'm okay with that.

Chapter 28

Susie

I think I'm in trouble. Why am I putting myself into the situation of being kissed by Paul Simmons? Because I like to torture myself, that's why.

But also, maybe this will be good for me? Kiss my best friend. Get it out of the way and go back to normal.

I find it sweet that he was adamant about me understanding what to do if I become uncomfortable, not that I think that will be a problem…

Still, he hasn't moved. He's still standing back with a devouring look in his eyes and the anticipation is killing me.

"Paul are you going–"

You know how some people say they see stars when they kiss? I always thought they were full of shit, until now. Because the feeling of Paul's lips crashing onto mine surpasses seeing stars, I think I'm floating in them.

He's just helping me out. He's just helping me out. It doesn't mean anything.

But when his calloused hands gently cup my face, it feels like it means something.

When my hands find themselves wrapped in his hair and he lets out a low groan, it feels like it means more.

And I should stop. I should tap his shoulder because I'm losing myself in him. In this. His hands continue to roam my body, goosebumps prickling my skin as one lands on the back of my head pulling me tight to him, his lips never leaving mine.

There's a lot of things Paul is great at. Hockey, being a friend and teacher, but kissing takes the cake.

This isn't just a kiss, though. His tongue slips into my mouth, his hand begins to travel around my waist as mine begin to do the same. The truth of how awkward this may make things comes washing over me. And that's the only reason I pull away. When I do, he gently rests his forehead against mine, his breathing is shallow and quick.

"Wow," is all he says.

"Some date," I tease, trying not to let on how breathless and flustered I am. "Did–did I do okay with my hands?"

He steps back as he combs his through his hair and I swear there's a faint color of red washed over his cheeks. "Uh, yeah," he clears his throat, "I–I thought it was sexy when you grabbed my hair."

Paul Simmons thinks something I did was sexy?

"I just kind of, uh…went with what felt right?"

He chuckles as he heads towards the kitchen, grabbing a cup out of the cabinet and filling it with water. "Did that help you?"

Help confuse me even more? Yeah.

"I–I kinda wanted to be in control more? Like–like if I wanted to push you–Jamee! I mean Jamee. If I wanted to push Jamee against the wall and be more touchy, would that be sexy?"

His eyes snap to mine with a dark, devouring look I've

never seen before as he sets his drink down and begins to walk, *no...stalk*, towards me.

"I think anything you do is sexy, Q. I know Jamee will think the same. But if you need to practice being in control," he grabs my shoulders, switching places with me as he says, "then practice with me."

I blink once, twice, maybe four times before I fully register that he's being serious. Clearly, he isn't as affected as I am by what just happened minutes ago or else he wouldn't offer himself as my practice. I mean, this is what we're here for. He's teaching me...but am I wrong for taking up his offer knowing that I just enjoyed what happened a bit too much?

Am I wrong for wanting one more chance to kiss him?

"Are you sure?" I ask, needing to hear it once more.

His adorable cocky smirk appears as he says, "Show me, Q."

I place one hand on his chest, his rock solid chest, as I push him back to the wall he just had me pinned against. He's in his normal evening outfit – sweatpants and a shirt – but he didn't opt for the compression tee tonight. Instead, it's one that hugs his broad shoulders but is loose enough to slip your hands under.

So, I step close and begin to toy with the bottom of his shirt, making sure to gently brush my fingers across his bare skin. Then, I bring my other hand up, never taking my eyes off of him as I get a bit braver and slip them both to his back and under his shirt completely.

I have no fucking clue how to be sexy but the way his honey-hooded eyes are staring down at me makes me feel like I don't have to try very hard.

"Tell me, Paul," I drag my nails up and down with one hand as I reach around the back of his head with the other, standing on my tiptoes, pulling his head close to mine. "How many other situations have you been in just like this?"

I lazily drag my nails around his body and up his chest, placing my hand flat against him where I can now feel his heart racing. "Is it more sexy when a girl barely kisses you, teasing you? Or do guys prefer it all at once?"

Genuinely, I don't know. I don't go around kissing a lot of guys for reference…

"I prefer you," he says. And he says it so fast that it catches us both by surprise. I'm just about to open my mouth, to question what he means when he laughs and quickly adds, "I mean, I prefer you to do what you want, Q."

Duh. Of course that's what he meant.

"I know we just literally made out but this won't make things awkward for you, will it?" Me? I'm already screwed, not because of anything Paul did, but because of how he made me feel. But my date with Jamee will help me get out of my mind about it, I just need to make sure this won't ruin our friendship.

"Use me, Susie. Use me however you need."

My sweet, sweet Paul.

I shouldn't because this moment is fueled by different desires now, but I do. I carefully push my lips to his, testing the waters, trying to figure out what I like. And when he kisses me back slowly, a warmth spreads in the bottom of my stomach I've never felt before.

But Paul isn't moving. His arms are glued to his side like he's afraid to move? I pull back, examining his face for any sign of what he's thinking.

"Is there a reason you resemble a statue right now? Did you change your mind?" I take a step back, "It's totally okay if you did! I shouldn't have asked. I'm fine. I feel good, ready to kiss the shit out of Jamee Locke tomorrow. We can watch a movie if you want!" I turn to walk towards the sofa but am stopped by his hand wrapping around my wrist and pulling me back into him.

"I was trying to let you take control, Q."

"Thank you for trying to be a gentleman but do whatever a guy would do in this situation, Paul. Be you. How am I supposed to know what to do if my teacher doesn't prepare me for all the situations?"

I can sit here all I want and say this is for learning reasons, but I know damn well I'm lying to myself.

"What's the rule?" he asks. "If you want me to stop, what's the rule?"

I reach up, tapping his left shoulder twice with a smile on my face. A smile on my face that is cut short by the force of Paul's lips crashing to mine as he does exactly what I asked of him.

He takes my face into his hands, tilting my head to the side, deepening the kiss. Before I know it, our tongues are intertwined and my hands have found their way back up his shirt. Not purposely, I suppose I got carried away, but he doesn't seem to mind.

My senses are on overdrive. My nipples are hard. My vagina is reacting like it hasn't been touched in years. But I'm not naive to how this is affecting Paul either, considering the bulge pushing against me. He doesn't seem to be embarrassed by it so I suppose I shouldn't be embarrassed by how my body is reacting either.

Next thing I know, I feel Paul's hands slip to my thighs as he hoists me up, my legs instinctively wrapping around his chiseled hips. Now this? This is foreign territory for me. Our bodies are touching too closely and I'm basically resting on his dick which definitely feels enormous.

But do I tap his shoulder? No. I wrap my arms around his

neck and bury myself in him. Paul is used to meaningless hookups, not that this is where that's leading because that's absolutely absurd. I just mean that he's used to things not meaning anything, so this? This isn't anything different for him.

"Fucking hell Susie," he breathes as he moves to my neck leaving a trail of kisses. "Do you know what you're doing to me?"

What *I'm* doing to *him*?

I lean to the opposite side giving him access as I close my eyes. "This is–this is some great practice." The words come out short and breathy as I try to keep my shit together while this man turns me into a pool of mush.

He pulls his face away from my neck with a lazy smirk on his face. "I–I think good. No, fuck. I think you did good. You took control, you followed my lead when you wanted, and your body…" he trails off, his face still inches from mine. "Uh, how your body and hands moved against me was–was pretty fucking sexy, Q."

How my body moved against him? It did that?

I still have my legs wrapped around his waist, and with his mouth so close to mine, I want nothing more than to lean into another kiss. To grab his face and show him that this isn't just practice for me anymore.

But I don't. Instead, I unwrap my legs as he gently places me back to the ground. Things will go back to normal after this lesson and this will be a funny memory for the both of us.

"I really appreciate you helping me out with all of this, Paul. Mrs. Baker may question our methods, but she'd be proud of me for working on myself again and that's all because of you."

He shoves his hands into his pockets as he says, "That's all you, Q-T. I didn't do anything but share what helps me.

You're the one that put them into practice." He walks past me, patting me on my shoulder as he takes a seat on the sofa. "What movie tonight?"

I take a seat next to him, closer than usual, handing him the remote as if we didn't just have two extremely hot makeout sessions. As if I'm not soaking wet. As if I'm not thinking of what it just felt like to have my legs wrapped around him. "It's your pick."

He takes the remote from my hand, pulling me into his side. "I'm feeling a funny movie tonight…have you ever seen *Dodgeball?*"

* * *

One hour later and I'm laughing my ass off snuggled into Paul's side. We haven't really talked about tonight's events and I think it's probably best that way.

It was a lesson, we kissed, *a lot*, and now we're back to our regular selves. And as the movie is coming to an end, I remember that we won't have these nights anymore, but that I want to. These last few evenings spent with Paul have been some of my favorites.

Just as I'm about to tell him that, to let him know I don't want this part of the arrangement to end, his phone dings. I imagine it's the boys asking where he's at, supposedly they've been on his ass this past week about him being out late, but I refrain from reading the message.

"Bullshit," he says, huffing out a breath.

I immediately sit up, turning to face him. "Is everything okay?"

"Yeah, normal shit," he tucks his phone back into his pocket.

"Do you want to talk about it?"

At first he looks hesitant, like he's not sure how to answer the question. I'm beginning to get the feeling that Paul might be really great at listening but not sharing.

"I'm a great listener, Pauline," I tease as I bump him with my shoulder.

"I don't talk about my shit," he confesses. "I don't want it to be other people's shit."

"Paul," I place my hand on his, "friends are here so you don't have to handle your shit alone and we're friends, aren't we?"

He looks down at my hand and then back to me as he begins to chew on his bottom lip. "It's Lisa again asking for money to help 'turn her life around,'" he says in quotation marks. "I just ignore her."

My back is immediately straight. I don't know much about his birth mother but I know she didn't treat Paul the way he deserves to be treated and that pisses me off.

"She texts you asking for money? Does she ever say anything else?"

He shrugs his shoulders and laughs. "That woman hasn't said anything else other than 'can I have' for as long as I can remember."

"I'm sorry, Paul. She–she's missing out on knowing and being around the most amazing guy," I lean back into his side. "I don't know how you feel and I won't pretend to. But it's okay to be angry or upset or hurt about the situation. That doesn't mean she wins, it just means you're human."

He goes quiet for a second and for a moment I'm worried I overstepped, until I feel his cheek rest on my head and he quietly says, "I spent my whole life convincing myself I didn't need her or anyone other than Meme. It pisses me off that she broke the part of me that could ever try to give someone more."

I move my head just enough to where I can look up at him, a blank expression written all over his face that consists of anger, hate, maybe both. "I don't think that part of you is broken, Paul. I think it's there," I place my hand on his heart, "I just think you haven't found it yet. And that's okay, you will."

He brings his large hand to my cheek, holding it as he lazily runs his thumbs back and forth. "I've never told anyone this but–but I know she's the reason I've never been interested in anything more than a hookup. Why risk getting hurt by someone leaving if you never let them close enough to leave?"

"Paul–"

"I know it's fucking ridiculous and stupid. I let my friends get close to me, you and the girls, but a relationship? Falling in love? That's serious shit and if there's one thing Lisa taught me, it's that trusting someone wholeheartedly just to be continuously let down fucking sucks," he chuckles, taking his hand away from my cheek. "So I just never put myself in that position."

And I swear I feel my heart snap into pieces for him. Having that type of mindset, especially created at such a young age, is heartbreaking. Sure, the shit that happened to me with Lane fucked me up, but having someone that's supposed to love me consistently choosing not to is an entirely different trauma that I can't imagine.

I stand up, offering him my hand. At first he's hesitant, his eyes squinted trying to figure out what I'm doing.

"Come on Pauline. Tonight the teacher becomes the student," I tease as he finally takes my hand and stands.

"What are we doing?" He asks as I lead him towards the bathroom and place him in front of the mirror, taking my place behind him and leaning to the side to look at us both.

"My teacher once told me that standing in front of a mirror and being able to see the positives in yourself helps. So, here we are."

He rolls his eyes as he tries to turn around but I keep a firm grip on his shoulders. "Your Paul Simmons and lord knows your ego is big enough to fill this entire bathroom, so this isn't about self-confidence. This is about how you feel and telling yourself it's okay to try. I can't begin to understand how your moth–Lisa's–actions affected you, Paul. I won't pretend that I understand because that's just plain stupid. But I will help remind you that you deserve love just as much as everyone else does."

I wrap my arms around his stomach, "So repeat after me. I deserve love." I raise my eyebrows at him in the mirror to show I'm being serious.

"I deserve love," he says as he leans forward, resting his hands on the bathroom counter.

"And I deserve to try." I nudge him as his lips tug upward.

"And I deserve to try," he repeats, staring back at me in the mirror.

Moving behind him, I tap his shoulders for him to turn around and when he does, his expression is unreadable.

"I–I know that won't fix how you're feeling and maybe it's stupid but it's the truth, Paul. You deserve everything and more. Sure, relationships can be messy and people get hurt. But your life won't always consist of people like Lisa."

He goes to open his mouth, his lips slightly parted, and I can tell there's words at the tip of his tongue he wants to say, but I see the moment he chooses not to. Instead it's replaced with his typical smile and twinkling eyes.

"You're one of the best friends I've ever had outside of the guys, Q," he wraps me into a hug. "And I'm a little bummed about our lessons ending. I–I've liked spending time with you."

"It's definitely different from hanging out in our large group, huh?" I slightly pull away from his embrace, motioning for him to follow me back into the living room.

It's 12:30a.m., we both have class tomorrow, Daytona announcements on top of the boys finding out about their season lineup, plus my date with Jamee.

And yet all I want to do is stay in this moment with Paul.

"In the best way," I hear him say from behind me.

I have a lot I could say. Like how tonight meant more to me than just a lesson. How I've started to…I don't know… fall for him? How I don't want what's become our normal to end…

"Paul, I think–"

And for the second time tonight, his phone interrupts us as it begins ringing, and at this point I'm taking it as a sign. A sign that just saved my ass from embarrassment.

He quickly hits ignore, flipping the phone over on the counter. "Sorry, Q. It was Liam probably asking for a late night McDonald's run, which fuck him if he thinks I forgot about the shit from last year with that shitty pizza he delivered cold. Anyway, what were you saying?"

"Oh, umm…I–I can't quite remember now," I lie, and I know he can tell, but he doesn't push it.

"Well, if you happen to remember, let me know," he says as he begins to grab his things. "I suppose I should probably get out of here, I didn't realize it was so late. I know you have an exciting day tomorrow," and he may not mean for it to, but it sounds almost sarcastic.

"I'll see you at the bar for our celebratory festivities, especially when I make the Daytona team with the girls," I flash my biggest smile. "My teacher taught me to think positively."

"Fuck yeah he did," he teases, pulling me into one more hug. I feel him bury his face into my hair, letting out a sigh. "I hope your date goes well, Q-T. We'll be at the game tomorrow and I'll see you afterwards," he pulls away, holding my shoulders. "Call me if you need an early out. If Jamee pisses you off, makes you uncomfortable, I don't give a shit. I'll be there in a heartbeat, Q."

And I know he's being serious.

"I'll be okay, Pauline. I hope the announcement for your team goes well."

He pats me on the head as he walks to the door. "Please, Q. It's me we're talking about. I'll be on the first line just like you'll be competing in April," he winks as he opens the door, "and I can't wait to cheer you on."

As he slips outside of my dorm, I immediately head to the shower, needing to take some time to think about what the hell just happened tonight.

I made out with my best friend, not once but twice, but it's okay, nothing's changed between us. We're still friends, everything is good.

Except for the fact that I can't get the feeling of his lips off mine...and I don't want to.

Chapter 29

Susie

"Susssieeee," Clara whines from beside me as I unpack my clothes, pulling out my outfit for tonight's date.

"Ssssh," I stick my finger over her mouth, "they're going to hear you and–"

"Is it her outfit?" Sara asks from the living room of the River Road house. "Keep it out! We're coming to see," she yells.

We've turned Clara and Liam's bedroom into our own personal dressing room as we get ready for tonight's game. The boys are in the living room taking celebratory shots in honor of their team announcement, and sure enough, all four of them are on the starting line, again.

I haven't seen Paul since last night, he wasn't home when we all got here, but I'm a bit...anxious...to see him since yesterday's events. Not because I think things will be weird, but because I don't know how to tell the butterflies in my stomach to disappear.

However, I'm trying not to think about that because tonight is all about Jamee and I.

The girls immediately burst into Clara and Liam's room

with little Rocky trailing right behind them, running over to the outfit I have laid out on the bed.

"Yes!" Leah yells. "I hate orange, but not on you, babe. It really makes your eyes pop!"

"But can we acknowledge this adorable black skirt and how I don't think I've ever seen you in a skirt outside of your cheer uniform," Lucy adds, bumping my shoulder. "Put it on so we can see the whole thing."

"Right nowwwww?" I whine. We were told to arrive early for Coach to announce the Daytona team. I'm already nervous as it is, pushing it on time doesn't sound ideal...

"Yes, right now," Leah says with a smirk on her face, taking a seat on the floor. "Let us see, Suse!"

Typical Susie would huff and immediately go put on the outfit. This Susie is ready to get to the locker room and a good friend of mine told me I need to learn how to speak what I feel.

"I need to get my uniform on so we can get going. I promise you girls will see my outfit when I show up to the bar after the date," I begin walking to the bathroom. "Give me ten minutes and I'll be ready to go!"

The girls make an audible reaction, mainly grumbling, as I disappear into the restroom. And as I get ready, looking into the mirror, I grin at the girl staring back at me. Realizing how much I love her.

I always have, but these last few lessons with Paul have helped my confidence shine and remind me who I am and how I can choose to be.

Ten minutes later and I'm ready to conquer the night. "Are you all done whining now?" I ask as I make my way back into the bedroom.

"That depends," the much deeper and all too familiar voice says, "does whining get me anything?"

I jerk my head up, immediately dropping my things. "Paul! What–what are you doing here?"

He starts to stalk towards me, never tearing his gaze away. "The girls sent me in here to let you know they were putting their bags in Lucy's car. I didn't mean to scare you," he chuckles as he stops right in front of me. "I also got to hear an earful about how sexy your outfit is for tonight." He grabs a strand of hair, gently tucking it behind my ear as he adds, "And how you refused to try it on for them right now."

"My teacher taught me to be assertive and speak my mind," I shrug. "And I listened."

"Good girl," he whispers, his eyes fixed on my mouth.

I've read some of Leah's books before and the females always swoon when they're called a *good girl*. I always thought how stupid that was. Who would want to be called a *good girl* like some dog?

Me.

Paul Simmons can call me a good girl any day of the week and just like now, a wetness that shouldn't be there would spread between my thighs.

"I–uh, heard about you guys being on the startling line," I say, trying to ignore the impact his words have on me. "Congratulations hot-shot goalie." I grab his bicep. "Not only do you wear number one, you are literally number one."

He steps closer, almost as close as we were last night, softly whispering, "You look fucking breathtaking, Q-T."

And now I have a lump in my throat, not knowing what to say because this seems a lot like flirting, meaningful flirting.

"You don't look so bad yourself," I smooth out his shirt. He's dressed in light washed blue jeans with a white tee tucked in and a grey button up hanging loose. Simple and super freaking attractive. "Any special lady you're dressed to impress?"

"Can I say you?" His fingers find their way under my chin, tipping it up to where I'm now looking into his eyes. "Maybe I wanted to impress you, Q."

Well, damn.

"I would say that you always impress me, Paul. But this outfit will definitely have all the girls clawing their way to you."

He leans closer, his smell engulfing me. A hint of vanilla mixed with something woodsy. Whatever it is, it has me leaning into him for more.

"As long as I'm impressing you, that's all I care about."

And maybe I imagine it, maybe it's my wishful thinking, but I swear his lips part slightly as if he's about to make a move but then we're both startled.

"Suse!" Lucy calls from the living room. "Are you ready?"

Paul pulls back, motioning his eyes to my bag. "I guess you better head out, Q. I'll see you tonight."

Rushing around, I grab my things and toss my bag over my shoulder hurrying out of the bedroom, stopping in the doorframe.

"You didn't wish me luck for my date?"

His smirk is small as he reaches one hand up, running his fingers through his hair. "You don't need it, Q. It'll go great."

* * *

"Alright ladies," Coach Hawkins says as she stands in front of us with her notebook. "You all have done fantastic work gearing up for Daytona. We have a lot of newbies on the team this year who've truly impressed me," she makes eye contact with me for a brief second before continuing.

"As a reminder, we'll have the competition team and

some alternatives in case, lord forbid, something happens. This is never an easy decision for me but just know that this is based on multiple factors. With that being said, we are a family first. We support and encourage others and anything other than that will not be tolerated."

I look around at my teammates realizing that some of these girls live and breathe for Daytona. Me? I would just be lucky to be an alternate.

"With that being said, let's get started."

Coach begins to read off the list of names, all girls who are incredibly deserving of a spot to compete and then one by one, my friends get listed. First Clara, followed by Sara, Lucy, and Leah. My hope is fading as she's getting ready to name the seventeenth–

"Susie Cobble."

My head snaps to the left where my friends are sitting because there's no freaking way I just heard that right. Coach made sure to tell us before the announcement to hold all the screaming until the end. So, as soon as she names the two alternates and leaves the room, chaos ensues.

The girls immediately fall on top of me, kissing my forehead, cheek, screaming, and I'm fairly sure Leah is crying.

"Holy shit!" Clara yells. "You're telling me I get to experience Daytona year two with all of my best friends? Guys, this is literally a dream come true," she squeals.

"Susie, you should be so fucking proud of yourself," Lucy says as we finally begin standing up. "Your first year making the cheer team and you're going to compete in Daytona!"

I smooth out my uniform when I feel the tears start to flood my eyes. Lucy's right. This is my first year as a cheerleader and I worked my ass off to earn my spot on the competition team. And there's only two people I want to tell right now.

"I love you all so much and truly cannot wait to celebrate but I–I have to make a call," I hurry out of the locker room with my phone. Firstly, I immediately FaceTime mom and dad to which of course mom gets all emotional.

"Oh honey," she says as she wipes a tear from her eye. "I am just so so proud of you for putting yourself out there. Your father and I will be there and we can't wait!"

Then I hear dad in the background, "Proud of you Susie cutie!"

And once I say my goodbyes, I'm immediately pulling up the contact for the second person that crossed my mind, the one I can't wait to share with. I pull up his number, but as soon as I'm getting ready to hit call, someone else grabs my attention.

"Susie!" I hear someone yell from behind me. "I've been looking for you."

I turn to see Jamee Locke jogging towards me in his football gear. His blonde hair is swaying back and forth as he holds his helmet in his hand. With everything that's gone on since we talked in the coffee shop, I forgot just how handsome he is.

"Jamee!" I say as he stops in front of me. "Hey! You were…looking for me?"

"Yeah," he says with a cocky grin, his blue eyes shining bright. "I wanted to see you before it got busy. I'll wait for you outside our locker room after the game if that works for you?"

I tuck my hair behind my ear, suddenly nervous. "Yeah–yeah that sounds great!"

He reaches out, grabbing my hand and pulling me close to him. "I have to be honest, Susie. I didn't just come over here to tell you where I'll be waiting."

"Oh?" I ask. "What else–"

And for the second time in two days I'm cut off by lips crashing to mine because Jamee Locke has his arms wrapped around me, holding me tight. I imagined what it would be like kissing Jamee. Would it live up to Paul and I's kiss? Will I see fireworks like I did yesterday? What would his lips feel like against mine?

Don't get me wrong, it's a great kiss. I find myself leaning into it, wrapping my arms around his neck, our lips locked together. It's not a frenzy make out session like Paul and I, it's simple and sweet, and when he pulls away, I feel the same butterflies in my stomach.

But there were no fireworks?

"I came over here to do that," he says in a low, deep voice. "Make sure to cheer for me tonight, Suse. I'll be listening for you only," he smirks as he jogs off.

I stand there stunned for a moment because I was not, in any way, prepared for Jamee to track me down and kiss me before the game. It was most definitely enjoyable…but what do I do if I was thinking of someone else the whole time?

Go to hell, probably.

"Suse," Sara sticks her head out of the door, "we're getting ready to head to the field, are you ready?"

I shake my head, locking my phone and putting it away. "I'm ready!"

"Why are your cheeks so red?" she asks.

"Because Jamee Locke just kissed me," I confess.

"Girls!" She yells, stopping me in my tracks. "Come here, hurry!"

"It's not a big–"

"What? What's wrong?" Clara asks as she hurries to me.

"Are you okay?" Leah grabs my shoulders. "What hurts?"

I roll my eyes because as much as I love my friends, they are extremely dramatic.

"I'm fine, I'm fine. I was just telling Sara that Jamee and I kissed, that's all."

"That's all?" Lucy repeats. "One of Barker University's hottest football players just kissed you and you're this calm?"

If she only knew all the shit that's going on in my mind.

"How was it? Is he a good kisser?" Sara raises her eyebrows up and down as we make our way to the field. "He looks like he'd be a really good kisser."

"I mean," Clara adds as she grabs my arm, "I am happily married with a fur baby, but the man is ungodly attractive and definitely looks like he knows what he's doing."

"Come on," Leah adds. "Spill the beans, Suse!"

As we take our place on the sideline, I look up to see the boys in the same spot as always, my eyes immediately drawn to the brown haired, honey-eyed boy as his face lights up while he waves at me.

I return the favor and then turn my eyes to the field where number nineteen is.

"It was a great kiss. And I'm looking forward to tonight."

And to getting Paul Simmons off my mind.

Chapter 30

Paul

"**D**o you think little Rocky's doing okay?" I yell over the music towards Clara. "He's just a baby, what if he's scared at home by himself?"

It's the third time I've asked her and each time she's given me the same answer, "Rocky is perfectly fine by himself, Paulie. Are you okay? You seem a bit…on edge tonight?"

I shrug my shoulders because what am I supposed to say? *Uh yeah, I am on edge. I fucking made out with your best friend yesterday, enjoyed it way too much, didn't tell her how I feel, and now she's out on a date with some prick asshole named Jamee.*

"I'm fine just–just worried about the little dude is all."

"Quit worrying about Rocky and have a fucking drink dude," Liam says as he wraps his arm around his wife's shoulder. "We're celebrating, remember?"

"Yes, I remember."

"Even Clay is drinking," Jake laughs as he points, Leah tucked into his side like normal.

"I've never seen my brother drunk and I don't know how to feel about it," she laughs. "He's actually…fun?"

"Please," Lucy scoffs. "Fun and Clay don't belong in the same sentence. Try miserable and sad."

That makes me laugh. "I knew I liked you, Lucy," which rewards me with a middle finger and a chuckle.

I want to enjoy tonight. I want to celebrate and let loose, but it's pretty fucking hard when I can't stop thinking about Susie Cobble.

Last night's lesson turned into so much more. Into *wanting* so much more.

Wanting her lips on mine. Wanting her hands wrapped in my hair. Wanting her body pressed against me.

Yesterday we crossed the line of no return. I will never be able to forget the taste of her lips or how her tongue felt tangled with mine.

And I have no idea if she feels the same. I don't think it matters and I definitely don't plan on asking her or confessing how I feel. She's on a date tonight, she's my best friend.

But I can't get her off my mind.

This fucking sucks.

"Okay," I interrupt the group's conversation, "I'm ready for shots."

* * *

"Bartender," Clay slurs, "another shot of Whiskey, Bourbon."

It's my fourth shot on top of six beers in a span of two hours and I have officially entered the dangerous game of word vomiting.

"What the fuck do I do, dude?" I slap Clay in the chest to get his attention. The man's eyes are bloodshot and I know he's in another universe.

"Abutt whaaat?" He slaps his hand on my shoulder.

I chose the wrong fucker to talk to.

"My girl problems, asshole."

"Fuuuuck girls," he shakes his head. "They're needy," he hiccups, "they're emotional, and they confuse the shit out of you."

"I'm not confused," I say as I throw the fifth shot back. "I know how I feel, I don't fucking know what to do about it."

"About what?" A gentle voice says next to me.

I snap my head to the right and see the most beautiful girl I've ever laid eyes on.

"Suse!" Clay all but screams from in front of me. I have no worry that he'll share what I said, there's no way he fucking remembers anything from tonight. "You're here!"

And wearing an almost too short skirt paired with an adorable orange top.

"Holy shit, Q-T," I say as I drink her in. "You look–you look–"

"Gorgeous," Clay finishes for me. My head swivels to him, eyeing him hard because I know his drunk ass isn't about to try to flirt with her.

"Oh," she says as she looks down, her cheeks red, "thank you guys. I–I just got here."

"Bartender!" Clay hollers, again. "A Vodka Cranberry for my friend here, please!"

I lower my mouth to Susie's ear so she can hear me, "If you don't want to drink it, I can. He's drunk off his ass and won't know the difference." I pull back to watch for her response, and when the voice in my head screams *fuck it, kiss her…*I realize just how drunk I am.

She laughs, shaking her head as she stands on her tiptoes, resting her hands against my shoulders. "Can we go talk somewhere quiet real quick?"

My brows furrow because she seems serious and a million

things race to my mind. Did Locke hurt her? Did he do something to make her uncomfortable? I'll kill a motherfucker.

But I probably shouldn't talk right now. I have no idea how to control what I say or do with the amount of alcohol coursing through my veins.

Eh, fuck it.

"Yeah. The bathroom hall is probably quiet," I yell over the music. She nods, grabbing my hand and leading us quickly to the hall. But she doesn't stop there. Instead, she bursts into the single restroom, locking the door behind us.

She rests her head against the door, giving me the perfect view of her ass.

God, give me strength.

I'm trying extremely hard to be a gentleman right now, to not look at how perfect her ass looks in her skirt. To not think about how I want to sit her on this countertop and bury my face between her thighs.

I have no idea why we're in here, but I need to start thinking with my head before my dick takes over.

"Susie?"

"I had my date," she says quickly as she turns around.

"You had your date," I repeat, taking a step closer. The memories of last night on replay in my head, and with the alcohol, I know my rational thoughts are out the fucking window.

"And here I am," she breathes out, "getting ready to ask you something that may make you feel uncomfortable. Something that definitely crosses the boundaries of our friendship but I'm only asking you this because–because I trust you."

"Ask me anything, Q," and I mean it. Hell, if she asked me how I felt about her right now, I'd probably tell her.

"I went on the date and it was great and we–we kissed

and then in his car...you know...it almost turned to more but–but I wasn't ready."

Immediately, I put my hands above her head, lowering my head to hers so she has to look into my eyes. I don't think I've ever sobered up as quickly as I did just by her sentence. My vision is still a bit blurry, but not from the alcohol. No, this is pure fucking red hot anger.

"Susie. Did he–did he touch you or do something you didn't want to? I swear I'll hunt the fucker down and break every goddamn bone in his body."

She rapidly shakes her head back and forth. "No, no! Nothing like that. I–I told him I enjoyed the date but that I really needed to get home and he was super respectful and we planned a second date. But I...I want to go further, it's just, I haven't had sex or done anything in a long time and I don't want to embarrass myself with Jamee."

I'm trying my best to understand, but I'm stuck on the part of how she wants to go further with stupid fucking Jamee.

"Q," I say as I continue to tower over her, "I'm a bit confused?"

She closes her eyes as she whispers, "I...umm...it–it's been a bit since I've had...relations with someone. And–and Jamee seems experienced and I, you know? I don't want to make a fool of myself not knowing how to handle myself in the bedroom?"

She lowers her head. "I think...that umm...I think that I would feel better about possibly going further if I, uh, practiced going further?"

"Oh? Oh!" I yell. "Like...porn? Watching porn and–and practicing on yourself? Nothing's wrong with that, Q. I–I think that's normal?"

She takes a deep breath, leaving her eyes fixed on the

floor as she says, "I don't want porn to help me, Paul. I–I want someone to help me that I trust. That knows me and what I've been through…" she trails off as her emerald-like eyes finally look up at me, her brows raised as if she's waiting for me to answer.

But what the fuck am I answering? What in the hell is going on right now?

"Q, what are you–"

"Oh for god's sake Paul, it's you. I–I am asking if you will help teach me more…personal skills…in, you know… inthebedroom," she quickly says in one breath.

I immediately lower my hands from the door, taking a step back, fairly positive my jaw is touching the floor. I'm drunk, but not *that* drunk. Susie Cobble is asking for our lessons to turn *more* physical. And I know for certain that my dick has sprung to life.

Her hands immediately fly to her face as she groans into them. "It sounds so embarrassing and stupid," she laughs. "It's just been a long time and–and I want to know what I'm doing before I make an idiot of myself."

Susie Cobble, the girl I'm falling for, is standing in front of me asking for me to help her discover herself sexually. I want nothing more than to say fuck yes. Hell, I'd even start the lessons here and now. But there's two factors I don't know how to handle.

One, this is to help her for anything that may happen with Jamee Locke and I don't like that one bit. Two, is it fair of me to agree without telling her how I feel?

What the fuck do I do?

I open my mouth but she quickly cuts me off. "I can't believe I just asked you that," her face turns a shade of red I've never seen before. "Pl–please forget I asked you this. It was stupid. I'm overthinking. I will literally be fine."

She gives me an awkward thumbs up, turning to open the door. She doesn't get it half-cracked before I slam my palm on there to shut it back.

"Susie," I wrap my other hand around her wrist, "are–are you sure you know what you're asking me?"

She doesn't turn around as she answers, "For more lessons by the most experienced teacher?"

"What about…our kiss last night–"

"Meant nothing, I know," she finishes for me. *Except that's not what I was thinking.* "I know this doesn't change anything between us," her body spins to face me, her beautiful eyes locked on mine. "Just a friend helping a friend. But really, Paul. If you aren't comfortable with what I'm asking you–"

"I'm in."

I'm fucked.

"You–you're in?" she repeats.

Too far in.

"I told you before, Q. I'm glad I'm the one helping you and I'll do anything I can. So, if showing off my best skills is what you need? You won't hear me complain," I smirk, trying to keep with my normal cocky attitude.

She begins nervously running her fingers through her hair. "I–I know it's a weird question to ask of you, Paul. You thought your teaching days were over and here I am asking for more…and I'm going to be honest with you, I–I don't exactly know what this looks like? I just…I know you can help."

And holy fuck do I want to help.

"Do…do you think we should–should we lay out some rules?" she asks.

"What kind of rules are you thinking, Q-T?"

"Like maybe we have safe words?"

I chuckle, stepping closer to her, very aware of how close we are. "I don't need safe words, Q. Do you want a safe word?"

Chewing on her lip, she answers, "I'll tap your left shoulder twice."

"What else are you thinking in that beautiful head of yours?"

There's that smile.

"How–how do you think we'll…you know?"

I chuckle as a million fucking things run through my mind. A million things I'd love to show Susie. A million things I want to do *to* her.

"What exactly are you looking for?"

She crosses her arms over her chest as her shoulders move up to her ears. "Jamee and I go out again Wednesday. I–I want to do as much as possible before then?"

"Come on, Q," I tap her nose with my pointer finger. "I can't create my lesson plans if I don't know the topic of study."

"Ummm…" she goes quiet and I can tell she's a bit over-whelmed, not sure where to start.

"Let's start with this, Q. Are you wanting to know what you like in the bedroom or how to be good at things in the bedroom?"

"Both?" Her eyebrows raise in uncertainty.

Fuck me.

I'm hard just thinking about the possibilities; something I hope she doesn't notice…

"I'm going to be honest with you, Q. All I want to do is help you, but I need to make sure you understand this means we'll be seeing each other in a way we never have before. Are–are you sure you're comfortable with that?"

"I understand," she lets out a deep breath. "I would rather jump back in the deep end with you than with anyone else."

And this would be the perfect moment to change my mind. To tell her the truth and explain why I can't do this — why I *shouldn't* do this. But what's the alternative? I say no and send her on her way with Jamee fucking Locke not knowing what she likes or dislikes?

No. I can put whatever it is I feel for Susie to the side for the sake of her.

"Three lessons just like before. Sunday, Monday and Tuesday night. Nothing you don't want to do, nothing that makes you feel uncomfortable and you have to swear you'll talk to me about how you're feeling, Q."

"I swear. And after…everything goes back to normal," she holds out her pinky. "Promise me I won't lose you because of this, Paul. I–I can't lose you as my friend."

Without hesitating, I link my pinky with hers. I can guarantee she won't lose me, but I can't promise I won't lose myself in her.

Chapter 31

Susie

I walk out of the restroom first to not cause suspicion, flabbergasted by what the hell I just did.

If I thought I was going to hell before for kissing my best friend while having feelings for him, I just sealed my one way ticket. Asking Paul Simmons to more than less teach me his ways in the bedroom was the craziest idea I've ever had. And he agreed.

But everything I said was true. Things got heated between Jamee and I…and I freaked.

It's not like I haven't had sex or been touched since the *event*…but I was the one to always take my bra off. I controlled that. When Jamee's fingers slipped behind the strap, my mind went right back to the party.

And while we're on the subject, it's not like any of my previous encounters set me up to feel like I'm the most experienced girl in the world. I've never been quick at making the guy come. I've never been told I was doing a good job. The guys I've been with were never vocal. They just laid there like a lump on the log which always made me feel like I was the most boring person to be with…

So, yeah. My mind began racing with the fear that I wouldn't be experienced enough, but I want to be. And I immediately knew what to do.

There's the whole feelings thing…yeah I know. But if I want to find out about myself in the bedroom, there's no better person to do that with, regardless of how I feel. I trust Paul. I trust that no matter what happens in the bedroom that he won't laugh at me or make me feel stupid. I feel safe with him.

I make my way to the group in their usual corner and see everyone is hammered. Maybe not as hammered as Clay, but at least tipsy.

"Suuusseee," Clara yells as she walks towards me, not in a straight line. "You're hurrr!" she slurs.

At that moment, Paul comes up beside me. "What did I miss?"

"Where the fuck did you disappear to?" Clay comes around, wrapping his arm around Paul's shoulders. "I missed you, buddy."

Paul chuckles as he says, "I missed you too, buddy."

"Suse here was just about to tell us about her date," Lucy says while looking at Clay. "Big bad Clay can't handle his alcohol?"

"I'm fine," he draws out. "Are you okay?" He points at her. "You always have a fucking stick up your–"

"And that's enough," Paul quickly interjects as he begins to walk away. "We'll be over here," he looks back, waving, shooting a wink in my direction.

I look to my left and see Leah with a glass of water in her hand as she watches the boys walk away.

"Are you not drinking?" I ask.

"Suse!" Leah holds her hand over her heart. "I can't believe you think I'd use a fake ID to drink!"

Rolling my eyes I say, "Don't forget I was there when Lucy delivered it and your brother freaked out."

"That was a greeeeat night," Clara says in a hiccup.

I take a second to look around at my best friends, soaking in how wonderful they are and how much I love them. I know I could tell them anything, yet the last thing I want them to know about is Paul and I...

They'd be supportive, I'm sure of it. There'd be no anger, they wouldn't think any less of me, hell, they'd probably be happy for me.

But if I share that, then I have to share the other part...

"Clara, sweetie," Liam appears beside her, "I think we all need to get out of here before Clay throws up on the table."

I look over to where Liam's pointing. Both Paul and Jake are holding up Clay, him gagging, which in turn has Paul looking away gagging while Jake is yelling at Paul to *"get his fucking shit together."*

Paul looks back, catching my eye and his gagging is immediately replaced with a smile. *My favorite smile.*

"Babeeee–"

"I know, I know, C. You're not ready to go, but Rocky's been alone for a while, Lucy is close to punching Clay in the face and I'm fairly positive Jake was about to take Leah into the restroom before I tasked him with helping our drunk as fuck captain." Liam bends down, kissing Clara on the cheek and wrapping his hand around her waist. "Come on sweetie, let's go see our baby."

Twenty minutes later, we've made it to the two Ubers out front. Sara didn't make it out tonight so we split the ride evenly, and for the first time in our friend group's history, Lucy and Clay are in the same car.

I'm in the back between him and Paul with Lucy in the

front and I'm fairly sure everyone is in their own world, except Paul and I.

Clay is staring out the window moaning and groaning while Lucy is blaring TikToks in the front, a very familiar feeling from our Daytona road trip.

"Susie," Paul says as he drapes an arm around me, leaning into my ear, "are you sure about what you asked me earlier?"

He's having second thoughts…

"I–I'm sure. Do you not–"

"No, I do. I just didn't know if you had a chance to think about it and maybe changed your mind?"

He doesn't know that I had plenty of time to think long and hard about what I asked him. He doesn't know that the entire drive back to my dorm with Jamee, I practiced on repeat in my brain exactly how I would ask him.

I look into his gorgeous, caramel eyes. "I won't change my mind, Paul. I–I want you to be the one to help me."

He pulls me in close, just like the other night on the sofa, and I comfortably snuggle into his side. A few seconds pass before he quietly says, "I'm proud of you for making the Daytona team, Q."

My eyes shoot to his, realizing I never finished calling to tell him the news.

"I–I meant to tell you, I just got–"

"Busy," he gives me his signature grin. "I know, Q-T, it's okay. I just wanted you to know I'm proud of you, and I can't wait to watch you compete." He lowers his voice as he adds, "Jamee Locke is one lucky guy."

Chapter 32

Paul

"Why the fuck did you guys let me drink so much?" Clay growls as he slides into Liam's jeep. "This is the worst kind of hell."

"You said, and I quote, *'it's senior year, I'm the hockey captain on a team with my three best friends, I'm getting fucked up tonight,'* and then when Liam tried to tell you to slow down, you told him to eat a bag of dicks," Jake shrugs. "So, this is on you Cap, and now you must suffer your consequences."

By consequences he means our early morning practice.

"And you know Coach is going to be on one today. We're a month out from our first game and he isn't happy with the line switches," I add. "I think if Shaffy could get his head out of his ass and focus more on passing than his damn stats, the line transition would go smoother."

"His giveaway percentage is fucking atrocious," Liam says.

"Leon," he hates when I use the name Clara used when they first met, "did you not have three giveaways during last practice?"

His eyes dart to the rearview mirror. "You mean when Clara texted beforehand saying she thought Rocky was injured because he wouldn't put his paw on the tile floor? Yes, Paul. I was worried for my son's fucking safety."

"You being a father is going to drive us up the fucking wall," Jake chimes in.

Liam doesn't respond, he offers a kind middle finger while Clay says, "You all are driving me up the fucking wall and my headache into overdrive."

I grab his shoulders from behind, "Thank god we've arrived, Cap."

"Why did you numbnuts have to choose a house so close to campus?" He whines as we unload our bags.

"Blame Liam," I say as I grab my stick from the trunk. "How are the girls feeling today?"

One in particular is on my mind.

"From what I've heard, not as bad as this guy," Jake jams his thumb in Clay's chest. "They had a fun girl's night at Susie's dorm, though. Leah was pretty bummed they didn't get to celebrate the Daytona announcement with Suse but said her date with Jamee went well."

I don't want to hear another fucking thing about Jamee and Susie's date. I hate that she even wants to go out with him again. I hate that the only reason she came to me for more *lessons* is because things might go further with him.

I hate Jamee fucking Locke.

Anyway…

I meant to congratulate Q about Daytona as soon as I saw her, but then when she got there, well…things didn't go how I expected by any means.

I'm most definitely blaming drunk Paul for the irrational and hasty response in agreeing to more lessons. But I know sober Paul wouldn't have thought twice.

* * *

"Dammit, Shaffy!" Coach yells. "If you give one more goddamn puck away, I'm giving your fucking spot away for the season."

I pull off my helmet as I walk into the locker room, wiping the sweat from my forehead with the back of my hand. Our two hour practice was all drills as we're continuing to mesh out the line change. I don't know how in the hell we expect to get to the Frozen Four when we can't even get the simple shit right.

The starting line, or first line, consists of me, Clay, Jake, Liam, Ronnie and Jay. A solid fucking line. We have Liam as our left-winger and Ronnie as our right, with Clay at the center while Jake and Jay are our two defensemen.

But there's some fucking disconnect when Coach is switching the lines and it never fails that Shaffy and Brandon shit the bed, giving up the puck within the first ten seconds.

"I–" Shaffy begins as Clay interjects.

"Coach?"

Coach Watt doesn't say anything but motions for Clay to take the floor.

"Look. Today fucking sucked and if we don't get our shit together before our game next month against Carnelly we might as well kiss any hope of making it to the championship goodbye," he lets out a sigh as he pushes his hair back. "Shaffy and Brandon, I know you're struggling with the line change but we all had some fuck ups today that could cost us a game."

"Jake, you let B team's right winger beat you twice when you pinched too tight and he slipped right past you. And Liam," he directs his attention to BU's golden boy, "you know better than anyone when to pass the puck in a pinch and you still tried to take the shot instead of setting Ronnie or I up."

He takes a breath as he turns around to Ronnie. "You were the last player to the opposite side every fucking time. Get faster or get replaced."

And then he turns to me and I know what's coming.

"Paul. You allowed three goals. You and I both know something was on your mind today and it affected practice. Don't let it happen again."

I don't say anything, I don't even acknowledge his comment because we both know he's right. The ice is usually the one place I don't have anything on my mind – the only thing I care about is the person with the puck.

Not today.

Today the only thing on my mind is tomorrow night with Susie Cobble. We're lucky I didn't get a fucking hard on out there.

And it most definitely affected my practice. Paul Simmons is being affected by a girl and I don't know what to do. I can't talk to the guys, Susie and I agreed this stays between us. There's only one person I know outside of this group that I can talk to…and lord knows how that'll go.

"I also fucked up," Clay continues. "No one was anywhere near perfect. Let's get our heads out of our asses, show up and do better, and go on to win the Frozen fucking Four."

The room erupts in chaos with sticks hitting the floor and you would think we just had the greatest pregame hype known to man. But for the boys who are just joining the team or the ones who shit the bed this morning, *like me*, it's good to hear. Clay waves us off as he takes a seat next to me while Coach dismisses us for the day.

"So? No comment on my call out?" he asks. "I expected at least some shit?"

I shrug my shoulders as I pack up my things. "Hard to say shit when you're right."

"Dude. You know you're the greatest goalie we've had and if there's ever a time we'll make the Frozen Four, it's with you in our net. And when we get to the Razers, they'll be just as fucking lucky."

"Careful, Harp. I'll begin to think you have a heart in that chest of yours."

"And that's the last time I'm nice to you, asshole."

"You were nice and I missed it?" Jake asks as he joins us. "Fuck. Do it again, let me get it on camera for Leah!"

"Good luck getting that again in your lifetime," Liam adds.

"Okay, fuck all of you," Clay huffs as he starts to grab his things.

While they continue with their shit, I finish getting my things together, grabbing my bag and hurrying towards the door.

"I have to call Meme. I'll walk home today," and before they can answer, I hurry out the door, waiting until I'm far away from the arena to call; I ain't risking those dickheads hearing this conversation...

"Did hell freeze over? My grandson is calling me?"

I chuckle through the phone. Meme can be a lot of things but dramatic is always on top of that list.

"Hell may have frozen over but not because I'm calling you. I–I need your advice."

I know I fucked up the moment the words left my mouth.

"Oh my god, it's a girl. It's the one I met on the phone a few days ago isn't it? 'Over at a friends' my ass, Henry."

"She is a friend," I sigh as I kick the rock in front of me. *"She's one of my best friends and…well…"*

I'm sure the gasp that comes out of her can be heard from outer space.

"Paul Henry Simmons, is this girl pregnant?"

"What!" I yell a bit too loudly. *"Jesus Christ Memes. No, she isn't pregnant. She doesn't know I like her and well…I've been helping her with things and that included kissing her and then she asked me to help her with…more…which I said yes but now I don't know what to do."*

"Honey," she says while slightly laughing. *"I don't know what you're saying."*

Dammit.

"I was helping her feel good and confident for her date and at first it was just an arrangement…" I laugh hearing myself say everything out loud. *"But it isn't just that anymore, but she doesn't know that, and I agreed to help her with even more…personal things, like sexual things,"* I whisper, *"And I like her a lot. So much so that I thought about her the entirety of practice this morning and fucked up an ungodly amount of times and now I think I should back out and not help her but then-"*

"You thought about her during practice?"

Really. Out of the whole conversation that's what she picks up?

"Well, yes. But did you hear the rest about us kissing and how she basically asked me to help her out in the bedroom? And how I agreed even though I'm into the girl?"

"You could've just led with how you thought about her during practice, that would've told me all I needed to know. And look, a little too much information on the sexual activities, Henry, but is she into you too?"

"I–I don't know because I haven't told her any of this."

"And why not?"

I think I'd rather take my chances with the boys next time.

"Because she trusted me with helping her out. She's trusting me with this huge thing and I don't want how I feel to ruin that or our friendship."

She goes silent for a while. Not completely silent because her chewing echoes through the phone.

"She's doing all this for another date with the same guy?"

Unfortunately.

"Yes."

"Do you want her to go on the date?"

"Fuck no," the easiest answer there is.

"Then tell her that."

"Now? What if–"

"Dammit, Billy Randall's dog is back. I gotta go, Henry. I love you!"

And then she hangs up, leaving me no closer to an answer than I was before the call.

Am I not in the same boat we gave Liam plenty of shit for with Clara and his secret feelings? Yes, yes I am.

But I swear this is different.

Susie asked me to help her with this. She *needs* this. And I don't want to let her down, even if that means torturing myself while doing it.

Chapter 33

Paul

For the first time since my debut college game, I think I may throw up.

I spent the entire day thinking of tonight, of the gorgeous black-haired girl standing in front of me. Is that what happens when you like someone? Do you think about them constantly?

How was her day? What did she have for lunch? Did she sleep well?

I couldn't focus. I changed my outfit three fucking times before coming over and the best I could come up with were black gym shorts and a grey t shirt.

It's been five minutes since Susie let me in the door and I can tell she's also nervous. She hasn't quit babbling, she keeps picking at her nails, and she's as far away from me as one could get.

But holy hell does she look good in her leggings and sweatshirt. So simple, so sexy.

Alright, I can do this. Help my best friend and don't let her know I'm feeling things I've never felt before. Easy.

"You're rambling, Q," I say as I stand with my arms crossed. "Don't get me wrong, it's cute," I wink.

She slouches her shoulders as she whines into her hands, "I–I don't know how to handle this?"

You and I both.

"Susie," I whisper as I move towards her. "It's not too late. We don't have to do this."

Moving her hands away from her face, she reaches out to grab my hand. "I trust you and I feel safe with you. I've done things since what happened to me but never once have I ever felt confident or sexy while doing those things. I–I don't even know if..." she trails off.

"Has a guy never made you," and because I'm twelve, I motion with my eyes to her pussy, "you know?"

I already have my answer just by the redness on her face.

"Uh...no? I–I don't think so? Is that bad? Does that mean there's something wrong with me?"

"Q. It's not your fault those boys were fucking useless in the bedroom."

She still has her hand in mine so I seize the opportunity, pulling her into me. "I promise to take care of you, Q. If this is what you need and want, I promise to help you."

And I think I've fallen for you, is something I should add.

"I know," she says softly. "Can–can we go to my room for tonight's lesson?"

I swallow hard because I know she didn't mean to, but that was the sexiest fucking sentence I've ever heard and my dick is having a hard time understanding this is about her, not me.

"Whatever makes you comfortable, Q."

She responds by turning on her heels and leading me down to her bedroom, again. And as soon as the door closes with us inside, the air changes. It's thick with tension, full of electricity. For a bit, we don't say anything. She's sitting on her bed as I continue to slowly scan the room, admiring her paintings.

"Soooo…" her sweet voice cracks the silence. "How do we go about this?"

Sex, making women feel good, I know how to go about that. How to make my best friend, a girl I care about feel good? That's new.

"Let's start with what you want from tonight's lesson, Q-T. What did you have in mind?"

Because my mind is racing with all the fucking possibilities, I wouldn't know where to begin. Not to mention I don't know where she *wants* to begin.

"I thought long and hard about this all day," she says as she rests her hands on her thighs. "I–I want to start slow? Like…basics?"

Basics, okay. This I can work with. But I need to ask her one last time before we enter the point of no return.

"I can do that, but I need to hear it one more time Susie. If I cross a line you don't want to be crossed, you'll immediately stop me. If you don't like what I'm doing, if it becomes awkward or you want to stop, you'll speak up. Promise me, Q."

"I promise, Paul. I give you permission to do whatever you need to do to help me figure out what I like and how to be good at these…things."

And I may regret this, *I know I will*, but having this girl sit in front of me so trusting and fragile? I'd burn the fucking world down to help her.

I walk towards her, trying to calm my brain of all the ideas running rampant.

"I know it's been a while for you, Q, but I'm not some fucking boy who doesn't know how to treat a girl. I'll talk you through things. I'll make you feel things you haven't felt before and the only thing I ask," I say as I lower my face to hers, "is that whatever you feel, don't be embarrassed. Don't be afraid. Let yourself feel good, Q."

I watch as she swallows, nodding her head as she follows my movements, my thumb and pointer finger grasping her chin. "Now, stand up, Q."

Go slow, Paul.

I reach my arms around my shirt pulling it over my head and can't help the pride swell in my chest as Susie gawks at the view. I'm used to women and the way their eyes grow when they see me shirtless, but Susie's look of approval is all I'll ever need.

"Oh my," she says with a blush on her face. "You're– you're shirtless."

I lean close towards her ear, "You're about to be."

I slip my fingers below the hem of her sweatshirt, pausing one last time. One final attempt to let her call this thing off, but she doesn't, instead she dips her head in agreement and I know I'm a fucking goner.

I carefully strip off her sweatshirt, tossing it to the floor and marveling at the girl standing in front of me. She has a few freckles on her chest with an adorable looking birth mark right above her hip. And holy shit does her black lace bra make her boobs look fucking perfect.

I have to keep myself from reaching up and touching her immediately, but goddamn…she's mesmerizing.

"So…what next?"

I don't bother answering. Instead, I loop my arm behind her waist and seal her lips to mine. I can feel whatever ounce of restraint I had moments ago slipping away. I've always found Susie breathtakingly gorgeous and up until recently I would have never imagined having the chance to show her just how gorgeous I think she is.

But she's giving me the chance, the chance to help her while enjoying every goddamn moment, and that's what I'm going to do.

There's nothing slow about this kiss. My tongue immediately finds hers and neither of us break for air. Next thing I know, I have my hands under her ass, lifting her up to straddle me. As if it's the most natural thing in the world, her legs wrap around my hips while my hand makes a fist in her hair.

I begin walking us to her bed, gently lying her down as I hover over her with my hands beside her head. Hands that are slightly shaking…

Her lips are plump and pink, begging for more, while her breathing is fast and cheeks flushed.

"You look so fucking beautiful like this," I say. We're past the boundaries, so fuck it.

Leaning down, I place a gentle kiss on her lips softly whispering, "I'm going to make you forget all the assholes who never made you come, Susie."

Her eyes shoot open as I pull back, moving my kisses to her neck. Inch by inch, I trail down her body stopping when I get to her bra, placing a tender kiss on top of each boob. I don't linger there long, even though I want nothing more than to rip it off so I can see all of her; I'm not sure if she's ready to be completely naked and I don't want to push her on it.

I take my time getting to know her body and what she likes – where she likes it most. I know that when I move to the side of her stomach, it must tickle because she can't stop laughing. I learn that when I kiss her lower stomach, her breathing becomes shallow and her hands find their way to my hair with a slight push downward. So of course, I oblige.

Watching for her reaction, my eyes are peering up at her as I move my mouth to the fabric right over her pussy. I don't kiss her yet, I want to hear what she wants. So, I just hover, breathing out my hot air and taking in the sweet, sweet scent of Susie Cobble.

"Paul–" she trails off, her eyes closed as her body shifts back and forth underneath me.

"What is it, Q?"

Her hand is still wrapped in my hair as she arches her back, pulling my head closer to her.. "I–I want…" her voice trails off.

"Tell me what you want, Susie."

"You know," she pants.

I move up her body to where I'm back hovering over her face. Her hooded eyes are on me, her lips parted as she clenches her thighs.

And holy fuck do I want her to clench them around my face.

"Tell me, baby. Tell me what you want."

She brings her petite hands to my cheeks, cupping them as she softly says, "I want you to make me feel good."

I can't help the cocky fuckboy grin come out as I say, "Easy."

I bend my head down to hers, placing a kiss on her lips as my finger trails down her stomach. Stopping at her waistband, I slip my pointer finger barely underneath to gauge how she feels.

She doesn't say anything but she also doesn't react. By now, my typical puck-bunnies have usually ripped their own leggings off and shoved their own fingers down there.

But Susie isn't a puck-bunny.

She's so much better.

"Susie?"

"Keep going," she says.

Happily.

I drag my finger further down, taking my sweet time as I explore her body. Her incredibly sexy body.

"I–I'm going to warn you that I'm pretty…turned on," she says with a shaky voice. "It–it may be a little embarrassing when you touch me."

"No, baby," I say as I move my finger over her slick entrance, "it's fucking sexy."

Her breath hitches as I circle my finger over her sensitive bud, her hips bucking to create more friction.

I feel like a teenage boy who's about to blow his fucking load in his jeans.

"Paul–" she breathes out. "That feels…"

I move my finger down, gently and barely slipping it into her pussy. Her wet and incredibly tight pussy.

"Fuck," I say as I rest my forehead against hers, "you're already so wet for me, Susie."

"Mmhmm," is all she manages to say.

I push a bit further as I say, "And so fucking tight."

"Is–is that bad?"

I place a tender kiss on her forehead. "Not at all. Are–are you doing okay?"

I feel her hips rise against my hand, forcing my finger further inside her and I imagine this is the feeling of entering Heaven.

"I–I'm perfect."

Chapter 34

Susie

There is no coherent sentence forming inside my head right now. It's too focused on the feeling of Paul's finger inside me – a feeling I would have never guessed I'd be experiencing, but here we are.

And I'm extremely glad we're here. I can think about how awful I am later for enjoying this much more than I should be…

But for now, I'm going to do exactly what he said to do: let myself feel good.

Of course I knew Paul would be good at this; *this* is what he does – lord knows how many times before. Meanwhile, this is entirely new to me.

Being fingered? No. The talking and embarrassing moans coming out of me? Yes.

I can tell he's holding back. Moving cautiously, and I hate that my leggings are limiting his movement.

My best friend has his finger inside my vagina, seeing me in my underwear won't change a damn thing.

I run my left hand from his lower back, which is just as muscular as the rest of his body, up to his left shoulder tapping two times and just like promised, he immediately stops. He yanks his hand out of my leggings, like my mother just walked in, and rolls to his side.

"What's wrong, Q? Fuck, did I–did I hurt you?"

I sit up, viciously shaking my head. "No, god no! I–I'm sorry I just needed to get your attention. I…I think I'd like to take my leggings off?"

His eyes roam my body as a small smirk forms on his lips.

"Go for it. I'll sit right here and watch, baby."

There's something about the way he calls me baby that sends shivers straight down my spine.

Confidence, Susie. Confidence.

I slip my fingers under my leggings as I slide them down my thighs. Thankful that I had time to prepare for tonight and basically gave myself a Brazilian bikini wax. I am as smooth as one could be.

Watching Paul watch me with such hunger in his eyes would make any girl feel sexy. But it also makes me feel something else, which is why once I'm lying here in nothing but my bra and underwear, I roll towards him and immediately push my mouth to his.

He doesn't seem to mind because the next I know, his hand is cupping my ass as he pulls my leg over his. I don't say anything but I can feel how turned on he is. It's hard to miss when the monstrous thing is poking you in the thigh.

As much as I love making out with Paul, I love his finger even more. I reach down, grabbing his wrist and gently guiding his hand to the top of my underwear. Thankfully, it doesn't take him more than five seconds to get the hint.

His finger goes right back to where it was before, circling my most sensitive spot and I swear I may come apart from just this alone.

"Do you like that, Q?"

My eyes are squeezed tight, my lips slightly parted as I focus on the tingling sensation building at the base of my spine and the warmth in my stomach.

"Yes," I say breathlessly.

He moves his finger a bit lower, pushing back inside me. The slight ting of pain that was there earlier is gone, replaced with the need of wanting more.

"Do you like this?"

I open my eyes to see Paul staring at me as I bob my head up and down. That damn cocky grin is back as he begins moving his finger in and out, lazily, teasingly, all while never taking his eyes off of me. This is a whole new level of intimacy I've never experienced.

I can't help the moan that leaves my mouth, or the way my body embarrassingly grinds on his hand. But his smile only widens.

"Good girl," he says as he picks up speed.

There's that damn sentence again.

I am losing my mind. This–this feeling is too overwhelming. Too good. My hands want to do something, anything, but mainly touch him.

So, I do. I move my hand to his chest as he keeps a steady rhythm inside of me while I begin to trail my fingers down his body, my eyes on his waiting for his reaction. When he doesn't react, I test the waters.

I carefully and softly move my hand over his bulge, and just as I begin to wrap my hand around his hard length, his other hand grabs my wrist.

"This isn't for me, Q."

I keep my hand where it is as I say, "I know but–but this would be for me. Making sure I'm doing what a guy would like in return?"

And because I want to touch you.

"I don't want you to think you need to," he says as he places a gentle kiss on my nose. "I'm a grown ass man who can go home and take care of myself, Q-T. And if a man ever makes you feel otherwise, call me immediately."

"Paul," I say as I roll my hips. "I want to."

His tongue darts out running over his bottom lip as he says, "Whatever my girl wants to do."

And when I continue gently running my hand over his hard outline, his finger picks up pace and I can feel myself getting close. At least I think so...I've never experienced the feeling before.

"That feels..." I try to say but lose all train of thought as his finger curls inside of me, hitting a spot that I don't think has ever been touched in my life.

There's nothing more that I want than to make him feel the same.

"Can I?" I barely manage to ask as I begin to slip my fingers into his shorts.

"You can do whatever you want to me, Susie," he says with his lips hovering barely above mine.

"Take off your shorts," I instruct, surprised at my demand.

He wastes no time as he does, never pulling his finger out of me. I can feel the pressure building, a tingling sensation growing from the base of my spine.

My eyes trail down his body as he tosses his shorts to the ground, his erection standing at attention, his boxers tight.

Paul Simmons is by far the sexiest man I've ever seen. Him in the bedroom? No woman would stand a chance.

I watch my hand disappear into his boxers, his breath hitching as I drag my nails lower. But when I graze his tip and feel the wetness leaking out of him, I know I'm in over my head. I also know I've never been with anyone as big as Paul.

"I'm going to add another finger, baby," he says. "If it's too much, you know what to do."

I immediately tense, not knowing what to expect.

"Breathe for me, Q."

And when I let out a breath, I immediately feel the pressure. At first it's uncomfortable, a bit painful, but when his mouth falls to my neck, I'm a goner.

Especially when he pushes them deeper.

"Paul, I–I think–"

"Come all over my finger, Q. Let me feel you."

I never knew talking would do the trick for me but holy hell.

My body begins trembling, my hand wrapping tightly around his thickness as he continues easing in and out of me.

"Fuck Susie," he says as he grabs my chin with his other hand, pulling it downwards. "You are fucking incredible," he whispers into my ear. "Watch yourself."

So I do. I focus my eyes on my leg draped over his while his finger works inside me.

"Oh fuck–" I lose all train of thought as I fall over the edge.

Paul continues moving in and out as I feel my vagina contract around his finger, pulsing with every push, my stomach tightening.

"Give me all of you, Susie," he says as he continues working me, taking it all. And I let him, riding out my orgasm with my head pressed against his chest, hand still holding on to his erection.

And when my body finally stops pulsing, when I can finally catch my breath again, I look up at Paul who carefully takes his finger out of me.

"Holy crap," I say, "I…that was–"

"Amazing," he finishes for me, pushing my hair back from my forehead, planting a kiss there. "You were amazing, Q."

It means nothing.

Looking down I ask, "What can I do about…" I motion towards the bulge pressed against his underwear.

He chuckles. "There's nothing you need to do, Q. I can take care of it," he tries to grab my wrist but I squeeze tighter.

"I–I want to."

He stills, and I can tell he's not sure what to say, so I save him the trouble.

"If that's okay?" I ask as I slightly sit up, my body still facing him.

He gives me a single nod as I bend down, placing a tender kiss on his chest. I begin moving my hand up and down, taking time to rub his wet tip with my finger as I place kisses up and down his chest, making my way to his neck just like he did mine.

And when I get to the spot right below his ear, his hand reaches around, grabbing my ass and pressing me tight against him. My pace becomes fast, my kisses sloppy as I try to find what he likes.

All of sudden his wrist wraps around mine, his hand pulling my face up to look at him.

"I'm pretty fucking close to coming on your hand like a fifteen year old boy, Susie," he fists his hand in my hair, "are you sure?"

I dip my head in agreement, his lips quickly finding mine as my hand continues its rhythm.

"Tighter," he says with a raspy voice.

I listen, squeezing my hand tighter as I keep sliding up and down.

"Holy shit, Susie," he breathes. "I can take over if you don't want to get it on your hand," he leans back on the pillow, his eyes closed tightly.

I seize the opportunity to kiss his throat, making my way to his mouth as I hover just inches above it. "Come all over my hand, Paul."

My name falls from his lips as he comes apart. I don't see it since his boxers are still on, but I can only imagine the sight. His thick release coats my hand as his body jerks. It isn't until I feel him still that I take my hand out, seeing the evidence of how I made him feel left behind. The sight is enough to turn me on...again.

He sits up, resting against my headboard. Now comes the awkward part. The part I don't know how to handle because for me, that was most definitely more than just a lesson...

"I'll be right back," I quickly say as I begin to move to the side of the bed, but before I can, he grabs my side, pulling me back into him.

"Not yet, Q," he says as he lays his chin on my head. "We're going to talk about it."

I rest my head on his chest, listening to his heartbeat as a million things race through my mind. Like how in the hell do I go back to just being his friend? How do I not think about this every hour of the day? How do I go on a date with Jamee Locke while it's Paul Simmons consuming my mind?

He runs his fingers up and down my back and I can tell he's thinking long and hard of what to say next, but I imagine this is normal for Paul. Meaningless hookups, no-strings-attached, letting a girl down easy. Not that he needs to do that for me, I know this is nothing more than our arrangement.

I suppose maybe I should clear that up so he doesn't feel he needs to.

Leaning up to look at him, I softly say, "I know this

changes nothing between us, Pauline. Just friends, best friends really, I don't want you to think I'm going to turn into some crazed girl who thinks you're in love with me," I tease, trying to lighten the mood.

"It changes nothing between us," he repeats as he's looking down at me. "I'm just helping out a fellow best friend discover herself," he cocks an eyebrow as if it's a question.

"Just two best friends, one helping the other," I sit up crossing my legs underneath me, "and–and I'm super thankful that you are, Paul."

He sits up alongside me, smiling as he reaches over, grabbing his shirt from the ground and tossing it to me.

"I'd do anything to help you, Q. However, my dick doesn't understand this whole friendship thing and looking at you shirtless isn't helping his situation." He moves off the bed, grabbing his shorts, "I'm going to go clean up real quick, be right back."

He begins walking down the hall, giving me the chance to admire him from behind. I felt his muscles during our lesson, but seeing each defined line spreading all the way up to his shoulders is otherworldly.

I stand, Paul's t-shirt falling right below my butt, and make my way over to my mirror. My hair is a mess and my cheeks are flushed – a look I've never seen on myself – and I can't help but smile.

For the first time in my life, I spoke up during sexual activities, and for the first time in my life, it was about me. I'd like to think that it can be this way with any guy…surely?

As I'm staring at myself, I see Paul come into frame at my doorway with a glass of water and a small bottle in his hand.

"I–I brought you some Ibuprofen? I wasn't sure if you were like…hurting or something?"

A simple, sweet gesture that makes those damn butterflies appear again.

I turn around and begin walking towards him, noticing that he's still looking in the mirror.

"Thank you, Paul." I take two pills out of the bottle, gulping down some water. "Let me grab my clothes and we can head back to the living room."

"I like you in this," he says quickly. "Come on," he grabs my hand, leading me towards the sofa. "We aren't done talking, yet."

"What more do we need to talk about?"

"Well, I think we need to debrief after these types of… lessons," he pauses on the word, "just to go over what you liked and didn't like that way you know how to communicate those needs to Jamee."

Jamee Locke. The guy I'm going on a date with in a few days. The guy that I've been texting throughout the day…

"First let me start by asking, was there anything you didn't like?"

I curl my feet under me, taking time to consider his question. The only part I didn't like was when his finger wasn't inside of me and that doesn't feel like a good thing to tell him.

"I really enjoyed all of it," I admit. "I–I think I really liked the talking?"

He hums, his eyes fixed on mine. "Not all guys like to talk but it's kind of my thing," he winks. "And did–did you experience anything new?" I know he already knows the answer, but I find it sweet he's letting me lead the conversation.

"I think I," I motion towards my vagina, "you know? I–I don't really know for sure because that was the first time?"

He rubs his hand across his jaw as his eyes rake me up

and down. "Did you like how it felt, Q? What sent you over the edge?"

You.

I think about how it felt with Paul kissing me, his finger moving in and out as he called me a good girl. Hell yes I liked how it felt.

"It was the best feeling I've ever had," I confess. "I've been missing out."

He laughs as he looks up at the ceiling, "You have no idea, Q."

"I liked when you added another finger and I think neck kisses are a huge turn on for me." I'm shocked at how honest I'm being and how comfortable this feels. How natural it seems.

His phone vibrates on the sofa, lighting up the time. 1:30a.m…

"Holy fuck," he hops up, "I didn't realize it was so late. I– I have an early class tomorrow, Q-T. I should probably get home," he begins gathering his things.

I stand, helping him. "Is this your normal way to get out of a girl's house after hooking up?" I joke.

He stops dead in his tracks, walking over to me, pulling me into a hug. Not exactly what I was expecting.

"I'd be perfectly fine staying in your dorm always," he pulls away, holding my chin with his thumb. "I hope tonight didn't make things awkward for you. If you don't want to do another lesson like this, I understand. We can just hang out tomorrow?"

I gently shake my head. "I–I feel good with you, Paul. You're helping me discover myself. I couldn't thank you enough."

He bends down and places a gentle kiss on my cheek. "In case you didn't know, you made me feel good too, Q."

Chapter 35

Susie

"What's up with you, Suse?" Leah asks as she nudges me with her shoulder. "You seem…different? But not in a bad way!"

I can feel the heat creep up my neck as I say, "I think I am?"

Leah, Lucy, Clara and I are all at dinner on campus for our typical Monday night, and of course, Sara couldn't make it. Still, I love this tradition of ours.

And Leah isn't wrong, I do feel different. One, last night with Paul helped me learn more about myself in the bedroom than I could have ever imagined. Two, last night with Paul has me confused as hell.

Then I woke up to his text this morning.

PAULINE

Good morning sunshine. I hope you have a
good day, Q. See you tonight.

That feels a lot like a text message that would come from someone that likes you? Right?

Clara said it herself that the signs are there, but would she say the same knowing it's Paul? The one who's DNA is literally made up of flirting and swooning women? Throw on top a man who's caring and kind and you get yourself in a confusing situation.

I'm not confused on how I feel about Paul – that's simple. I'm confused about what to do.

"Oh my god!" Clara yells as she practically spits out her cheeseburger. "You two had sex, didn't you?!"

"No, no, no," I wave my hands in front of her face, "we didn't have sex!"

"But you did something?" Lucy asks with her too perfectly sculpted eyebrows raised to her hairline. "Spill the beans."

Absolutely not.

"Guys, I swear–"

"You don't have to tell us, Suse," Leah says. "But when you want to, we're here to listen," she leans over, kissing me on my cheek.

"Freshie, don't give her an easy out!"

"Again with the freshie shit?" Clara turns her head towards Lucy. "Give it up, babe."

"Never," she says as she steals a french fry from Clara's plate. "Now, back to you Suse. You don't have to tell us everything, although I am literally dying to know, but at least, like, a snippet?"

I know these girls, they won't let it go. But I've learned a thing or two from my teacher.

"I love you all very much but all I'm going to say is that I've never experienced anything like it in my life."

The absolute truth.

I–I still struggle to wrap my head around it myself. How good Paul Simmons made me feel. How intimate it was. The way he called me baby like he'd done it a thousand times and the feeling of his *excitement* all over me.

I told Paul Simmons to come all over my hand and he did. I did that…

And sure, afterwards was a bit awkward, but him wanting to talk it out solidified every reason as to why I felt safe doing these things with him.

I just hope things with Jamee feel the same as they do with Paul. And yes, I feel absolutely awful doing all of this knowing I'm going on a date in two days with another guy, but that's the whole purpose of Paul and I's arrangement…

Building up my self-confidence for our date? Check.

Finding out what I like in the bedroom and getting my nerves out of the way with my best friend? Getting there.

Enjoying the lessons with my extremely attractive hockey player best friend whom I happen to have feelings for? Also check.

* * *

"So…who do you think out of the boys has the biggest dick?"

All of our heads immediately snap in Lucy's direction as we exit the campus dining room. And before anyone says anything, we all break out hysterically laughing.

"Come on," Lucy adds. "We were all thinking it, I'm just the only one brave enough to ask."

"I can promise you I wasn't thinking it," Leah makes a gag face as she finishes her sentence. "One of the four we're talking about is my brother. I don't want to be involved–"

"Involved with what, darlin'?" Jake appears out of thin air, wrapping his arm around her.

"Ah, there's Mrs. Russell," Liam beams as he, Clay and Paul walk towards us.

I will never grow tired of seeing my best friend light up at the sound of her last name.

In a few swift steps, we're joined by the entire group on the campus lawn. As everyone, *except Lucy and Clay*, begin saying hi to one another, my eyes are stuck on the one in the Razers hat and grey sweats.

"Hey Q," Paul says with a cocky grin, "long time no see," he winks.

I can't help but roll my eyes at his comment; a lie only he and I know. He walks over, wrapping his arm around my shoulder as he usually does.

"This is my favorite color," he plays with the strap of my tank top. It's hot pink and I know for a fact that Paul's favorite color is a navy green because it's the color of the Razers logo.

"I thought green was your favorite color," I say as I pull down the front of his hat.

He turns his head towards my ear, looking over me as he softly says, "My favorite color is whatever you're wearing."

And I'm fairly positive someone brought out a heater because my whole body just warmed up.

"What were you guys up to?" Liam asks as he stands behind Clara, his arms wrapped around her stomach.

"We were just discussing some very important matters," Lucy answers. "Matters you boys can help us with."

"NO!" Leah yells.

Jake nuzzles her into his chest. "Sssh. Sshhh," he says while turning her head away. "What matters, Lucy?"

She looks at us girls and judging by the shit-eating grin on Clara's face, she wants this chaos just as much as Lucy. So, I shrug my shoulders as I look up at Paul.

"We were just discussing which one of you has the biggest package."

If there were ever a sentence to break the boys' brain, it was that one.

Paul immediately looks at me asking, "This was a discussion?"

"No," I say immediately. "She asked the question and then Jake showed up. No dicks were discussed and they don't need to be," I try to pull out of his embrace but his other arm reaches up, grabbing my arm and holding me tight against him.

"You're right Susie Q," he says with that stupidly attractive grin. "Mine wins."

And here it comes.

"Wait a fucking minute," Jake says. "We all know it's mine. Right darlin'? Tell them."

Leah's eyes look between Jake and Clay, her cheeks red.

"He referred to it the other night as the…trouser titan," she confesses, causing an uproar of laughter.

Jake chuckles as he leans down, placing a kiss on her temple. "What can I say? It's enor–"

"Fuck off, Wiley," Clay interjects. "I'm excluding myself from this conversation, you fucking weirdos."

"Or is it because your micropenis doesn't compare?" Lucy challenges as she crosses her arms across her chest, staring straight into Clay's soul.

"Ask the boys here who had to size up on hockey pants due to dick si–"

"La-la-la-la-la," Leah yells while she puts her fingers in her ears.

"I can promise you it wasn't any of these dickwads, sweetie," he winks at Lucy which earns him the middle finger. Her most common response.

Liam leans around, kissing Clara on the cheek as he says, "Should we go measure mine, C?"

"Sorry girls, see you tomorrow!"

Next thing I know, Jake is bent down, whispering in Leah's ear as she begins to giggle. "Uh, love you girls but I–I need to go with Wiley. It's our turn with Rocky!"

"And that's my cue," Lucy says. "Want a ride to your dorm, Suse?"

"You didn't want to test your theory?" Clay asks.

"Over my fucking dead body would I ever," she says.

He winks as he says, "Whatever you say, Lucy."

Paul looks at me and then to the other two. "I'll take her. I–I need to stop and grab something from a friend anyways."

"Does this friend come to the games in a Simmons jersey, scream your name and ask you to show her how you use your personal stick?" Lucy asks while opening her mouth, pointing her finger towards her tongue to act like she's gagging. "I'll never understand the hype of hockey players."

Paul shakes his head as he begins walking us away from Clay and Lucy, and I swear I can still hear them bickering.

He doesn't let go of me as we walk towards my dorm. Meanwhile, I'm trying to figure out who it is he needs to see and what it is he needs to grab?

And why do I feel jealous thinking about what Lucy said?

"Which dorm room?"

"Huh?" He asks as he moves his hand down to the lower part of my back, gently wrapping his hand around my waist.

"You said you needed to stop and grab something from someone?"

He smirks as he looks over at me. "It's lesson number two tonight, Q. My night consists of you and only you."

Chapter 36

Paul

I've been looking forward to tonight way too much.

Fucking christ…

After tonight we only have one more lesson. One more night of me having to act like this shit doesn't mean more.

Like this isn't something that's knocked me on my ass. Feelings I've never felt before, things I've never wanted all wrapped up in a five-foot-something, black-haired ray of sunshine.

"Paul?" Susie's sweet voice jolts me out of my thoughts. "Did you hear me?"

"Sorry, Q. I–I was in my head. What's up?" We haven't been in her dorm for more than five minutes and I'm already struggling to keep my head on straight. I think part of that is because ever since last night, I haven't been able to get her sexy fucking moans out of my mind or the way her hand fit perfectly around my dick. How her goddamn pussy felt when it tightened around my fin–

"I asked…uhh…what's–what's on tonight's agenda?"

The same question I've been racking my brain for since I

walked out of her dorm yesterday. I pause, thinking long and hard with what I want to say.

I don't think "come sit on my face so I can see just how good you taste" is an acceptable answer.

"Because I kind of had something I wanted to try?" she says innocently. Her cheeks are red, she won't look me in my eyes and her knee is shaking up and down. "But–but you have every right to say no, Paul."

She has no idea the things I would say yes to with her.

I nudge her knee with mine to get her attention, those gorgeous jaded eyes fix on mine with a nervous look on her face.

"I–I've never…had a guy like…go down on me?"

Oh holy fucking shit. God, if this is a test, I'm accepting failure now.

"You want me to go down on you, Q?"

Her already red cheeks burn brighter as she slowly nods her head up and down. "Only if you're comfortable with that?"

I chuckle as I stand. "Q-T, there isn't a thing in this world I wouldn't do for you." I hold out my hand which is immediately met by hers.

On the outside, I'm Paul Simmons – cool, calm and collected. On the inside, I'm fucking losing it. I fingered her, I came all over her hand like a twelve year old boy, yet here we are like everything is completely normal.

Like I'm not about to take one of Susie's first. And I hate to admit it, but some twisted asshole part of me loves knowing that I get this part of her.

And that same part of me gets pissed off knowing this is all for her to be comfortable doing this with Jamee, or whoever else the fuck she feels like doing this stuff with.

"Are you okay?" I feel a gentle hand on my shoulder as

we make it to her room. Turning, I see Susie with a soft smile on her face. "If you're having second thoughts–"

Fuck this.

I bend down, locking my lips to hers as my hands gently but forcefully cup her cheeks while I begin walking her backwards towards her bed. She kisses me back with as much eagerness as I have, nipping my bottom lip as her hands find their way under my shirt, attempting to lift it up over my head. I pull away enough to finish lifting it off, her cold fingers grazing over the contour of my abs as her eyes trace her every move.

"You're unbelievable," she breathes out. The compliment alone sends my dick throbbing.

I push her shoulders down to the bed so she's now sitting at the edge as I very slowly drop to my knees.

As I would any time she asks me to.

I run my palms from her feet all the way to her hips, hovering my fingers over the button of her jeans.

"Are you sure, Q? Once I have a taste of you, there's no going back."

I'll be ruined, I know it.

She brings her hand up to the hem of her shirt, lifting it over her head, leaning back on her palms. "I–I just don't know what to do? You'll...you'll have to tell me and–and please don't get upset if I don't, you know...from this. I don't know if I'll like it?"

I chuckle as I continue to work the button of her jeans, sliding the fabric down her legs leaving her in her underwear. I sit back on my heels as I take in the sight of Susie Cobble before me; the wetness coating her underwear, her chest rising and falling quickly. A sight I'll want to remember forever.

"Sit here and relax, baby. I'll teach you how every guy from here on out should make you feel."

I lean forward, placing a gentle kiss on the inside of her thighs, gently breathing out as I tease her.

Her hips roll as her hands find their way to the nape of my neck, pulling me flush to her. Cautiously, I bring my finger up her body, pulling her panties to the side revealing the prettiest fucking pussy I've ever seen. Glistening wet, pink and ready.

"What's the rule?"

I feel her tap my shoulder two times.

"Good girl. Now, lean back and let me feast on what I know will become my favorite fucking dinner."

The plan is to go slow. To let her discover what she likes, what makes her feel good. My tongue darts out swiping up her wet slit, her salty taste coating my tongue.

"Paul…that feels so go-good."

And I know for a goddamn fact that the only time I've loved hearing my name is when it's falling from Susie's lips.

I continue with what she likes, only pausing to stop and suck on her clit, my dick aching in response to her moans. I keep at a steady pace, lapping up every fucking drop she has to give. And when my eyes look up, I'm met with the most jaw-dropping view. At some point, Susie took her bra off and she's lying in front of me completely bare. Her nipples rock hard, her boobs sitting perfectly, practically begging for my mouth.

I pull back to look at the beautiful girl in front of me as I wipe my mouth with the back of my hand. "Holy shit."

She shoots up, immediately covering herself. "I–I can put my shirt back on," she reaches beside her. My hand immediately finds her wrist.

"You're a goddamn goddess on earth," I lean in, placing a

gentle kiss on her lips when all of a sudden, I feel a tear hit my cheek.

"Susie? What's wrong?"

She chuckles as she reaches up to wipe under her eye. "I–I just haven't ever felt as beautiful and sexy as I do right now with you looking at me like this. I'm...I'm most insecure about my boobs," she confesses.

"Why in the hell would you be insecure about such a breathtaking body?" My mind can't grasp the concept.

"Because that's what happened to me in high school, Paul. A–a guy untied my bikini top and flashed me to everyone at a party. They all–" her voice wavers. "They all pointed and laughed at me. *Who'd want to date an ugly girl with an ugly body,*" another tear escapes her eye. "And here you are, making me feel like I'm the most gorgeous girl you've ever seen."

I reach up, swiping the tear away from her face with my thumb. "You are the most gorgeous girl I've ever seen, Susie."

I'm trying to focus on the moment, but all I can see is red. All I can feel is piping hot anger at whatever asshole decided to dim Susie's light all those years ago. I'll dim the light in his eyes if I ever see him.

"What that asshole did is fucking disgusting, Q. I–I can't even begin to imagine how that affected you, how it hurt you. But I know one thing," I push her hair back from her forehead, "you are the toughest fucking girl I know. The sunshine on a cloudy day. The most gorgeous woman I've ever laid my eyes on. What you went through, what that prick did..." my voice breaks. "I'd fucking kill him if I ever had the chance, Susie."

"I know," she says quietly. "It broke me, but I–I've been

healing piece by piece, and you…" she sniffles. "You're healing the rest of me, Paul."

"That–that isn't because of me, Q. That's all you, baby."

"I didn't mean to ruin the moment," she chuckles. "I–I understand if we need to pause the lesson."

I hover over her lips as I say, "Fuck that."

I start with kissing her forehead and begin making my way down her entire body. I'm in no rush, I want to savor every moment, every moan, every sound.

When I make it to her nipple, I stop, my tongue rolling each one around before I take the entirety of it in my mouth.

"Oh fuuck…"

"You like that baby?"

"Mhmm," she manages to hum.

I give one final tug with my teeth before continuing my trail of kisses down her body. And when I make it back to Heaven between her thighs, I can't help it. My tongue moves in a frenzy like I'm a starved man as I bring one finger up, teasing her entrance. The other reaches up, taking her nipple in between my thumb and pointer finger.

"Holy shit," she says in a raspy voice. "More. Pl–please, Paul."

So I do. I push my finger all the way inside as I continue licking and sucking, her nipple hard enough to cut glass. And when I curve my finger just like last night, I know she's close. She's grinding her pussy against my face, her thighs squeezing my head as my name continues to fall from her lips.

"Fuck, Q," I slightly lean back as I watch my finger work her. "You're so fucking breathtaking like this."

I lower my face, my tongue circling her clit as she wraps her hands tighter in my hair, legs quivering.

"Paul. I–I think–"

"That's it, baby. Come all over my face. Let me taste how fucking perfect you are."

As if that's all she needed to hear, her hips buck up, thighs trembling as her pleasure explodes and just like I thought, it's the best taste I've ever had. A taste I could never get enough of. As I make sure to not miss a single fucking drop, her panting slows as she relaxes into the bed.

"Holy shit," she says.

"Holy shit is right." I stand, my dick sore from how hard it is. "I'll be right–" but before I can finish the sentence her hands are in my waistband pulling down my sweats.

"Q, what are you doing?"

Her innocent eyes look up at me saying nine words that send me spiraling. "I want to do it all with you, Paul."

Chapter 37

Paul

I suppose this was what everything was leading up to. I just...I wasn't prepared for how I'd feel when those words left her mouth. I was supposed to have one more night to mentally prepare for having her in a way that I shouldn't.

Her hands work fast as she pulls my sweats down my thighs, and as I watch her take her bottom lip between her teeth, part of me wonders if this is more for her too?

Is there any possibility Susie Cobble could have feelings for *me*?

The fuckboy who's never dated with mommy issues?

Of course not, she's turned on just like I am...this is strictly an arrangement for her.

But it isn't for me and it hasn't been for a while...and I can't do this without her knowing that.

"Susie," I say as I grab her wrist. "We-we can't." I mean to go on, to explain, but my sentence stops there.

For some fucking reason, I can't open my mouth to tell her how I feel.

Her face falls as she yanks her wrist back. "You don't want to?"

The opposite, baby. I want you in ways I've never wanted anyone before.

My sweats are halfway down my thighs as I stand here gathering my thoughts. Trying to figure out exactly what to say.

"I–I'm sorry. This...this was a mistake," she says as she scurries up from the bed putting her clothes on.

I pull my sweats up as I ask, "What was a mistake?"

She motions to the bed, "Me asking you to do that... we've done plenty. Enough for me to feel comfortable in the bedroom. Enough for me to know what I like and want with others and you're right. I think that's where we should stop, we don't need to cross the last line."

That line was crossed a long time ago.

"I think we end things here," she says confidently. "Not our friendship of course, but–but this," she points between us. "The lessons? I–I truly feel like a better version of myself because of you Paul. And I have my date with Jamee in two days and–and I think it'll go well. I feel better...should something between us happen."

"Q–" I try to interject, to explain my hesitancy. I don't know what is happening here but I don't fucking like it. I'm not ready for our nights like this to end...

She walks up to me, wrapping her arms around my waist in a tight hug. "Really. You've done enough for me, Paul. I–I can't thank you enough for helping me with these things. For being someone I could trust with a huge broken part of me," she rests her chin on my chest looking up at me. "You are the greatest friend I have ever had. I mean...you just had your head between my thighs," she chuckles.

The greatest friend. The greatest reminder of what this is to her.

Which is why I say nothing about how I feel.

Shit. I have become Liam fucking Russell.

I peel away from the hug, doing my best to put on my typical cocky grin. "A teacher is only as great as their student," I wink. "I'm glad I was able to help you, Q. I–I'll never forget this little…arrangement of ours."

She reaches her hand up, cupping my cheek as her eyes meet mine and I think I need to see a doctor. Why? My heart just stopped for a fraction of a second.

"There's so much more to you than Barker's playboy, Paul Simmons. And–and I hope one day that the girl you decide to let in sees that in you."

She does.

"I suppose I should head out," I stick out my hand just like I did a few weeks ago when this began. "Can we make a new deal?"

Her eyebrows quirk up with an intrigued look on her face.

"I don't want this to change anything. I want to watch movies with you and eat takeout. I want to hear about your paintings and listen to you gripe about practice. I–I want to still hang out without needing an arrangement to do so."

I watch as her adorable fucking dimples appear.

"I would love that."

Chapter 38

Susie

"Wow," Jamee says as he stands next to his car, "you–you look beautiful, Susie."

I can feel my cheeks heat at his compliment because holy crap does this man look good. He's in black jeans with a grey button up that hugs his biceps nicely with the top button undone.

"Thank you," I say as I stop in front of him. His sandalwood and vanilla cologne surrounding me. We haven't seen each other since our date last Friday; practices have been insane but we've talked almost every day.

"Thank *you*," he repeats as he bends down, planting a kiss on my cheek, "for being my date."

And as I sit in his car, I smile and nod along as he tells me about his week. I laugh at his jokes and admire how gorgeous he looks from the side. Physically, I'm present.

Mentally, I am not.

Because just like the last two days, my mind has been consumed by Paul Simmons.

How I asked him to have sex with me…how badly I wanted to. *Want to.*

And how he told me we couldn't. Any small hope I had that just maybe this man had or was beginning to have feelings died with that statement.

I know it was for the best. I know I was in over my head asking while I had fallen for him. I don't know how our friendship would've survived giving that part of myself to him. Hell, it's probably already damaged.

He said he didn't want it to change anything and I agreed, but how could it not?

Because now I can't stop thinking about him. I can't help that the last two nights my mind has drifted to the feeling of his fingers inside me. How I can still hear him calling me a *good girl*. How for the first time in my life I got myself off last night while imagining him between my legs.

But it's not just that part of Paul Simmons I find myself thinking about. I think about the boy who loves his Meme above everyone. I think about his childhood and how if I ever had the chance, I'd give his piece of shit mom an earful. How he's the greatest friend to the guys and girls, but most importantly to me.

I'm thinking about Paul Simmons while I'm on a date with someone else, wishing it was him.

"Something on your mind, Suse?"

My head snaps towards Jamee, worried that may not have all been in my head.

"Wha–what?"

He grins as he pulls into the restaurant; a fancy, over-priced steakhouse he chose. Not that anything's wrong with that, I'm just not deserving.

"Long day," I say as I step out of his car in my blue jeans and skin tight black body suit.

"Well," he says as he holds the door open for me. "Let's get you some food so I can hear all about it."

So we do. And I thought that as the date would go on, that I'd get out of my head. I've been telling myself that for the last forty-five minutes…

I hear him talking about the upcoming game and how he's currently number one in receptions. The top spot he's recently taken over since Chase Ryker, Clara's ex, switched positions. Apparently, Barker's previous quarterback suffered a horrendous knee injury and Chase took over last year, securing his new spot and giving Jamee the star receiver role. I intently listen to him describe him and Chase's friendship, and I answer the questions he asks me about cheer and Daytona.

But I don't feel the sparks I felt with Paul. It doesn't feel as easy. Our silence is uncomfortable and I feel like I need to fill it with conversation.

Don't get me wrong, Jamee is amazing and kind and as sexy as they come.

But I fell for my best friend and–and I don't know how to get over that. I know dragging someone like Jamee along isn't the answer.

"Jamee," I interrupt as the waitress walks away. "I'm–"

"Not interested?" He finishes for me with a soft chuckle. "Gotta say, Suse. This is a first for me," he pushes his shaggy blonde hair back. "You look like you've had something on your mind all night. Clearly it's not how amazing this date is," he teases, "so what's up?"

"I'm so, so sorry. You're amazing and hot and literally any girl would be lucky to be on a date right now with you. And–and I was interested. I suppose I still kind of am but–"

"There's someone else?" He asks, nodding his head up and down. "Well, fuck. Who's the lucky bastard?"

I peer up through my lashes, too afraid to tell him the truth.

"I see," he says as he reaches for his wallet. I grab his hand as I pull my card out.

"I can cover mine. This–this was expensive for you to get nothing out of it. I wasn't even a good date, we're literally talking about my crush right now."

He laughs as he swats my hand away. "If anything, I gained a new friend and that's good enough for me."

Damn. If only every guy handled rejection like Jamee Locke.

"So, he doesn't know?"

I shake my head back and forth.

"You have to tell him, Susie."

Sighing, I sit back in my chair. "I–I can't tell him."

"Why not?"

"Because he's like my best friend. Is my best friend…and I don't want to ruin that."

He stands, holding out his hand. "Is there any part of you that thinks he may feel the same?"

We're walking towards his car as my phone vibrates and I can feel my pulse pick up as I see the name across my screen.

And then I'm immediately brought back to reality.

PAULINE

Hope the date is going good, Q. Call me if
you need anything. I'm here.

I turn the phone towards Jamee, making sure to cover the name. "Would someone who has feelings wish you luck on your date?" I huff as he squints his eyes to read the message. I get into the car, shutting the door behind me, watching him chuckle as he walks around the front.

"Why are you laughing?" I angle my body towards his, arms crossed tightly with a deadpan look on my face.

"Because the obvious answer is yes, Suse. If he's your best friend, he's going to support you."

"But if he was into me, why wouldn't he tell me before the date?"

"Did you?"

I open my mouth to protest but immediately snap it shut. I suppose he has a point but how do I tell if a guy likes me if I'm the one that asked him to do all these things? How do I know if it was real versus him simply being my teacher?

"Has he ever done anything that has made you think he likes you?"

I take a deep breath in as I go into the story of Paul and I, being careful to leave his name out of the equation. How it started with us, with our *arrangement*. How it was always me pushing for more, asking for more and how he simply obliged – helped me. I even talk about our latest *lessons*.

As he's pulling up to my dorm he cuts the engine. "Suse. I'd bet money that this guy has had feelings for you since before the lessons turned more *personal*," he uses air-quotations around the word. "You need to talk to him. Let him know you passed up on Barker's most eligible and sought after football player for him," he winks.

I chuckle, thinking about his words, knowing I should tell Paul how I've come to feel even if he doesn't feel the same way. I need to be honest with him.

"I bet this wasn't the date you had in mind, huh?"

"I thought we'd be making out in the back seat of my car by now," he laughs. "But honestly? This hasn't been so bad. I'm going to sound like a bitch when I say this but having a female friend is nice. I mean...I know this is literally our second date turned non-date, but I think by helping you out with your little situation that automatically makes me your friend."

"Well then," I stick my hand out, "until next time, friend?"

He slides his hand into mine with a gigantic smile across his face. "See you next game, Suse. Better still cheer for me."

"What else are friends for?"

* * *

It's been thirty minutes since what was supposed to be an amazing date with Jamee came to an end. But as I'm lying in bed, I have time to be honest with myself.

And the truth is that from the moment Paul and I kissed, I knew the date didn't matter to me anymore. I told myself it did, I tried my hardest to convince myself that if I could just go, fall for a nice, attractive man, I'd get Paul off my mind… all would be good.

Boy was I an idiot.

The only positive to come from this whole shitty situation is that I gained a new friend in an unexpected turn of events.

And now I have to make a decision. Do I–

I'm interrupted from my thoughts by the sound of my phone ringing; a FaceTime request from Clara. I knew she'd be calling tonight, I was just hoping to have my thoughts together beforehand.

Still, her face filling the screen with her auburn hair pulled up in a messy bun is enough to put a smile on my face.

"Bestieeeeeeee," she squeals. "Tell me everything! Was he sweet? Did he treat you well? Did you two fuck? Is it true that he has a way with his–"

"C, baby. Just a reminder your husband is here," Liam leans into the frame. "Please don't answer that for her, Suse."

I wave, laughing at the pained expression on Liam's face. An expression that quickly changes when Clara leans into his ear, whispering lord knows what because he immediately begins ogling his wife.

"Continue," she says, not looking at me.

"I–uh…it went…great," I manage to say, as if that was convincing at all.

Both Liam and Clara look at me, their eyes narrowed.

"That sounded like a load of shit, Suse," Liam says.

"Was it not a good date?" Clara asks, pushing Liam out of the frame.

"Hey, I was talking to her too," I hear him whine as he reaches for the phone, and in the chaos of them fighting, more voices appear.

I should've known everyone would be there…

"Suse," Leah presses her cheek to Clara's, "what happened?"

Then Jake appears behind them. "Darlin', she may not want to talk about it right now," he waves. "Hey Suse, sorry to hear it didn't go well."

"We tell each other everything," Leah says with a wink.

Everything except for how I messed up and got in over my head with Paul Simmons.

"I never said it didn't go well?"

"You might as well have," Clara adds. "What happened? Just a couple of days ago we were talking about how the dude was calling you beautiful and sharing past trauma and shit–"

"What did you just say?"

All of their heads immediately turn to the right, following the voice that just two nights ago was whispering in my ear.

"About?" Clara asks.

"Did you just say how he shared his trauma?"

"Oh, that?" She looks at me and the others. "Yeah, Suse here was asking how to tell if a guy likes her and gave some examples of things he had said along with how he shared some deep level shit. I told her that it sounded like the dude was into her but she's saying her date didn't go well so we're…" she trails off.

"Yo, where are you going?" Jake yells towards their door.

"Everything okay?" I hear Liam ask as he goes to stand up, followed by Clay.

"Can you stop by Checker's on the way back, bud?"

I can't see Paul in the frame but I hear him answer. "Everything's fine. I'll–I'll be back soon. I just realized I forgot part of my homework at the locker room and needed to run to the library to finish some shit."

"You know where the library is?" Clay asks.

"No Checker's for you, fuck face."

Not shortly after he finishes his sentence, the front door slams and everyone begins looking around at one another, probably just as confused as I am.

Liam begins scratching his forehead as he says, "What the fuck just happened?"

"Fuck if I know," Jake says as he wraps his arm around Leah. "The dude's been MIA and we all know something was on his mind the other day at practice. He was dog shit, and he's never dog shit."

"Okay," Clara stands with the phone. "Y'all keep chatting about Paulie and figure out what's going on. I'm going to listen to my girl's date night."

And then it dawns on me.

Does Paul think I shared his trauma?

No, no, no.

"Actually," I say as I begin hustling around the dorm, "I–I need to go. I'll fill you in tomorrow but," I fake yawn, "I'm pretty tired, Clare Bear."

"But–"

"I love you guys, talk to you tomorrow!"

I quickly hang up the phone, pulling on my sweats and sweatshirt as I call Paul. I don't know if I'm right, but I have to make sure he knows I didn't share anything he told me.

Please pick up. Please pick up.

Nothing. Straight to voicemail. He's ignoring my calls… but can I blame him? He trusted me, opened up to me, and he thinks I took that for granted.

Three more times and still nothing. Finally on the fourth I decide to leave a voicemail.

Paul, it's Q. I–I know what Clara said and how it sounded but I swear I didn't share anything you told me. I did lie to you but not about that and–and if I could just explain to you what I mean I think it would clear this up.

I swing the door open, hustling downstairs to make my way to the library in hopes that he actually is there studying. I should probably take some time to think about what I'm going to say. To understand that by me telling him how I've felt I may be driving a stake through our friendship, but I rather that happen than he believes that I shared the deepest parts of him.

By the time I make it to the library, I'm slightly sweaty and embarrassingly tired. Coach Hawkins would kill me if she saw how that jog wore me out.

As I hastily look around the library, going up and down the floors in every study corner, my heart sinks a bit further because he's not here. My second guess would be the practice arena but students can't get in after hours, so…I truthfully have no freaking clue where he could be.

He hasn't called back and he hasn't responded to any text messages.

So, with nothing else to do except hope that he gets my pathetic voicemail and gives me the time of day, I start my trek back to the dorm room, with plenty of time to practice the things I would say if I could.

I promise this arrangement didn't start because I liked you. I truly needed help and felt comfortable with that person being you. It wasn't like I went into this expecting to fall for my best friend.

Strong start.

But everything changed after our first kiss. Things weren't fake anymore, and I should have told you instead of asking you to help me with more. But I got to know Paul Simmons and there's so much more than the star hockey goalie. I fell for every part of you and didn't know how to tell you, but here I am.

I have literally resorted to practice conversations in my head…

Shaking my head at myself, I drag my feet up the stairs and down the hall, pulling out my phone. Still nothing–

"Susie?"

Chapter 39

Paul

Two fucking days.

That's how long it's been since I walked out of Susie Cobble's dorm like everything was normal between us. Like I was still faking this shit and completely fine walking away from it.

"You are the greatest friend I have ever had."

Fuck me.

This wasn't supposed to happen. It goes against everything I've always wanted; keep them at a distance and they can't hurt you.

I suppose I didn't account for someone like Q to walk in my life.

A girl who made it easy to share parts about me I always try to hide. A girl who sees me as more than the fuckboy.

I spent two days trying to convince myself this is how it's supposed to be with her and I. Hell, I even texted her good luck on her date, and I meant it. Susie Cobble is sunshine, *my sunshine,* and she deserves happiness. And at first I told myself that if that's Jamee, then it would be okay. I could sit back and watch her fall in love if she's happy.

But then I overheard Clara and it seemed like too much of a fucking coincidence. Calling her beautiful, talking about trauma? That's not Jamee, that's *me*. Which means Susie was talking about us.

What was she talking about? I don't fucking know. That's the reason I'm sitting outside her dorm room right now in full fucking panic mode because what in the hell am I supposed to say when I see her?

And where the hell is she? I booked it over here when she was on FaceTime with Clara and now she's gone? Maybe she went to talk with Jamee? Maybe I was wrong about this whole fucking thing and it *was* him she talked to Clara about?

My head is spiraling because clearly I've never been in this situation before. Caring about a girl, in my head about if she likes me or not? It's always been simple for me: fuck her, give her the best orgasm of her life, and then it's over. No texting afterwards, no checking-in, no repeats.

But these last two weeks with Susie changed…everything. And maybe it hasn't changed a single fucking thing for her, but I have to know and I have to tell her. I will not go down in history as being a Liam Russell and letting the girl make the first move.

I pull out my phone, not realizing it's been on *do not disturb* the entire time. Four missed calls, one voicemail and several text messages – a few from the *BUFHP* chat but mostly all from Susie. I scan through them, all of them mentioning something about how she swears she didn't tell Clara my secrets but it's the voicemail I care about.

As I press play and bring the phone to my ear, I don't make it more than four words in when she appears at the top of the stairs with her head fixed on the floor.

Fucking breathtakingly gorgeous as ever in her sweats and oversized sweatshirt with her short hair pulled back in a claw-looking thing. I immediately shoot to my feet, and before I can think about what I want to say, her name leaves my mouth like it's been waiting for her.

"Susie?"

Her head snaps up and for a moment, I lose my breath. Her eyes are wide as she stares at me, phone gripped tightly in her hand, but she stays planted where she is, clearly not sure what to do.

And neither am I, but here it goes.

"I–I know this looks pretty fucking weird but–"

"I didn't tell Clara anything you told me," she interjects, still staying locked in place. "I swear I would never share about your mom or how she made you feel, Paul. You're– you're my best friend and I wouldn't do that to you."

My brows pinch together as I take a step closer to her. "What are you talking about, Q?"

She begins nervously fidgeting with her sweatshirt, rolling her bottom lip in between her teeth. "When Clara said I told her about Jamee sharing his trauma? I heard you asking her what she was talking about and then you left," she begins shaking her head. "I–I was indirectly talking about you, but I never mentioned anything about what you shared with me. I...I needed you to know that."

A smile spreads across my face, stupidly big, but I don't give a fuck. She was talking about me. She was thinking about me. Now, to find out why.

"You're...you're smiling?"

Fuck yes I am baby.

It never even crossed my mind that Susie may have shared about my mom. I trust this girl as much as I trust the guys. Hell, probably even Meme.

Stepping closer I ask, "You were talking about me? You know what that does to my ego right, Q-T?"

A faint smirk touches her lips. "That's what you care about?" This time, she steps closer. We aren't close enough to touch yet, but if the whole electricity shit is real, I'm feeling it. I want nothing more than to reach out and pull her into me, showing her how I feel, why I'm here.

"Why were you talking about me, Q?"

Her cheeks immediately redden as she begins to chew on the inside of her lip. I'm not entirely sure what she wants to say, but whatever it is, it's making her nervous.

"A truth for a truth?" I ask just like before.

"You first?"

I move to where I'm standing directly in front of her, my heart fucking racing. Maybe it's a heart attack? I don't fucking know. I've never even experienced this feeling at games so it's very possible I'm dying.

"You know I'm a flirt, right?"

She scoffs as she rolls her eyes. "Like it's built in your DNA."

"Possibly," I shrug. "And you know I've never wanted more, right? Sure, I thought maybe one day in the future I could," I reach my hand behind, scratching the nape of my neck as I search for the right words. "Excuse me for my bluntness, but fucking around was perfectly fine with me, Q. I didn't care to share myself with one girl for the time being."

I watch as her eyes scan my face, her expression almost… hurt?

Shit, I'm fucking this up.

I take a deep breath, exhaling as I say, "And then this fucking arrangement started and my head hasn't been straight since."

Reaching out, I grab her hips, gently pushing her against the wall. Her breath hitches as she latches onto my bicep.

"What–what are you–"

"It's never been a secret that I flirt with you, Q. And at first that's all it was…my normal asshole, cocky personality. But these damn lessons," my hand reaches up, cupping her cheek and bringing my forehead to hers. "It's not fake for me anymore, Q. The whole teacher shit ended a long time ago. I can't get you out of my head. I can't stop thinking about you. I can't stop fucking missing you."

Her eyes are closed like she's soaking up every word.

"I–I don't know how to do this whole feelings thing but I need you to know that the other night when I stopped you…it wasn't because I didn't want you. Fuck, Susie. All I can think about is how much I want you. But–but it wasn't just about me helping you anymore." Her eyes fly open as they peer up at me, bouncing back and forth as they search my face.

"It hadn't been about that for me since the moment we almost kissed. And–and I should've said something before, I know that. I shouldn't have let it get this far without you knowing how I felt, but I promised to help you and above everything, you feeling confident was what mattered most, plus the whole date with Jamee–"

"Paul?" Her soft voice cuts through the air. "Are–are you saying you're…into me?" I feel her hand tighten its grip.

Bending down, I lean close to her as I whisper in her ear.

"I'm so fucking into you, Susie Cobble."

The smile that stretches from ear to ear is all I need.

"Q?"

Her breathing is heavy and I can practically feel the rise and fall of her chest pressed against mine. "Yeah?" She says in a heavy voice.

"Can I kiss you now? Not as your teacher or some fake ass lesson, but as Paul Simmons. Barker University's hockey goalie hotshot with mommy issues?"

One gentle nod is all it takes for me to fist my hands into her hair, pulling her tight to me.

A kiss that feels a lot like home.

We stay like that for a moment, soaking it in before a throat behind us clears, causing both of us to quickly turn our heads.

"You guys are in front of my door," the redhead says. "Can you move, please?"

Chuckling, I pull away as I slide my hand into Susie's and start pulling her towards her room.

"My bad, I've missed my girl."

Susie's head snaps up to mine with a twinkle in her eye. "Your girl?"

I open the door, pulling Susie in and only letting go to lock the deadbolt. Turning around, I see her standing there with her fingers combing through her hair.

Fuck, did I let that slip?

"I mean–"

She turns around, walking to her room giving me the perfect view of just how good she looks in sweats. Right before she enters her room, she turns around saying, "A truth for a truth, right?"

Chapter 40

Paul

In four strides I'm standing outside her room, leaning against the doorframe watching her as she takes a seat on her bed.

Is my heart still racing? Fuck yes it is. I don't know if that's from waiting to hear what she has to say or the blood pumping through me from that goddamn kiss.

"The truth is that I've–I've had feelings towards you for…a while now."

There's that heart thing again. *I really need to make an appointment with my doctor.*

My brow quirks up as I walk in, taking a seat next to her. "Describe a while, Q."

She moves so she's facing me, her legs underneath her. "It didn't start that way but…I knew I had feelings for you before I asked you to help me with more lessons…" she trails off as she begins twirling a strand of hair. "I didn't want to say anything and ruin everything, plus I was doing all this for a date and thought that I'd give it a shot and see how things went with Jamee–"

"You've known for that long?"

"Honestly, I think it's when you started to open up to me. I've known Paul Simmons the hockey player, but getting to know Paul Simmons, the guy who loves his Meme? The guy who did everything in his power to help me? Yeah, it was super freaking easy to fall for him. Not to mention that first kiss really sealed my fate," she chuckles.

"And then when things started turning physical, I was torn. I was afraid if I told you after all that, it would break our friendship, and I didn't want to lose you," she places her hand on my thigh. "You're my best friend, Paul. But you're also so much more."

I stand, placing myself in front of her, leaning down with both hands beside her.

"What does that mean, Q?"

She leans back, enough to where our lips are mere inches from each other.

"It means that this stopped being fake for me a long time ago. It means I'm into you, too. It means that I really like hearing you call me your girl."

And fuck do I like knowing she is. But also, does this mean we're dating? Did I just make her my girlfriend without even asking like a proper gentleman?

She chuckles and I realize how it's easily become my favorite fucking sound.

"I can see your mind racing," she reaches up, gently touching my temple. "We–we don't have to label this," she points between the two of us, "I–I like you, you like me and we can figure the rest out?"

I click my tongue on the roof of my mouth as I grab her chin. I want to tell her fuck that, as long as it's with her, I'll gladly do the labels. But I also have no idea how to be a boyfriend…and I want to be the best she's ever had.

"Fuck yes I like you, Q, And I want you to know that

even without labels, you're my girl. The only girl. And should a fucker try to mess with what's mine, I will use my hockey stick as a personal spear to kill him."

"Wow. Paul Simmons is a softie," she laughs as her hand travels down to my sweats, toying with the string. "I knew it."

"Maybe," I grab her hand, moving it over my rock hard dick, "but most of the time, around you, I'm hard."

Okay well, that sounded a lot creepier than I meant. *Come on Paul, get your shit together.*

"Shit. Fuck. Not like, not like I'm *always* hard around you. I–I'm not some crazed high school boy just walking around thinking of all the ways I want to make you scream my name. I mean, yes. I do think that, a lot. But also, like just normal shit too. My dick isn't always just on stand by waiting–"

"Paul?" Her green eyes bounce between mine.

"Yeah, Q?" I ask as I clear my throat.

"You can stop rambling now."

Her eyes trail down my body as she palms the bulge pressed against my sweats. Immediately, my eyes roll back. Who knew you could miss a simple fucking touch so much? And when I open them, I see Susie eyeing my dick like she's starved for it. Like she's missed this as much as I have, biting her bottom lip while her hand is moving back and forth over my sweats.

There is nothing more that I want than to pick up right where we left off, but I need her to know that's not what this is for me.

"Q-T, I want you to know we could sit and watch a movie and I'd be perfectly fucking happy. Just because we did these types of things for your lessons doesn't mean–"

"You know," she says as she moves her hand to the

bottom of her sweatshirt, stripping it off. "My teacher once said that I should say what's on my mind. That confidence is about being in charge and telling people how it is," she throws her sweatshirt to the side, revealing what I hoped.

Nothing underneath…

"Fuck." The word comes out deep and quiet as I take in the sight of how breathtakingly gorgeous she is.

"I want you, Paul. Not as Susie Cobble, the girl you're helping, but as Susie Cobble, your girl."

Four words that send my mind into a frenzy because holy fuck do I want *my* girl.

"I don't think you know what you're asking for, baby," I whisper into her neck as I run my fingers down her belly and into her sweats, her slickness coating my finger. I pull away, just enough so she can see me as I bring that same finger to my mouth. My eyes never leave hers as I suck her taste off me.

"I walked away once but that won't happen again, Q. You're stuck with me and this," I slide my finger back down her sweats, this time gently pushing inside her. "You? I want you all to myself."

She moans as my finger pumps in and out of her, and I take back what I said earlier. Her laughter is *one* of my favorite sounds, but hearing Susie moan my name? Pure fucking Heaven.

"I'm…" she takes in a sharp breath when my second finger slips inside her. "Oh fuckkkk."

I pull both out, circling her sensitive clit with one as I repeat myself. "Say you're all mine, Susie."

It's not a question because there's no option – it's her and me. And yes, I realize that makes me sound like a crazy obsessed asshole, but for Susie, I am.

I can't promise I won't beat a motherfucker for so much as looking at her.

"I'm…" her nails move to my back, gliding up and down, desperate to touch me. "I'm all yours."

Without a second thought, I sink to my knees, prepared to take my sweet ass time with *my* girl.

My hands wrap around her waistband as I pull her sweats down. I begin placing lazy kisses on the inside of her thighs as she goes to lean back on the bed, but before she can, I grab her wrist.

"Oh no, baby," I move my hand down her leg, grabbing her ankle and tossing it over my shoulder. "Suffocate me and I'll die a happy man."

She hesitates for a moment and I can see the rush of nerves flood her face. My sweet, sexy girl.

"Susie, there's only one thing I love more than hockey and that's your sweet fucking pussy. Throw that leg over my shoulder and let me show you just how much."

"Such a gentleman," she teases, cautiously draping her leg gently over my shoulder.

I reach my hands around, grabbing her ass and pulling her flush to my face.

"I haven't tasted you in two days and I'm going out of my goddamn mind."

She doesn't get a word out before I bury my face in her sweet scent, my tongue darting out lapping up all her wetness, each lick met with a moan of approval. Her hands dart to my hair as she wraps her fingers at the base, guiding my head with the pace she wants, pushing and pulling me where she wants my mouth.

"Fuuuuck Q," I lean back, looking up at her. She's panting, her eyes heavy as she desperately moves her hips for friction.

"Pauuulll."

I hover right above her clit, breathing out a heavy breath as I grin. "Yes, baby?"

"I–I need you."

I lean down, gently sucking before pulling back again. "Need what? Tell me what you want, Q."

"I want your mouth and your finger," she says without hesitation.

No need to tell me twice; I'll give this girl anything she asks of me. I go back to before, except this time, I add my finger and stay with a steady pace of pumping in and out.

"Oh…oh my god…"

"You're so fucking perfect. I could feast on you all day every day and never grow tired of this, Q."

I pick up speed, twisting my finger the way she likes and I can feel her pussy immediately tighten around my finger. Her hands are holding my head tight to her as she begins grinding against my tongue.

"Fuck," I grit through my teeth, trying to think of anything but how I'm about to come in my sweats. "Ride my face, baby. Come all over me."

Adding a second finger, she begins fucking my face harder and faster, but when I bring my thumb up to massage circles around her clit, she loses all control. My name falls from her lips as she clenches around my finger, pulsing as her legs tighten around my back.

"Give it all to me, baby."

I keep going, not slowing down as she rides out her orgasm, until her legs go limp against me and she lays down backwards, exhausted.

Slowly, I begin climbing over her, hovering above her perfect body with my dick at attention. Bending down, I place a tender kiss on her forehead. "You okay, Q-T?"

No words come out of her mouth, only a mumble of *"mhmm."*

Laughing, I roll beside her to adjust myself, and also because I don't fucking know what to do now? Usually, I leave or I kick the girl out. And before tonight with Susie, there were no expectations for the after. But now? It's not exactly a *"well, bye"* situation.

Do I…cuddle?

Do I thank her for what just happened?

Do we talk more about our…um…feelings?

Fuck it.

Carefully, I drape my hand over her stomach as I face her, drawing circles on her chest. Entirely out of my comfort zone, but still content.

"Is–is this okay?"

"You were amazing," she says with her eyes still closed. Chuckling, I bury my face in her neck.

"I meant my cuddling skills, Q."

Her eyes shoot open as she sits up.

"Paul Simmons," she faces me, "have you never cuddled before?"

I shrug my shoulders as I lift my hands behind my head. "There's a first for everything, Q-T, and I'm pretty fucking glad you're my first for this."

"One could say the teacher has become the student," she lays back down, this time facing me. "I'm a pro-cuddler. The girls say so all the time during our sleep overs," she chuckles.

She brings her hand up, running her nails up and down my jaw line. "You know you're pretty handsome?"

I lean forward, placing a kiss on the tip of her nose. "The boys have admitted to me being the best looking out of them all, but hearing it come from you sounds so much better."

She throws her head back laughing. Her short hair messy

from the claw thing and her face still flushed from the last few minutes. "Is this insane? You know you're like one of my best friends?"

I run my fingers up and down her back, thinking about her question. Is it insane that Susie Cobble and I are…whatever we are? Yes. I would have never guessed this shit would be real.

"Our friends may shit a fucking brick, but I don't give a damn. There's no one else I would rather be insane with than you, Susie Cobble."

"I like insane with you," her fingers slip underneath my sweats and into my boxers, gently grazing my happy trail. "In fact, it's insane that we never finished our last lesson, yeah?"

"Susie," I warn.

"Paul?" She mimics as her hand wraps tightly around my cock.

"Fuck me," I grit out.

"Yes, please," her voice is barely above a whisper. And as I look down at her jade-green eyes peering up at me, I don't see the girl who struggled with her confidence, I see a girl who's sure of herself.

"You know you're pretty fucking beautiful?" I ask as I sit up, taking my shirt off.

She doesn't answer, instead, she gets comfortable underneath me as she motions her eyes toward my dick pressed against my sweats.

"Be gentle with me? It's–it's been a while…"

"Good fucking answer." Bending down, I give her a kiss as I unattractively pull my sweats and boxers off. My dick springs out like it's been deprived of attention for a fucking year and I immediately know I'm going to have to focus real hard on not blowing my load two pumps in.

But that's pretty damn hard when Susie is under me naked.

I watch her expression change as her wide eyes stare at me. I can't tell if it's shock, admiration or pure fucking horror.

"Oh...um. Why–why is it so...big? Not in a bad way! Like, your dick is really pretty. I–um...is pretty the right word? Huge? Girthy? I–I don't know but I've never seen something so...gigantic before?"

"Baby...telling me my dick is the biggest dick you've ever seen is going to cause me to come on your stomach right here and now."

"I...uh–uh...I don't think it's going to fit?"

Smiling, I bend down, placing a kiss on her lips. "It's going to fit, Q." I move my hand down, feeling how wet she is already. "Fuck, you're soaked for me."

Pushing my finger inside, I lower my voice and say, "Are you going to be a good girl and take all of me, Susie?"

"I–I want to."

Taking my finger out, I line my dick up with her slick entrance, resting my forehead on hers.

"We're going to go slow, baby. If it's too uncomfortable or it hurts you too much, what will you do?"

She taps my shoulder two times, the same rule we've had since this started.

"I'm going to grab a condom," I reach over to my wallet, pulling out my emergency stash. A stash I haven't used in a while.

"Keep them handy, huh?"

And I know it's meant to be a joke, but I don't miss the slight seriousness in her tone.

"I haven't been with anyone for months, Q. Ever since Daytona..."

"I–I didn't mean–"

"No, I want you to know. I haven't been with anyone since Daytona because I think in the back of my mind it was always you there. Ever since that damn car ride of twenty questions. It's only been you for me, Q."

"I never imagined we'd be here," she says as she grabs my arm, "but I sure am glad we are."

Chapter 41

Susie

I should be thinking about how we got here. How the evening started with me concerned Paul was going to be pissed thinking I shared parts of him with Clara. I would have never imagined we'd be *here*. Paul Simmons – the incredible hockey goalie, the irresistible ladies man, my best friend – has had the same feelings for me that I've had for him.

We almost pulled the same crap Liam and Clara did.

But we didn't, we're here.

And I'm happy.

And extremely nervous because his dick is inches away from my vagina.

"Susie?" His gravely voice cuts through the air. "Are you okay?"

"Yes, I'm perfect," I say, rapidly nodding my head.

He places the condom over himself. His huge self I should add. I mean seriously, how could any girl ever fit *that* into *them*?

"What's going on, Q?" He brushes a stray hair off of my forehead. "We don't have to do this."

"I want to. I really, really do," I reach my hands up, cupping his face. "I–I just started thinking how–"

He hangs his head, taking in a deep breath. "How many girls have I been with? We–we both know how my reputation used to be–"

"I don't give a shit about that, Paul," I lean up, placing a kiss on his lips. "You and I both know your past doesn't define you. I was more or less thinking how in the hell could anyone fit *that* inside them," I feel my cheeks redden, "and how badly I want it to…"

There's a physical change in his face, immediately going from concerned to almost primal? His eyes lock on mine, jaw ticking as his biceps flex beside me.

"Saying things like that isn't good for my ego and sure as hell isn't good for my self-restraint."

Still inches away from his lips, I softly say, "Who said you need to restrain yourself?"

Before I have time to think, he moves his hands to my wrist, pinning them above my head as he holds them together tightly. "You sure, baby?"

"Do I need to beg?"

He moves forward just enough to where his dick presses against my entrance, carefully moving back and forth. "I'd like that," he lets go of my wrists, moving one hand to my hair and the other to my boob. Pulling my hair back, he bends down placing a gentle kiss on my throat as he says, "Beg for me, Susie."

Well, I wasn't being literal, but I suppose I can try?

How does one sound sexy while begging?

He continues his slow, tortuous pace of teasing as his finger circles my nipple. My very, very hard nipple. I bring my hands down to wrap around his arms, but his shoot up pinning my wrists above my head, again.

"Hands up here, baby."

"I want to touch you," I pout.

"And I want to do this," bending down, his tongue darts out as it takes over for his finger, circling my nipple.

Instinctively, I find myself pushing my hips up, aching for friction as his tongue roams over my body. And as he pulls back, his eyes lock with mine, it allows a brief moment to rake my eyes over the entirety of him. I've admired Paul's looks before, but from this angle, it's entirely different.

Each muscle, from his bicep down to the incredibly sexy v-cut on his hips, are perfectly sculpted. This is a man who's dedicated his life to being fit for his sport and bless him for it. Dropping my eyes past his stomach, I land on his *pretty* dick. *God, I can't believe I called it that... could I be more embarrassing?*

The sound of Paul clearing his throat brings my attention back to his face. A face with a cocky smirk. "Like what you see, Q?"

"I'd like it more inside me."

Did I just say that?

He quirks an eyebrow, like he's waiting for more.

"Please, Paul? Please have sex with me."

Bringing his forehead to mine, he moves forward and I expect him to tease again.

But he doesn't.

This time, he pushes in and the feeling is overwhelming. Painful and filling at the same time. He isn't moving, his dick is literally just sitting inside me right now, and I'm fairly certain I'm about to begin clawing like a rabid animal.

"Holy shit," I say, circling my hips back and forth. Still, nothing. He's frozen solid.

"Paul? Why–why are you not moving? Am I doing something wrong?"

With his forehead still resting on mine he says, "I can't move yet, Q."

"Oh, the begging?" Disobeying his rule, I drape my arms around his neck. "Please fuck me like I'm yours Paul. I–I want you so bad."

His head shoots up, eyes peering down at me, and I can feel his muscles contracting, like he's fighting a battle with himself.

"Fuck, you have no idea what that does to me, baby. But–but I can't fuck you yet."

"More begging, huh? For your information, you should know I've never begged once in my life so…this is new to me." Grabbing his back, I begin to push into him, trying to angle him deeper. Needing him to be deeper.

"I want you to go fast, hard, I–I don't give a shit. But I want you, Paul."

He quickly places his palm flat against my stomach to keep me from pushing against him.

"Paaaulll," I whine.

"Baby, if you want fast and hard, I'll give it to you. I'll give you anything you want. But I can't with just the tip inside of you."

My eyes widen as I look at where we're joined together and sure enough, Paul's freaking girthy dick is sticking halfway out of me. My eyes shoot to his and that gosh dang adorable smirk.

"I–I already feel so full. I don't know if I can take the rest of you!" I don't mean to, but it comes out as a scream which just causes him to chuckle even more, vibrating his dick inside me.

"You can take it, Q-T." Bringing a hand to my cheek, he says, "I'm going to push further now and I want you to take a deep breath. Okay, baby?"

Eagerly, *and very anxiously,* I nod. And as I inhale a deep breath, I feel Paul push deeper. The sensation much more painful than before. I can't imagine my wincing in pain is making for an attractive face, but I can't help it. It feels like my vagina is literally splitting in half right now.

"That's it, Q. Look at you taking me like the good girl you are," he reaches his hands up, intertwining his fingers in mine. "How are you feeling?"

"Mhm," is all I can say. I'm too focused on the feeling of how full I am. How tightly stretched I feel.

His honey-filled eyes are still fixed on mine, his long fingers still intertwined above my head as he slightly pulls out, pushing his hips forward teasingly.

"Fuck you're so tight, Q. So perfect. Like you were made just for me and me only," he continues his slow pace.

The painful sensation from moments ago is still there, but it's met with the feeling of wanting, *needing*, more.

"More. I want...more," although it may not sound very convincing judging by the quiver in my voice. Letting go of his hands, I bring my fingers to his chest, running them over him. His solid, golden chest peppered with freckles mixed with bruises from what I can only assume is from some seriously hard-hitting pucks.

Moving them down, I scrape my nails up and down his toned stomach, his muscles flexing under my touch.

"I want all of you, Paul."

His lips twitch upward as he places a tender kiss on my lips.

"I'm all yours, baby."

And when he pushes into me for the second time tonight, I don't focus on the pain. Pure instinct and desire takes over. Wrapping my arms around his back, I pull him flesh to me. His chest pressed against mine as he continues his pace.

"Fuuuckk," he growls through his teeth. "You feel so fucking good, Susie."

My mind isn't coherent enough to make sound responses, moans are all that's coming out. The pressure, his lips on my neck, the way he's praising me is all too much. My senses are on overdrive. And when he reaches down, grabbing my ankles and wrapping them around his back, the new angle is so much more intense.

I thought he was deep the first time? I swear he's touching my fucking rib.

"You look so fucking intoxicating like this," he pulls back, slamming forward with his hips, causing me to gasp.

"So fucking beautiful on your back," and again. "So fucking sexy while you're full of me," once more.

Each time is met by the sound of our skin slapping together. Each thrust forward is met by my moan of approval.

"God, Paul. That feels…that feels so good."

He picks up the pace, one thrust after the other, the next sloppier than the last, and I love it. I love knowing I make him feel this way.

Finally, I work up the courage to meet him thrust for thrust, snapping my hips forward at the same time his snap to mine again.

"That's my girl. Give it to me, baby."

I never knew I liked the vocal part of sex, but holy hell does it do things to me.

And I do as he commands. Digging my nails into his back, I push harder as he goes deeper. My stomach begins to warm deep down low, a feeling I'm becoming to know all too well thanks to Paul.

My hands become frantic, moving along his muscular back. My breathing quick as I feel his fingers trail down my belly.

"Fuck do I love seeing you like this. Sweaty," he leans down, placing a gentle kiss on my forehead. "Coming apart," his finger brushes over my most sensitive area all while never changing his pace.

The feeling of his finger rubbing circles around my bud while his dick continues to fill me is enough to send me over the edge. The sensation building and building until I can't take it anymore.

"Paul, I–I think I'm going to–"

"Come all over my dick, baby."

Yep, that was hot. And yep, I do come all over him.

"Paul—I…"

My legs are shaking, hands trembling, and I can feel my vagina pulsing as my orgasm takes over. "Holy fuu–shit. Don't–don't stop."

His hips continue snapping forward, harder, faster.

"Where do you want me to come, Q?" he asks. His usual perfectly pushed back hair falling over his face, his jaw clenched tightly.

"You have a condom on. You can–you can come inside me?"

"Fuck," he says as he bends down, biting my shoulder. I can feel his back muscles tightening under my hands, his breathing becoming quick.

"Fucking hell," is all he says before I feel his dick pulse inside me, my name falling from his mouth.

And as we both come down from the high of the Heaven we just experienced, we don't move, we don't say anything. We just lay there, his head still resting on my shoulder, the quiet filled by only the sound of our breathing.

There's a million things racing through my mind. One, the fact I just experienced this with Paul. Two, how Paul

Simmons just rocked my freaking world. Three, what do we do now?

We just established the whole no labels concept, which is fine. I'm okay with no labels – we know how we feel about each other and for now, that's enough for me. I don't want to scare him away by thinking he has to ask me to be his girl-friend right here and now. I mean eventually I'd like to be, yeah. I could see myself dating Paul. Going to his games, holding his hand as we walk to class.

I'd be fine with it all.

But would he?

He carefully pulls out of me, a tinge of pain shooting through me at the loss of contact. I watch as he rolls off the side of the bed, his bare ass facing me as he takes the condom off, discarding it in the trash can.

Then I watch as he pulls his sweats on, still shirtless and not saying a word, as he slips into the hallway.

Well, definitely not the strangest post-sex interaction, but not what I expected for us?

I quickly stand, pulling my own sweats on and throwing my sweatshirt over my head. Taking a look in the mirror, I comb out my hair with my fingers. My cheeks are flushed, skin warm, and although I'm confused by the interaction after, I can't help but smile thinking about tonight.

Everything I was in my head about, the not knowing, convincing myself the feelings were one-sided – we ended up here.

I, Susie Cobble, have fallen for my best friend and he fell for me, too.

It isn't until I hear Paul's deep voice from behind me that I'm snapped out of my trance.

"Well, this feels like deja vu."

He's leaning against the door frame with his arms crossed

against his chest. His messy brown hair pushed back from his face showcasing all his gorgeous features. I watch in the mirror as he approaches me, but it isn't until he wraps his arms around my waist that I see what's in his hand.

He wrests his chin on my head as he brings the items up to my face. "I know you're going to be sore from my pretty dick," he winks, "so I got you Tylenol and Ibuprofen because I wasn't sure which was stronger. A towel for me to wash you off and some water," he sets the items down on the dresser in front of us, grabbing my hips to turn me around.

"How's my girl feeling?"

Like that sentence just sent the butterflies in my stomach flying rampant.

His six-foot figure towers over my five-foot-one. My neck has to crane back just to look up at him.

"I–that…you felt…awesome, you know?"

Jesus Christ, Susie. Awesome? What are you even saying…

He chuckles, "Awesome, huh?" The next thing I know, he has me lifted up, my legs wrapped around his hips as he begins walking me back to the bed. His veiny hands are holding tight as he places me on my back against the headboard.

"Take them off," he motions to my clothes.

"Oh…uh–I don't know if I can go for round two right now?"

Holy hell this man's stamina…

"Baby, as much as I want and could go another round with you right now, this isn't that. Take your sweats off so I can clean you up."

"That isn't–"

He raises an eyebrow as if he's daring me to argue, and if

I had the energy, I might. But he did just tire me out so lucky for him, I'll obey.

I slowly wiggle off my sweats, remaining in my sweatshirt as he heads towards the dresser again.

"Which drawer is your underwear?"

"Uhh, the second?"

He opens the drawer, grabbing the first pair he sees with the washcloth, making his way to the bed, crawling over me as he plops down next to me. He places the underwear between us while he rests his chin on his forearm, carefully running the towel down my thighs and between my legs, gently wiping the inside. I fully believe this is more intimate than the sex we just had.

I know Paul has never been in a relationship before, but the man knows how to treat a woman, that's for sure.

"Do you feel okay, Q?"

Grabbing his wrist, I roll over to face him, slipping the pair of underwear on before pulling the covers up as he lays his head against the pillow.

"Tonight was amazing, Paul. You…this."

"I meant what I said earlier, Q. I'm all yours. I don't give a fuck if we spend every evening watching more of those cheesy-ass romance movies. I want to spend my evenings with you just like this, looking into those gorgeous eyes of yours."

No more lessons, just us. I like the sound of that.

"Do you maybe want to–to stay over? You can totally say no, it won't hurt my feelings. I understand if you need to get home so the guys don't question–"

"I thought you'd never ask," he maneuvers under the covers with me. "Need to practice my cuddling skills a bit more." He winks as he flips me over in one smooth motion, my ass now pressed against him.

His long arms wrap around me, pulling me into him as he buries his face into my neck. The smell of sandalwood cologne mixed with the scent of sex filling the room. I'm relaxed in a matter of seconds, snuggled up to the man who just made me feel things I've never felt before.

The room is dark, only the light from the telephone pole outside is slightly creeping through the window, and I have no clue what time it is. It's a Wednesday evening which means I have classes tomorrow, but I think I'll be staying in. Skipping one lecture won't kill me…

"Susie Q?"

His voice sounds heavy, tired maybe?

"Yes, Pauline?"

"I've never let a girl stay over with me before, let alone me crash at her place. You're–you're my first."

I know he can't see it, but I can't help the smile that stretches ear-to-ear.

"I'll gladly take that first from you."

Maybe he doesn't mean to say it out loud considering it's barely above a whisper, but the next sentence out of his mouth sends my heart racing and stomach fluttering.

"I think I'm going to share a lot of my firsts with you, Q."

Chapter 42

Paul

One Week Later

"Holy fuck," Clay clasps me on the shoulder as we're exiting the ice, "you were on fucking fire tonight dude."

"Always am," I wink.

"If I remember correctly, you also received the disappointed dad speech from Clay a week or so ago, Paulie," Liam chirps.

Ignoring him, I pull my shirt off, grabbing my change of clothes as I pull my phone out of my bag. And fuck me for smiling so goddamn hard at a text message.

SUSIE Q

Soo...I know I just saw you yesterday but... kind of missing you?

And fuck do I miss her.

Is that possible? To miss being away from someone after one day? So much so that I stared at our photo from the wedding? The photo strip she gave me a few days ago, a memory I didn't know she even kept but am sure fucking glad she did.

I don't necessarily care for photos, but I remember everything about her pulling me into that stupid photo booth. Her smile wide, dimples on full display, green eyes focused on the screen in front of us. We did pose after pose, and although we were only friends back then, I still could never take my eyes off of her.

"Yo," Clay says as he waves a hand in front of my face. "Who in the hell has you smiling at your phone like a dumbass?"

Quickly locking it, I pull my shirt over my head. "No one. I–I was reading up on my stats," a quick lie, but a believable one.

"I'm convinced if you could suck your own dick you would," Jake scoffs as he begins to undress.

"Your mom takes care of that for me, buddy."

"Why do you always have to bring my mom into this you fucking weirdo?"

"You know you made a 'your mom' joke to me last year, right? Payback is a bitch," I shrug my shoulders as I continue gathering my things.

"But you don't even have a–"

"Dude," Clay punches him in the shoulder. "Too far."

I place my hand over my heart, acting offended. "How could you joke about something so serious, Jake?"

"Jake," Liam says as he joins us. "Too far dude."

His face turns a light shade of red as he begins to rub the back of his neck. "Ah, fuck. I–I'm sorry, Paul. I didn't even realize I made a mom joke beforehand and–and I didn't mean to make one just now either."

Grabbing my bag, I toss it over my shoulder as I pat Jake's arm. "No worries man," then lowering my voice, I add, "I'll have your mom make it up to me."

He steps back quickly, pointing at me like a child tattling

in a classroom. "Guys, guys! Did you just fucking hear him? He did it again, talking about Laurie!"

The other two roll their eyes as they begin changing, so of course, I flip Jake the middle finger as I walk out the doors.

As always, we all rode together, but if there's one thing I know about Clay, it's that he takes his sweet ass time getting around. I don't mind though, I have something I've been dying to do.

Ring. Ring. Ring. After the fourth, I'm convinced it'll go to voicemail, but just as I pull the phone away from my ear to hang up, her voice fills the speaker.

"Paul?"

"Hey, Q. What's my girl up to?"

Fuck that feels so good to say. *My girl.* I know, I know. I haven't made things official yet, but I don't need her labeled as my girlfriend to know she's mine, and she sure as hell has nothing to worry about from my end. I'm hers, through and through.

"I–uh...was honestly about to lay down and go to sleep. Practice was tough, I can barely keep my eyes open."

The girls are gearing up for Daytona in April, months away, but they start that shit early and based on watching last year's performance, I can see why. There's a lot of behind-the-scenes work that goes into being able to flip and throw girls in the air like that. And I know Susie's extra nervous with this being her first year as a cheerleader and now on the competition team.

"Did you get your flippy thing down yet?"

She softly chuckles through the phone. *"My roundoff back handspring tuck? Not quite, but,"* her voice gets excited, *"I had the guy only slightly touch my back so that's progress!"*

"Guy?"

I can't see her, but I can only imagine how high her eyebrow is raised and the smirk she's wearing on that gorgeous face.

"Is that...jealousy I hear?"

"Fuck yeah it is."

"Jealousy sounds kind of sexy on you."

Leaning back against the jeep, I can see it clearly. Susie lying on her bed, her stupidly short pajama shorts basically showing her ass cheeks, her nipples fucking hard under her satin tank top, bottom lip curled under her teeth.

Shit. Now I have a fucking boner.

"Pa–"

"I miss you."

Not just the sex. Not the way she moans my name every time I make her come – although yes, that is pretty fucking amazing – I just miss her. Her laugh, her dimples, the way her ass snuggles into me during the night.

"Come over tomorrow?"

I'd come over right now if it weren't for the fact that it's movie marathon night and the guys would definitely know something's up if I missed out on our tradition, especially considering I'm forcing them to watch yet another Marvel movie.

"I'll be there bright and early, baby. Get some rest."

She doesn't hang up, but she does go silent for a moment.

"Q, are you–"

"I don't know how I managed to snag you Paul Simmons, but I sure am glad I did." And then she hangs up, right on cue as the boys make their way out of the arena.

As I climb into Liam's jeep, her sentence replays over and over in my head. I don't think Susie realizes how fucking lucky *I am to have her.* I was fine living life going from one casual fuck to the next, at least I thought I was.

I think that had a lot to do with me holding on to the shit with my mom – which I still do – but it wasn't until I started spending more time with Susie that I realized just how much I was letting it affect me.

So, here I am. Paul Simmons, falling hard for a girl.

And I'm more than okay with it. I would never choose to go back to a time in my life when it wasn't consumed by Susie Cobble.

I literally almost pulled a Liam fucking Russell, and I would have never lived that shit down with the boys.

Now, I'm pulling a Jake Wiley, and that's probably worse. To be fair, we aren't dating yet so maybe not as shitty, but still there. Susie and I have been keeping a secret from them ever since this whole arrangement started a few weeks ago, who's to say a few more would be any worse?

It's not that I want to, but telling the group *'ah yes, Susie and I have been fucking and while I am head over heels for the girl, I haven't exactly done the whole official shit yet but hey, that's that,'* doesn't seem like it would go over very well, especially with the girls.

So, no. I'm not ready to tell the three dipshits currently discussing dinner that I'm no longer living by the *'fuck around, never tied down'* motto.

But sooner or later I'll need to, because two days ago was our first group hang out since confessing how we feel, and I already almost fucked it up.

* * *

"Babe, Rocky does not need to be held all the time," Clara huffs as she plops down on the sofa next to Liam and their floppy-eared pup.

Liam, in his pathetic baby voice, leans closer towards

Rocky saying, "Tell momma yes you do. You do need to be held all the time," he looks up, giving her his signature smirk – the one that always earns him the same in return.

Everyone is over for spaghetti night, even Sara was able to get away from her internship for the evening. Susie, Leah and Lucy are in the kitchen cooking with Jake and Clay close by while I sit in the living room with the two lovebirds and Sara. I know there's a conversation going on that I probably should be part of, but I can't focus on anything when Susie is fifteen feet away from me looking like she is.

She has the top part of her hair pulled up in a bun with half of it down. Her leggings hug her ass so fucking perfectly that I'm fairly positive I've drooled a few times, and her smile is enough to light up the whole damn room.

In a room full of people, my eyes will always drift to her.

And before I know what I'm doing, I'm walking towards the kitchen. It doesn't take long before I'm at the island, leaning on my elbows as I watch their conversation take place. More like an argument between, you guessed it, Lucy and Clay.

"I know how to make spaghetti," Lucy snaps.

"Sure as hell doesn't look like it." Clay grabs the salt, sprinkling some in the meat that's warming. "You have to fucking season the meat for it to taste good."

"Give me that!" She stands on her tippy toes, trying to grab the salt out of his hand.

"Sweetheart, give it up. You can't–"

And that's when all hell breaks loose. Lucy jumps on Clay, kind of resembling a spider monkey clinging to a big tree trunk, and I know I should help a friend out, but watching is much more entertaining.

"Guys," Susie says as she steps forward, trying to get Lucy down. "Can't you two just get along?"

At the same time, they both stop moving as they yell, "No," and then continue on their path of destruction. Finally, Lucy manages to get the salt shaker out of his hand, but as she does, she flings it backward sending salt flying everywhere.

Right into the eyes of Susie.

"Shit!" She yells, immediately throwing her hands over her eyes.

Lucy immediately lets go of Clay, jumping down to help her friend as I hurry around the kitchen island, all but pushing Lucy out of the way.

"Q, are you okay?"

She shakes her head back and forth as she frantically wipes at her eyes, "It just burns really bad."

"Is everything okay?" Clara yells from the living room. "What happened?"

Without thinking, I grab Susie's hand and lead her down the hall to the restroom. "Susie got salt in her eye, I'm going to help her flush it out. Make sure the two in the kitchen don't murder each other."

As I pull Susie into the bathroom, closing the door behind us, I can still hear the two bickering, only now it's about who's fault the salt catastrophe was.

"Q, baby. I need to see your eyes," I gently grab her wrists, pulling them away from her face. She has them squeezed tight, her adorable nose scrunched as a small tear slips down the side. Carefully, I reach my thumb up, brushing it away as I cup her face.

"This next part is going to suck, but we need to flush your eyes, Q."

"No, not happening." She brings her hands back up, trying to rub her eyes again. I drape my hand over hers as I place a soft kiss on her forehead.

"It has to happen, baby. You can't keep rubbing your eyes. Let me help you, okay?"

And fuck do I want to help her. Seeing her in pain, even if it is from stupid fucking salt, makes me want to march in there and punch Clay right in his goddamn face for having to cause issues with Lucy.

Hesitantly, she nods her head up and down.

"Good girl," I brush my knuckles across her cheek. Carefully, I pick her up and place her on the counter next to the sink. Even with her sitting here like this, I still have a few inches on her.

I rummage around in our cabinet, looking for Clay's saline solution – his eyes are always getting irritated from his contacts. Quickly, I pour just a bit in the lid as I tilt Susie's head back. And I know now isn't the time, but watching her throat bob as she swallows, her mouth slightly parted and her spread out on the bathroom counter is sending blood straight to my cock.

Focus, Paul. Focus.

"Okay, Q. I'm going to hold your left eye open with my fingers and pour this saline in there, okay? Then, you're going to blink a few times and not rub it once I'm done. Okay?"

She rapidly bobs her head as she grabs my free hand, squeezing it tight. I carefully pry her eye open, pouring the saline in it as she squeezes my hand tighter, blinking quickly.

"Ow, ow, ow," she repeats. "Go ahead and do the other to get it out of the way."

"That's my girl."

Following her instructions, I do the same for her right eye, and after a moment of sitting there with them both squeezed shut as the solution drips down the side, she reluc-

tantly opens them, looking straight ahead at me. They're red and watery, but still gorgeous shades of green.

"How's that feel?"

"Well," she stays planted on the counter top, wrapping her arms around me. "I can sort of see your handsome face now, so I'd say better," she grins. "Hi." Leaning forward, she rests her cheek on my shoulder as she inhales a deep breath.

Wrapping my arms around her back, I turn, placing a kiss on her cheek. "Hey there, baby. Looking awfully cute for a girl with salt in her eye."

She pulls back, searching my face with a smile on hers. "They still burn a little."

I feel her hands flinch, knowing she's once again going to attempt to rub them. Placing my hands over hers, I hold them against the countertop as I gently begin blowing on her eye.

"I'm not going to let you rub them, baby."

She pouts, an adorable pout, but still not going to work.

I lean forward, just a bit closer, fully aware of how close we are to one another. Fully aware that our friends are down the hall.

And maybe I should put some distance between us, but all common sense goes out the window when her hands slide up my arm, fingers gently scratching up and down my bicep.

"Thank you for taking care of me," she whispers. Her hand moves to the front of the counter where my body is pressed against hers. I'm already very aware of her straddling my legs, the last thing I need is her hand near my hard dick.

Clearing my throat, I meet her whisper. "I'll always take care of you, Q."

She bats her eyes, peering up at me through her thick lashes as her tongue swipes over her bottom lip.

"Don't do this to me here, baby," I groan.

"Do what?" Her hand slides closer to my dick. "Am I doing something?"

Placing my hand on her thigh, I give it a tight squeeze. "Q," I warn. "I'm two seconds away from dropping to my knees and ripping these fucking leggings off of you."

She shrugs her shoulders, ignoring me as her hand gently grazes over my boner.

Tightening my jaw, I grab her wrist, placing it back on the counter. I'm so fucking crazy for this girl it's unreal.

"I'm about to go eat dinner with our friends thinking about how I'd much rather be feasting on you." I reach up, tilting her chin back so she's looking up at me. "What are you going to be thinking about, Q?"

Her lips part as her head rolls to the side, and I know it's because she's picturing it. Her legs draped over my shoulders, her pussy dripping wet as I bury my face between her thighs. Leaning forward, I brush a faint kiss over her lips. "I bet you're already wet just thinking about it, huh baby?"

She wraps her arms around my neck, pulling me flush to her as a sinister smirk spreads across her face. And just as I'm about to fully lose myself in the moment, the sound of footsteps scurrying down the hall breaks up the moment.

"Suse, are you okay?" Lucy ask loudly. "Is Paul still helping you? What's going on?" The door flings open as I quickly step back, Susie's hands dropping to her side as she lets out a grunt of disapproval.

"All-all good here," she throws a thumbs up as I flash Lucy my teeth. Both of us acting as normal as possible.

Lucy looks to me and then back at Susie with narrowed eyes, and it's at this moment I realize I didn't fix my fucking boner. One wandering eye and it's game over. Her face doesn't scream convinced, but she doesn't question more.

"Right, well. Your eyes look better. Sorry about what

happened back there. That dumbass always knows how to piss me off."

"Maybe you two should hate fuck and get it out of your system?" I shrug.

She scoffs, "Fuck that. I wouldn't touch his conceited ass with a ten-foot pole," then proceeds to shiver for dramatic effect. "Maybe you two should fuck and get rid of whatever is happening," she points between the two of us, "here."

Susie's eyebrows shoot up to her forehead as she tries to find the right words. "Uh–what? Why would–no why would you–that's insane," she nervously laughs.

There's an opportunity staring straight at me to be a fucking man and claim this girl as mine. Tell all of our friends together what's going on between us.

But I don't.

We're not labeling things right now. Once I grow the balls to make Susie Cobble officially mine, I'll tell them.

"I've been saying the same thing for months," I wink at Susie, trying to be my normal flirty self. "Still no fucking luck."

Susie brings her shoulders up to her ears as she says, "I hear football guys do it better anyway," then proceeds to throw a wink right back at me.

"Damn, Suse. When did you get so good at being sassy with comebacks?"

Her smile widens as she says, "I suppose I've learned a thing or two."

* * *

"Dude. Why are you very creepily smiling out the window?" Jake asks.

Shit. Is this what happens when you're into someone? When you like someone? You just daydream about them?

"Thinking about Laurie," I tease, knowing how much it pushes his buttons.

He closes his eyes, taking a deep breath – clearly annoyed – as the other two laugh.

Jake deserves all the shit I give him considering I kept his and Leah's little secret last year. I caught them making out in the hotel hallway in Daytona. I knew it was a bad idea, I knew the shit that would go down with Clay, her older brother, when he found out, but I kept my promise.

It wasn't my secret to tell. And yes, shit did go down, the whole fucking group almost imploded, but Clay came around.

They got their shit sorted and now, Leah basically lives with us. In fact, after this semester, her and Clara both will.

And for as much shit as I give Jake, it's nice to see how happy he is. How happy Leah makes him. It was always clear Jake didn't care for relationships. He and I were alike in the sense that hookups were perfect, we never needed more.

Then Leah walked into his life.

And Susie walked into mine.

Jake fell in love with his girl. Liam fell in love with his best friend.

Is that what's happening with me?

Chapter 43

Paul

"*M*emes, *there's no need to feel bad,*" I chuckle through the phone as I gather my clothes for Susie's. "*You can stream the game, it's no big deal.*"

Except I know it is to her. I know she thinks that missing out on something important makes her resemble my egg donor, but it doesn't. Not to me, anyway.

"*It's been a while since I've been to one. I'm making the trip next week, staying in a hotel, and you can save me a seat next to that pretty girl of yours at the game.*"

For the seventieth time tonight, I roll my eyes at no one but the phone, knowing what she's trying to do. I talked with her a few weeks ago about how I felt, ignored her advice the first time around, so she's waiting for an *'I told you so'* moment, something Meme never passes up.

"*Paul Henry? You didn't listen to my advice, did you?*"

I swear she has telepathic abilities.

"*Technically, yes. Just not immediately after your recom-mendation?*"

I hear her squeal in the background, a sound I've only

ever heard once before and that was when she found a snake in the backyard of the house, so I know I'm in for it.

"Ignoring the part where you didn't listen to your dearest immediately. What does this mean? You do in fact have a lady? I never thought I'd actually see the day my grandson settled down. I was sure I'd be dead before then."

"Calm down, calm down. I–I'm not entirely settled down because I haven't exactly asked her to be my girlfriend yet?"

"And why not?"

I'm putting my shoes on as I answer her complicated question. *"Well, we only just said how we feel about each other? I mean, I want to...I know that. I know I've never felt this way before, didn't think I cared to. But I just, um, need to do it right?"*

Ever since I met Susie I knew two things. One, the girl is effortlessly gorgeous. Two, she deserves it all.

I look at her and I forget how to breathe. She smiles at me and my day immediately brightens. She is sunshine wrapped in beauty, and I will never let her forget that.

So, yeah. I have to do this right. And yes, plans are in the works.

"Wow," Meme says, and for a second I forgot I was on the phone. *"You care about her, yeah?"*

I don't need a moment to consider it. *"So fucking much."*

And I know I can't see her, but I know she's smiling. Hell, maybe even crying.

"Do me a favor and get your shit together before next week so I can meet her as your girlfriend, Paul Henry."

"Love you Memes, goodnight."

"Love you always, sweet boy."

Throwing my bag over my shoulder, I check my phone and see I have a text from Susie.

SUSIE Q

How do you feel about quesadillas for
dinner? • •

Heading out of my bedroom, I type out a quick response.

I feel like I could probably eat ten of them
and they sound fucking delicious. Heading
your way. See you soon baby.

As I head down the stairs, I come to a halt when the cutest floppy-eared boy is sitting at the bottom of the steps.

"Well, hey there buddy. Were you the goodest boy today?" Bending down, I pat him on the head, trying to hurry out the door.

"No, he was not the goodest boy today," Clara's voice appears, but no Clara?

"God?"

Laughing, she answers, "Over here."

Circling the sofa, I see her on her hands and knees, scrubbing a spot in the rug.

"Are you okay?"

She looks up at me with an annoyed expression plastered all over her face. "Rocky had an accident. I was just trying to clean it up."

"I'll take care of it," I hold out my hand. "Come hold the little booger." I motion to Rocky who's currently chewing on a shoe by the door.

"Rocky!" She yells as she stands. "No! Put it down!" Stomping over to him, she quickly snatches him up as she takes a seat on the sofa while I get to work.

"You don't have to clean that for me, Paulie." She leans back against the sofa yawning, "I can get it." Then, her eyes land on my bag as her lips tug upwards. "Where are you heading?"

I freeze for just a moment, feeling bad that I'm about to lie to one of my best friends.

"I–uh, was going to crash at a friend's," I avoid making eye contact, knowing it's game over if I do.

"A friend, huh? Do I know her?"

Very well, I almost say.

"Maybe in passing?"

That peaks her interest. Shit. I couldn't have just said no?

"Who is she?!" She almost yells. I stand, looking around to see if anyone heard.

"She–I, um…" I've already said enough, more than I wanted. "No, you know what? No. I'm not sharing anymore. And this," I point between us, "stays between us. I don't want the three fucking amigos ganging up on me with this shit."

She smiles as she stands with Rocky still in her hands as he chews on a stand of her hair.

"Wow. Not just a normal hookup, huh?"

"No, not a normal hookup."

She begins to walk past me, stopping next to me as she places her hand on my shoulder. "You know if you're happy, we're happy, right?"

I teasingly roll my eyes as I bend down, kissing the top of her head. Clara is one of my good, good friends. Someone I know means every word she says and loves all of her friends deeply.

"I know. Thanks, Clara."

She motions towards the door as the sound of Liam and Clay's voices begin to get louder. "Go on, your secret is safe with me."

* * *

I'm lying on the sofa with Susie snuggled up against me. The scent of berries and vanilla tickling my nose as her ass is pressed against my cock.

The quesadillas were in fact delicious, and we settled on a romcom tonight, *Anyone but You.* And I hate to admit it, but it's funny as fuck. Lying here, snuggled up with my girl, watching a movie? I can't imagine anything better.

These are what my nights have become, a routine of me coming over and staying cuddled up with her until the sun rises. The best part of my day.

But there's one thing on my mind tonight, especially since my phone call with Memes.

"Q?"

"Mhmm?"

Her head is tucked under my chin, and I know she can feel my heart racing. I can't help it, I'm nervous. I–I've never asked a girl on a proper date before and although I'm fairly positive she'll say yes, I still want to shit a fucking brick.

"Do you, um…maybe want to go on a date this Saturday…with me?"

No shit with you, dumbass.

In all honesty, I already know every single detail of what I want to do for this date. A fancy as fuck dinner somewhere with pasta since she loves that shit, flowers, the whole nine yards. Nothing less for my girl.

She turns to face me, her face bare of make-up, my personal favorite look of hers. Smiling, she brings her hand to my arm, wrapping it around her as she buries herself in my chest.

"You want to go on a date? Like, out? In public?"

"Fuck yes in public. You think I want to keep you hidden, Q?"

She chuckles as she squeezes tighter. "What–what if our friends find out?"

"Then they find out. Besides, after the date you'll be my girlfriend, we'll have to tell them anyway."

I feel her freeze at the exact moment I realize what I just said.

"Did you just–"

I pull her tighter into my chest, muffling her sentence. "Ssh, ssh. I think you're tired, huh baby?"

I expect her to fight it, but she doesn't. Maybe it's because she can still feel how quick my heart is beating. I'm nervous enough about the date, more so to ask this girl to officially be mine. How do you make something perfect for the perfect girl?

Hell if I know, but I'll find out.

"I actually am pretty tired," she says in my chest. "Do I get another night with Paul Simmons?"

She can have all my nights for all I care.

Without answering, I sit up, turning around and looping my arms underneath her.

"What are you doing?" She squeals as I pick her up.

"Taking my girl to bed?" As if it isn't obvious.

"Does this mean you're staying over again?" The smile on her face stretches ear-to-ear, and I love knowing that smile is for me and me only.

"You may not ever be able to get rid of me, Q."

Leaning in, she plants a kiss on my cheek. "Good."

When we make it to her room, I gently place her on the bed as I kick off my sweats, quickly climbing over to what has become my side of the bed. Keeping her pajamas on, she curls into me just like we were on the sofa, my arm wrapped around her waist, her fingers tightly gripping my arm.

A week ago, I could have never imagined this – there's no

way Susie and I would be here right now. She'd be with Jamee fucking Locke and I'd be miserable.

She'd be in his arms, me in my room sulking like a bitch. And yet, here we are. My girl. My arms. Mine.

The strangest part? None of this with Susie feels *too fast*. The dinners, the staying over, us. It feels normal, dare I say, perfect.

Just as I'm about to close my eyes and drift to sleep, my bright ass phone illuminates the room, the vibration buzzing her nightstand. Text, after text, after text.

"Do you want me to hand it to you?" Susie's voice cuts through the darkness.

Grumbling into her neck I mumble, "Can you check them for me?"

"You–you want me to read your texts?"

"If you don't mind?"

Is that a bad thing to ask of your girl but non-girlfriend?

"Not worried it's a puck bunny of yours?"

Well, shit. I'm not worried what she'll see, I haven't talked or fucked a girl since before Daytona. Does that mean a girl wouldn't text me for a late night hookup? No. In fact, it's fairly normal. But I don't give a shit about anyone else, and I want Susie to know that.

"I'm not worried, baby. That's not to say it isn't, but I could give a flying fuck if it is. My girl is right next to me and that's all I care about."

She squeezes my arm tighter before reaching over to grab my phone as she begins to read off the messages.

"You have like five just from a BUFHP group chat?" She chuckles, "Paul, what does BUFHP mean and why is the icon a photo of Clay asleep?"

A chuckle escapes me, reminiscing on the night not so long ago when Cap decided to let loose. His mouth is hanging open as he's passed out in the backseat of the Uber.

"Obviously it stands for Barker University's Finest Hockey Players, Q. What else could it mean?" I wink. "Will you read them to me?"

"Read you all your messages?"

"I'm too comfortable to move," I nuzzle further into her neck. "Plus, your voice is soothing."

"Clay texted first asking what size Rocky would be in dog clothes," she laughs. "Awwwww! He's buying him a dog shirt with hockey sticks all over it. Adorable." She continues scrolling through the chat. "There's a few messages from Liam about how you all need to stop spoiling Rocky so much because he, and I quote, *'doesn't even know he's a dog anymore.'* And honestly, he's probably right. I can't even imagine how rotten he is being surrounded by you guys all the time."

"No comment."

"Ummm, one from Jake telling Liam to shut the fuck up, they'll spoil Rocky however they want and the last chat is from Liam asking..." trailing off, she clears her throat, "asking if you're too busy fucking to answer the group chat?"

Placing a kiss on the back of her neck, I say, "Text back saying snuggling, not fucking. And it's much better."

I feel her body shake from silent laughter. "I–I can't tell them that. They'll ask who you're snuggling with?"

"Just snap a picture and send it, that'll shut them up."

"Yeah, that's one way to let the friend group know we're...something." She chuckles, cutting it short as she adds, "There's one more text, but–but I don't know if you want me to read it?"

"Q, baby. I have nothing to hide–"

"The contact name is egg donor?"

Of course it is.

"Ah. Well, I can tell you what that says without you needing to read it." Because it's the same shit every time.

Sweetie, it's been too long. I think I could make it to town to see you if you could spot me a few hundred? I swear it's the last time I ask. Your grandma hasn't been responding.

I get that text about twice a month, and I haven't answered since junior year of high school. You'd think she would remember me telling her she's a worthless "mother", or that I want absolutely nothing to do with her. More specifically, she was as disappointing as they come.

But she doesn't remember, she never does. I suppose drugs do that to people.

"Paul?" Her sweet voice breaks my thoughts. "Are–are you okay?"

Reaching around, I lock my phone and toss it to the floor. "You know, I used to be disappointed by her time after time. The promises when I was younger, the phone calls with plans she never kept. I believed them all." I begin running my hand up and down her arm to calm the memories. "And then Meme was left picking up the pieces when she didn't follow through. She'd have to answer my questions, explain that mom was sick and often forgot things. When I had my eighth birthday party and she didn't show, again, she sat me down and told me. Lisa had been on drugs even while she was pregnant with me, and when I was born, Meme didn't hesitate. Sure, Lisa was living at her house and in my younger years she was around, but never present."

Q squeezes me tighter around her, and I know at any moment I could stop talking about it…but I don't want to.

"At some point, Meme officially kicked her out. After that, she never cared to reach out or visit unless she needed money." I think back, blurred memories of Lisa at the door,

her arguing with Meme and the door being slammed. "And–
and I suppose I never realized how much I let her fuck with
my head until you came around, Q."

She doesn't say anything, giving me the space to talk,
which I'm thankful for considering this is the first time I'm
ever sharing this part of me out loud.

"I never had a problem fucking around with someone
because I never cared what came of it. Never cared to get her
name, never cared to get to know her, one and done – that
was all I wanted. And then I saw you outside of Liam's jeep
and I didn't know any different, but I knew I wanted to be
around you. And then you made me feel ways I never had
before, and I ignored every part of it. Lisa fucked me up more
than I realized, I know that. Why open myself up to someone
when they can be just like her? Use me, leave me, like it was
nothing – like I was nothing? I tried fighting it. I tried
convincing myself this wasn't anything more than an attraction," I lean up, turning her cheek to face me, "but I was so
fucking wrong, Susie. And I've never been happier about
being wrong in my life."

"I know Lisa made you nervous to trust, to let people in,"
reaching up, she places her hand on my heart, "and I don't
take it lightly that you trust me, Paul. I like every part of you,
nothing can change that for me."

Chapter 44

Susie

"Leah, babe," Clara brushes her hair out of her face. "You're going to get the stunt in no time. Give yourself some grace, it's a hard fucking stunt."

We're out for dinner after a very, very crappy practice. Daytona full-outs are in full swing which means so is my stress. Everything that could've gone wrong in practice today? Yeah, it did. Kicked in the boob? Yep. Fallen on? Yep. Yelled at by Coach? Yep.

And for Leah who's a flyer, she's feeling a little bit more pressure to get everything perfect. So, we've wound up at a burger joint in Evanston that carries the essentials, ice cream of course, as we talk about the away game tomorrow.

"You make it look so easy," Leah sniffles. "I'm just frustrated that it's taking me longer…"

"It doesn't help that LeAnne and Sadie are fucking up their grips. It's hard to do your job when you aren't standing on a solid platform, freshie," Lucy chimes in.

Leah's eyes fix on hers with a glare. "You can't call me freshie when I am in fact not a freshman anymore, Lu."

She laughs. "Got you to quit sulking, huh?"

Flipping her off, Leah continues on. "Whatever, can we talk about the seating arrangements for tomorrow? I do not want to get stuck next to LeAnne and her stupid humming. I'm still pissed I drew the short straw."

"I heard you humming along too, Leah," I wink. We've only had one prior away game and since we're an odd number, we drew straws for seating. Whoever had the smallest sat in the seat by themself and had to deal with whomever sat next to them. "No need to worry, I'll take the seat by myself. I–I have some homework I need to focus on."

"Are you sure?" Sara asks.

Nodding my head, I take a bite of my burger, knowing damn well I don't have any homework, I made sure to finish it earlier this week. But I do have an incredibly attractive hockey player to keep me company.

One I'm going on a legitimate date with.

And I know I didn't bring it up or fixate on what he said, but casually dropping that I'll be his girlfriend after Saturday has had my stomach in knots. Part of me realizes how insane this may seem, *will seem*, to others. To everyone else, we've been friends, best friends, which is absolutely true. But he's so much more. He's been the one who anchors me. The one who knows all of me, sees all of me.

So, is it fast? Maybe. But I have never fallen for someone like I've fallen for Paul.

And I could fall straight on my face, but something tells me he'd cushion the blow if I did.

"Care to share what you're smiling about there, Suse?" Lucy raises an eyebrow, her long brown hair falling in perfect waves.

Clearing my throat, I do my best at changing the subject. "Heard anymore about the mentor shit you have to do, Lu?" I know that'll rile her up.

"Har, har," she mocks. "Nothing more than our mentees will be assigned in the first week of spring semester. And I swear to fucking god I'll choke someone out if they choose not to take it seriously."

'We know you would," Leah chimes in, snickering as she says, "you're kind of aggressive, Lu."

Throwing a hand over her heart with a hurt expression on her face, she replies, "When have I ever?"

Still chuckling, Leah starts to hold a finger up for every instance. We're already on number four and they're all in relation to her brother, of course. "Oh, and just the other day when we ran into him outside of the practice arena, you told him to eat a bag of dicks."

Scoffing while rolling her eyes, Lucy responds, "He was staring at me with that stupid fucking grin on his face. Arguably, I'm not aggressive. I'm just aggressive to your brother," she shrugs.

"Did you two just meet that first night and decide right then and there you hated each other?"

It does feel that way; there was a whole situation with Clay being a bit of an asshole towards Leah the evening she first joined our group dinner. We had no idea he was her brother and Lucy definitely didn't care for him, and clearly, she still doesn't.

"I just don't like his arrogant, cocky, too-good-for-others attitude," she says matter of factly.

"You know, he isn't that bad," Leah adds. "Sure, my brother is as arrogant as they come and definitely cocky, but there's a sweet side to him. I've seen it before, just not since–"

"Since ever? Leah, I love you and I will continue to love you while hating your brother." Leaning over, she places a fat kiss on her forehead. "Nothing could change my mind about that, babe."

"Not even how hot he is?" Sara chimes in, all eyes shooting to her.

"Please tell me you didn't just call my brother hot," Leah gags.

Laughing, Sara adds, "Not my type, but objectively speaking, the man is pretty nice to look at."

We all laugh while Lucy runs her hands over her face and Leah plugs her ears.

"He isn't all that," Lucy grunts. "There's plenty of good looking men out there and I'd rather fuck one who couldn't get me off than ever let Clay Harper think he's hot."

"Moving on," Clara waves her hand in the air. "Can we talk about how since I've been out of the house, which has been a total of four hours, I've received three photos from Liam of him and Rocky? One is a family picture of all the boys around the dinner table eating with Rocky in his own chair and a text from Paul asking if he could feed him a french fry," she turns the phone around to show us the photo. "There's four grown ass men in our house all acting like this puppy is our newborn baby."

And I have to admit, it's an adorable photo. Sure, all the boys look happy and it's cute they care so much about the pup, but my eyes are fixed on the brown-haired goalie with his dreamy hazel eyes.

"Imagine when it is a newborn baby," Leah winks. "Spoiled won't even begin to describe how these boys will treat your little one. Jake has already asked me if he's an honorary godparent since he was the best man at the wedding and I'm fairly positive he has a few things in his Amazon cart on standby for when the time comes."

"Well, it's not happening for a while," Clara pats Leah's

knee. "Tell your man we want to experience life and marriage before immediately popping out a child."

I sit back, watching my friends as I take a bite of my ice cream, realizing how incredibly lucky I am. We get to experience seasons of life together – there's nothing I love more than that.

But it's not just them I'm thankful for. I'm just as thankful for the guys – they're as much my friends as the girls are. I know in a heartbeat they'd be there for me if I needed them, no questions asked.

Still, I am partial to favoring one more than the others…

* * *

"You're not even going to take the aisle seat?" Sara asks as she sits next to Lucy.

And risk them seeing my text messages? Nope.

"Concentrating is hard while sitting next to Clara who gives a play-by-play of the movie she's watching." Which isn't a lie, the girl narrates everything, regardless if we've seen it or not…

"I'd argue, but that's fairly accurate," she chuckles.

As I slide into the window seat while another teammate of mine plops down next to me, I slip my headphones in my ear and eagerly pull out my phone. When I told Paul the other night about our away game and the long drive, he insisted the ride be spent talking to him. So, when I see that there's a text already waiting for me, I can't help the smile that spreads across my face.

PAULINE

Thinking of you.

If only he knew he's the only one I'm always thinking about.

> Just got on the bus, maybe thinking about you too...

PAULINE
Oh yeah? Care to share specifics, baby?

Baby. He's called me that name more times than I can count and each time it sends a flutter to my stomach.

> About our date tomorrow night?

He hasn't told me much about it, refuses to, but I could tell he was nervous the other day when he asked, and I thought it was absolutely adorable considering Paul Simmons rarely gets nervous. I've been thinking about what to wear ever since. Do I go for cute casual or fancy and sexy? I know Paul doesn't do anything half-assed, he proved that during the whole *teacher* gig. Something that feels like another lifetime ago but was literally a few weeks back.

I suppose time flies when you're having fun? Or when you're falling for your best friend.

PAULINE
I've been thinking about the date too, Q.

Like how the fuck did I manage to snag one with Susie Cobble?

> Haha, yeah right. I think it's the other way around, Pauline.

PAULINE

I'm a lucky motherfucker, Q-T.

Now, tell me. What's my girl's idea of the
perfect date?

I…I don't expect a lot, Paul. Food, talking,
and ending the night with you over sounds
perfect enough to me.

Apart from my date with Jamee, which I don't even consider a date since the night ended with me telling him how I felt about someone else, I haven't been out with a guy. And if so, it was typically dinner at a burger joint, casual and relaxed.

PAULINE

Me staying over? Missing me already, baby?

More than I should admit.

I may or may not be missing a specific
hockey goalie?

But in all seriousness, I'm just looking
forward to going out with you, Paul. No
matter what, it'll be great.

That much I know to be true. There's a sense of comforta-bility knowing I'm with the man who's been my friend above everything else. He knows every part of me – my insecurities, my past, what I like in and out of the bedroom – and I'm fairly positive that Paul Simmons is the closest I've ever been to knowing and understanding love.

Crazy considering we're just going on our first date? Probably. But I can see it, and I think that's because it's already happening. There is no second-guessing with Paul, I feel safe and comfortable and confident.

> PAULINE
>
> Prepare for the greatest fucking date of your life, Q. I have to go all out for my first date, it's a must.

First date?

> As in first date together or...?

Sure, I know Paul has only ever been into hookups, but surely he's been on a date before?

> PAULINE
>
> Once more, you're taking a first of mine, Q.

I can't help the blush that begins to creep up my neck. I know it's stupid, but I enjoy knowing that I get to share some of Paul's first experiences like he has with me.

> The other girls will be devastated to know that.
>
> Paul, the most attractive BU hockey player, sharing firsts with someone?

> PAULINE
>
> Take them all, Q-T. I would be fucking honored.

Chapter 45

Paul

"*What do you think about this, Memes?*" I ask as I sit the phone down and step back, showing her the full fit. I'm dressed in a navy blue button-up, with the sleeves rolled, tucked into black slacks, hoping it outlines the hard work I've put into my physique.

I couldn't ask the guys, they'd just follow-up with a million damn questions. Questions I can't answer right now.

But that changes tonight, something I didn't mean to tell her but accidentally let slip last time we were together.

"*Sweetie,*" Meme says as she brings her face closer to the screen, the most precious smile illuminating the screen. "*You look very handsome. You looked very handsome in the last two outfits you had as well.*"

"I just...I want tonight to be perfect, you know? She deserves perfect, Memes."

"*What did the guys say? Did they say that you look bussin?*"

Oh for fuck's sake. My grandma who sits at the young age of sixty-seven years old has discovered new words thanks to TikTok. Unfortunate for me.

"One, stop trying to use new hip words, Memes. And secondly, no. They umm...don't exactly know about her yet?"

I hear her tsk as she shakes her head back and forth. *"Keeping a woman a secret is never good, Henry. That for sure would make someone feel like shit."*

"No, no. She...it's not like that," I put my shoes on, realizing I'm running behind due to my horrible fucking time management. *"We've been keeping us a secret because she's um, she's the best friend of Liam's wife and consequently she's become our friend, part of our group. And–and we just haven't told the group...yet. But before you begin chewing my ass, that's changing because after tonight, I will officially be a taken man."*

A year ago I would have never guessed this would be the conversation I'd be having. A year ago I simply thought I found the most beautiful girl in the world. And while that's true, I would have never known I'd have the opportunity to make her mine, or that I'd be in a position to feel like I could.

Lisa Simmons convinced me that it was easier to keep my heart guarded. Susie Cobble convinced me that I didn't have to.

"I'm happy for you, Henry. I can tell this girl makes you happy. I can't wait to meet her."

I grin thinking about the interaction, knowing how smothering Meme will be towards Susie. Asking her question after question, desperate to get to know the girl who changed her grandson's mind about dating.

"Speaking of my girl, I need to get going. I'll talk to you later and tell you how it goes." I pick up the phone, smiling at my grandma who's staring out her window, listening to her grumble about the dog in her yard.

"I love you Memes."

"I love you, Henry. Be safe, use protection."

Shaking my head, I hang up and begin gathering my car keys and the flowers I bought earlier today. Like I said, my sunshine girl deserves the world, the perfect date, and I'm going to give it to her. Cracking the door, I stick my head out, listening for the sound of voices downstairs, and sure enough, Liam and Jake's echo through the house. Sneaking downstairs isn't exactly easy; the stairs creak and if they so much as see me dressed how I am, they'll know something's up.

There's only one person I can count on to get me out of here without being caught.

> Sandy D, my favorite wife of the group.
> What's up?

Almost instantly, she replies.

CLARA RUSSELL

I'm the only wife in the group…

Chuckling, I quickly type out my request.

> And yet the statement still stands. I'm
> hoping you can help me out?

> Please. Please. Please. Please. Please…🙏
> 🙏

> Without telling your husband?

I can only imagine the grin on her face. If there's one thing Clara Russell loves as much as her husband, it's secrets.

CLARA RUSSELL

Do tell, Paulie.

> I need a way to get out of the house without
> the guys seeing me?

CLARA RUSSELL

Come on Paul, I need more than that...

Snapping a photo of me in the mirror with a thumbs up, I attach it to the message.

It's date night for me, bestie. And if the guys saw me come downstairs in this, they'd for sure give me shit. I need a distraction so I can sneak out and get to my date...

I watch the text bubbles appear then disappear, tapping my foot as I sit on the bed, watching the minutes tick by. And just as I'm about to type out another text message, I hear Clara scream.

"WHAT THE FUCK! Liam, babe, come quick! There's a raccoon outside!! It–it's as big as Rocky!"

When I hear Liam yell to Jake, *get the net*, with the sound of their heavy fucking feet scurrying outside, I quickly step outside my door and hurry to my truck. As I'm heading down the street, I get a photo message from Clara of Jake shining a flashlight under the house with Liam next to him aimed ready with the net.

CLARA RUSSELL

You owe me. Have fun, bestie. Soon enough, I need to meet this mystery girl and your best friends need to know you have a girl...

I don't bother answering, especially because the last thing on my mind is thinking about how to carefully explain to my friends how I've fallen for a girl. The girl.

It doesn't take long before I'm pulling into Susie's parking lot. But before I get out, I take one final look at myself in the rearview mirror, smoothing down the few curls I have, making sure they look perfect as I give one final pep talk.

"I'm Paul fucking Simmons. It's a date with the most stunning girl who already knows every part of me and hasn't run yet. She's your sunshine, be hers for the night."

With a nod to myself, I hop out of the truck, flowers in hand as I make my way to her door. I've planned everything tonight. The reservation, the specific table I wanted for us, hell, I already tipped the server, instructing him to only show up to take our order and refill our glasses. My time is solely dedicated to Susie Cobble – I want to spend every goddamn second I can soaking in tonight's moments.

And as I knock on her door, I can't help the shit-eating grin that spreads across my face, knowing that on the other side is the girl who I've thought about since the moment I met her a year ago. But when the door swings open and her green eyes beam up at me, I'm at a loss for words. Everything I planned to say is taken away at the sight of her.

Including my breath.

"Wow," I run my hand across my jaw, fumbling through my thoughts. "Susie, you–you're...fuck. No! Not fuck. You're–awesome. Gorgeous. A lot gorgeous."

A lot gorgeous? What the fuck does that even mean?

Her cheeks heat as her eyes roam up and down my body. "You clean up very nice, Paul Simmons. A lot handsome," she winks.

She moves to the side of the door, giving me space to walk in. And as I do, I pause in front of her, bending down as I capture her mouth with mine.

A single kiss, my lips lingering on hers much longer than I anticipated, but I can't help myself. She's intoxicating in the best way. It doesn't help that I haven't seen her since her away game. Her hands snake around my waist as she pulls me into her, our lips only parting for a breath of air.

"Fuck, I've missed you."

She rests her cheek on my chest, breathing me in as she says, "I haven't stopped thinking about you since the last time I saw you, and you're still even better looking than I remember." Her hand moves to my stomach as she pulls away. "Let me grab my shoes and then I'm ready."

Reluctantly, I let her go, admiring the view as she shuffles around. She's in a baby blue dress that falls just above her knees with the straps hanging off her shoulders. The dress itself hugs her boobs and waist tightly, showing off every tempting curve while the bottom flares out, and when she bends down to grab her shoes, I know I'm in trouble.

"Susie, baby. Your dress is awfully close to showing your ass." I slowly walk towards her as she stands up straight, turning to face me.

"Does it? Hmm, I hadn't noticed," she rolls her bottom lip between her teeth, a playful smirk pulling at the corner of her mouth.

Reaching around, I slide my hand under the dress, ruffling it up until I clasp my palm over her ass cheek. "Not that far from the bottom of your dress at all." She gasps as I pull her into me, my other hand coming to the bottom of her chin. "And it's taking a lot of self-control to keep from sitting you on this counter, pushing that dress up, pulling your flimsy underwear to the side and slipping my finger in your perfect fucking pussy that I know is already wet."

Her eyes flutter closed for a moment as her tongue wets her lips. My poor fucking cock is aching, pressed against my slacks.

We haven't even made it to the restaurant and I'm already hard for her.

"That sounds better than dinner." She brings her hand to my stomach, running her fingers down to my belt. "Should we skip and stay here? I–I like your idea."

Bending my mouth to her ear, I softly say, "I can promise you, Q-T, the night will end with you on this counter, screaming my name while you come around my fingers, might as well make sure you're fed first."

* * *

As I pull up to the valet line of *Étoile Endroit,* I can't help but chuckle when I turn to see Susie's jaw hanging open and I'm really hoping that means I chose well.

"Q, baby. You better be careful or you'll be eating a fly tonight." I put the truck in park, quickly making my way around the front to Susie's door, grabbing onto her hand as she hops down.

"Paul, this place is brand spanking new! How…" her eyes roam around the building illuminated by the lights lining the outside. "How did you manage to get a reservation here?"

Her gorgeous jade eyes find mine as they twinkle in the light. Her smile is contagious and I can't help but mimic her. "I told you, Q-T. A perfect date for my perfect girl."

Honestly? It was a fucking headache getting a table here. A lot of calling and trying to convince anyone to let me talk to the owner. My research showed he's Barker alumni, and a deep dive into the archives showed him smiling at the Beavers Bin – the hockey arena that still houses all of our games. So, when I offered him season tickets, he folded like a fucking lawn chair; it sweetened the deal when I told him I could get him behind the bench.

The deal being Susie and I in our own private area without a single fucking soul around.

"This is insane," she says as she squeezes my hand tighter. As the door opens to the restaurant, I'm even taken aback. *Étoile Endroit* is a little taste of France here in Chicago, only thirty minutes from Evanston, and everything about this place is living up to its reputation. Tall ceilings lined with murals, elegant chandeliers, a fucking mini Eiffel Tower in the middle of the room.

It's insane.

It's not even half of what Susie Cobble deserves.

We walk hand in hand as the waiter leads us to the secluded area, the nicest seating in the restaurant. It's upstairs, *yes – this place has an upstairs*, in a dimly lit booth area with no one around. And just like I requested, there's wine already at the table with another dozen roses sitting in water.

I take off my jacket, placing it on the table, turning to wave at our waiter, Brian, letting him know I got it from here.

"I'll be back in a moment to take your order, sir." And off he goes.

Turning my attention back to Susie, I see she's already taken a seat in the booth and has somehow plucked the white envelope that was tucked in my jacket pocket.

"What's this?" Her face is lit up with a playful grin.

Taking a seat beside her, I quickly snatch it out of her hands. "That comes later, baby." I lean back, draping my arm around her as I lean in and kiss her cheek. "What do you think of the restaurant?"

"Seriously? Paul this," she waves her hands around, "is actually breathtaking. I–I have never been anywhere so fancy in my life."

Fuck, yes. Paul's non-dating skills, point one.

"I want this to be perfect," I shrug, trying to play off how incredibly nervous I am. I think the knee bouncing up and down is a dead giveaway, especially considering that she rests her gentle hand on my thigh.

"For someone who's never been on a date before, you're doing a great job, handsome."

She leans into the crook of my arm, bringing the menu up to my eyesight. I know I should be looking at the food options, but I can't bring myself to take my eyes off the beautiful face in front of me.

I don't know the first thing about being a boyfriend, but I'll do anything for moments like this with Susie.

"What sounds good, Q-T?"

Turning towards me with a mischievous grin on her face, she says, "Your idea from earlier."

Holy shit my girl is sexy.

Clearing my throat, I bring the hand I had wrapped around her shoulder to her hair, brushing it away as I place my lips on her collarbone.

"You are breathtaking."

"Changing the subject, huh Pauline?"

"It's that or we go fuck in their fancy-ass bathroom, baby. But I don't feel like sharing your moans with the entire restaurant. They're mine, and mine only."

"So sure of yourself," she winks. "What are you thinking about for dinner?"

"I have not a fucking idea. What are you thinking, Q?"

"Hmmm…" she brings her finger up to her mouth, truly thinking hard about what she's wanting. "The Fettuccine Chicken Alfredo sounds delicious. But good god Paul, this place is so dang expensive," her eyes roam up and down the menu. "The cheapest plate is twenty-three dollars," she lowers her voice as she turns to me. "We can leave right now and get McDonald's. I wouldn't complain."

"We are not going anywhere, and I don't give a fuck

about the price. If you want the Fettuccine Chicken Alfredo, get it. If you want an appetizer, fine by me. If you want three fucking courses so you can try them all, order them. Whatever you want, I want."

Is this what falling for someone does to you? Turns you into a man who does and says sappy shit? Because if so, I'm game as long as it means I get to see Susie's smile for the rest of my life.

"I want the Fettuccine," her eyes begin searching mine, "and I want you to know that this is the best date I've ever been on."

I can't help the way my mouth pulls into a cocky grin as I look around the restaurant. "It is a pretty fancy place, huh?"

"It is," her hands cup my cheek as she pulls my gaze to hers, "but this being the best date has nothing to do with the place. It has everything to do with who I'm sharing it with."

"Holy shit," I say as I push the plate away from me – a very empty plate – "that was fucking delicious."

"I think I'll throw up if I take another bite," she laughs. "I'm assuming your steak was good?"

"The best steak I've ever had." Worth every penny of my thirty-three dollars.

Dinner was quick, our waiter doing everything he was told to do – only checking in when he noticed our drinks were empty – and now we're sitting here as Susie finishes off the glass of wine.

And because I'm driving, Susie has had the majority of the bottle, and I can tell she's starting to feel it, especially because her hand keeps getting higher and higher on my thigh.

"This wine is my favorite ever," she draws out the end of the word. Turning to me, she boops me on the nose. "Just like you're my favorite ever."

"Ever?" I raise a brow as I brush a strand of hair behind her ear.

She hiccups as she leans into my touch. "A truth for a truth?"

"Always."

Opening her eyes as she flutters her lashes, she lays her head back on the seat. "I have fallen so hard for you, Paul. I–I know it's been a short time from the arrangement to now, but it hasn't taken me long to know how I feel about you. To know that you are the one I feel safest with. To know that I can count on you, trust you. I–I know we took an unconventional way of getting here, but I'm glad we did."

Unconventional is one way to put it...but I wouldn't change it for the fucking world. Reaching into my jacket, I pull out the envelope she tried grabbing earlier, handing it over. I had planned to wait until we got back to her dorm, but I know all too well plans don't always work.

"What's this?"

"My truth."

The truth I rewrote three times.

"This is new to me, you know that, Q. And I was worried I wouldn't say everything I wanted to, needed to, so I wrote it. Another first for me, by the way. A letter to a girl? I felt like I should've called for a pigeon while I was at it."

She takes a look at the chicken-scratch scribbled on the outside of the letter, smiling up at me as she tucks it into her purse. "Are you ready to go home?"

Twisting my neck, I ask, "You don't want to read it?"

She places a kiss on my cheek. "I want you to read it to

me so you can say everything you want to, need to. And I want it to be a moment for only us."

"Does that mean you're ready to go home?"

She eagerly bobs her head up and down.

I stand, smoothing out my slacks as she slides out of the booth. She starts for the stairs but not before I grab her wrist, leading her over to the balcony overlooking the restaurant, pulling out my phone.

And I know it's extremely cliché, maybe even embarrassing, but I motion the waiter over, handing him my phone as I pull Susie into my embrace.

"Taking a photo to remember one of my firsts."

I snake my arm around her waist just as she looks at me, my eyes finding hers.

She's usually about a foot shorter than me, but not in the heels she's wearing tonight. She stands right under my chin, and I know we're supposed to be taking a photo, but I can't help that my mouth is drawn to hers. And I definitely can't help the fact that my tongue slips inside her mouth, or that I pull her into me, or that her hands fist into my hair.

I'm lost in her, and for a brief moment, I forget the waiter is there until the sound of his throat clearing pulls us apart.

"I'm ready to go now," she says breathlessly, cheeks red, and I know exactly what she means. I haven't gotten the image of me finger fucking her on her counter out of my head since we left the dorm room.

Five minutes later, we're in the truck heading back to the dorm, the sound of the radio playing low as Susie laughs.

"Your Meme did not say that!"

Reaching across the console, I pull her hand into mine as I continue telling her the story.

"Q, I swear to god my grandma told me to use protection before coming on our date. She also gave me an earful when she thought I was keeping you a secret from my friends." I bring her knuckles to my lips, placing a kiss on each one.

"What did you tell her?"

"That soon you won't have to be my secret because you'll be my girlfriend. And then I can walk into the River Road house holding your hand, telling the guys to eat shit because I'm happily in a relationship."

"Oh, is that right?"

"You're stuck with me, Q-T. The sooner you accept that, the better," I wink.

"You know you have to ask someone to be in a relationship, right? And," she looks around, "I don't think that's happened yet?"

"The night is young, Q. So, so young."

"And if I say no?"

My head snaps to hers, lowering my voice as I say, "Not an option."

She throws her head back laughing as she says, "No need to worry, Paul. If the question were to come, you'd be stuck with me, too."

Chapter 46

Susie

Tonight was perfect. Absolutely perfect, and as if it wasn't already obvious, I am a complete goner for Paul Simmons. The man who has helped me discover confidence in myself and in the bedroom. The man who is so much more than just Barker's star hockey goalie. A man who once favored one-night stands, choosing to open himself up to the possibility of more.

With me.

He wouldn't admit it, and he may not see it, but he's braver than he knows. Paul has every reason to close himself off, to choose the surface level relationships – his mom consistently chose drugs over him – I could easily see how trusting someone on a deeper level would be hard.

Yet, here we are. A card in my hand, a date that exceeded all dates, and a very handsome, very sexy man in front of me.

He's standing against the front door as I sit my purse down, eager to pull out the card that's been carefully tucked away since the moment he handed it to me. He doesn't move as I carefully trace my name on the front. And I'm sure he

                    M. J. Hughes

can't hear it from where he's standing, but my heart is beating a mile a minute.

Turning, I catch him smiling at me like I have throughout the entire night, and just like before, I can't help the blush that spreads across my cheeks.

"What?" I manage to squeak as he stalks towards me.

And yes, I mean stalk.

His jacket comes off first, revealing his biceps bulging against his rolled up button-up. His shirt stretched tightly against his chest and shoulders, outlining his very muscular body. His eyes are roaming up and down in a devouring way, as if he's undressing me with them.

"You and this damn dress," he stops in front of me, running his hand over my off-shoulder strap. "You look so breathtakingly sexy."

He reaches behind me, lifting me up as my legs wrap around his waist, my dress bunched up as the wetness pools between my thighs by the mere contact of his body. In two steps, he's sitting me on the counter as he nudges my thighs apart with his body, standing between them as he carefully pries the card out of my hand.

"Do you want me to read this now or after you come all over my face, Q-T?"

I can't help the way my breath hitches or how my eyes immediately dart to his bulge pressed against his slacks.

"N–now," I wrap my arms around his neck, my vagina throbbing in anticipation at his words. "Please?"

His signature smirk comes across his lips as I drop my hands, wrapping them around his waist as he takes the card out of the envelope. I carefully watch him, the loose strands of his hair falling over his forehead. His hazel brown eyes focused on the paper in his hand as he clears his throat.

"This is all new to me," his voice low, "falling for

someone is new to me, Q. But learning with you has been my favorite experience."

I squeeze his waist tighter as I intently listen.

"You've easily become my favorite person, Susie Cobble. I wake up and I look forward to seeing you. I go through the day constantly thinking about you. I fall asleep and I'm picturing your goddamn adorable dimples. You consume my every fucking thought and I wouldn't want it any other way. You're pure sunshine. You're perfection. You're someone who deserves the world and I'm the lucky son-of-a-bitch who gets the chance to give it to you."

His eyes stay glued to the paper as he continues. "Our whole arrangement started with the thought that if I could just be around you, if I could help you, that would be enough for me. And I quickly realized there is never enough of you, Q." He finally looks up, tossing the card to the side as he takes my cheeks in his hands.

"How am I doing?" He quietly whispers.

"Absolutely perfect."

He runs his fingers through his hair as he continues.

"I have a lot to learn. I'll fuck up, I'll probably piss you off, but I wouldn't want to do this with anyone else, Susie. It's you or no one," he rests his forehead against mine, taking in a deep breath. "And it would make me the happiest motherfucker if you would officially be mine. If I could show you off to the world and let everyone know that I, Paul Henry Simmons, am happily taken by the most beautiful girl with the kindest fucking heart."

He doesn't move as the sentence lingers in the air. His eyes are closed as he waits for me to say something, as if anything needs to be said, clearly I'm already his and have been for a while now.

"I remember when this arrangement started," I run my

hands through his hair, "and how I promised myself this was simple. The flirting, the feelings…they were just because of us spending so much time together." I lean back, my eyes never leaving his as I say, "I've never been happier about being wrong."

As quickly as the words leave my mouth, he's pulling me into him, his lips finding mine. It's a tender kiss, one that holds the three unspoken words I can't bring myself to say yet, but I can feel it. It's in the way his hands move to the nape of my neck holding me tighter against him, not coming up for air until we have to.

"Does this mean…"

"It means you're stuck with me, Paul."

He pumps his fist in the air as he takes a step back. "Fuck yes. My girlfriend," he runs his hands up the side of my thighs, pulling me to the edge as he gently pushes me flat against the cold countertop. "I think my first duty as your boyfriend is to circle back around to that promise from earlier. What do you say, Q?"

I pull my bottom lip in between my teeth, unable to keep from squirming as his long fingers reach under my dress, slipping off my underwear and tossing them to the side.

"Use your words, Susie baby."

"Ye–yes. God, yes."

His jaw flexes as he pulls my dress up as I lay here naked, my bare ass on the counter.

"Fuck, Q. Look at you, so fucking wet. All for me, baby?"

"Only you."

He places his hands next to me, peering up as his head hovers above my most sensitive area.

"Say it again," he commands. "Tell me who this pussy belongs to."

Oh...oh wow.

"Only you," I repeat instantly.

"Such a fucking good girl."

His tongue darts out, running through my slit as he laps up my slickness, a moan escaping my mouth from the contact. I push my hips to his mouth, chasing the pressure I crave as he continues his slow, tortuous pace.

"Tell me what you want, baby."

"You." A one worded answer is all I can muster.

"Come on, Q. I taught you to be more specific than that."

I look down at his face between my thighs, seeing his signature grin spread across his face.

"I–I want your finger inside me. No–no. I want you inside me."

I feel his thumb circle over my clit. "How about we do both, Q? How about I make you come right here on this counter and then carry you to bed so I can properly fuck my girlfriend."

Yep. Sounds great to me. Perfect, actually. And when I open my mouth to agree, I'm cut off by his finger pushing inside me, that damn sexy smirk still on his face. "Is that okay with you, Q?"

He continues to watch me as he pumps his finger in and out, his thumb continuing its slow circle. His other hand snakes up my dress, and thank god I opted for the no bra option tonight. My nipple is a solid pebble underneath and when he pinches it between his fingers, I know I'm five seconds away from being a goner.

"It's completely okay." I toss my head back, squeezing my eyes shut as the familiar warm feeling builds low in my stomach. I can still feel the smirk on his face when his mouth goes back to work. And holy shit is his mouth good at its job.

The feeling of his tongue as he continues to finger me has

me spiraling, in the best way. My body is moving on its own accord, grinding into his hand, desperate for more. Reaching down, I grab his hair, pushing him harder against me while the other hand continues teasing my nipple.

But when he curls his finger inside of me, hitting a spot that only he has ever found, the waves of pleasure wash over me as I call out his name, my thighs clenching together as his tongue continues working over me.

As I come down from the high of all things related to Paul Simmons, my arms stretched across my face, his gravely voice brings my eyes to his.

"I could live off of your pussy and never starve," he winks. "In fact, eating you out is now officially part of my meal plan, baby." He worms his arm under my back, the other grabbing onto my hand as he helps me sit up. My heart is still racing as his hands run over my hair while he says, "Susie Cobble, you are the most mesmerizing girl I've ever fucking seen, and you're all mine."

"This spot right here," he drops his mouth to my neck, placing a kiss as his hands reach around to my ass, pulling me flush to him. "Mine."

Moving to my collarbone, he repeats the words, something he continues to do as he places playful kisses on my skin. But when his lips make their way to mine, he hovers an inch away.

"And I'm all yours, Susie."

Threading my fingers through his hair, I pull his lips to mine. My tongue collides with his as a deep groan escapes from the back of his throat. When he tries to pull away, I wrap my heels around his waist, keeping my fingers locked.

"I would like to have sex with my boyfriend now…"

I don't know who this confident, outspoken Susie Cobble is, but I like her…I'm proud of her.

Without saying a word, his long fingers slide behind my thighs as he lifts me onto him. "You don't have to ask me twice, Q. I live to please my girl."

We make it to the bed in what feels like record time. I'm slipping my dress off as I sit against the headboard, watching Paul pull his shirt over his head. A sight I will never get tired of seeing, the man is simply otherworldly. I try to be patient, to bask in the show of Paul undressing, but patience goes out the window when I see the outline of his dick in his slacks.

I slowly crawl towards the end of the bed, standing on my knees in front of him as I bring my hand to his chest.

"Your heart is racing." Keeping my eyes locked on where my hand is, I lean forward, placing a kiss on his chest.

"The sight of you usually does that to me," he says so quickly it causes me to snap my eyes to his.

"Are you sure you've never done the whole boyfriend gig?" My hand drops to his stomach, grazing over every crevice of muscle.

He brings his hands to my cheeks, a proud grin on his face. "I can absolutely say with certainty you are the one and only girlfriend I've had, Q-T. And I think you'll be the last," he speaks with confidence, a statement that makes my chest warm.

"I like taking your firsts," my hand travels to his belt, "and I'd like for you to take another one of mine..."

"What—what would that be, baby?"

"An enjoyable blowjob? I've only done two or three. But—but I know I'd enjoy it with you."

He palms his bulge over his slacks, his honey eyes deep, *darker*, if that's possible.

"I want to enjoy it with you, Paul."

I want to enjoy everything with this man. I want to experience it all with him.

"How do you want me, Q?"

Well, hell if I know. The two or three previously were god awful. Maybe that's my fault? Maybe I didn't know what to do or what the guy liked, but that's not a concern with Paul because I know he'll talk me through it. I know he'll tell me what he likes, what I'm doing well, what I don't need to do. And because of that, I feel sure of myself.

"Just like this." I undo his belt, pulling his slacks down as I silently thank the sport of hockey. Paul puts his body through the ringer for the game, I know that. But the game has rewarded Paul with a god's body – perfectly sculpted, solid, breathtakingly gorgeous. I never knew I could find thighs attractive, but the outlines of Paul's muscles? Downright sexy.

I can see the pre-cum on his grey boxers, and I swear my mouth is salivating at the sight. Knowing that I'm the reason for how turned on he is only fuels my hunger more.

"Will you," I motion to his boxers, "help me out?"

"Happily," he says as he not-so-gracefully shimmies them off, an adorable grin on his face. I've seen Paul's impressive dick many times, but knowing that–that it's about to be in my mouth is a bit more intimidating. And I think he can tell, because his hand gently cups my chin as he brings my eyes to his.

"Say the word and we stop. If it's too much, if it hurts, if you don't like it. I don't give a shit, you tell me, Q."

I nod as I inch closer to him, bringing my finger up to the tip, circling the wetness dripping out of him. His eyes close, head rolling back as he lets out a low hum of approval. I teasingly run my fingers over the length of him, coating him with his own wetness leaking out of him. Remembering how he liked it the first time I touched him here, I wrap my hand and squeeze tightly, my eyes fixed on his face. His throat bobbing as he swallows, his jaw flexing, his chest quickly rising and falling.

Leaning forward, I bring my tongue to his length, licking him from base to tip as a deep *fuck* falls from his lips. I continue my pace and I can feel his thighs flex, his hands wrapped in my hair but frozen solid. Not an ounce of movement...

"Am–am I doing something wrong?"

I sit back on my heels as his head snaps up, eyebrows lowered. "Why would you–"

"You...you aren't moving or saying anything? Does it not feel good? Should I do something diff–"

"I'm going to stop you there, Q. Fuck," he runs his hand over his jaw. "All I want is to grab you by the back of your head and fill your throat with my cum, but–but I'm trying to be a gentleman and have you set the pace. You're fucking amazing. Your mouth..." he trails off rolling his head to the side. "Your mouth is fucking Heaven, Susie."

I have no doubt that Paul means what he says, he's the most honest person I've come to know. Without saying anything, I bend forward again, wrapping my mouth around him, my tongue swiping over his tip.

"Holy shit," he exhales, his hand tangling in my short hair. "That feels so good, baby."

I push further, trying to take him all. I wrap my hand around his base, trying to guide myself down the length of him, gagging the entire time.

"Q, sweetie. If you keep making those noises I'm going to come in record time."

I pop his penis out of my mouth as I look up through my eyelashes, "Is gagging good or bad?"

"Hot as hell, baby."

Dropping my gaze to his dick, I say, "I don't know if you'll fit all the way inside my mouth?"

Smirking, he says, "That's too good for my ego, Q." Then adds, "What you were just doing was fucking perfect. But…if you want to try, breathing through your nose might help."

I'm a girl on a mission when I wrap my mouth around him the second time. This time, I move my hand to his balls, cupping them, gently massaging as I continue sucking and licking. And when I push my head forward, I take a deep breath in my nose, going slow as the tip of him hits the back of my throat. The gagging is still there, my eyes filled with water – tears maybe – as I adjust to the feel of him.

"Fuck, that's it Q. You take my cock so fucking good."

God, this man's words do things to me…

I begin rocking back and forth, continuing to breathe through my nose. My lips stay rounded, my tongue darting out every so often as his grip on my hair tightens. Softly, he begins pushing forward into my mouth, meeting me thrust for thrust. It's still a lot, the water-maybe-tears now sliding down my cheeks, but I don't mind.

This is the hottest thing I've ever done.

I wrap my hands around his ass, holding on as I begin to pick up my pace, him doing the same. And when I pull my mouth off completely, his dick sliding out, I quickly push it back in. I can tell the act unleashes any type of control he was holding onto.

His hips snap forward as he guides me with his fist in my hair. His movements are quick, sloppy, needy, and I can feel my vagina throbbing, just as needy for him – his touch.

"I'm–I'm going to come, Q. Where do you want me to come, baby?"

I pry my lips off of him, biting the inside of my cheek as I confess, "I…I don't think I want it in my mouth? I'm sorry–"

"Don't you fucking dare say you're sorry for how you feel, Q. You don't want me to come in your mouth? That's fine, I'll happily come all over your body. Nothing is hotter than seeing how you're mine with my cum spread across your chest."

A small whimper leaves my mouth because how in the hell is Paul Simmons real? How has this man been my best friend for a year and I never knew this part of him existed? Of course, I assumed the playboy god was good in bed, that's a given with his reputation. But the talking, the praising, the sweet, caring Paul who makes sure I feel nothing but safe and satisfied?

I flash him my dimples before pulling him into my mouth again. After a few strokes, his deep voice cuts through the air.

"Lean back."

Immediately, I do as I'm told. *As I would every time when it comes to this man.* I lean onto my elbows as he climbs over me, hovering as his next command comes. "Wrap your hand around me and jack me off, Q."

Again, without hesitation, I do as he says. His eyes on mine as I pump up and down, making sure to run my thumb over his tip. His hand comes to my nipple, taking my hard bud in his fingers, pinching it as I pick up my pace.

And when he leans forward on his hands, capturing my mouth in his, I feel his warmth coat my skin. His tongue circling my mouth as my hand continues working him until I feel his thrusts slow, his mouth resting on my lips in a gentle kiss.

We stay like that for a moment as our breathing slows. When he pulls away, he rests his forehead on mine, the cockiest of grins on his face.

"How was that for enjoyable, baby?"

I chew on my bottom lip, acting like I have to think real hard about the answer.

"Hmmm…it was okay."

His grin grows bigger. "Okay, huh?" He lies beside me, him naked, me still in my dress. "I–I didn't hurt you, did I?"

"My throat will most likely be sore tomorrow…"

He closes his eyes as he grimaces at what I'm saying. Genuine worry etched on his face.

"Yet I loved every moment of it."

He rolls over, now facing me as he brings a hand to my cheek. "My girlfriend did such a great fucking job."

I place my hand over his as I say, "I love hearing you call me that."

"I love saying it," he places a kiss on my nose. "How about we go wash up so we can get some sleep?"

Nodding my head in agreement, I chuckle as he rolls over me, standing and scooping me in his arms.

If this is what nights with Paul as my boyfriend consist of, I'm going to be one happy, lucky girl.

Chapter 47

Paul

Honestly, where the fuck does time go? One minute, you're agreeing to help your best friend find her confidence, the next you're fucking her in her bed while she moans your name.

One minute you're hesitant about falling in love, the next you're head over heels.

One minute you're practicing in the arena for a game day that's three weeks away, the next it's here.

And that's where I am. The locker room of Beaver's Bin – my home for the last three years with my three best friends. And I'm also in love with Susie Cobble – my best friend and now girlfriend. My sunshine girl. She just doesn't know that yet…

We're about forty minutes away from our opening game and tonight we're facing off against the Carnelly Raptors, a college not too far from Susie's hometown. They aren't anything special; they have a few key players, a left winger with a nasty fucking temper, nothing we can't handle. They're a non-conference game, not a typical opponent of ours, but Coach thought it would be good to play outside the normal.

Doesn't mean dick all to me or the guys, a puck is a puck and a win is a win.

I'm sitting here going through my pre-game ritual, which doesn't consist of much compared to others. Our shit for brains teammate Shaffy has a thing where he won't look anyone in the eyes until we take the ice; something about how unlucky it is to make eye contact beforehand. I don't fucking know, and I don't care.

Brandon, one of our left-wingers who has finally started meshing on the line, refuses to touch his necklace until we huddle up.

I know what you're thinking…how could I know these strange things? It's easy to pick up on habits when you spend as much time as we do together.

I've never been much for superstition, I don't believe that a nasty-ass pair of socks can bring me a win, but I do focus on getting my head in the game. For Liam, it's avoiding his phone. For Clay, it's avoiding everyone. For Jake and I? It's giving each other shit and going over the game.

"No, no. I can guarantee you Carnelly is going to rely heavily on Gantser for their slap shots. They know we're aware of Ross and how great of a fucking player he is. They'll expect us to focus our defense on him, leaving Gantser open," Jake says as he pops his bubblegum loudly.

"They can try. But they're out of their fucking minds if they think I'm allowing a single puck past me," I scoff.

He smirks, typing away quickly on his phone. "It's Carnelly, Paul. They aren't known for being the smartest fucking team, but you'll put them in their place. We know that," he finishes, never once looking up from his screen.

"Something on your mind, buddy?" I nudge his thigh with

my knee. "You seem awfully focused on something, and the fact it's not me pisses me off," I laugh.

"Leah's on her way with the girls," he turns the phone towards me, all five of them smiling big in the mirror for the photo. Their smiles are almost as big as Jake's while he's staring at his girl. *Almost.* "Call me a bitch if you want, but I'd spend the rest of my days making a fool of myself if it meant I could see that smile on Leah Harper's face."

And at one point, a month ago or so, I wouldn't have understood what he meant. But not anymore, because the way Jake feels about Leah is the exact way I feel about Susie. It's how I know I'm just as in love as the two goons next to me.

I've watched them fall in love – I watched them deny it, hide it, whatever the fuck you want to call it, but not me. There's nothing more that I want than to wrap her in my arms after the game, pulling her into me, letting the entire arena know she's mine. That I'm hers.

So, when Jake goes back to focusing on his conversation with his girl, I seize the opportunity to talk to mine.

> How's my girl doing today?

I will never grow tired of calling her that.

I don't have to wait long before a text comes through.

> SUSIE Q
>
> Well…I'm on my way to watch my hotshot goalie boyfriend kick ass with my best friends. I'm doing pretty good. 🐾 How about you, Pauline?

Better than I've ever been.

Well...my girlfriend is on her way to watch me kick ass. And I'm really praying I'll be seeing a certain name spread across her back when she gets here?

Two days ago, I showed up to Susie's dorm with a gift. It wasn't enough to see her in a regular Barker sweater, jersey if we're being common and simple, I wanted to see her sporting my name. So...I had a custom jersey made for her: Simmons with the number one underneath it.

If this isn't an announcement to our friends, I don't know what would be.

Her response comes through as a photo and fuck me, it's the hottest photo I've ever seen.

Susie Cobble has her back turned to the mirror, throwing a smirk over her shoulder as my name sits across her shoulders in big letters. The jersey comes to her mid-thigh and I can almost guarantee there's nothing underneath it in the photo…

And I can guarantee I'm sitting next to my best friend with a damn hard-on.

I suppose I never knew what type of boyfriend I'd be, but it's fair to say possessiveness is a strong characteristic of mine.

Two words, Q-T. Holy fuck.

SUSIE Q

Remind me again how in the world you came up with that nickname?

Well, I told you it stood for Susie Q the terrific. But truthfully, it's always been short for cutie.

Like I said, I've always been a flirt, especially for Susie.

SUSIE Q

Paul Simmons! You made me believe you've been calling me terrific this entire time and really you've been flirting with me?!

What can I say, Q? I've had it bad.

I was just too stubborn to admit it.

Have you told the girls yet?

SUSIE Q

I thought what better way to tell them than showing them my outfit when we get to the rink? I'm not worried, though. I know they'll be happy. Why…are you worried? What did the guys say?

It was part of our talk the other night – how we'd go about telling our friends. What better way to hard launch our relationship than Susie Cobble showing up in my jersey? I told her we technically don't have to tell them…they'd figure it out after the game when I wrap my arms around her and pull her into a kiss, but she thought it'd be best if we told them separately before I kissed her for the world to see.

I know the boys know something's going on. I've been gone almost every night for the last few weeks. But I think it's the fact that I haven't exactly been the *"normal Paul"* for a few months now that's gotten their attention. Especially during dinner the other night.

* * *

"Are you sure you're feeling okay?" Liam asks as he places the back of his hand on my forehead.

We're out eating after an exhausting practice, and all I

want is to order food and get to my girl, but that doesn't seem to be happening.

"Why wouldn't I feel okay, Leon?"

"That girl just asked for your number and you said you weren't interested?"

"Because I'm not?"

Clay scoffs. "When are you ever not interested, Paulie?"

To be fair, I haven't been interested in a girl for some time now, ever since I looked into those captivating green eyes, I've been a goner.

But they don't know that yet, and they can't.

"I'm just...focusing on hockey right now..."

"Oh, fuck off," Jake laughs. "That's the Cap's excuse, it can't be yours, too."

Clay gives him the finger. "Nothing is wrong with focusing on a sport I love instead of pussy."

"No one said it was," Liam clasps him on the shoulder, "we're just saying having fun isn't against the rules of playing hockey and being captain. And Paul," he points at me with his finger, "I call bullshit. There's something else going on and has been for a while now. You're Paul fucking Simmons. There used to not be a Friday night you weren't hooking up with a girl. Now, it's been months?"

"I'm just not interested," I shrug my shoulders.

No need to be when I have the perfect one.

Thankfully, they drop it for now. And I can't help but wonder how they'll feel when they find out the real reason behind me not being interested.

* * *

So...I was supposed to already tell the guys, and no...that hasn't happened yet. Not because I don't want to or that I'm pussy-ing out, but there hasn't been a right time. I planned to tell them on the car ride here but Clay went into captain mode before we even left the house – earbuds in the entire drive. And if there's one thing I've learned it's that interrupting a game-focused Harp is a hard fucking no.

There's definitely no sharing the news now. I suppose it'll have to be a surprise moment later on. It's truthfully quite the day, not to mention Meme is coming to the game. She's made it to a handful throughout my time at Barker, but the chance to watch me play and meet my girlfriend? She wouldn't miss the opportunity.

Of course I warned Susie. I didn't want her to be caught off guard when my foul-mouthed grandma started asking her questions about us, because she most definitely will. Even so, I am pretty fucking excited to see Memes, it's been too long. And I'm even more excited for her to meet Susie.

> About that...

SUSIE Q

PAUL.

> I know baby, I'm sorry. I didn't have the chance I thought beforehand.

> This changes nothing. I'll tell them, Q.

> And I don't give a fuck if it's before or during the moment you're in my arms.

SUSIE Q

Do you think it'll be okay? That everyone will be okay with us?

> They will be, baby.

> Say hi to Memes for me. I'll see you after
> the game.

I lock my phone without waiting for her reply. I could spend the entirety of my time before the game talking to her, but I should somewhat focus. Tonight's our opening game and although I've been drafted to the Razer's, my performance is still under review and at any moment they could withdraw their offer.

It's something I try not to worry about too much. My college record is fairly impressive. I've had twelve shutouts in the span of two years and I'm sitting at a save percentage of ninety-one. I just need to keep my shit together and finish these next two years strong – simple, easy. Playing hockey with my best friends with Susie Cobble cheering me on?

What the fuck could go wrong?

Chapter 48

Susie

My hands are clammy as we pull up to the hockey rink for so many reasons…

One, it's the first game I'm watching as Paul's girlfriend.

Two, I'm meeting his Meme.

Three, tonight we tell our friends about *us*.

Time with Paul has been a blur filled with happiness, laughter, orgasms and cuddles. I suppose it's been over a month since the entire arrangement began, two weeks since we finally shared how we felt about one another. I know that's not long, but the feelings I have for him are almost overwhelming, in the best way.

And keeping us a secret has been exhausting, especially because I hate keeping it from my girls. But before I walk into the arena, I want to be able to walk in as Paul Simmons' girlfriend, which means it's time to come clean.

We file out of Lucy's car, and as we do, I unzip my jacket leaving it behind, stepping out into the cool October night. The girls take off towards the door and I swear I can feel my heart beating a mile a minute.

I clear my throat as I holler at them. "Wait!"

Immediately, they all turn around.

"What is it Suse?" Clara's eyes are wide as she hurries back to me, scanning my face. "Do you feel sick?"

"Do you need water, babe? I have some in my car but it may be lukewarm?" Lucy asks as she heads to her trunk.

"Sitting might help you feel better? Here," Leah grabs my hand as she tries to lower me to the ground. "Sara, do you have a snack in that gigantic ass purse of yours?"

"Firstly, my purse is not that gigantic. But yes," she begins rummaging through it, "I have a granola bar!"

I can't help but be in awe of my best friends. So caring and loving; I am truly lucky to have such amazing friends.

"No, no…it's not that," I scrunch my nose as I shrug my shoulders. They're all side-eyeing one another, trying to figure out what's going on. I practiced what I was going to say, the entire story of how Paul and I started, how we got to where we are. A carefully thought out explanation of why I kept it from them for so long. But all that goes out the window when I yell, "Paul and I are dating!"

Their reactions come in waves and I watch each one wash over their face. Shock turned to confusion turned to… cheering?

"Shut up!" Clara says as she grabs my cheeks with her hands. "Since when?! How…oh my god you were the date weren't you?! No wonder he was being so secretive!!"

"Please share every detail," Leah beams.

"I knew you had a sex glow about you," Lucy grins as she grabs my shoulders, turning me around. "I'm assuming he bought you this?"

I think the smile I'm sporting answers her question.

"We were going to tell you guys sooner but…but we sort of just officially started dating and–"

"And nothing," Sara cuts me off. "You don't have to

explain yourself to us, Suse. You're happy, we're happy. Plus, I think you and Paul are adorable. Always have," she pulls me into a hug.

"You don't *have* to explain," Clara kisses my cheek, "but if you want, I would definitely love to hear all about you and Paul!"

"I do," I say quickly. "I have a lot to tell you guys."

So, I do. I share the entire truth. The quick details about what happened in high school, how this *thing* between Paul and I started because of Jamee and I's date, how it quickly turned from me needing help with self-confidence to just needing...him.

I tell them how I started to develop feelings, how sweet and caring he's been through the entire journey of discovering myself, how he's so much more than the playboy we've always known him as.

Five minutes later, I'm wrapping up my story, *our story.*

"Wow," Clara says as she loops her arm in mine. "I'm sorry you felt those feelings alone, Suse. You're beautiful, radiant, so smart and the kindest person I've ever met. Whoever this fucker was in high school that did that to you better count his lucky stars we don't know where he is now."

"I'm not above murder," Lucy shrugs, making me laugh as a tear escapes my eye. Not because I'm sad, but because their responses are so refreshing. No animosity for not telling them. For keeping Paul and I a secret. For not coming to them for advice.

Pure love.

"Oh shit balls," Sara pulls a tissue out of her purse, handing it to me. "Why are you crying, Suse?"

"Because I truly have the best friends one could ever ask for," I look around at the girls. "I thought about coming to y'all and telling you what was going on, but...I had already let Lane affect me so much that I didn't want it to affect this, too. I didn't want to put the burden of my issues on all of you."

"Suse," Leah says as she grabs my other arm. "A burden? If your shoulders are heavy, so are ours. You can't carry everything, but if you try and need some help, we're here. Always."

Sniffling, I rest my head on her shoulder. "I know. I love you all."

I wipe my nose, sure that my eyes are red, mascara probably on my face from the few tears that slid down my cheek, and nod towards the door. "Think we can go inside to watch my boyfriend play now?"

"Fuck yes," Clara chuckles. "Speaking of the boys. Do they know?"

"Paul is telling them tonight," I shrug. "Do you think they'll be okay with it?"

"Please," Lucy huffs. "If the asshole we know as Clay can get over Leah and Jake fucking behind his back, no offense freshie, the boys can get over anything."

I look at Leah who's cheeks are slightly red as she says, "I mean…you aren't wrong."

"Yeah…yeah, you're right. All will be great. Tonight will be great. Oh, and I'm meeting Paul's Meme for the first time. She's sitting with us so what a night, right?" I chuckle nervously.

"What a night indeed," Clara winks.

"Okay, okay," Sara says as she opens the door to the rink, "can we go admire the boy aquarium now?"

✳ ✳ ✳

"Wow, it's insane here!" I shout over the loudness of cheers. The boys have just taken the ice for warmups and immediately I spot my number one. He effortlessly glides around the rink next to Jake with Liam and Clay in front of them. And when his hazel eyes meet mine, I swear my heart stops.

He's so dangerously sexy. Dangerous because I'd give this man whatever he wanted, whenever he wanted – that's the kind of hold he has on me.

And I'm perfectly okay with that. More than, actually.

Him, along with Liam, Jake and Clay, stop in front of us. I've seen hockey games before, but being able to openly admire Paul in his gear is really doing something to me. His usual perfectly styled hair is messy, the pads he's dressed in make him look ten times his size, and it's even hotter knowing everything that lies underneath.

"Sweetie, you're almost drooling," Charlotte's sweet voice jolts me out of my thoughts.

Shit. Shit. Shit. I completely forgot I was sitting next to Paul's grandma, who definitely just say me eye-fuck her grandson...

"Oh, I–I wasn't–"

"He deserves to be gawked at," she pats my arm, waving at Paul. We're about five rows back from the glass, so we can't hear what the boys are saying to one another, but I watch as Paul nudges Jake, pointing to Charlotte beside me.

Both of their faces light up, smiling wide. Paul points at her, mouthing very big for us to see, *MIND YOUR MANNERS*, before giving me a wink, sliding his helmet on and skating to the net located directly in front of us. Did I maybe encourage choosing seats behind the net so I can admire Paul all night? Possibly...

He drops to his knees, a sight I've come to love when we're alone, and begins stretching and holy hell. There's a very strong possibility I'm turned on just by watching this man do his awkward, but incredibly sexy, hip thrusts.

And I must be staring for a while because Leah, who's next to me, nudges me with her shoulder.

"We have so much to be thankful for with hockey, don't we? It's absolutely insane what they put their bodies through, but I'm not complaining about the perks of their intensive workouts," she laughs.

"It's so…hot," I admit with red cheeks.

"Are you warm, sweetie?" Charlotte asks, causing my cheeks to turn to flames.

I literally am making a fool of myself in front of Paul's most loved human.

"Nope, no I am fine!" I squeal. "How was the trip in, Char–"

"Meme, works perfectly, dear."

I find it endearing she prefers for me to use the same name Paul's called her all his life.

"How was the trip in, Meme?" I correct myself with a grin, turning to face her.

It's at this moment I can see Paul so vividly in her. I know she isn't his mother, but the similarities are there. They have the same nose, hazel colored eyes and thick eyebrows. At sixty-seven years young, she looks pretty remarkable. Her hair is different shades of grey, natural and lovely.

Paul hasn't shared much about his grandma's personal life. I don't know much about his grandpa, but looking at the strong-willed lady in front of me who raised her grandson since birth, I have nothing but respect and love for her.

"I despise flying," she chuckles. "Airports are crazy and the one I flew out of in Lancaster doesn't nearly compare to O'Hare's airport. But that damn taxi driver," she shivers, "almost gave me a goddamn heart attack while driving through Chicago."

Paul is an Ohio boy, that was the first thing I learned about him during our twenty question game back during our Daytona road trip – he grew up in Lancaster – and although he never quite told me how he found Barker University, I sure am glad he did.

"Well, Paul must be so happy you're here." My eyes drift back to where the boys are now lining up by the net, practicing shots as Paul blocks every single one of them. "He told me how much you mean to him and…" I clear my throat, "and I'm so happy I was able to meet you tonight."

"When Paul told me there was a girl he was thinking about during practice, I knew he was in trouble," she pats my thigh as she looks at Paul. "He's never…he's never had a relationship before, so I know this is serious for him and it makes an old grandmother's heart happy to know he's found someone to let in."

Don't cry. Don't cry. Don't cry.

"You did a great job raising him. You should be proud."

"Of my boy, Paul?" She looks at me with tears in her eyes. "Always."

Chapter 49

Paul

Taking the ice tonight felt different, and I think a large part of that is knowing there's two women in the crowd that I can't stop thinking about.

During warm ups, I couldn't help but sneak some looks at my girl smiling ear to ear as she talked with Memes. Tonight has everything I love – my guys, my game, my girls.

And yes, I am so fucking in love with Susie Cobble. I am in love with my best friend and I can't wait to tell her.

But first, we have a game to win.

And so far, we're unstoppable. The line changes are damn near perfect. Liam scored a point in the first three minutes of the game and our defense isn't allowing Carnelly the chance. Jake has checked the right-winger every time he touches the puck, slamming him into the boards and getting the puck to Clay to set up the offensive plays.

And for Clay's first game as captain, he's doing a great fucking job. Controlling the momentum, winning the face-offs, and most importantly, backing the team no matter what zone we're playing. He's a goddamn beast.

"Left, left, left!" I yell down the ice at Shaffy who's not

paying attention to number five barreling towards him. Just as quick as the words leave my mouth, he's being slammed into the boards, falling to the ice as five slaps the puck to eighteen – Carnelly's golden boy, Ross.

The boys are on him, but he's one hell of a player and when he makes it past Clay, I know it's up to me. He lines up the shot, the lean of his shoulders indicates he's going left, so when he shoots, I slide. And he does shoot left, but to fucking Gantser who sends it right past me on the right.

Fucking dammit.

I'm standing up, Clay making his way to me, when I hear Ross and Ganster celebrating.

"Fuck yes!" He yells as he headbutts Ganster, taking off his helmet as he smooths his hair back. "Great fucking shot dude."

"Nice set up," Ganster looks back at me. "Simmons there didn't know what the fuck was happening."

"He was drafted to the Razers, no surpr–holy shit," Ross stops mid-sentence as he grabs Ganster's chest. "It's the bitch from high school," he laughs.

I'm not paying much attention to them, as Clay's now talking with me about the play that just took place, but I also can't help but overhear him.

"The one you–"

"The one I humiliated. Fuck, I had no idea she went here. Haven't seen that bitch since her family tried getting me into legal trouble. Goddamn cunt."

My head begins to turn in the direction they're looking, trying to figure out what poor girl he's talking about when Clay snaps his fingers in front of my face.

"Don't get in your fucking head about this Paul. It's one score, all at the hands of Shaffy for not getting his head out of his ass."

"We're good, we're good," I tell him, slapping him on his helmet. "Have to let them think they have a chance," I wink.

Chuckling, he skates back to center ice for the next face-off, while Liam and Jake do a quick pass tapping my stick with theirs.

"I know this may not be the time," Jake shrugs, "but I told you so about Ganster."

"Yeah, yeah," I drop my stick in front of his skate, tripping him as he rolls to the ice.

"Shithead," he huffs as he flips me off, skating back to his zone as Liam laughs, giving me a thumbs up.

I sway back and forth, and I know I should keep my eyes focused ahead of me, but I can't help that my head swivels to the stands behind me. One look, one look at my girl and I'll be good.

Except she isn't there…

Chapter 50

Susie

"Let's go Russell!" Clara yells from my left. "That's my husband!" She says as she points to Liam who just scored.

The boys are on fire. I don't know much about hockey, actually...I know nothing. It's on my list of things to ask Paul to teach me, just the basics at least. But I do know that watching the boys together on the ice is incredible. As for the rest of their teammates, I couldn't tell you their names.

I can tell how at ease Paul feels in the net. He's gliding back and forth, relaxed, and it's honestly impressive to watch.

And I may or may not be checking out his ass periodically...

"Great fucking stop, Henry!" Charlotte, Meme, hollers from my right. Paul doesn't look, but I know he can hear and I can only imagine how big his grin is.

"So," Leah lowers her voice, "how does it feel to be dating Barker University's star hockey goalie?"

I turn, her eyebrows raising as she waits for an answer.

"Like it isn't real...I mean, look at him," I motion to where Paul is. "He's hot and can have any girl he wants. Yet here I am wearing his name. I never thought this would be where he and I would end up, you know?"

She grins as she looks out to the ice, looping her arm through mine. "I mean…the man was always flirting with you, Suse. Maybe neither of you expected to end up here, but I think it's great you did," she squeezes the arm she's holding. "I think from just hearing the snippet about you two outside, that it's obvious he makes you happy and treats you like the queen you deserve to be treated as. I know he's a great friend and I bet he's an even greater boyfriend."

"He really is," I smile as the sound of Paul's yelling brings my gaze back to the rink.

"Left, left, left!"

And just as he says it, the Barker player is slammed into the wall with a Carnelly player quickly making his way towards Paul. He gets in position as his other teammate crowds the player with the puck. It all happens so fast, and I'm not entirely sure what happened, but the puck goes flying into the open space on Paul's right.

Carnelly's players go wild as they celebrate the score while my eyes stay locked on Paul. Clay starts making his way over as the Carnelly player in front of him takes off his helmet.

I watch his eyes lock on mine.

I feel the blood drain from my face.

I hear nothing as the sound of my heartbeat rings loudly in my ears, like I'm on the verge of fainting.

There's no way. No fucking way. It's not him…can't be.

Except I can tell by the shit-eating grin on his face that it is.

Lane Ross is staring into my eyes, smirking and laughing with his friend.

Suddenly, I'm not the confident Susie Cobble. I'm the

Susie Cobble that was being pointed and laughed at during a party.

I jolt to my feet as he turns, skating away. I can feel my stomach churning, vomit rising to my throat. I–I have to get out of here.

"I–uh…excuse me, please," I say to Charlotte, quickly scooting past her.

"Dear, are you okay?" She stands, placing a hand on my back. "You look awfully pale?"

"I…" looking back at my friends, I know if I tell them here and now I'll break down in tears, and the last thing I want is to give Lane Ross any type of satisfaction. "I just got a little sick to my stomach. I'll be right back," I plaster a tight-lipped grin on my face.

"Do you want one of us to come–"

"No–no, I'm okay."

I don't give them a chance to answer as I hurry up the stairs and to the restroom, throwing myself into a stall as I sit, placing a hand over my chest to slow my breathing.

How is this happening? I–I knew he played a sport in high school, I sure don't remember that sport being hockey?

I never expected to see him again, let alone as he plays against my college…my boyfriend.

Seeing him brings so many emotions. Anger, hurt, sadness. I don't know if I want to cry because of the old feelings that are bubbling up or because I'm so fucking pissed that he had the audacity to smirk at me. Like he didn't try, *and almost*, ruin my life. Like he didn't walk away from the whole situation without facing any type of consequence…

He's so smug, stupid, and he's only gotten uglier with age, fucking asshole.

Even so, I don't want to face him. I don't want him to know how much he took from me…how I struggled with such a big part of myself because of him. How until recently, I still let what he did affect the deepest parts of me.

I close my eyes, focusing on my breathing. Mrs. Baker used to tell me to think of my happy place, focus on what's good, what I love, what makes me happy instead of letting one moment cloud my thinking.

So, as I slowly breathe in and out, I do just that. *My happy place? Barker. What's good? My life. What I love? The girls and Paul Simmons.*

My happy place? Barker…

I continue repeating the three, allowing myself to focus on the now. Of the friends I have out there that would ride or die for me. Of Paul, my best friend – my boyfriend – who has helped me find myself again.

I gradually open my eyes, continuing my breathing as my heart rate comes back to normal.

"Lane Ross is nothing," I quietly say to myself. "What he did to me has no control over my life. He's an asshole who probably has a micro-peni–"

The bathroom door flies open so fast it slams against the wall, causing me to jump.

"Suse?" I recognize Clara's voice immediately. "Are you in here?" she asks, laced with worry.

"Yeah…I'm–I'm coming out." Standing, I take one deep breath before opening the door. I feel better, but I still dread seeing him out there. His face is one I had hoped to never see again…

"Babe, are you okay? You still look a bit pale?"

"I…I don't feel sick, but there is something going on."

"Should I tell the girls to come here?"

"No, no. I–I don't want to make it a big thing because he doesn't deserve it. But…number eighteen on Carnelly is *him*…"

She runs her fingers through her auburn-brown hair as she bites her bottom lip. "Him as in?"

"The asshole from high school. The one who–um…pulled my top down–"

"THAT FUCKER?" She yells, her face turning as red as the top she's wearing. "Oh just fucking wait until we find him after the game. A good kick to his fucking balls would be good for him." She begins pacing, laughing like a mad woman.

"As sweet as that is Clare Bear, he isn't worth it."

She makes her way next to me as I'm washing my hands, staring at me in the mirror. "Do you want to tell someone? See if they would remove him?"

Shaking my head, I smile at my friend through the reflection. "I love you tons, but there's nothing we can do. He got away with the shit he did and it was years ago, Clara. Yeah, I kind of freaked out when I saw him…it's been four years since what happened and this was the first time our paths have crossed again. Plus, him smirking at me really set me off…but I'm going to be okay. Seeing him just kind of brought all those old feelings up and for a moment I panicked, but then I remembered all the amazing people I have, all the ways I've grown since then and realized he isn't fucking worth it."

Grabbing my shoulders, she turns me towards her. "You are the strongest person I know, Suse. Resilient, kind, full of love and one of the greatest friends I've had. You're absolutely right, a dickhead like that isn't worth it." Pulling me into a hug, she softly whispers, "But if that motherfucker tries to approach you tonight, I'm kneeing him in the dick and punching him in the nose."

I can't help but laugh as I pull away from her, grabbing

her arm as I lead us towards the bathroom door. "You never cease to amaze me, Clare bear."

"Well, I'll keep amazing you till the day I die, babe," she winks. "Are you ready to go watch the boys kick ass?"

And although I still have my feelings and hesitations about having to see Lane out there, I feel at ease knowing I'm never alone.

Chapter 51

Paul

We're four minutes out from the first intermission. All I need to do is focus on not letting them score, and apart from Shaffy's error earlier, that's been fairly easy.

Carnelly isn't full of amazing players – they have one great player. And even with Ross being a great fucking scorer, if his team can't pick their shit up and play defense to keep the puck, it does no good.

I'm watching Jake pressure Gantser as he battles him for the puck to my left, trying to keep him away from the net and get the puck back to Liam or Shaffy. After a check into the boards, he makes it out, sending a cross-ice pass to Clay as Liam moves in behind him.

It's a play I've watched many times in games, one that always throws off the defense.

Clay brings his stick back, making it appear that he's taking a slap shot to the left-hand side, but at the last minute he drops the pass, leaving the puck behind as he veers left while Liam comes in sending it flying to the right side of the net with his signature wrist-shot.

The crowd erupts in cheers as the players surround

Liam, clasping him on his shoulders and helmet congratulating him while our teammates on the bench slap their sticks against the boards. Atmospheres like tonight are my favorite.

As Carnelly's players begin making their way to the center of the ice, I allow myself to turn around, searching for those addicting green eyes once again. This time, Susie is standing there, her head turned towards Clara as she's clapping. When she faces the ice again, our eyes connect instantly. Pulling my face mask off, I shake the sweat from my hair as I point at her, winking. Her face immediately turns a shade of red as she rolls her eyes. God, I love when she blushes.

Excitingly, she points to my Memes beside her. I can only imagine the things they're talking about, but seeing my two favorite women together, cheering me on, makes tonight feel pretty damn special.

There's girls calling my name to the left, trying to get my attention, but I don't give a fuck. I have all I need right in front of me. But I do see Susie look, and I watch the look of disgust spread over her face with one of the girls yells, "*You can score with me, number one!*"

My head doesn't even flinch in her direction. Maybe once it would have, but not this Paul Simmons. Not the one who's got the girl and doesn't want to let her go.

So, instead, I bring my glove to my mouth as I look into Susie's eyes and blow her a kiss. I don't give a shit if no one knows who it's going to, she does.

Pulling my helmet back over my face, I turn around and see Ross and Ganster standing there, looking past me in the direction I was just looking. Liam and Jake have now made their way over to me as well as Clay gets ready for yet another face off.

"Hope your body isn't too sore from eating shit against the walls over there, Ganster," Jake says.

"I'm good, it's your girl you should check in on. The other night when she was taking my cock–"

Jake gets in close as he grabs a fistful of his jersey. "I fucking dare you to finish that sentence. Give me a goddamn reason to knock your fucking teeth out."

Liam comes beside Jake, grabbing his arm as Ross puts a hand on Ganster's chest.

"Okay, okay. You know how the game goes, fucking relax," Ganster throws his hands up.

He means the chirping – years of hockey helps you develop thick skin – it's easy not to react, especially with NCAA's strict rules about fighting. But talking about someone's girl isn't the same as shit-talking about the game.

"I suggest you keep the jawing game related or you'll have a bigger fucking problem than just the scoreboard." Liam spits.

Laughing, Ross says, "Game related, got it." He goes to skate off, but not before stopping and motioning behind me. "I'm not much into black-haired bitches with small tits anyways."

Liam and Jake ignore him, turning to me as they begin talking about the game, but something isn't sitting right with me.

Because I know he was looking towards our girls and I know the only girl back there with short hair is–

The one I humiliated. Her family tried getting me into legal trouble.

Motherfucker.

Without thinking, I rush forward, grabbing him by the back of his jersey and yanking him towards me. He quickly spins around, his eyes wide.

"What the fuck are you doing Simmons?"

"You're the fucker that got away with the shit you did to her at that party, aren't you?"

I should calm down, I know I should. But I can't. All I see right now is red, my fists are balled tightly at my side and I can feel Liam and Jake next to me, ready to intervene at any moment.

"Ah, she told you, huh? Four years later and she's still hung up about it? I did her a solid by giving people a reason to talk about her." He goes to look past me, but over my dead fucking body will he ever look Susie's way again.

"I suggest you look at me and me only." I step closer, our face guards only inches away.

"Paul, what's going on?" Liam asks as he places his hand on my chest, trying to push me away. For a moment I almost do, until Ross opens his mouth again.

"She's not worth it, you know? Still has the small tits and probably still a bitch. I suppose the rest of her body doesn't look half–"

I don't give him a chance to finish his sentence before I'm shoving him backwards, pulling his guard off with one hand as I rip mine off as well. I hear the gasps from the crowd as my fist connects with his face, as we begin trading swing for swing, but I don't care about anything other than hurting him for hurting Susie.

For standing here like he isn't the scum of the fucking earth. For once dimming the most beautiful ray of sunshine I've ever met.

I keep throwing punches while Liam and Jake try pulling me off of him. Whistles are blowing, fans are cheering, Coach is most definitely yelling, but it isn't until Clay grabs my arm that I take a moment to breathe.

I drop my arm from Ross's jersey, but the son-of-a-bitch won't stop.

He spits blood on the ice as he says, "Can't believe a cunt like her has you this worked up."

I start to lunge for him again but Clay's words slice through the air. "Simmons get your fucking ass to that bench right now!"

My eyes snap to his and back to Ross who's now being held back by his teammates as well.

I made my point. He hurt my girl, I hurt him. Simple.

Skating to the side to face whatever repercussions come my way, I throw one last look over my shoulder. "Talk about my girlfriend again and it'll be more than your fucking nose that I break."

"Are you out of your damn mind, Simmons?!" Coach repeats for probably the third time. "Fighting during the first game? What the hell came over you out there?! You know–"

"Yes Coach, I know about NCAA's rules." I keep my eyes locked on him, knowing if I don't this will be ten times worse.

"Then why in the hell did you start a goddamn brawl with Carnelly's number one player? Was it over some girl? Lord help me Simmons, I might actually murder you."

I look over at Clay, Liam and Jake who are just as confused as Coach. Susie's story isn't mine to share, so I won't.

"Coach," I sigh, "I know I fucked up." I look around at my teammates. "I know I put us in a shitty position and I take full responsibility for my actions and whatever consequences I have to face. But sir, Lane Ross did an awful fucking thing years ago to someone I love and never had to face the consequences. He deserves more than a broken fucking nose."

Coach Watt runs his hands over his face as he takes a deep breath. "Look, son. I know you and I know this is out of your ordinary, and that is the only fucking reason I'm not throwing you out of the locker room right now. But from now on, that shit stays off my ice or you will."

He turns to Clay as he picks up his clipboard. "Now, I have to go talk to the officials to find out what exactly this is going to cost you. Clay, please come up with a game plan for the next two periods, and Paul, don't leave this fucking room."

"Yes, Coach," I say as I stand, tearing my pads off. I don't know what will happen, but I know I'm not going back out for tonight's game.

And I have not a single ounce of regret. I'd do anything for Susie. Beating up the asshole who broke her so long ago was the least I could do. How will she feel about it? I'm not too sure…

I sit, my knee bouncing in anticipation as I wait, listening to Clay discuss line changes and updates to the roster.

"Hennigan, you're going in as goalie. I suggest you talk with Paul about what he's noticed in their shooting habits and talk fast because we have five minutes before we take the ice again."

Miles Hennigan, a sophomore transfer from Wyoming, bounces over to me as we go through Carnelly's tendencies. I imagine Ross will be out too, so at least that takes care of their top scorer. For the next three minutes, I walk him through the tell-tale signs of their shooters patterns.

"Every time Ganster has taken a shot, he'll look right where he's aiming the second before he sends it to the net.

Don't go too early on him and you'll know exactly where you need to–"

"Alright," Clay calls. "Time to head out. Shaffy, practice some different shots and drills with Hennigan. We'll be out there in a second."

One by one, the team files out of the locker room as Jake, Clay and Liam hang back. Going on my third year of college hockey, over forty games I've played with the boys, and I've never so much as threatened to fight.

I know they're confused and I owe them some of the truth.

"Paul, buddy," Clay crosses his arms like a disappointed dad. "What the fuck was that out there?"

"Fuck what happened with Ross, that asshole deserved what was coming to him. I'm more focused on the fact you mentioned your girlfriend?" Jake chuckles. "Um…what's that about, Paulie?"

"I just want to say I told you so," Liam shrugs his shoulders. "I called bullshit and that something's been going on and here we are finding out something has in fact been going on." He takes a seat next to me. "We have two minutes so fucking spill it."

Well, this wasn't exactly what I had in mind when I told the boys about Susie and I, but I guess it'll work.

"I do have a girlfriend."

"I knew you seemed like less of a prick," Clay teases.

Jake holds his fist out like a middle schooler. "Hell yes, bud! I'm happy for you. Who is she? How did you meet? How long–"

"Jake, dude. Chill it with the questions," Liam shakes his head as he clasps my shoulders. "What's her name? Is she here tonight? Do the girls know her?"

"Asshole," Jake kicks Liam in the shin. "I wanted to ask all the questions."

"We know," Clay chimes in. "Please get them to shut up and answer the questions, Paul."

Chuckling, I rub my hand over my jaw. "Well, she's pretty fucking great. I–I didn't exactly know I was falling for her, or expect to. You guys know me, I thought it was just the same shit – I found her attractive and flirted with her. But–"

"But it was more than a hookup?" Jake asks, finishing my sentence.

"It wasn't even about that. It was spending time with her, watching the silly ass rom-coms she would choose, seeing her smile…I became addicted to all things Susie and before I knew it I was falling–"

"SUSIE?" Liam repeats. "As in Susie Cobble, our friend? Clara's fucking bridesmaid and roommate? The one I told you no chance last year? That Susie??"

"Well–"

"Wait a minute!" Jake yells. "You told me she wasn't your type last year. That you weren't hers? What the hell changed, dude?"

I saw this going a little bit better in my head.

"I changed," I confess. "You guys know about Lisa and how I feel about her. I–I didn't want to let someone in just for them to fucking leave like she has all my life. I thought I'd be better off not letting someone in at all. And then Susie and I started hanging out and…and I realized being with her would be worth it. I'd gladly give my all to Susie. I mean…fuck guys, I'm in love with her."

I'm tempted to grab my phone from my bag to snap a photo at how wide Liam and Jake's mouths are right now. As for Clay, I think after the fiasco with Jake and Leah, nothing phases him.

"How long have you two…?" he asks.

"A month or so? But I just made things official a few weeks ago?"

"A MONTH OR SO?" Jake throws his head back. "Dude, you've been keeping this secret from us for a few months?"

Slowly, we all turn to face him and of course, Clay's the first one to speak.

"Like hell you're giving shit for keeping a secret," he laughs. "Do you not remember getting with my sister behind my back for *MONTHS*," he emphasizes.

Jake scratches the back of his neck as he says, "Well…I suppose you're right."

"I'm always right," Clay adds.

I turn towards Liam who's been awfully quiet and at the moment, he's hard to read. I can't tell if he wants to hug me or punch me. I think I'd be fine with either if it meant he'd just fucking say something.

"Leon, buddy. If you want to punch me, just do it. You know I hate silence."

"Why the hell would I punch you, Paul?"

"Because I'm with Susie? Clara's best friend and I specifically remember you tried warning me away from her."

He drapes his arm over my shoulder. "Dude. No fucking way would I be mad about you being happy. I know you've been through some shit with your moth–egg donor, and out of all of us, you deserve to have someone. Did I expect that someone to be Susie? Umm…no. But I don't give a shit, bud. I'm happy for you."

"We're happy for you," Jake says with a smile, wrapping his arm around Clay's shoulder. "Hmmm," he turns towards him, "we all have someone who happens to be friends with Clara? Should we expect a certain someone to–"

"Fuck off. One," Clay says as he grabs Jake's hand from

off his shoulder, "I'm focused on hockey and hockey only. Two, Sara's sweet and attractive, but not my type."

"I think we all know he isn't talking about Sara," Liam lowers his eyes.

"I've said it from the start," I say as I stand, "you two are either going to hate fuck or legitimately kill each other."

"She's the equivalent of nails scratching a chalkboard for me. The sight of her alone pisses me off," Clay groans.

"We'll see," I tease. "You guys better get out there and win this game."

"What did he do?" Liam asks as he stands. "Three years and you've never been pissed like that. He did something to Susie?"

I continue gathering my things to shower as I answer. "He hurt my girl pretty bad back in high school, not physically but…emotionally. And he never had to face consequences for what he did so tonight, I made sure he did. He still deserves more, broken hands would be preferable, but this helped."

"We would've had your back had we known," Jake shakes his head. "If I had the chance, I'd probably murder the asshole Leah had problems with in high school. So," he grabs his stick, tapping me on the leg to look at him, "we'll miss you out there, but that asshole got what was coming for him."

He heads out the door, Liam following behind him. "Proud of you, buddy. Not just for breaking the fuckers nose, but for putting yourself out there. Falling in love with my best friend was the greatest thing that's happened to me, and I know you'll be good for Susie.

"She's good for me," I say without hesitation.

The two head out the door and to the ice, with Clay still standing here staring at me.

"Tell them two fuckers this and I'll suffocate you in your sleep," he hangs his head. "I love you all like my brothers.

My incredibly annoying, idiotic brothers. And although I hate not having you on the ice tonight, and probably for a while, I'm proud of you for standing up for your girl, Paul. I'm happy for you."

"One second," I say as I pull out my phone, "can you say that again for the camera?"

"And the moment's gone," he turns around, walking out the door.

"Clay!" I holler as the door begins to shut. He doesn't turn around, but he does stop. "I'm honored to be your brother."

Chapter 52

Susie

The rest of the game was a blur.

Barker won three to two, and the boys were ecstatic as they celebrated on the ice, but you could tell they were missing a piece of them.

Paul Simmons.

My boyfriend who beat the shit out of Lane Ross on the ice.

I don't know how he put two and two together, I was hoping he wouldn't for this exact reason.

Lane wasn't worth Paul getting kicked out of the game, missing the season opener and probably more, from what his Meme said.

"That little piece of shit must have done something pretty bad to piss off my boy like that," she says as we stand, waiting for the crowd to clear to make our way to the lobby.

"I–I think he was defending me," I confess. "I swear I didn't tell him to…I didn't even know he played for Carnelly."

"This boy, did he hurt you?" Her tone serious.

"Not physically, but something he did took a toll on me

emotionally in a pretty rough way…" I begin chewing on the inside of my mouth. "It was back in high school, something that I should've gotten over a long time ago, but parts of what happened still haunted me. Paul helped me gain back a lot of the confidence I once lost, and I don't know how he figured out who he was but–"

"But nothing. My boy stood up for someone he cares about, sweetie. That makes a mother's heart happy no matter the consequences he has to face."

I can't help the tear that escapes my eye. "You raised a great man."

"That boy had everything going against him," she looks out towards the ice. "Hockey has been the love of his life for so long, a constant." Her brown eyes meet mine as she smiles. "But getting to spend time with you tonight, Susie. I think he may have found a new love, and nothing makes my heart happier."

* * *

The girls and I are circled around the lobby after explaining to the rest of them why Paul did what he did.

And just like Charlotte, they were proud of him.

Now, we're sharing stories about ourselves and the boys as we continue to wait for the team to emerge from the locker room. I imagine they're having to have a lengthy discussion surrounding tonight's events and what happens now.

From what Charlotte explained, it won't affect his NHL dreams of playing for the Razers – he's already been drafted – but he'll most likely be facing suspension from a few games this season.

"Charlotte, you're a badass," Clara laughs, wiping a tear from her eye.

"Please, call me Meme," she grins as she continues her story. "So, yeah. For the last two weeks I've been stealing his flowers from his flowerbed. If he thinks his dog can come shit in my yard and eat my flowers, he's got another thing coming for him."

"Has he noticed?" Lucy asks.

"It's only a matter of time, and when he does, I pray he comes over and asks. I'm liable to kick him in the pecker."

"Meme, pecker is so outdated," a deep voice comes from behind me. I know it's Paul without needing to look, but when I turn around and see him standing there, a mix of emotions run through me.

He's in his signature grey sweats and t-shirt, hair tousled and wet, but his face is bruised. There's a scratch on his chin, his eye is already purple and swollen, and his lip is busted.

I want nothing more than to wrap him in my arms, kiss every cut and bruise he has, but I know his Meme has been just as excited to see him and I should really let them have this moment.

"Oh, Henry," she pulls him in a hug.

"Memes, you're kind of suffocating me," he teases as he tries to pull away.

"I know, I know. I've just missed you is all," she grabs his cheeks. "One hell of a punch you threw out there and one much deserved. I'm proud of you, Henry."

He looks past her at me with his brows drawn together in confusion. I open my mouth to say something but we're joined by the rest of the boys.

"Hey wifey," Liam snakes his arms around Clara's waist. "Looking gorgeous as ever." He directs his attention to Charlotte, pulling her into a hug. "I know I'm your favorite of his friends, Memes."

Laughing, she hugs him back. "Oh, Liam. Maybe one

day," she pats his back. "Is this beautiful auburn-haired gal Mrs. Russell?"

"The one and only," he moves back to Clara. "This is Clara Russell, the absolute love of my life," he says proudly.

"We met earlier," Charlotte says, "and sweetie if I would've known you're the one putting up with this one's antics, I would've offered a lot more advice," she winks.

"Okay, okay, let me through," Jake says. He plants a kiss on Leah's cheek, then heads directly to Charlotte. "Her actual favorite has arrived." Wrapping her in a hug, he flips Liam off. And when he pulls away, he keeps his arms on her shoulders as his face lights up. "Memes, meet my girl, Leah Harper."

"I had the privilege of sitting and getting to know each of these wonderful ladies," she smiles. "All of you boys deserve someone who brings you happiness. You too, Clay," she waves him forward, "I see you back there. It's nice to meet you other than just FaceTime." And before he knows it, he's wrapped in a Charlotte hug, too.

It's funny watching him hesitate and eventually give in, wrapping his arms around her petite body.

"It's nice to meet you too, ma'am," he nods as he pulls away.

"Wow," Lucy says, "he has manners?"

"To people I respect, yeah. To girls–"

"Nope," Leah shoves her finger over Clay's mouth. "Not tonight. Tonight we're celebrating your first win and Paul being a badass boyfriend."

All eyes go to him and I.

And before I have time to think, he has me wrapped in his arms with my feet off the ground.

"Are you okay, baby?" He whispers into my hair. "If

you're mad at me, I understand. I know that maybe violence isn't the answer, but that asshole deserv–"

"I love you," I softly say into his neck, feeling his body go rigid at my confession.

For a moment we don't move, he keeps me tucked into him as he keeps holding me. Finally, I hear someone speak, but it's not Paul.

"Dude, I can't read your fucking lips, what are you saying?" Liam asks.

Paul shakes his head back and forth as Jake chimes in. "Oh, you want us to give you a minute? Yeah, yeah. We'll be outside."

He puts me down as everyone begins gathering their things.

"Yeah, we'll see you two lovebirds outside," Sara winks.

"Take your time," Leah smiles.

We watch them walk off as Charlotte stays behind.

"I should get back to my hotel. I imagine tonight's an IHOP or B-dabs type of night?"

"B-dabs, Memes? B-Dubs…and I'm not sure where we'll go tonight," he reaches down, lacing his fingers through mine, "but I'm happy either way."

She looks between Paul and I, a grin stretching ear-to-ear.

"Happy looks good on you, Henry," she leans in to hug him. "I love you very much." Then she moves to me. "And Susie, it was an absolute joy talking with you this evening. Thank you for bringing my grandson so much happiness."

I can feel tears forming as I look at the man beside me. The one who's been my best friend, my personal teacher, and now, the one I'm madly in love with.

"I think he's the one I should be thanking."

Chapter 53

Paul

"So," Liam clears his throat, "another secret relationship within the group?"

I had planned to hang back and talk with Susie after the game, after she told me she loved me, I had a whole fucking speech planned. But when Meme left, I didn't get the chance. We walked her out, rode here with our friends, and that's that.

Now, we're sitting in our normal booth at IHOP but I'm still over the fucking moon.

Yes, I'm happy the team won.

Yes, I'm exceptionally happy that I was able to beat the shit out of Lane Ross.

But the biggest reason for my happiness is sitting right next to me.

A year…a whole year I've stood next to Susie as her friend, a fucking idiot who was afraid to want more. It took an arrangement of me helping her to realize I was the one who needed help.

"To be fair," I bend down, planting a kiss on Susie's forehead, "our secret didn't almost destroy the friend group."

"Fuck you," Jake snickers. "Clay," he points to him and then Lucy, "I suppose it's y'alls turn."

Lucy doesn't even look Clay's way as she says, "You got me fucked up if you think I'd ever be into...*that.*" At the same time he says, "I'd rather stick my dick through a meat grinder than go anywhere near her."

They'll fuck before they graduate.

Or commit murder, both are likely possibilities.

"I'm just so excited my Suse has found a good man," Clara winks at me. "I knew there was a certain glow about her. I suppose Vitamin D will do that," she laughs.

I can feel Susie's cheeks heat as she's leaned against me while Liam practically chokes on his food.

"C, sweetie. Please don't mention Vitamin D when talking about my friend..."

"Intimidated by my Vitamin D, Liam?" I cock a brow at him. "Worried that mine may be better?"

"Fucking kill me," Clay huffs to my right.

"It could be arranged," Lucy shrugs.

"Enough, enough," Leah waves them off. "So, Paul," she directs her attention to me, a wide smile on her face as she looks between me and Susie. "You kicked Ross's ass and I couldn't be more proud to call you my friend."

I pull Susie tighter into me as I drop my hand to her thigh. I don't know what she told the girls, but the slight nod she gives me tells me they know enough and I love knowing that she has the girls for moments like tonight.

Just like how I have my boys.

"We don't know what the asshole did, Suse," Jake speaks up, "but I hope you know that if we would have known, it wouldn't have just been Paul getting kicked off the ice."

Clay clears his throat as he brushes his hair out of his

face. "As captain, I don't condone violence. As your friend, we would've all been sitting in the locker room together."

"We'll always have your back, Suse," Liam adds as he kisses Clara on the top of her head. "All of you," he looks at the rest of the girls. "You're our friends, too. If someone fucks with you, they fuck with all of us."

* * *

An hour later, we're finishing up dinner, sitting around listening to the girls talk about their Daytona practices and how they're feeling about the competition in April.

I know one thing for sure…this time when we go to Daytona, I'll be Susie's boyfriend and there will be no mistaking who I'm there to cheer for. We're talking a custom shirt, hat, foam finger, I don't give a fuck. If it can be custom made to support my girl, it will be.

"Oh my god!" Susie yells as she turns to me, grabbing my bicep. "What happens now with hockey? Do–do you still get to play?"

Waiting in the locker room for Coach to tell me what was decided was the longest minutes of my life. He gave me an earful during the first intermission, the second, and post-game, all of which were deserved. But, after he was done ripping me a new asshole, he did finally share the news.

"Well," I say as I tuck a strand of hair behind her ear. "I am most definitely suspended for the next two games. My scholarship is on a very strict no-violence tolerated behavior moving forward, and Coach said I'll be spending an hour after practice with him for some extra conditioning."

I can tell she's not happy about the consequences by the way her shoulders are slumped and the way she's nervously chewing on her bottom lip.

"Paul, that's…I wish–"

"I'd do it all again, Q. I'd take any fucking consequence there is to hurt any asshole who hurts you." I take her cheeks between my hands, ignoring our friends at the table. "I have not a single regret with what happened tonight," I move my thumb back and forth. "Not when that prick didn't get what he deserved for hurting the girl I love."

"I…I don't want you to think you need to say it back," she whispers.

"Susie…" I drop my hands, running one through my hair. "I–"

"I think it's time to go pay," Liam interrupts as he grabs Clara's hand, standing from the table.

"Yep, right behind you," Jake and Leah spring up out of their chairs, followed by the rest of the group.

We don't even have time to say our goodbyes before they're at the register. The only goodbye we get is Clara yelling, "Be good to my girl, Paul Simmons. We all love you both!"

Moments later, they're out the door and we're left alone.

"Well," she chuckles as she turns towards me, "I–I was just saying–"

"That you don't want me to think I need to say it back," I shrug. "Yeah, I heard you. And Q, baby, let me make myself clear…"

Is IHOP the place to tell the girl of my dreams how in love I am? Maybe not. But fuck it.

"I've loved one woman my entire life and she's as stubborn as they come with the kindest heart, and I thought that was enough. But you changed everything, Q. I'm man enough to admit I was afraid to fall in love, afraid of what it would do to me if it ended like it did with Lisa. I guess it took a stunning girl with piercing green eyes to walk into my life to help me realize it."

I reach behind her, grabbing the back of her head as I pull her close to me, resting my forehead on hers. "And here's what I've realized, Q. Love can be fucking terrifying, and I am still convinced I don't know everything I'm doing with the whole boyfriend thing, but it all seems a lot less terrifying with you. So, yes. I love you, Susie Cobble. You are my sunshine girl. The strongest person I know with the biggest fucking heart, and I'm a lucky bastard to be loved by that heart of yours."

She pulls away, bringing her palm to my cheek as a tear slides down hers. "I love you, Paul Simmons. From the moment I asked you to become my teacher, I knew I was in over my head...but this moment, here with you? It was worth it."

I reach up, swiping the tear away with my thumb. "You're worth everything, Q. And I won't ever let you forget it. Now," I say with a cocky grin on my face, "can I take my girlfriend back to my room and show her just how much she's worth?"

Chuckling, she asks, "How do you plan to do that?"

"Worshipping her until she screams my name for the entire house to hear?"

I climb out of the booth, grabbing her hand and pulling her into me. "Poor Rocky might be scarred for life."

"You–you want me to come stay with you at your house tonight?"

"Q, baby. I want you to stay with me forever."

I throw an arm over her shoulder, holding her tight as we walk out of IHOP. She has her hand wrapped around mine with a twinkle in her eyes as she looks up at me. And I know that no matter where I go in life, I couldn't give two shits as long as it's with her by my side.

My best friend.

The girl who started this whole arrangement.

The girl who has my whole fucking heart.

Chapter 54

Epilogue: Paul

One Month Later

"Rocky! Rocky, no!" Clara yells as she runs out of the kitchen and into the living room.

"What's he got this time?" Liam bends down, scooping the ornery pup into his arms. "Come on, bud. Open up," he pries the dog's mouth open. "C, babe. It's just lettuce. Is it safe for him to eat?"

"Not when he's a bad boy and doesn't listen to mom," she says as she grabs the lettuce out of his mouth.

As Liam sets Rocky down, he runs over to the sofa where Jake, Leah and I are sitting.

"Don't worry bud, I'll sneak you some goodies later," Jake whispers.

"Wiley," Leah chuckles, "you're going to make him fatter with all the shit you give him."

He quickly clamps his hands over Rocky's ears. "Darlin'. He can hear you."

It's Thanksgiving day and the entire group is together. Our house smells like a mixture of turkey, pumpkin pie and slightly burnt food, probably at the hands of Clay who's in the kitchen helping the girls.

Apparently, he loves cooking. Who would've thought considering the asshole has never once offered to cook for us.

It's 11:00a.m., the Macy's parade is on – courtesy of Lucy – and it's shaping up to be my favorite holiday ever.

Why?

Because there's a gorgeous black-haired girl bouncing my way in an adorable *talk turkey to me* sweater. Not to mention there's a bit of flour on her face.

The best fucking decision I ever made was agreeing to help Susie Cobble all those weeks ago. Because now? Now, my mornings are spent waking up to her beautiful smile. My days are spent thinking about her. My evenings are spent making her cry out my name.

And I have no fucking doubt that my life will be spent making her happy because the smile on her face as she sits next to me? It's all I ever want to see.

"There's my girl," I drape my arm over her shoulder, pulling her into me. "How's cooking duty going?" Reaching up, I wipe the flour off her face with my thumb, replacing it with a kiss.

"Well," she chuckles, "let's just say that if the potatoes turn out a bit too runny, it was all Sara's fault." She leans into me, her eyes fixed on the TV in front of us as she whispers, "You look really handsome."

"With the help of my girlfriend, I dress up nice, huh?"

I'm wearing her favorite pair of black jeans paired with her favorite grey sweater and collared white shirt underneath – she asked if she could pick my outfit, said something about how cute Thanksgiving photos will be, and I of course said fuck yes.

"She has a great eye for choosing an outfit that really highlights your…features."

Lowering my voice, I say, "If my features are what you want to see, they look better with no clothes on, baby."

She sits up, looking around us, a blush painting her cheeks. "I think I forgot between this morning and now exactly what your features look like under the clothes. Maybe we should take a field trip to your bedroom to jog my memory?"

"Our bedroom," I correct her. No, she hasn't officially moved in, but might as well. She's over every night, she has a whole ass drawer for her over-night clothes and her own space on my dresser for her morning makeup-slash-skin care routine.

"Paul–"

"Susie, I'll remind you every fucking day if need be. My bedroom, my house, my clothes, my time, my heart, whatever the hell it is that belongs to me, belongs to you, too."

Turning to face me, she places a gentle kiss on my lips, and if it weren't for the audience we have, I'd lie her down right here on this sofa and show her how my tongue also belongs to her and her perfect fucking pussy. Instead, I slowly pull away, looking into her deep green eyes.

But as soon as she opens her mouth to say something, Clay's voice cuts through the house.

"Alright girls and assholes, dinner is ready."

* * *

"Holy shit, Suse!" Jake says with a mouthful of potatoes. "These are fucking delicious."

I place a hand on her thigh under the table, mouthing *so fucking good* as Clara chimes in.

"Hands down the best potatoes I've ever had. Look at you, you little chef."

She shakes her head, slightly laughing. "Guys, I appreciate you, but it's just potatoes. The turkey though? Lucy, I'm going to need you to make this every month."

Lucy waves her fork towards Susie as she says, "For the fair price of a new manicure to take care of the nasty turkey shit underneath my nails, sold."

"I must say," Clay shoves a piece in his mouth, "it is pretty fucking good."

She hesitates, almost like she was caught off guard by his compliment, but quickly recovers. "Thanks. Your green beans are edible I suppose."

Holy shit. A Thanksgiving miracle. Clay Harper and Lucy Hayes getting along.

"If they weren't made by an arrogant asshole like you, they'd be perfect," she flashes him a *fuck you* smirk and the Thanksgiving miracle vanishes.

The table erupts in laughter as he flips her off.

"Yeah, yeah. One day you all will be able to say you ate the green beans cooked by a Frozen Four champion and who will be laughing then, huh?"

The Frozen Four seemed like a distant fucking dream during practices. But now, we're eleven games in with six of those being in conference and we're sitting at a 4-2 conference record, 8-3 overall.

A hell of a start to the season with the Frozen Four not looking so far away now.

As normal, our conversation divides, the girls talking about cheer while we go on about hockey and upcoming games. Sitting here, listening and looking around at all my friends, it hits me how fucking lucky I am.

I may only have one blood relative in my life, but I have a huge fucking family.

Three annoying-ass bastards I call my best friends and five girls who could put all of us in our place at any moment.

There's one in particular, who I know without a doubt, will become an official part of my family sometime in the future.

The girl who taught me everything about falling in love and being loved.

My sunshine girl.

Acknowledgments

How incredibly insane is it that we are here yet again?

I am truly so moved by the love and encouragement I have received throughout my author journey. Your love for my series never ceases to amaze me.

I mean it when I say that I would not be where I am if it weren't for individuals like you who take a chance on an indie author like me. From your kind words to your love for my characters, my heart is full.

Of course, I would not be here if it weren't for the individuals in my life who have consistently supported me chasing my dreams.

To my husband, thank you for your unwavering support of my dreams. Thank you for reminding me that I am capable of reaching them and encouraging me to do so. I love you 3000.

To my mom and dad, thank you for always voicing how proud you are of me and my 'basically porn' romances. You taught me to dream big and that anything is possible.

To my cousin Jenna who has to suffer the initial draft of every book, thank you for being my voice of reason.

To Lex, my amazing beta reader, words cannot express how thankful I am for your help in polishing this book.

To Gravy (Gracie Rose), my insanely talented best friend, every book is a process of my many requests and visions for its cover. You continue to amaze me with each book and your hard work never goes unnoticed. Thank you for bringing my characters to life.

To my ARC readers, thank you for sharing your excitement surrounding Paul and Susie's story.

To my street team members, thank you for believing in my books and my journey.

I am blessed to be living out my dreams, and excited to see where we go from here.

About the Author

M.J. Hughes is a self-published romance novelist from the small-town of Kellyville, Oklahoma. An Okie girl through and through, where she continues to reside as she chases her dreams of becoming a USA Bestselling Author.

Her journey began in 2024 with the publication of her debut novel, *What If*. A year filled with happiness as it also marked the beginning of her marriage to her high school sweetheart. Since then, she has published two more romances within her series, *What Now and What Next*, and reached milestones with the first two books being recognized as Oklahoma Fiction Bestsellers.

Her current series in progress, a *River Road* series, only marks the beginning of her author journey, with one more book to be released for our hockey boys of Barker University.

While M.J. isn't writing, she enjoys spending time at home with her husband and dog, Rocket, as well as participating in activities such as fishing, thrifting, and finding hidden treasures at garage sales with her parents.

M.J. welcomes readers to join her on her journey as she continues to bring stories to life, and would love to connect through social media where you'll find all the latest updates!

instagram.com/author_mjhughes
tiktok.com/@miranda_parham98
amazon.com/author/m.j.hughes

9 798218 893378